# ARMY

## Night Rebels Motorcycle Club

## CHIAH WILDER

D1360331

I love hearing from my readers. You can email me at chiahwilder@gmail.com.

Make sure you sign up for my newsletter so you can keep up with my new releases, special sales, free short stories, and other treats only available to newsletter readers. When you sign up, you will receive a FREE hot and steamy novella. Sign up at: http://eepurl.com/bACCL1.

Visit me on facebook at facebook.com/AuthorChiahWilder

# Other Books by Chiah Wilder

## Insurgent MC Series:

Hawk's Property

Jax's Dilemma

Chas's Fervor

Axe's Fall

Banger's Ride

Jerry's Passion

Throttle's Seduction

Rock's Redemption

An Insurgent's Wedding

Outlaw Xmas

Wheelie's Challenge

Insurgents MC Romance Series: Insurgents Motorcycle Club Box Set
(Books 1 – 4)

Insurgents MC Romance Series: Insurgents Motorcycle Club Box Set
(Books 5 – 8)

## Night Rebels MC Series:

STEEL

MUERTO

DIABLO

GOLDIE

PACO

SANGRE

## Steamy Contemporary Romance:

My Sexy Boss

# Chapter One

ARMY SMACKED WILLOW'S ass as he sat up in bed, his eyes squinting against the setting sun's rays that poured through the open window.

"You're leaving so soon?" she asked and grabbed hold of Army's bicep to pull him back toward her.

He jerked out of her grasp and stood up. "I'll be late for my brother's fight if I stay for another round." He walked to the bathroom.

"Can I go with you?"

"Nope. The event's sold out," he said over his shoulder before closing the door. Not wanting Willow to follow him into the shower, he pushed in the lock. Army was meeting up with several of his Night Rebels MC brothers at the Durango Center, and the last person he wanted glued to his side was Willow.

The doorknob turned slightly and then a soft knock tapped against the wood. Army turned on the water and stepped into the shower, welcoming the warm spray as he tuned out Willow's muffled voice. Hooking up with her while he was in Durango was supposed to be fun, and for the most part it was, but for the past few months, Willow had begun to change what they had. She wanted to hang out after sex, hear from him when he was back in Alina, and even make future plans, but Army wanted no part of that. He had no intention of dating Willow or any other woman, and if she kept pushing him, he would lose her number and move on to the next.

Attracting women wasn't a problem for the tall, well-built biker, and he liked a variety of chicks to choose from. The club girls were always fun, and the citizen women he hung out with were usually cool with his no-strings-attached requirement, but every once in a while a citizen wanted to change what they shared, and that's when he'd bail. Willow was quickly rising to the top of his "too complicated" list.

As he came out of the bathroom, relief washed over him when he saw that Willow wasn't waiting for him in bed. He grabbed his keys and spare change off the dresser and walked out of the room.

Willow sat on the couch and turned her lips up in a huge grin as she gestured to a plate of nachos and two beers on the coffee table. "I thought you'd be hungry and thirsty after all your hard work." She winked at him.

He grabbed his leather jacket and slipped it on. "Sorry, but I don't have time. I'm meeting some of my friends, and I'm already running late."

Her lips turned downward. "But I made the nachos for you. I don't eat fried food, even chips."

"I know and I appreciate the effort, but I didn't ask you to do it. I told you I had to go." There was no way he was going to let her guilt him into doing something he didn't want. No one told him what to do. Plain and simple.

"Since your brother's fighting tonight, I'm sure he could get a ticket for me." Willow rose to her feet and came over to him, curling her arms around his neck. "Please?" She kissed him softly along his jaw.

Army stiffened then gently pushed her back. "I told you it's sold out. Anyway, that's not what we do. Didn't I give you a good time?"

"Yes, but I thought we could start doing more than just having sex." She crossed and uncrossed her arms.

Sighing, he shook his head. "We hook up when I'm in Durango. It's just for fun. You know I'm not looking for anything more than that. If you want to move on, I'm good with that."

Panic flashed across her face. "No … I didn't say that. I just thought we could go out once in a while for dinner or a movie."

"Sorry, I'm not your guy for that. I thought you were dating. That's what you told me a few weeks ago. Go to dinner and the movies with those dudes." Army took out his phone and read a text from Chains asking where the hell he was. "I'm outta here."

"Wait!" Willow pulled at his sleeve. "Can we see each other again before you go back?"

"I don't have time. I'm leaving tomorrow." He opened the front door.

"You'll call me when you come back in town, right?" Her voice quivered slightly.

"I don't know when I'll be back."

Willow fidgeted with the button on her robe. "You know, I'm good with what we have. I don't know why I said what I did." She came up to him and placed her hands on either side of his face. "Kiss me."

Army pressed his lips against hers for a second then broke away. "Everyone's waiting for me. I'll see ya." He walked out of the apartment and headed toward the elevator. Willow was standing in the hallway waving to him as the doors closed, but he just stared at her while making a mental note to send her a text when he returned home. The look on her face and the break in her voice told him the affair was over, at least for him.

Pulling up in front of the Durango Center, he saw the motorcycles of Chains, Crow, Eagle, Sangre, Paco, Cueball, Goldie, and Steel. After parking next to them, he entered the lobby and walked up to his brothers.

"It's about fuckin' time," Chains said as he bumped fists with Army. "What took you so long?"

Before Army could answer, Eagle punched him in the arm. "Fucking up a storm with Willow?" The men laughed.

"What can I say? She couldn't leave me alone," Army replied as he took the tickets out of his pocket.

"When you're done with her, give me her number. She's hot as hell," Eagle said, a smile in his voice.

"I'm moving on. I'll give it to you in Alina." Army walked toward the entrance. "Have the fights started?"

"Yeah. They've gone through two matches so far. Why're you done with Willow?" Eagle asked as he came behind Army.

"She wants to change our arrangement." Army pushed open the doors.

"They always do, dude, so that's why I only hookup with the club girls," Chains said.

The sour scent of sweat and a wall of warm air greeted them as they walked into the medium-sized room. Rows of chairs filled with men and a few women framed the cage standing in the middle of the room. It was set high above the audience, where the two men punched, kicked, and drew blood inside of it. Jeers mixed with cheers surrounded them as the fighters went down on the floor, writhing and grunting loudly.

"Here we are," Army said, pointing to a row close to the ring.

"When's Taylor on?" Goldie asked as he took his seat.

"The ring girls are fuckin' hot," Crow said, sliding into the row.

"Does your brother know any of them? Maybe we can party with them after the fights," Eagle said.

"He probably does. I'll ask him. I could go for the dark-haired one with the Daisy Dukes. Fuck, I love a woman in short shorts." Army sat down and shrugged off his jacket, then he uncrumpled the schedule and looked at it. "Taylor's the fourth one. He's won his last five matches, so I hope he nails this fucker's ass too." He turned to face his brothers and added, "Two recruiters are here looking for fighters to go pro, and I think Taylor's got a real good chance. It'd be fuckin' awesome for him."

"He's a damn good fighter, bro," Sangre said as Paco and Steel nodded in agreement.

"He deserves to go pro," Cueball said. "He works so damn hard. When I came by here a couple of weeks ago, I asked if he wanted to shoot some pool and have a few beers at Harry's Hall, but he said he was in training and he had to go to the gym and wasn't gonna drink until after the fight. I was fuckin' impressed. To pass up beer? Damn ... that's discipline." He motioned over a woman with a bright orange strap over her shoulders and a vending tray in front of her filled with cups of beer.

Then he held up four fingers.

"Twenty dollars," the woman said, smiling widely at Army. Cueball handed her a twenty and passed two beers to Army, then took the other two for himself. "Thank you." The usherette's gaze lingered on Army then she licked her lips and looked at Eagle, who yelled out his order.

"Thanks, bro," Army said to Cueball as he brought one of the cups to his lips. He watched the woman as she handed glasses of beer to Eagle and the others. The woman looked hot in her uniform, which consisted of tight spandex shorts and a low-cut blouse, and he knew all he had to do was give her a wink and they'd be tearing up the sheets later that night. She glanced over at him and bit the corner of her mouth, but he looked away; he'd promised Taylor that they'd hang out.

The bell rang and the fighter in bright yellow shorts held up his arms in victory as blood streamed down his face. "And 'Torturer' does it again!" the ring announcer yelled. "Elio Sandoval is hot right now. This is his seventh win in a row."

"Has Taylor fought that dude?" Cueball asked.

"No. He's in the heavyweight division. Taylor's middleweight." Army motioned for the beer girl to come over.

She winked at him and rushed over, leaning in deeply to show off her stunning cleavage. For a split second, Army debated on whether he should fuck her later that night, but decided that he could catch her the next time he came up to see Taylor fight.

"What'll you have, sugar?"

"She didn't call *me* sugar," Cueball said under his breath.

"Because you don't have my blue eyes," Army said as he held up two fingers. Women were always complimenting him on his gunmetal blue eyes. "Brown eyes are damn boring."

"Fuck you," Cueball said, taking the cup Army handed him.

Sangre nudged Army's side. "Taylor's up next."

A rush of adrenaline surged through him as the announcer stood in the middle of the ring. He saw his brother seated on a stool in the right corner as two muscular men hovered over him, most likely giving Taylor last minute pep talks and instructions. Then Taylor rose to his feet and moved to the middle of the ring, meeting his opponent with a scowl etched across his brow.

*Fuckin' nail him.* Army perched on the edge of the chair, his left hand gripping the metal corner of the seat. Taylor's opponent was a stocky guy, a couple of inches shorter than him. Army didn't think he looked any more or less muscular than Taylor, but anything could happen at a mixed martial arts match.

The bell rang. "Fuck," Army whispered under his breath as he watched his brother and Calvin "Destroyer" Hemsley assess each other. Suddenly, red and green gloved fists threw punches: fast and hard, over and over.

"Taylor's gonna own this fucker," Eagle said, his eyes fixed on the two fighters.

Before Army could agree, Taylor's fist connected with a right punch behind Destroyer's ear and it was done; he'd knocked out his opponent in the first round. The crowd went wild and Army leapt to his feet, screaming out his brother's name as his chest swelled.

"Mayhem takes the win!" the ring announcer yelled.

"That was so fuckin' awesome!" Paco said, clasping Army's shoulder.

"That's my brother. That damn Destroyer didn't stand a chance." A grin spread across his face as he continued to pump his fist in the air. The two men who'd been around Taylor before the fight started ushered him away from the ring. Glancing at his friends, Army said, "I'll be back. I'm gonna congratulate my little brother."

"The next match is between Stiletto and Athena. They're competing in the lightweight division." The ring announcer's voice filled the room.

"They're chicks," Cueball said.

Army glanced at the ring then stopped dead in his tracks. A woman with long, toned legs wearing high-as-hell red heels walked up the steps. She turned to the audience and flashed a seductive smile. Then she looked at him—her eyes held his and suddenly he felt as if he was drowning in their depths. They were a beautiful golden amber and shone like the glow of morning sunlight.

"You going or staying?" Eagle asked.

"What?" Jerked back to the moment, Army realized that he'd spent the last thirty seconds staring at this captivating woman.

"Damn, these chicks are hot. All they need is a vat of mud," Cueball said.

Army sat back down and watched the amber-eyed fighter slowly take off her high heels. Her caramel brown hair was in braided cornrows that came together to form a bun on top of her head. Simple movements like slipping on black open-fingered gloves, shaking out her arms, and tucking in a few stray strands of hair into her bun struck him as the sexiest moves he'd seen from a woman in a long time. The fighter wore tight black shorts that fit around her high, rounded ass perfectly, and a neon purple sports bra, which showcased her tits. *Fuck. Why the hell didn't Taylor tell me about this fighter?* His brother would call him and share some gossip and anecdotes about the different fighters, but he hadn't remembered Taylor ever mentioning this hot-as-sin MMA fighter.

"Maybe they'll pull each other's tops down," Eagle said and Cueball and Crow laughed.

"Get serious," Army said, his voice laced with irritation. "The women fighters work just as hard ... maybe even harder than the dudes. They have to prove themselves to everyone."

"You got a hard-on for one of them?" Eagle laughed. "There's no way you're giving us a lecture on chick fighters unless you want to get into one ... or maybe both of their shorts. With all that strength and flexibility, I bet they'd be great fucks."

Chains and Crow busted out, and Cueball slapped Eagle's back. "Good point, bro." He turned to Army. "Maybe Taylor can introduce them to us after the fights ... and the ring girls, for sure."

The bell rang, and Army watched, transfixed, as Stiletto and Athena squared off. The way she moved with her hands punching Athena's face in a series of boxing strikes, and her toned arms flexing with each hit, caused a surge of heat to burn through Army's body. The people in the row ahead of him were on their feet, and he stood up just as Athena delivered a kick to the side of Stiletto's head that made her fall to the floor. Army held his breath, his insides tight, as Athena pounced and caught Stiletto, forcing her into submission. For a few seconds it looked like Athena would be the victor, but the lithe fighter escaped from the hold, leapt to her feet, and continued her assault on Athena with elbow strikes and several strong kicks. Taut skin, shiny from sweat, covered her well-toned muscles, and a wicked dragon tattoo glared while it hugged the fighter's side, disappearing around her back. Fire blazed out of its fanged mouth with its blood-dripping talons raised as if to strike. It was mesmerizing, but not as enthralling as the way Stiletto delivered high kicks and Brazilian jiu-jitsu moves. Then a devastating elbow jab and right kick knocked Athena to the ground.

"Damn. These chicks can fight," Crow said.

"Afraid they'd beat your ass?" Goldie laughed.

"They'd definitely make me break some sweat," Crow answered. "My money's on the chick with the sexy as hell purple bra."

"I'll bet on the other chick. The one on the floor with her legs spread wide. Fuck, what a waste." Cueball took out a twenty-dollar bill. "Who you betting on?" he asked Army.

Without taking his eyes off the fight for one second, Army crossed his powerful arms. "Stiletto, all the way. She knows her shit and can she move."

Before any of the other guys placed their bets, Stiletto had her legs closed together, one of them on Athena's neck, the other right below her armpit. As Stiletto straightened, she held her opponent's wrist tightly, bending it in a way a wrist wasn't supposed to be bent. Tears streamed down Athena's face.

"Stiletto has her in an arm bar. Pay up." Army held out his hand, his gaze still fixed on the fighters. Then he saw Athena tap the ground, signaling the referee to stop the match, and he closed his hand around the crisp twenty-dollar bill.

"I wanted Athena to win," Cueball said, shaking his head. "I'm a sucker for blondes."

"That was the hottest thing I've seen in a while," Eagle said.

"Hailey should've been here to watch that fight. She's getting into mixed martial arts." Goldie plopped down on the metal chair.

"Really? I didn't think there were any MMA training gyms in Alina," Army said as he watched a large muscular guy escort Stiletto down the stairs, his bulging arm wrapped around her.

"She goes to Alina Martial Arts."

"I bet the training is weak as shit over there. I still say there isn't a decent training gym in the whole damn county."

"Breanna goes to their self-defense classes. She's trying to get Chelsea to join her," Steel said as he glanced down at the schedule.

"Hailey doesn't want to compete. She just wants to learn some tactics and self-defense. I tried teaching her but we always ended up fucking at some point, so she decided to go to the gym." Goldie laughed.

"I've been there with Breanna, bro. We never finished a full lesson." Steel tipped his chair backward.

"Are there any more chicks fighting tonight?" Chains asked.

"Doesn't look like it," Goldie replied, laying the schedule on his denim-clad thigh.

"I'm gonna see how Taylor is. I'll be back in a few," Army said.

"Bullshit. You wanna see that Stiletto chick up close. You've got a boner for her," Eagle said as Army slipped past him.

Ignoring his comment, Army made his way toward the ring. Two burly men stood sentry at the door leading to the back area.

"Where's your badge?" one of them asked.

"Taylor 'Mayhem' Conway is my brother, dude."

Stone-faced, he stared at Army. "That means shit. You got a badge?"

Anger pricked his nerves and he took two steps until he was almost nose to nose with the man. "I just fuckin' told you, Taylor's my brother."

"Anyone can say that. Step back. Now."

Army's hands clenched into fists and blood rushed to his throbbing temples.

"He's cool, Rocky. I know him," a sultry voice said behind him.

Army whirled around and the air sucked out of his lungs as his eyes locked with Stiletto's.

"If you say so," Rocky said dully.

Army tore his gaze from her face and ran it slowly over her body, tensing when it landed on the swell of her tits, which spilled over the top of her tight-fitting sports bra. Desire raced through him as he drew in a raspy breath.

"I'm up here," she said, a frown creasing her forehead. He snapped his gaze back to her face. She shook her head then brushed past him and went through the door Rocky held open. "Get in, or your chance is lost."

Army watched her hips sway and her ass bounce as he followed her. "You did a great job in the ring."

Stiletto looked over her shoulder as she kept walking, her high heels clacking on the concrete floor. "Thanks. Taylor's in there." She pointed to a door on the right.

"Wait up. How about a drink or something after the fights?"

She stopped so abruptly that he ran into her, her fine ass bumping against his hardness. Turning around, her face wore a mask of contempt. "I was just helping you out because Taylor's been talking about you coming to the fight for the past week."

"You sure that's the only reason?" Army leaned back on his heels.

"Don't flatter yourself. I'm not into cocky jerks."

"Army," Taylor's voice said behind him. "Way to go, Stiletto. You kicked Athena's ass good."

Her chuckle was slow and warm like honey. Army stared at her lips. *I wonder if she tastes as sweet as she sounds.*

"I'm glad I broke my losing streak. Later." Stiletto glanced at Army. "You can stop fantasizing now." She spun around and walked away. Army watched the tattoos on her back move until a firm clasp on his shoulder diverted his attention.

"Did you catch my fight? I looked for you earlier but didn't see you," Taylor said.

Army pulled his brother into a bear hug. "I wouldn't miss your match. You fuckin' nailed the bastard. A knockout in less than five minutes? The recruiters will be banging down your door."

Taylor patted Army's back then stepped back. "Let's not get ahead of ourselves. I still have losses in matches I should've easily won."

"That was a while ago. Your last several fights were great. No way the UMMAC doesn't want you." He glanced around the small room and spotted a mini-fridge in the corner. "You got some beer in there? We gotta celebrate." He went over and bent down.

"Get one for you," Taylor answered.

"I'm not drinking alone. You can have one fuckin' beer. Your fight's over, bro." Army took out two cans and handed one to Taylor. "Don't argue about it. Just drink the damn thing." He sat on the small couch, cracked open the top, and took a deep gulp, then he motioned his brother to drink up.

Taylor plopped down in an armchair. "Did any of the Night Rebels come?" He slowly brought the can to his lips and stared at it as though it were poison.

"Yeah. My prez and VP are here."

"Steel and Paco came?" Army nodded. "That's cool," Taylor said before he took a small sip.

"Cueball's here too and some of the others. They wanna go to Harry's Hall after the fights. They'll expect you to join them." Army shook his head. "Don't give me that look, dude. You can come out to play for an hour. Damn, you can't train all the time. You gotta have some fun too."

"Now you sound like Dad." Taylor put his beer down on the table. "It's hard for you guys to understand, but I'm trying to go pro. It's all I think about. Once that happens, I'll slow down a bit."

"I get it, but you need to relax. When's the last time you got laid?"

Army crushed his can, tossed it in the trash, then went over to the fridge and took out another beer.

Taylor snorted. "How the hell is that your business?"

Army rubbed his hand on Taylor's smooth head then sat down again. "It's not, but as your big brother, I'm just making sure that you're keeping *all* of your parts toned."

"I'm doing just fine." The corners of his mouth curled up.

"What's the story with the chick in the high heels?" Army stared at the metallic writing on the can.

"Stiletto? I don't know. She's an MMA fighter."

"I fuckin' know *that*. I mean, how long has she been training at the gym with you? I don't remember seeing her before."

"She's been there for a while. You probably didn't pay any attention. You like your women blonde, stacked, and with a ton of curves."

"She's been there for years? No way." *I definitely would've remembered her, and she's stacked just fine.*

"Not that long. She moved to Durango from Arizona. She's been with us for a year or so. You've only been to the gym a few times in the past year, so I'm not surprised you didn't run into her. She usually trains at night. Anyway, she's really good. When she came to Champion, she was in the middle of a losing streak."

"She kicked ass tonight." Army wanted to ask if the dude he saw escorting her from the ring was her man, but he didn't want Taylor to give him *that* look. He was also pretty sure Taylor would do everything in his power to make sure he kept Stiletto away from his big brother. Army had the reputation of being a heartbreaker, and neither of his two brothers would ever hook him up with any women. Not that he *wanted* to hook up with Stiletto, he was just curious, that was all.

"She fought real well. Mia's worked hard for tonight's win. I'm happy for her." Taylor looked down at his phone. "Dad's saying he's sorry he missed the fight."

"He'll make it to the next one. So Stiletto's name is Mia?"

"What?" Taylor looked up.

"The chick who fights." Army hated himself for asking.

"Oh … yeah. Her name's Mia. Why all the questions?"

The hair on the back of his neck bristled. "Are you going to Harry's or not?"

"Yeah, I'll go. Why're you pissed all of a sudden?"

"I'm not pissed." Army rose to his feet. "I gotta get back to my seat. I rode my bike, so we can just meet at Harry's after the fights."

"Okay. Are you sure you're not mad?"

"Yep." The truth was—flames of anger licked through him. He wasn't the type to ask questions about a chick. If he saw a woman who piqued his interest, he'd lock eyes with her then give her his boyish grin, and by the end of the night, they'd be fucking up a storm at her place. Asking about Stiletto or Mia or whatever the hell her name was reeked of weakness, and it pissed the hell out of him. Big time.

"Come in," Taylor said.

Army jerked his head back; he hadn't even heard anyone knock. Taylor opened the door and *she* stood there. Long, glossy caramel-brown hair with toffee streaks running through it tumbled loosely over her shoulders. Stiletto had changed into a short-as-hell black dress that hugged her hips and thighs and showed off the tempting swell of her breasts. Army ran his gaze down the length of her, his pants growing snug as he took in her shapely legs, the chain tattoo around one of her ankles, and the high heels. For a split second, all he could see was himself pounding inside her with those fuck-me heels digging into his ass.

"What's up?" Taylor asked.

Taylor's voice took Army out of the moment, and he lifted his gaze to Stiletto's face. She glared at him with high color in her cheeks. *If you didn't want me to stare at you, sweetheart, you shouldn't have worn that sexy-as-hell dress. You came over here to see me. You're not fooling me one fuckin' bit.*

"Goliath wants to see you," she said, diverting her attention away from Army.

Army walked over, and the scent of lemongrass and basil swirled around him. "You smell good," he said in a low voice.

Ignoring him, Stiletto leaned against the doorframe.

"If you don't want me to rub against you then get out of the way. But ... maybe that's exactly what you want." He quirked his lips.

"Army!" Taylor's voice boomed behind him as Stiletto moved away.

"See you at Harry's. Oh ... and bring the ring girls. Me and the guys wanna have some fun."

From his peripheral vision, he saw Stiletto's eyes widen and a bolt of satisfaction raced through him. Feeling her gaze on him, he swaggered down the hall with a big smile plastered across his face.

*We'll be fucking by the end of next week.*

He went back inside the arena.

# Chapter Two

MIA STARED AFTER Army until he disappeared through the door. He was so much of an arrogant sonofabitch, it didn't matter that he was such a hunk. Not at all. Who cared that he had blue eyes that pulled her in or that his strong jaw and high cheekbones made him ruggedly handsome. And the last thing she cared about was his sculpted, inked arms and his narrow waist. Nope ... she didn't care at all that he was just her type. *The guy's a fucking jerk.*

"Sorry about my brother. He can be ... uh ... kind of—"

"An asshole?" She smiled at Taylor. "No worries. I've dealt with worse. I just can't believe he's your brother. You're so nice and polite."

Taylor threw his head back. "I'm just better at filtering than Army is. He comes off too strong until you get to know him, and then he's a pretty cool guy."

"I guess I'll never know that since I don't plan to get to know him." Mia rubbed the sides of her arms. "I wish they'd turn down the damn AC. It's freezing around here. By the way, you did awesome out there against Destroyer. If the UMMAC doesn't pick you up, it'll be their loss. I saw a couple of recruits out there. Maybe that's what Goliath wants to talk to you about."

Taylor's face flushed. "I don't want to get my hopes up. He probably wants to chew me out on my weak back kicks. They totally sucked. Are you sticking around?"

"No. I'm meeting up with a few friends I've ignored for the last three weeks. I'll see you at the gym on Monday."

She stood aside until Taylor walked toward the office, then she went to the door leading out to the arena and slowly cracked it open.

"Coming out?" Rocky asked, his gaze raking over her body.

Folding her arms over her chest, she shook her head. "Just checking out how Perry's doing."

"He's getting his ass kicked by Babyface."

"That's too bad." Stiletto glanced at the ring and saw Perry wrestling with Babyface on the floor, then she scanned the crowd and spotted Army standing up and pumping his fists in the air, which made the muscles in his arms ripple. There was no doubt that he was deliciously buffed, and the way he wore his dark brown hair short on the sides but just full enough on top surely invited women's fingers to test its softness. Army's features were chiseled; his straight nose, sensuously full mouth, and the right amount of stubble covering his angular jaw would make most women drool. Then there were his eyes—those incredible blue eyes that resembled the color of stormy skies. She sucked in a deep breath and let it out slowly.

And that was all above his neck. She groaned. *Why the fuck is he so good looking?* Her gaze traveled downward; broad shoulders, a tapered, narrow waist, and sculpted arms probably had women sighing with pure desire. *I bet he has taut pecs and killer six-pack abs under his shirt. Fuck.* She groaned again. "Why do you have to be such a misogynist jackass?" she muttered under her breath.

The bell rang and before she could turn her attention to the ring, steely eyes captured hers. She held her breath.

A couple of seconds passed.

He smirked.

*Fuckface.* Anger rushed down her spine, and she flipped him off. Right there, in front of everyone, including her trainer, Rick.

Then the rugged bastard had the nerve to laugh and nudge the guy next to him while pointing at her. Mia spun around and slammed the door, but all the cheering for Babyface's win dulled the dramatic effect she'd wanted. "Grrr …!" She stalked down the hall, went into her room, grabbed her purse and gym bag, and left the building.

On the way over to Cricket on the Hill, Mia cranked the radio at full volume as if that would exorcize *him* from her mind. She swung into the parking lot and nabbed a space close to the front door. A last minute glance in the mirror told her that she did a killer job concealing the marks Athena had given her during their match. Mia finger-combed her hair then got out of the car.

"Mia! Over here," Ronica cried out as she entered the popular bar and eatery. Ronica and Mia had clicked when they first met at Salon on the Boulevard a little over a year ago. Ronica rented the booth catty-corner to hers. She had been beyond nervous about going into business for herself and forgoing a guaranteed paycheck each week, but Ronica had been her motivational coach during those few months when the clients were low but the bills were high.

"How'd it go?" Ronica's dark eyes swept over Mia's face then body. "No broken bones. Just a bit of swelling on the cheeks. That's a good sign, right?"

"I ruled tonight," Mia answered as she pulled the chair out and sat down.

"I still don't know how you guys can go into a ring and punch the shit out of each other. I could never do it … I'd be scared stiff," Danielle said. She was another hair stylist at the salon, and Mia had become friendly with her over the past few months.

"You'd be freaked about breaking a nail," Peyton added, and the other women laughed.

Danielle held up her hands in front of her. "I bet you can't even have long nails."

"You're right, you can't." Mia picked up the drink specials menu.

With her hands still up in front of her, Danielle shook her head. "See that just wouldn't work for me. I'd die without my nail art."

"Having to keep my nails ultra short has been the hardest part since I began training." Mia looked up at the waiter and ordered a Mudslide. When the waiter left, guilt pangs stabbed at her. "Maybe I should change my order to a glass of chardonnay."

Ronica tossed her dark hair over her shoulders. "Don't you dare.

You can afford to have a decadent drink, especially since you won your fight."

"And you don't have an ounce of fat on you, so it won't kill you," Peyton added.

"Guilt attack over. I'm pigging out tonight. Let's order appetizers." Mia giggled.

As they sipped their drinks, the women's eyes lit up when the waiter put a large platter in front of them. Carrots, celery, and pita chips surrounded a crock of hot artichoke-and-spinach dip.

"That looks fucking awesome," Ronica said as she picked up a chip.

"Good choice," Danielle injected, swiping the carrot stick through the gooey dip.

Mia crunched down on a celery stalk, and her mouth danced from the sweet, nutty flavor of the dip and the tang from the feta cheese. "This is so good," she said.

"How can you concentrate at the gym with all those buffed guys working out?" Danielle asked.

Mia laughed. "I'm so focused on what I'm doing and trying not to get my face smashed in that I don't even notice."

"Not even your trainer?" Ronica said.

"Rick? He's not really my type." Mia picked up her creamy drink.

"What's your type?" Peyton asked.

Mia tilted her head back. "I like ruggedly handsome guys who have a bad boy vibe." *Like Taylor's asshole brother.*

"Give me a guy in a fine-tailored suit any day," Danielle said.

"Who're you thinking of?" Ronica asked Mia.

She frowned slightly. "No one."

"You didn't blush for *no one*. I know you too well." Ronica pushed her plate away and leaned back in the chair, staring at Mia. "Give it up."

"It's nothing, really. I just met Taylor's brother today, and he's my type except that he's in love with himself. You know the kind."

"Oh ... one of *those*. It's best to stay far away from him," Peyton said.

"I love difficult men," Danielle added. "They're a challenge, and so damn masculine." She licked her lips.

"I've got enough difficult shit to deal with in my life. I don't need a conceited idiot making it worse," Mia replied.

Ronica clapped her hands. "He's gotten under your skin. I love it!"

Mia's jaw tightened and she smoothed out her napkin over and over as if her hand were an iron. "*He's* done no such thing. I can't even imagine what it'd be like to go out with someone like him. He's a total sexist ... probably one of those who think women MMA fighters are akin to mud wrestlers or wet T-shirt contestants. He's disgusting." Anger flushed over her neck and face. *Why am I getting so mad?*

"He does seem to have gotten to you," Peyton said, handing her a clean napkin.

Mia dabbed it over her damp face determined to change the subject.

"Who had the Tequila Chicken Salad?" the waiter asked as he took it off a large tray he carried.

Relieved for the distraction, Mia yelled, "Me!" then looked sheepishly down at the silverware as diners at tables around hers stared over.

After distributing all the dinners, the server dashed away with promises of refilling their water glasses.

"Hey, Mia," a jovial voice said behind her.

She looked up and into Taylor's face. "Hi. What're you doing here?"

"Harry's Hall was too crowded so we came over here. He gestured to a group of men making their way to the back of the restaurant. Several of the ring girls hung onto some of the men's arms, including Army's. All of a sudden, the creamy tequila-lime vinaigrette made her stomach sour. Tearing her gaze away from Dessie, who was molded to Army's side, she put her fork down. "Are the fights finished so soon?"

"The guys wanted to cut out early." He scanned the table.

With her senses returning to her, she waved her hand around. "These are my friends ... Peyton, Danielle, and Ronica." She pointed at him. "And this is Taylor. He's got a real good chance of going pro, and he's a super nice guy."

He laughed. "I need to hire you for all my PR."

"What's going on here, buddy?" The smooth-as-whiskey voice slid over her.

She kept her head down, counting the packets of sugar in the dispenser.

"Is that you, Stiletto?" The warmth of his breath made the back of her neck tingle.

She cocked her head back and almost hit his chin—he was *that* close. "Hey." She put on the best fake smile she could muster. His gaze shifted downward then his eyes gleamed and she realized that the fucker had a great view down the top of her dress.

"Seriously?" she gritted, folding her arms against her chest. His mouth curved into a smug smile as he snagged her gaze.

"Who's your friend?" Peyton asked as she leaned forward.

"He's not my friend."

Army glanced at the women. "I'm Army," he pointed behind him, "Taylor's brother."

"I thought you were a fighter." Peyton's gaze blatantly ran over his body. "You certainly look like one."

"Thanks for the compliment," he said smoothly.

*He's so fucking charming. What a damn act. I can't believe Peyton's feeding into his already inflated ego.*

Then his fingers grazed lightly on the back of her neck and her body shivered. *Fucking traitor.*

"I'm glad you're feeling what I am," he whispered into her ear.

"Don't you have to get back to Dessie?" The minute the words tumbled out of her mouth, she regretted them.

Squeezing her gently, he chuckled. "Good to know it bothers you." Straightening up, he nodded at her friends. "Another time?" He strode away with Taylor following behind him.

"What the fuck just happened?" Peyton looked over her shoulder, only turning back around when Army sat down. "You need to hook me up with him. Now." Her expression was on the edge of desperate as she stared at Mia.

Mia shook her head. "I don't know him. I just sorta met him at the fights. Anyway, he's a total asshole. Can't you see that? He'd eat you alive."

"*That's* the guy who's got you all twisted." Ronica craned her neck and looked at Army's table. "He's perfect for you. You need a strong man. Jorge was a weakling."

"Jorge was a gentleman. He was sweet, understanding, compliant, and—"

"Boring. Isn't that what you told me all the time?" Ronica smiled.

At that moment, Mia regretted telling Ronica so much about her last relationship. The truth was that Jorge was the type of man parents wanted for their daughters, and she should've been thrilled to have finally found a decent man, but ... she wasn't. *He* was *boring. He agreed with me on everything. I made all the decisions on where we'd go for dates, what we'd do, and how often we'd see each other, and he was too damn tame in the bedroom.* Mia's sexual appetite preferred rough sex that teetered on the edge of darkness.

"Your silence tells me I'm right." Ronica picked up her white Russian and took a sip.

"You're not right. He sent me flowers and romantic texts. He was a good guy. Any woman would be lucky to have him in her life."

"If he's so great, then why aren't you two together?" Danielle asked.

Ronica and Peyton sniggered and a current of anger sizzled up Mia's spine. "Because Jorge wanted to get married, and I wasn't ready. If I was, I'd be Mrs. Salvador right now."

"Yeah ... right." Ronica shook her head. "You keep telling me you can't find the right guy, and that's because you keep going out with guys you *think* you should like instead of guys that you *know* you'd like. It's like trying to fit a square peg into a circle. It doesn't work, girl."

"And you're saying that *he's*"—Mia waved her hand in Army's direction—"the one for me?" She laughed dryly. "I'm not *that* desperate. If I ever am, then shoot me."

Peyton looked over her shoulder again. "I'm that desperate. Please … *please* see if he's available. You seemed to be friendly with his brother. Just ask. He's so gorgeous. I've never gone out with a guy who oozed so much testosterone."

"Damn, girl, calm down," Danielle said, gently touching Peyton's arm. "Mia's right—he's a real heartbreaker. You can tell just by the way he walks and by the smug expression he wore the whole time he was at the table. I bet he'd be awesome in bed, but he'd be gone the moment you'd fall asleep. Definitely not a good bet."

"That's what I've been saying," Mia said.

"What you need is a mix of Jorge and this Army dude. I still like a confident man in a well-tailored suit. I should've been a legal secretary instead of a hair stylist. My mom always told me that if I wanted to meet classy men then I needed to get a job where I'd have those kind of connections. I blew that advice," Danielle added.

"Who listens to our moms' advice? If I had, I wouldn't be engaged to Stuart. He's just about the most perfect man in the world." Ronica beamed.

"How are the wedding plans coming?" Danielle asked.

"My mom's driving me crazy. The other day we were looking at invitations and she …"

Mia tuned out her friend and sneaked peeks at Army. Dessie had that goofy look women get when they're crushing on a guy and think he's the best thing in life. The way Army leaned down low and whispered into the ring girl's ear made Mia clench her teeth. *He's probably trying to get a good look at her boobs. That seems to be his thing. Although, Dessie isn't really covering them up. I know they're fake. She's too damn skinny to have such big breasts, but if she's ever in a flood, she's gold—her boobs will keep her afloat for sure.* Her eyes narrowed as Dessie planted a kiss on Army's cheek.

"I'll be right back." Mia scooted her chair back and jumped up. She needed to get a breath of fresh air. She hated that she'd stooped so low as to be jealous of Dessie's boob job, and she was pissed as hell at why it even mattered that the ring girl was hitting on Army or how he seemed to be enjoying it too much.

Outside, Mia welcomed the autumn breeze which tousled her hair and pinked her cheeks. The warmth that had been in the wind earlier that day had evaporated into the sky, and a chill had crept into the air. Not the bite of wintry gusts, but there was enough of a nip to make Mia shiver and wish she would've brought her jacket. Leaves skittered down the pavement, and the aroma of cinnamon and warm spices rode on the breeze, curling around her and whispering of warm winter fires yet to come.

Mia leaned against the restaurant's brick wall and inhaled and exhaled several deep breaths. She couldn't let this stranger get to her. It was ridiculous and totally out of character for her. It was probably the release of all the adrenaline she'd had coursing through her since she'd begun to prepare for the fight a few weeks ago.

"Aren't you cold?"

Mia jumped at the sound of the deep voice—she didn't hear anyone come out. She pushed away from the wall and let her gaze fall on Army. The yellow glow of the streetlights made his features soft against the darkness of the night. She ran her hands up and down her pebbled skin. "I am. I was just going to head back inside."

He stood in front of her, blocking her. "Stay for a few minutes." He shrugged off his leather jacket and draped it around her shoulders before she could protest. The heat from his body felt absurdly intimate, and she was extremely aware of his fingers brushing the back of her neck. He smelled of leather and caramelized dark coffee beans with a tang of salty herbs to it, and it was the most sensual aroma she'd ever come across. It wrapped around her, and much to her chagrin, desire rippled through her.

"Thanks," she croaked, her throat dry with tension.

"We never really met each other. I'm Army."

"Mia," she said softly. He still stood close behind her.

"That's a pretty name," his breath whispered over the curve of her neck, threatening to ensnare her.

Without thinking, she leaned back into him, and he ran a thumb along her jaw as his calloused skin scratched her lightly. "I couldn't keep my eyes off of you during the fight. You were amazing." His breath was warm on her cheek and her inner thighs clenched in reaction.

Army cupped Mia's chin and tilted her head back so she gazed into his desire-filled eyes. Her lips parted when he dipped his head down as his grip tightened on her chin.

Her brain screamed at her to stop, but her traitorous body relaxed in his powerful arms. Danger radiated from him, but it only heightened her excitement.

"Mia," he said, his low voice a mixture of sensual and gruff masculinity.

Her stomach fluttered as she closed her eyes in anticipation of his kiss.

"Army! You promised you'd be right back," Dessie whined.

The mood snapped all at once. Mia stepped away from Army and ignored the daggers shooting from Dessie's eyes. She threw off the leather jacket and handed it to Army.

He grabbed her hand. "Don't go." He waved his hand back and forth between him and Dessie. "This doesn't mean anything."

Dessie gasped and put her hands on her hips. "What the fuck?"

Mia yanked her hand away. "I'm sure none of your hookups do."

Army reached out for her again but she glared at him. "Don't touch me. Go back to wherever you came from, and leave me the hell alone."

"Mia, there's nothing going on with Dessie."

"You're a real jerk!" Dessie yelled.

"For once we agree on something," Mia said to her as she opened the front door. "Are you coming in or staying out here?"

Dessie tossed her bleached blonde hair and stormed past Mia, who looked at Army before she went back inside. "You're the worst kind of asshole. You pretend to be decent just to further your game."

Army glowered. "I didn't see you objecting, sweetheart. If Dessie hadn't come out, you'd be rubbing against me like a cat in heat while I had my tongue halfway down your throat. You're just fuckin' pissed because you know I'm right. You want me and I want you. Grow the fuck up, lady, and get over here."

"Are you for real? You talk like you're in a low-budget porn film. Unbelievable."

"Good luck with your next fight, *Stiletto*. That name suits you way better." Army stalked toward her, and she quickly stepped inside as he marched by. She watched as he walked back to his table, said something to Taylor, then headed to the back exit of the eatery.

Mia sat down and her friends stared at her. She didn't want to tell them how she almost made a complete fool of herself outside. She was madder than hell at Army, mostly because what he said was true—she was pissed because she wanted him. *Your body did. It's natural to be aroused by an attractive man.* Mia would just have to make sure she kept her body in check. It wouldn't be that hard, especially since she doubted she'd ever see him again. A macho guy like Army had too much pride to seek her out, and in the off chance he did, she'd have to be strong. She was an athlete and used to discipline and sacrifice. *Ignoring the fuckface shouldn't be too hard.* If she could withstand Goliath's grueling workouts, she could handle anything, especially Army.

"So, are you going to tell us what happened with Mr. Super Stud?" Danielle asked.

Mia shrugged and quirked her lips. "Nothing to tell."

"You looked pretty pissed when you came back and Mr. Super Stud stormed by the table. That doesn't sound like nothing." Danielle plopped a bite of cheesecake in her mouth.

"He's a jerk, and I put him in his place. Sorry to disappoint you, but that's all there is to it." Mia waved the waiter over and ordered a Manhattan—her go-to comfort drink when life got jumbled. Ronica's penetrating stare told her that her best friend wasn't buying her nonchalant act for one minute. In time, she'd tell Ronica what happened, but at that moment, Army, and how he made her feel, were the last things she wanted to talk about.

Not paying attention to Ronica, Mia leaned back in her chair and brought up a subject they all loved—hair color.

As the women chatted and she sipped her drink, thoughts of Army invaded her mind. The sound of his voice, his touch, his manly scent, and his sexy, but annoying walk all played havoc with her emotions. Mia knew the score with a guy like him, and she could guarantee that she wasn't on his mind. Nope, Mia just couldn't get involved with someone like Army no matter how much her body wanted him.

*I have to focus on my business and my training. That's the key. In a few days, I won't even remember his name.*

All would be good if only she believed it.

# Chapter Three

ARMY STACKED BOTTLES of vodka, whiskey, and gin on the glass shelves behind the bar, glancing every once in a while at Tawny as she gyrated around the pole in the middle of the stage. From the way the audience whistled, he knew he'd made the right decision in hiring her for the gentlemen's club. Army was the manager of Lust—one of the many businesses the Night Rebels owned in Alina.

"Do you have any kahlúa in those boxes? A couple of customers are asking." Aspen bent down low and rearranged her tits in the barely-there glitter top she wore.

"Lemme check." Army took out his knife and sliced open the top of a box. "There are a few bottles in here. What do they want? Black Russians or straight up?"

Aspen looked down at the notepad. "One Black Russian and a double shot with one ice cube in it." She hopped up on the stool and placed her leg over her thigh, then took off her high heels and massaged her foot. "That feels so damn good. These heels are killing me tonight."

Army glanced at her five-inch heels, and Stiletto popped into his mind. It'd been two weeks since he'd been in Durango, and every fucking day he thought about her. He shoved open the ice bin and filled both glasses.

"Whoa. One of the dudes just wants one ice cube," Aspen said.

Army grabbed another glass. "What kind of a pussy order is that? One fuckin' ice cube." He placed a cube inside the glass then poured the shots in it.

Aspen giggled. "Are you having one of those days too?"

He grunted and placed the two drinks at the station. "There you go."

"If you need to unwind, Charlie just came in and he can take over. You want me to get him?" She put on her shoe and grimaced when she stepped down from the barstool.

"I don't need you to tell me how the fuck to run the place." Army bent over again and pulled out liquor bottles.

"I was just trying to help," Aspen said, her voice quivering.

He looked up and saw her crestfallen face. "Don't pay any attention to me, Aspen. I'm just in a pissed-off mood. Nothing personal."

"You've been in that mood for a couple of weeks. Anything I can help you with?" She smiled warmly at him.

"I'll get over it. If you see Charlie, tell him to get the last two boxes of inventory in the back room and bring them to the bar."

"Will do." Aspen's eyes shone and she blew him a small kiss then walked away, balancing the drinks on a tray.

Aspen had been crushing on him since she'd first come to Lust as an exotic dancer. Army had hoped that her infatuation with him would lessen over time, but it'd been over a year and it seemed like her feelings for him were even stronger. He'd explained to her that club members were not allowed to date or hook up with any of the employees at any of their businesses, but that didn't seem to dampen her ardor for him.

"Aspen said that you needed these boxes." Charlie put them on the bar.

"I wanna stock the shelves and the cupboards before the evening crowd gets here. Give me a hand. I'll be back in a few." Army walked through the semi-full bar and slipped behind the black curtain. Several dancers ran around in various stages of nakedness, but Army didn't pay any attention as he made his way out to the back patio.

Leaning against the stucco wall, he dug into his cut's pocket, took out a joint, and lit it. As he inhaled deeply, he watched the red and gold leaves tumble from the oak tree that took up more than half of the back area. Bright gaps of sunlight broke through the thick interlocking branches, which would soon be sparse and bare. Army stomped his boot on the terra-cotta tiles. "Why the fuck can't I get her out of my mind? This fuckin' blows." He threw the joint on the ground and stubbed it out; it was supposed to relax him, but instead, it made him antsy and madder than ever.

"Hey," Eagle said as he came outside. "Taking a break?"

"Yeah. Once the Saturday night crowd fills up the place, there'll be hardly enough time to take a piss."

"Seems like it's always that way," Eagle replied. "Rooster's looking forward to his birthday bash tonight. I'm sure his old lady ain't." He chuckled.

"Shannon's always on his ass about cheating. She called me last night and told me she'd hold me personally responsible if one of the dancers gives him a lap dance." Army shook his head. "I told her he's gonna be at a fuckin' strip bar and if she had a problem with it to take it up with Rooster and leave me the fuck alone. She can be such a bitch sometimes."

"She shouldn't be telling a brother anything." Eagle took out a joint. "Want one?"

"Nah. Most of the dudes from the Fallen Slayers are gonna be here tonight."

"Steel said we're closing down at midnight for the party. It'll spill over to the clubhouse after two." Eagle glanced over at Army. "You planning to go to Durango anytime soon?"

Army stiffened. "Why?"

"Taylor was asking Cueball. He said you told him if the recruits were interested, you'd go up more often. Said he hasn't seen or heard from you in about two weeks." A cloud of smoke enveloped the two men.

"Is that why you're here? To relay a message that came through Cueball? How the fuck is what I say to Taylor or when I go to Durango any of yours or Cueball's goddamn business?" Heat flushed through his body.

Eagle threw his half-finished joint to the ground then cracked his knuckles as he glared at Army. "If you got a problem with me, then let's go a few rounds."

For several seconds a tense silence filled the patio until the door swung open and Aspen stepped out.

"I don't mean to interrupt, but Charlie needs some help. Wyatt called in sick and he's getting slammed." Aspen smiled weakly at the two men who glared at each other.

"I'm on it," Army said gruffly. He turned and went to the door.

"Is everything okay with him?" He heard Aspen's soft voice asking Eagle. Army slammed the door behind him and stalked to the bar.

For the next couple of hours, Army didn't have a chance to think about anything but making drinks and running credit cards—it was a welcome relief. As he was pouring whiskey shots, he saw Brutus coming over to the bar. He jerked his head at the Night Rebels' member.

"It's fuckin' packed in here," Brutus said as he pushed through several people leaning against the counter.

"Tell me about it. Jaxon and Caleb are here already." Army jerked his head toward the front door.

"I saw them when I came in. Do you need some help back here? It looks like they've got everything covered at the door. I told them to let me know if they need help in throwing anyone out."

"I could use a break," Army said.

"You got it, brother." Brutus went over to the screen and began reading orders. "Anything special I should know?"

"No. Charlie can fill you in if you need some help with the more exotic drinks. I'll be back in a bit."

Army went out back and called Taylor. He'd been avoiding a trip up to see his brother because of Stiletto. A part of him was surprised she hadn't tried to contact him through Taylor. There definitely were some sparks between them, and he knew she felt it too. It was a new sensation for him because he'd never felt such an intense connection with a woman who he'd just met. The way Stiletto had closed her eyes and parted her sweet lips let him know that her body had won over her reason.

"It's about time I heard from you," Taylor said.

Army shut the back door tighter, blocking out all the noise from inside the club. "I've meant to call you, but I've been busier than hell. How's it going?"

"Good. I'm preparing for another fight in a few weeks. The recruit says the UMMAC wants to see me win the next couple of fights, then they'll pick me up. I'm so damn pumped about it."

"They'll be lucky to have you. Are you nervous about your opponents?"

"Jason 'Ironman' Swick, I've fought against before. I know his strong and weak points, so I'm good with that. The other fighter, 'New Breed,' I've never been in the ring with. His name's Chad Torrent, and he's a real contender. I'm going cross-eyed watching all the videos of his fights over and over."

"That's the best way to figure out his moves. What else have you been up to besides training?"

Taylor laughed. "That's about it."

"You haven't gone out in the last couple of weeks?"

"I've gone out with people from the gym. We usually go to Berriegood on Wednesdays and Fridays. They've got great protein bowls and smoothies."

"I'm glad you're going out even if it's with the same people you see every fuckin' day." *There's no damn way I'm asking about her.*

"Don't you hang around the guys from the club every day?"

"That's different—we're family ... a brotherhood."

"I guess. When are you coming up?"

"I was thinking in a few days. I have to double-check with Steel to see if I can take some time off."

"It sounds like you're going to stay longer than your usual day or two. Dad'll be happy about that."

Army ran his fingers through his hair. "Yeah ... well ... I need a break. I can't remember when I've been away for more than a couple of days. Maybe I'll join you on one of your protein bowl nights. Do they put steak in them?"

Taylor's hearty laugh warmed Army. "That's too funny. I'll have to share that with the others next time we go. The bowl has peanut butter, chia seeds, whey protein, and a bunch of other high protein stuff in it. It's really good."

"No meat? Damn."

"Don't knock it until you've tried it. Mia got me hooked on it. I held out for a long time, but I finally went and now I crave it. It's fucking weird."

Army stood silent as the image of Stiletto in her killer black dress crashed through his mind. "How's she doing?" *Fuck!*

"Mia's good. She's just training right now because she had some things come up with her family. Not sure what it is. What're you doing tonight?"

He wanted Taylor to keep talking about the sexy fighter, but Army would just have to wait until he went to Durango. Of course, he was only going to support Taylor and see his dad.

"Are you still with me?" Taylor's question broke through his thoughts.

"Yeah. Uh …"

"What're your plans for tonight?"

"Oh. I'm working at Lust. Rooster's having his big birthday bash over here, then we'll finish it up at the club. Should be fun."

"I bet there'll be a lot of pretty women."

"Always are. You should come to one of the club's parties sometime. They can be wild, but that's what makes them fun. Anything goes, you know?"

Taylor chuckled. "So, who's your woman for the night?"

"I haven't decided yet." The truth was Army wished Stiletto were there keeping him busy.

"I don't know how you do it. You're gonna be thirty. Don't you ever want to just be with one woman?"

"Settle down? Nah. Dad's done it three times and *he's* alone. The last one cleaned out all his bank accounts. And our mother? She took off when you were barely four years old. Nope. I'll stick to my no-strings-attached policy."

"I don't really remember Mom, but I know you do. It's always been harder on you that she left us than on me, but Asher's only two years younger than you and he's married."

"Good for Asher. He was always lookin' for a mommy to take care of him. He found it in Kali. She packs his damn lunches when he goes to work. No fuckin' thanks. I'm doing just fine."

"I didn't mean to piss you off." An audible sigh hit Army's ears. "I know Dad's worried about you."

"He's worried about you, too, but we each have our own lives. Anyway, when's the last time you had a girlfriend? And don't give me that MMA shit. Plenty of fighters have a woman." Army took out a joint and lit it.

"I'm still getting over Penny."

Army snorted. "She married the fucker she cheated on you with. Damn, dude—grow some fuckin' balls." He kicked the side of the building.

"I'm sorry women are such a sore spot for you. We can—"

"Chicks aren't anything to me but a good time. They're warm and soft and I couldn't live without them, but I have no intention of hooking up with one just because you, Dad, or Aunt Rosemary think I should. I'm just fuckin' sick and tired of having to explain that all the time. Live your life and let me live mine." It took all the willpower Army possessed to keep from throwing his phone against the wall then stomping on it. Why did his family have to keep butting into his life? His aunt Rosemary had stepped in when his mom had abandoned them, and he loved and respected her for that, but he hated when she'd call him up and try to fix him up with another "perfect" woman. *Fuck!* He kicked the wall again and dust from the stucco finish glowed under the patio light as it floated in the air.

"Chill, dude. Let's change the damn subject," Taylor said.

"I gotta get going. I'm helping tend bar. I'll send you a text to let you know when I'll be coming."

"Are you staying with Willow?"

Army cleared his throat. "We're done. I'll figure it out. Later." He shoved his phone in his pocket and stretched his arms high above his head then dropped them down, shaking them out. The small clock on the wall next to the door told him he had at least five more hours before he could cut out and go for a long ride. Army needed to lose himself into the darkness and have the chilly wind invigorate him as it whipped around him. Once two in the morning rolled around, he'd help clean and lock up, and then he had a date with his bike.

The cacophony of music and chatter spilled out when he opened the back door. Scrubbing his hand over his face, he walked inside.

ARMY SAT AT the back of the room watching the last of the members as they filed in and quickly took their seats in the meeting room. Steel and Paco stood at the front of the big wooden table, and the minute the second hand hit twelve, Steel hit the gavel on the block. All eyes were on the president as he called church to order.

"We're going to put off talking about the fall rally until next week. Paco, Sangre, and Diablo all got some disturbing news about the fucking Satan's Pistons. They got this shit from different sources, and Chains has been doing his computer magic to make sure it's true." Steel picked up his beer bottle and drank then set it down with a thud. "It is. The word is that the Pistons are trying to get a hold of the drug money in Colorado."

"When the fuck are they gonna learn that they need to stay their asses in Arizona? We already warned them a couple of years back. We never should've left until we knew each one of them was dead," Army said.

"They're sonsofbitches. We have to stomp them out for good." Crow jerked his head to Army. "He's right. We shouldn't have let anyone live the night we attacked them. Now we got this shit to deal with. Again." He slammed his fist on the table.

"Are they still trying to get in with the 39th Street Gang in Durango?" Muerto asked.

"Yeah. That's what the grapevine is saying." Paco splayed his hands on the table. "We gotta shut them down for good. They don't have many members, but since we hit them, they've opened a couple more chapters. They're hell-bent in getting a foothold in our territory."

"Banger's not gonna like this shit," Army said, and several members yelled out in agreement.

Steel held up his hand. "The Insurgents know what's going on. They're on board if we need them. Considering the size of the punk gang in Durango, we may need them and the Fallen Slayers. If things go the way I think they're headed, it'll be an all-out war."

A contemplative silence descended over the room. Going to war with a rival club meant total lockdown for women, children, and even siblings and parents. The Night Rebels couldn't leave anything to chance. Satan's Pistons MC and the 39th Street Gang had the reputation of dirty warfare—taking out family members and children. Lives would be lost, and the war could drag out for years. No one wanted it, but the Night Rebels wouldn't sit back and let any other MC or gang come into their territory. The 39th Street Gang was involved in dog fights, sex trafficking, and drugs, and the Night Rebels didn't want any of that on their turf.

"When would we attack?" Eagle asked, breaking the silence.

Steel shook his head. "Not sure yet. We're monitoring the situation, but knowing Shark, he's chomping at the bit to start his shit with us."

The president of Satan's Pistons was ruthless and vindictive. He survived the attack on his clubhouse along with the vice president, Demon, and a couple of club members. He'd been slowly recruiting new members to bring the MC back to life. Diablo had been monitoring it along with Chains. The Night Rebels knew it was only a matter of time before they'd have to deal with the Pistons again. The Pistons' recent alliance with the 39th Street Gang would make the fight more challenging than when the Rebels had kicked their ass the last time.

"Right now they're in the talking stage. The fucking punk gang is only hooking up with the Pistons because they want to get into southern Arizona. They can't be trusted, so that shows what a bunch of dumbasses the Pistons are," Steel said.

"We already knew that about the fuckers," Goldie said, and the members guffawed and cheered.

"Let's hope we can still have the rally. I know the biker community looks forward to it as well as the women and kids. It also brings in some good revenue for Alina," Paco added.

"What if they start their shit at the rally?" Tattoo Mike asked.

"We're gonna have security tighter than Fort Knox. I'm working with the Insurgents. They said they'll hit up their chapters in Nebraska, Kansas, and Montana for help. Maybe even in California. The Fallen Slayers are on board, and even the Twisted Warriors in Ohio said they'd help out. We got allies in Louisiana, Utah, and Idaho. We've got this." Diablo crossed his large arms against his chest and rocked back on his heels.

"Any questions?" Steel asked. When no one answered, he hit the gavel down on the table. "Church is over."

The scraping of chairs and heavy footsteps bounced off the walls as the brothers left the meeting room. Army hung back until everyone but Steel, Paco, Diablo, and Chains had gone. The four members huddled in the front of the room no doubt discussing the impending declaration of war.

Paco looked up and motioned Army to come over. "What's up, bro?"

"I don't know if this is the right time now that all this shit about the fuckin' Pistons has come to light, but I wanted to take about a week or so to visit my family in Durango. It's not that far, so if something blows, I can be back here in under an hour." Army shifted from one foot to another. "If it won't work out, that's cool. I can just go for the day."

Steel and Paco exchanged looks, then Steel said, "I don't see a problem. You can help out and meet with our snitch to see what he knows about the punk gang. We can get another brother to cover you at Lust."

"Brutus does a kickass job, but you'll need to get another brother to help out with the door and kicking assholes out." A rush of excitement surged through Army.

"I could help out," Diablo said.

"When are you thinking of leaving?" Steel asked.

"In a couple of days."

"Wednesday?" Paco said. Army tilted his head. "I'll talk to Brutus. Have a good trip if I don't see you before you leave. If you find anything out, let us know."

Army bumped fists with the brothers then walked to the main room and sidled up to Crow and Patches. The prospect, Ink, put a bottle of beer in front of him.

"You're actually cracking a smile. First time in a while," Crow said as he picked up his glass.

"I'm gonna take a week off and visit my family. I need the fuckin' break." He pushed down the strands of anticipation that knotted in his stomach at the prospect of seeing Stiletto again.

"I heard Willow's history. Who's her replacement?" Patches asked.

*Stiletto, if things go the way I'm planning.* "Just there to see the family." Army guzzled the rest of the beer. "Gotta get to Lust and make sure everything's set up."

"You up for going to Cuervos tonight, or do you have to be at Lust all night?" Crow said.

"What time are you guys going?" Army pulled the keys out of his jacket.

"Nine or ten," Crow replied.

"That'll work. See you then."

Army walked out to the parking lot feeling better than he had for a while. There wasn't a chance in hell he'd admit it was because he'd be seeing Stiletto soon. *No fuckin' way. It's about having some time with*

*Dad.* And if he just ended up with Stiletto pinned to the wall, her sexy legs wrapped around him while he pummeled into her, then all the better.

He sped down the back road to Alina with the sun to his back and the scent of crisp apples and cinnamon in the air.

# Chapter Four

MIA GROANED IN frustration as Kat held her down in a submission she couldn't get out of.

"What the fuck's wrong with you, Stiletto?" Rick yelled. "This is an easy move to get away from. Focus!"

Kat pulled away and tapped Mia on the back. "We can go another round if you want to."

"She's not doing anything but laps and the speed bag." Rick narrowed his eyes at Mia. "Now!"

She leapt to her feet and went over to the water station to grab a cold bottle. From her peripheral vision she saw Goliath approaching, and her stomach twisted. *I should've stayed home tonight.*

"Do you want to tell me what's going on?" Goliath asked, his burning gaze scanned her face.

She ran the cool bottle over her face and neck then gave a half shrug. "I don't know. I guess the stuff with my family is interfering." She took a deep gulp, the cold water refreshing her dry throat.

"We all got shit to deal with. You've had it before. I don't approve of this hiatus you're taking, but just because you won't be fighting for a while doesn't mean you still don't give it your all during practice and training. Rick's in demand, and I've got a waiting list a mile long for people who want to join Champion. If you can't focus, then maybe you should move on."

Her chest tightened. *Is Goliath saying what I think he is?* "Are you kicking me out?" she blurted. She rubbed the back of her neck as her stomach churned.

For several seconds, the silence between them was deafening. Mia bounced from one foot to another in an attempt to quell her fear. If Goliath kicked her out of the gym, a huge part of her would shrivel up. The gym she'd trained at in Tucson had nothing of the camaraderie of Champion, and she'd made some really good friends at the training center. Goliath, the owner, was a retired three-time MMA heavyweight titleholder, and he was phenomenal as a coach. Rick Rodriguez was one of the most sought-after trainers in Durango, and she'd been pleasantly shocked when he'd agreed to work with her the year before. *I can't lose everything I've worked so hard for. I can't lose Champion.* It was the beacon that forced away the darkness which threatened to invade her psyche at every opportunity. After she'd been beaten and date-raped, her sense of security had evaporated. That night, she hadn't been able to fight off Gavin no matter how hard she tried. She'd been powerless, and it was the worse feeling in the world.

"You need to step up your game. We're not fucking psychologists ... we're trainers. If you need a break, you'll have a spot if you decide to come back." Goliath's gruff voice pulled her back from the past.

"I don't want a break. I'm back in." Mia let out a breath she didn't know she'd been holding.

"Make sure you are. None of us wants to waste our fucking time with a fighter who doesn't give it her all. Got it?" Mia nodded. "I heard Rick tell you to do laps. Get your ass running." Goliath stalked away, and she threw the bottle into the recycle bin, warmed up, then began running.

A couple of hours later, Mia dried off after a welcoming shower. Pushing her body and focusing on her breathing was just what she needed to take her outside her head. For the past couple of weeks, all that had been swirling around in her mind was Army and the mess her younger brother was in. Mia's mother had called the week before to tell her that Finn had been arrested for armed robbery in Phoenix. It seemed that during the course of one night, he'd robbed five convenience stores at gunpoint. Her mother had cried and kept saying that "my baby's gone," and it'd really grated on her nerves because for most of their growing years, her mother hadn't given much of a shit about any of them, especially Mia and her two brothers, Finn and Tucker. The only one her mom seemed to kind of give a damn about was Mia's oldest brother, Vic. All her mom really cared about back then—and now—was partying and having a man.

"You want to join us at Berriegood?" Kat asked, breaking through her thoughts.

"Not tonight. I'm pretty beat."

"Goliath and Rick were pretty hard on you. We all have off days."

Mia slipped on her high-heeled pumps. "But not bad weeks. I've been off my game for too long. I don't blame them for being pissed at me."

"They're always pissed at someone." Kat chuckled. "I still don't know how you can wear those damn heels all the time."

"I don't know how you can't." Mia smiled, stuffing her workout clothes in her gym bag.

Mia's love affair with high heels started when she was a freshman in high school and saw Abby Boothe's elegant four-inch strappy heels. Never mind that they were Jimmy Choo and had cost more than her family's monthly assistance check; they were magical, and from that day on, she'd been hooked.

When she'd first come to Champion, Goliath and the other trainers tried to come up with a good fighter name for her and they soon landed on "Stiletto."

"Are you coming in tomorrow?" Kat slipped a T-shirt over her head.

"I don't think so. My last appointment at the salon is at seven thirty. I'm just going to chill at home and enjoy a rare evening off. I'll see you on Friday. Maybe you'll want to join me and my friends for a drink on Saturday?"

"I'd love to. Thanks." Kat slammed her locker shut, and the two women walked outside.

A golden harvest moon hung low, occasionally obscured by ribbons of black clouds scudding across the sky. The scent of burning firewood permeated the air, and fallen leaves scattered across the road as the cool breeze gently stung Mia's cheeks.

"Winter's in the air," Kat said, wrapping her sweater tighter around herself.

"I hope it doesn't come too soon. I love the fall." Mia dug her keys out of her purse. "See you." She walked to the parking lot and hit the Unlock button on her fob. The headlights from her navy blue Chevy Cruze blinked on, illuminating a figure standing to the left of her car. Instantly, her muscles tensed, and she dropped her gym bag. A figure came toward her, and for a split second she thought it was Army. Tingles skipped over her skin but quickly stopped when her ex-boyfriend came into full view.

"What're you doing here, Jorge?" Mia picked up her gym bag and slung it over her shoulder.

"I was in the area and wanted to talk to you," he answered in a low voice.

"Why didn't you wait outside the gym instead of lurking in the parking lot?" She opened the car door. "I'm really beat tonight. What did you want to talk about?" A small frown furrowed her brow. She'd broken up with Jorge over five months ago, and he didn't want to admit it was over.

"My mom wanted me to ask you to come over on Saturday for my parents' anniversary party. They're celebrating twenty-five years."

"That's a long time. Good for them." A wide smile cracked Jorge's face. Mia meant it. If a married couple made it past five years, that was amazing, but twenty-five years? *That* was a miracle.

"Can you go? My parents would love it if you came." The plea in Jorge's voice reminded her why she dumped him.

She threw her gym bag on the passenger seat. "I've already got plans for Saturday." The way he hung his head down made her feel guilty even though she had no reason to. Jorge was famous for making her feel bad about things she shouldn't. *Just like good old Mom.* Turning to him, she sighed. "Look, we're broken up."

"But we can be friends," he said.

"We can't. I mean, *I* can't. I'm not the type to be friendly with my exes. I just move on. It eliminates a lot of drama down the road, you know? You're a great guy who deserves a woman who is into setting up house, making babies, and playing wife-of-the-year. I'm *so* not that person. You know that." Jorge just stared at her, his mouth turned downward. "I have to go. Tell your parents thanks for the invite. Bye, Jorge." She slipped into the car, started the engine, and drove out of the parking lot. In her rearview mirror, she saw him standing on the sidewalk, watching her, until she turned the corner.

Mia pounded the steering wheel. "Why can't Jorge move the fuck on? Men are a major pain in the ass," she said aloud. Army's face pushed into her mind. "And he's the biggest one of all." She turned on the radio and cranked it all the way up as she drove to her townhouse.

★ ★ ★

"WILL YOU PLEASE call Peyton back? She's bugging the crap out of me," Ronica said as she sat in the salon chair at Mia's booth.

Mia, checking the timer she'd set for her client, shook her head. "I'll call her when I have a minute to breathe. I've had back-to-back clients all day. My last one is at seven thirty. What does she want anyway?"

Ronica picked up one of Mia's hairstyling magazines and thumbed through it. "Something stupid. She's drooling and desperate over that guy. I can't remember his name. Something military sounding."

Mia froze, her insides clenching. "Army?" she said in a small voice.

"That's it. I guess she went by the gym this morning thinking you'd be there and saw him. She wants to know when you're going so she can get you to ask Taylor if the four of you can go out for a drink or something. I can't believe the way she's carrying on about him. He's good-looking, but he's not the only handsome man in Durango."

"Army's at Champion?" Fierce licks of excitement leapt through her.

Ronica looked up, her gaze fixed on Mia. "Are you glad he's here?"

Mia turned away and pretended to be engrossed in the hair dye mixing bowls. "You know I'm not interested in him. Oh … I forgot to tell you that Jorge was waiting for me in the gym's parking lot last night. Why can't he just move the fuck on?"

"You need to be firmer with him. Tell him …"

Mia smiled knowing Ronica loved giving advice. As her friend rambled on, Mia dwelled on the news that Army was back. Her brain told her body to stop humming with anticipation but it wouldn't listen. Her phone's ringtone interrupted Ronica's monologue, and a startled Mia dropped the bowls on the tile floor. "Crap," she muttered.

"I'll get them," Ronica said, sliding out of the chair. "If it's Peyton, do me a favor and answer it."

Peyton's name flashed across the screen, and Mia put the phone to her ear.

"Finally! I've been trying to get a hold of you for the last few hours. Didn't Ronica tell you?"

"She just now mentioned it. We've both been crazy busy today."

"Did she tell you why I was calling?" Peyton's voiced pitched higher.

"It's about Taylor's brother. He's at Champion." Mia took the bowls from Ronica and mouthed "thank you" to her.

"I'm begging you to set up an outing with you, me, and Taylor, and ask him to bring Army along. From what I've heard, he's not seeing anyone."

"Maybe not just one woman, but I'll bet my month's income that he's seeing a bunch. Do you really want someone like that, Peyton? Can't you find a nice guy at work?"

"Are you joking? I'm a nail tech. Almost all my customers are women. The rest are gay men or straight and married. Worst job to meet men … ever. I've never been this close to meeting a guy like Army. Those kinds of guys just blitz right past me without even giving me a *first* look. I just want to see how it feels to have all the women envy me. Just for one night."

The timer went off and Mia glanced at her client who sat with three outer-space-looking heat lamps positioned around her head. She ran her teeth over the bottom corner of her lip.

"If you don't want to, I understand. Actually, just forget about it. I don't know what got into me. It's been too long since I've had a date."

Mia inhaled a deep breath and blew it out, her gaze still on Mrs. Shapiro and the lamps. Against her better judgment, she agreed to talk to Taylor.

"Thank you so much! I'll do your nails for free for the next six months. Are you going to the gym after work?"

"No. I'm finishing up late tonight. I'll talk to him tomorrow and let you know. Army may only be in town for one night."

"I know. Let me know. Thanks. You're a good friend."

*More like a stupid one.* "I better go before my client's hair turns platinum blonde." Mia put the phone down and avoided Ronica's stare.

"You caved in. You know this is going to be a disaster, and for sure Army's going to think you arranged this because *you* wanted a date with him. He's too cocky to think anything else. He'll never believe the 'my-friend-wants-to-meet-you' story."

Mia walked over to the middle-aged woman and checked a strand of her hair. "It's time. The color is beautiful. Let's wash it out." As she passed Ronica, Mia grimaced. "You're right. What the hell have I done?" she whispered, her client following her.

"Created a monster with some of the best inked arms I've seen." Ronica's words fell over Mia as she led Mrs. Shapiro to the sink.

The hours flew by and when Mia pulled into her garage, she was exhausted. The minute she opened the back door, her two cats, Snickers and Pumpkin, meowed and rubbed against her legs.

"How're you girls doing? Sorry I'm late." She bent down and scratched them behind their ears. "I'm starving, what about you?"

Mia went over to the cupboard and took down two cans of food. As she open them, Snickers jumped up on the counter and rubbed her face against Mia's shirt while Pumpkin sat patiently on the floor, looking up at her with luminous green eyes. She set their dishes on the floor, and they ran over and began to eat. Mia watched them and smiled.

She'd rescued both, the tabby and the tricolored feline, at a Tucson shelter a few months after her attack. Her therapist had recommended that she consider getting a pet, so Mia went into the shelter that night with the intention of adopting a cat. But after she'd picked Snickers, she saw Pumpkin's light orange fur with snow-white markings on her belly, paws, and chin and fell in love with her. Now, with her late hours, she was glad her pets had each other.

Mia made a quick omelet and poured a generous portion of white wine into her water glass, ignoring the images of Goliath's and Rick's disapproving faces. "It's been a rough two weeks," she said aloud as she padded to the family room and sank into the couch. Snickers settled in behind Mia on top of the couch, and Pumpkin burrowed next to her.

A feeling of dread wove through her as she ate, and Mia was sorry for promising Peyton that she'd talk to Taylor about the four of them going out. *What the hell was I thinking? I don't want to spend five minutes with Army, let alone an evening. Ugh!* Even though she found him physically attractive, she wasn't crazy about his attitude and how he thought he was every woman's sexual fantasy.

Picking up the remote, she switched on the television and slowly sipped her wine, wishing tomorrow would never come.

# Chapter Five

ARMY TUGGED THE hem of his T-shirt down as he walked into the kitchen at Taylor's apartment. Squatting down in front of the open refrigerator, he took out two beers.

"Grab me a water," Taylor said from the small living room.

Army came into the room and tossed the bottle at his brother then sat down on the recliner in the corner of the room. "What's on the agenda for tonight?" He pulled the tab on the can and took a drink. The night before, he'd joined his brother at Berriegood, had a protein bowl which he hated, and endured two hours of martial arts talk just for the chance of seeing Stiletto. *Just like a fuckin' pussy.* She never showed up, and Army had decided he was done thinking about the chick. There were plenty of hot women he could pick up, and from the way Sela and Kat, the two MMA fighters from Champion, were checking him out, he was sure he could split his time in Durango between the two of them.

"Do you want to go to a nightclub?" Taylor asked.

"Fuck yeah. I'm itching to meet some babes tonight. I've been to the Mayan before, and a lot of pretty Latina women hang out there. The music is a mix of reggaeton and pop, and it rocks."

"I've never been there. I was thinking more along the lines of EDM. Sound Nightclub is fucking awesome."

"You know me, I'm a metal and rock guy, but I'm game." Army opened the second can of beer.

"Would you be cool if I asked a couple of girls to go with us?"

Army grinned. "Have you been holding out on me? Does your chick want me to be her sister or friend's date?"

"Something like that, but it's more my friend's friend who really wants to meet you. You met her at Cricket on the Hill a couple of weeks ago." Taylor shifted in place. "I told my friend I'm not sure you'd go for it."

"Who's your friend?" A smug half-grin raised up the corner of Army's mouth.

"Mia. Her friend, Peyton, is interested in you. She was the one sitting across from Mia. The one with the short hair that had streaks of pink in it. Do you remember her?"

*So this is Stiletto's game—a friend wants to hook up with me. Okay, sweetheart, I'll play along.* "Not really. I remember Stiletto, though."

"Uh ... Mia doesn't like to be called Stiletto outside the ring."

"I'll remember that." Army tipped his head back and finished his beer.

"So is that something you'd want to do? I told Mia I'd let her know. If you'd rather not, that's cool. We can still go to the club."

"I'm up for it." Army rubbed his finger across his lips. "Are you interested in Stiletto?"

Taylor shook his and laughed. "Not in that way. We're just friends. You better remember not to call her Stiletto tonight, or she'll ream you out."

"I wouldn't want *that*." Army stood up. "I got some club business I need to do. Text me the time we're gonna meet up with the ladies."

"Okay. Are you planning to go over to Dad's on Sunday? Starla's making dinner."

"Is she the one you told me about the other day? The one he just met?" Taylor nodded. "I'll pass."

"I think Dad wants you over. Asher and Kali will be there with Joshua. Don't you want to see your nephew?"

"I'm going over to Asher's tomorrow. Don't push me on this, okay?" Army threw Taylor a warning look.

"Okay. I'll text you soon with the details about tonight."

"Sounds good," Army said as he walked out the door.

The crumbling three-story building in the run-down part of the city looked like it belonged in a horror film. Broken windows, graffiti, and an air of death surrounded the abandoned building. Army drove slowly around the narrow street that circled the place. Rusted cans, piles of trash, and tangled balls of tumbleweed cluttered the road. Even though blackness stared out of the windows, and an eerie stillness surrounded the place, he could smell the desperation from scores of junkies who made the dilapidated building their home.

He turned off the motor and walked toward the rusted door that had a screaming ghoul painted on it. It looked like the stuff nightmares were made of, but then, Army figured that living in this hellhole must be a nightmare. Sand crunched under his boots, and he spied used syringes littering the ground. The closer he got to the building, the more prevalent the scent of urine, sweat, and feces grew.

He walked up the decaying concrete stairs then touched the gun that was tucked away in his waistband under his loose T-shirt before opening the door and entering. It took a few seconds for his eyes to adjust to the dimness, but soon he saw shadowy figures scurrying away to darkened corners and other rooms.

"Do you got any smack?" a female voice asked him.

Army turned to the left and saw a skinny woman huddled against the wall. "No. I'm here to buy. Is Lil' Donnie around?"

The woman pushed herself up and staggered toward him. The sunlight behind him cast a diffused illumination on her as she came closer. Army stepped back, his senses on high alert. The woman smelled like she hadn't bathed in a long time. Her face and arms were covered with scabs and sores, and her eyes were puffy and bloodshot. She grabbed the hem of her dirty shirt with one hand and lifted it up to reveal two small breasts. "I can give you this"—her other hand slid down between her thighs—"if you give me a hit," she slurred.

"I told you, I'm here to buy." Army wanted to throw her a twenty-dollar bill, but he didn't; he knew that gesture would circulate like wildfire, and he'd be surrounded by junkies begging for their next fix. Keeping her in his peripheral view, he glanced around and wondered where the hell Lil' Donnie was.

The snitch had told Army he'd be at the building at three p.m. Anger sizzled his nerves. Four years in the army made punctuality second nature for him. Another addict came out of the shadows and stared at him. The man looked to be in his teens and had long, straggly hair. Like the woman, who had now slumped down on the floor, scabs and sores dotted the young man's face and limbs. He shoved his hands in his jeans.

"I want a nickel bag," he rasped as he opened his hand.

Army looked at the wadded-up bills and shook his head. "I'm here to buy. Looking for Lil' Donnie."

"Over here," a voice whispered.

Army stepped back cautiously and placed his hand on the gun. From the corner of his eye, he saw a man plastered against the wall.

"How much do you want?" the man asked.

Army turned around and recognized the droopy eyes and lazy smile of the dealer. "I'm looking for a couple of baggies of your best stuff." Army came in close.

"I got you covered, dude. I don't keep the good stuff on me. Follow me." Lil' Donnie climbed up a flight of stairs and headed to a closed door. He turned the lock and went inside.

Army assessed the area then entered the room and locked the door behind him. "You sure no one can hear us?" he asked in a low voice.

"Yeah. Youse got the money?"

"After you talk."

Army watched Lil' Donnie go over to the window and look out. The dealer was one of several snitches the Night Rebels used to gather information. He'd been on the MC's payroll for the last two years. So far, he'd proved to be reliable and as honest as they could expect from a two-bit dealer.

"The word is that the 39th Street Gang is setting up a meeting with Satan's Pistons in a few weeks. They hate the Arizona bastards and they're planning to rip them off by giving them less quantity and quality. The word is that the biker motherfuckers are paying a fuckload of money for what's gonna be a shit product. They'll be diluting the smack with starch and powdered milk."

Army scrubbed his face with his fist. "The Pistons will never fall for that. Are you sure about your info?"

The man bobbed his head. "Yeah. The 39th dudes are gonna have the top and middle layer of the shipment with the pure stuff, but the rest is gonna be fucked."

"Then the 39th fuckers aren't planning to team up with the Pistons."

"Nope. They see it like the fuckers need them. The 39th Street Gang don't need the Pistons except for the easy money they're handing to them." Lil' Donnie laughed.

"Where's the meeting gonna be at?"

"I don't know yet. It'll cost more when I find out." The snitch glanced out the window.

"You expecting someone?" Army's voice had an edge to it as he slipped his hand under his T-shirt.

"No. I just don't like staying here too long. I'm usually in and outta here pretty quick."

Army stared at the dealer. "You better go then. I'll go after you've left." He slipped his hand in his pocket and took out a roll of bills. "Let me know about the meeting."

Lil' Donnie counted out the bills, shoved them in the inner pocket of his sports jacket, and grinned. "It's always good doing business with you." He opened the door and closed it quietly.

Army watched him leave and waited for a while to make sure no one was creeping around. He took out his gun and walked down the stairs. The woman and young man were no longer there, but in their place were three teenagers huddled over lighters, and under the flickering flames, their faces resembled ghoulish masks.

He stepped out into the sunshine and didn't relax until he settled down on Taylor's couch. His brother wasn't home, so Army gave Steel a call to update him on what he'd learned from their snitch.

Right after he hung up from talking to the president, Army's phone pinged. He glanced at the text.

**Taylor:** *We'll meet the women @ 7 for dinner.*

As Army kicked off his boots and plopped his feet up on the coffee table, excitement surged through him. It was a new sensation for him in regard to a woman. The only time he felt that way with women was when they were fucking, but then again, that was the way men were wired.

**Army:** *We still going dancing?*

**Taylor:** *Yeah. It was my idea about dinner. Cool?*

Army grinned.

**Army:** *Sure. I'm @ ur place now.*

**Taylor:** *I'll be home from the gym in an hr.*

Army wanted to ask if the sexy fighter was at the gym, but he put down his phone instead, then went into the kitchen to grab a couple of beers. Settling back on the couch, he stared at the big-ass TV screen in front of him; it almost took up the entire room. Army took a swig of beer and leaned back against the cushions.

Army hated to admit it, but he was looking forward to seeing Stiletto. He didn't even know what it was about her that had struck him so forcefully that night at the fights, but he'd been thrown off balance when he'd first seen her. *It was her eyes that drew me in, and after that, it was all her.* There was something about the way she'd walked to the middle of the ring, the sexy tilt of her chin, which seemed to exude confidence, and the way she moved in a sensual yet violently charged dance that ensnared him. Afterward, when he saw her in those fuck-me heels and wickedly tight dress with her hair falling over her shoulders, he knew he had to have her. *But she acted like she wasn't interested.* He snorted. *Bullshit. You're not fooling me.* The light flush that had spread up her neck when their eyes met, along with the way she'd gasped from his touch outside the restaurant after that crazy spark had passed between them, confirmed what he already knew—she wanted him as bad as he wanted her.

"If you want me to chase you, *sweetheart*, the hunt's on," Army said under his breath.

He interlaced his fingers behind his head and stretched back, a slow smile spreading over his face. He hadn't had this much fun with a woman in a very long time.

# Chapter Six

MIA SWIPED ANOTHER coat of burgundy mascara on her lashes and stepped back to look at herself in the full-length mirror in the corner of the bedroom. Sweeping her eyes over her eggplant-colored mesh mini-dress with spaghetti straps, and her five-inch peep-toe lace-up heels, she wondered if she should change into a pair of leggings and a top.

Snickers sat at the base of the mirror, looking up at her. Mia smiled. "You like my shiny dress? Is it too much?" If it was a regular Friday night with her friends, she'd already have been out the door, not giving a second thought about her outfit, but this wasn't an ordinary clubbing night—Army would be there.

"Why the hell am I second-guessing my wardrobe?" Snickers meowed and blinked her blues. Mia shook her head. "I guess I don't want him to think I got all dressed up for *him* ... and I don't want him ogling me all night." She glanced back at her reflection; the sheath draped over her body, enhancing every feminine aspect of her figure. *I love this dress.* The minutes slipped away ... Then, she turned away from the mirror, snatched her black clutch that sat on the dresser, and went downstairs.

After refilling her cats' dry food bowls, she stroked each one behind the ears then picked up her car keys and went into the garage. Butterflies fluttered about inside her as she drove to the restaurant, and she groaned in frustration. *How the hell am I going to make it through tonight? I should call Taylor and say I just threw up.* The way her sour stomach churned, she wouldn't be that far off with the white lie. *Why did I agree to this!* Loyalty weighed her down; she couldn't disappoint Peyton or Taylor. *I'll just have to make sure I keep my distance from Army and not let him get under my skin.* His smugness irked the crap out of her, and she suspected he knew that and got a kick out of egging her on. She vowed not to let him suck her into his childish game. *I'll be polite, but distant.* Relieved that she'd come up with a plan, she loosened her death grip on the steering wheel and turned on the radio.

LongHorn was one of Durango's newer restaurants, and it had a more modern look than the traditional dark woods and burgundy leather chairs that had become the stereotypical décor for steakhouses. Warm burnt-orange-colored walls, maple wood floors, brushed-steel tables, as well as chairs upholstered in a mélange of colors and patterns, and copper animal and landscape wall hangings gave the fine-dining restaurant a cozy but urban ambiance. A spectacular view of the San Juan Mountains helped to keep the place packed almost every night.

After circling the parking lot a few times, Mia finally landed a parking spot. As she slid out of the car, her phone rang.

"Hi. I just got here. Are you inside already?" she asked Peyton.

"I'm not feeling so good," Peyton replied. Mia's heartbeat raced as she leaned against the car, her fingers touching her parted lips as Peyton continued, "I know ... I'm the one who made you set this whole thing up. I feel terrible about it."

"I'm at the fucking restaurant. I don't even want to be here. And you're bagging out on me? No fucking way."

"I'm just sick to my stomach. I don't know what I was thinking," Peyton said.

"You're just nervous." Mia's mind raced. *How can she be canceling?*

"I'm terrified."

"He's just a guy. I'm going to be there and so is Taylor. Taylor's real easygoing, and if things don't click with you and his brother, it's no big deal. You're not on a blind date alone with him. Anyway, Taylor didn't set this up like a date." *At least I don't think he did.* "You have to come. It'll be fun. Remember how much fun it was the last time we went to Sound?" *It really wasn't—too many guys who touched before asking.*

"Yes ... we did have fun," Peyton replied in a soft voice.

"And I hear the steak is superb at LongHorn. If nothing else, we'll get a good dinner and a few drinks at Sound. You love EDM." Mia tapped her foot on the asphalt while crossing her fingers.

"All right, but you can't leave early, okay?" Peyton said.

Irritation pricked along her skin. Peyton was giving *her* conditions when the whole damn idea had been Peyton's. *Whatever.* "Yeah, okay. Deal. Are you dressed?"

"Yes. I just need to do my hair."

"How long until you get here?"

"Twenty-five minutes?" Peyton replied.

"I'll meet you inside. Just hurry." Mia put the phone in her clutch and walked across the parking lot. "I definitely need a drink," she muttered.

"Hi, Mia." Taylor's voice rode on the breeze.

She looked around and saw him standing in front of the restaurant. She waved. "Hey." Then Army appeared and she gasped at how handsome he looked in a dove gray button-down shirt and black dress pants that fit him to perfection. A dark rim of stubble bracketed his strong jaw and framed his full mouth. Wisps of inked shapes curled around his wrists and reached up under his fitted shirt, which was unbuttoned at the collar. Then he looked directly at her and his eyes sparkled like storm clouds right before lightning hit. A thrill worked its way up her spine.

Army lifted his chin then smirked, his twist of lips almost lethal. Mia broke eye contact with him and smiled at Taylor as she swallowed in a vain attempt to moisten her dry mouth. "You look beautiful." Army's voice washed over her, making her insides melt.

They hadn't even gone into the restaurant and her body was already misbehaving. This was ridiculous. "Thanks," she sputtered.

"Where's Peyton?" Taylor asked.

Grateful for breaking through their lust, Mia cleared her throat and walked up to Taylor. "She's running a little late but should be here soon. Let's go in. I could use a drink."

Army opened the door for Mia as she walked past; the heat of his body caressed her, and the intensity of his stare made things inside her clench. She made a beeline to the bar and leaned against the polished stainless steel counter pretending that everything was normal.

"What do you want?" Army asked.

His scent wrapped around Mia and filled her senses. She turned around only to find him close behind with his gaze locked on hers. She wondered where on his body he'd put his cologne. Her eyes drifted to his chest—the outline of his taut muscles visible against the shirt, and she imagined dabbing some of the spicy-scented liquid lightly over his pecs, abs, and the sculpted V that she was positive he had. Touching him. Smelling him. Taking him in as she pressed her bare breasts against his delectable chest. Suddenly lightheaded, she swayed, and his powerful arm gripped her waist.

"Let me find a seat for you," Army said.

"No … I'm okay. It's just so crowded and stuffy in here."

"Our table's ready," Taylor said as he approached them.

*Thank God.* Mia slid by Army and followed Taylor, making a mental note to ignore any sinfully delicious scents of sandalwood, tangy herbs, and spicy pepper emanating from him for the rest of the night.

Mia sat down at the square table and immediately placed her clutch on the chair to the right of her while tapping the empty place on the other side of her. "Come sit here, Taylor." She gave a saccharin-sweet smile and a thread of satisfaction wove through her as Taylor edged out Army, then sat down.

The chair across from her scraped on the hardwood floor, and Army sank down, leaned back, and winked at her, the corner of his mouth lifting in a sly half-smile. "I like the view better from here."

As they ordered their drinks, Mia was acutely aware of Army's unwavering eyes on her, which she refused to acknowledge, hoping it would convince him that she wasn't interested. By the time her Manhattan arrived, she'd talked nonstop to Taylor, and the confused look on his face made her feel like an idiot. Army was making her act like a pathetic girl rather than a strong and confident woman. *Why am I so nervous? This is ridiculous. And where the fuck is Peyton?* She glanced at her phone, cursing her friend for being so late.

"Peyton should be here at any moment." She glanced quickly at Army then gripped the glass and took a deep drink in an attempt to quell the flutters in the pit of her stomach.

"So is Peyton my date?" Army asked.

Mia felt her throat constrict and panic seized her as she coughed and choked.

"Are you okay?" Taylor asked as concern laced his voice.

Not able to talk, she nodded and placed a napkin over her mouth. Diners at the table next to theirs stared at her, and the waiter rushed over.

"Can I help with anything?" he asked.

As she shook her head, all Mia wanted to do was slide down her chair and disappear. "I just swallowed wrong," she managed to spit out. "It's okay." The whole time she was making a fool of herself, Army's gaze remained steadfast. *He's infuriating!* She dabbed the corners of her eyes with the napkin.

After a few seconds of silence, Army leaned forward and propped his elbows on the table. "You never answered me. Is Peyton my date for the night?"

"She wanted to meet you," Taylor said, handing Mia his unused napkin. "You don't date, remember?" he smiled weakly at Mia.

"So this is a date for her, but not for me. Is your friend cool with that, Stiletto?"

She wanted to slap the arrogant smile right off his face. "I'm only called Stiletto in the ring, and Peyton just wanted to meet up and have dinner with us." She took a small sip of water.

A low chuckle escaped Army's lips before he took a mouthful of his drink. "Then it's a hookup." He studied her over the rim of the glass. "Right?"

His words goaded her. *The bastard's enjoying this.* Mia lifted her chin and met his intense gaze. "It's whatever you want to call it."

They stared at each other until Taylor cleared his throat. "Uh ... to me, it's just friends—Mia and me—getting together with my brother and her friend. I can get to know Peyton and so can you." He lifted his chin at Army.

"And"—Army ran his finger up and down the side of the glass then threw back the whiskey—"Stiletto and I can get to know each other as well."

"I already know one thing about you," Mia said, gesturing to the waiter for another drink. "You don't listen. I told you, Stiletto's my ring name only."

"I listen just fine, *sweetheart.* Stiletto suits you better—slender and lethal, like the knife." His gaze drifted to her lips.

"Sorry, I'm late," Peyton said, breaking the intensity between Army and Mia. She put Mia's clutch on the table then sat down. "Have you ordered yet?"

From the slight tremor in Peyton's voice, Mia knew she was nervous as hell. "Just our drinks." She nodded at Taylor. "You remember Taylor," she said. "And his brother, Army."

Shifting his eyes to Peyton's face, he tilted his head then looked back at Mia.

"This is going to be so fun," Mia lied as she picked up the menu. "I don't know about anyone else, but I'm starving." She looked down at the selections, ignoring the insane chemistry crackling between her and Army.

"What do you recommend?" Army asked.

Mia's amber eyes glanced up, and as they connected, the heated stare from Army's blue ones made her squirm. "This is my first time here."

"It's too expensive for our ... or at least *my* budget," Peyton said breathlessly.

Poor Peyton was a basket case, but if Army kept looking at her that way, she'd be joining her. *Crap!* The toe of Army's boot was running up and down her calf, leaving a trail of electric sparks in its wake while it dampened her lace panties. *It's just a physical reaction. It doesn't mean anything.* She pulled her legs in and wrapped them around the bottom of the chair.

"I thought you'd been here," Taylor said.

Mia smiled softly. "After buying my townhouse, I'm on a pretty strict budget, but I've been wanting to try it out. Good choice." She lightly touched his hand and thought she heard Army growl low and deep from his chest. When she glanced over at him, his gaze was hard, like glacial ice, and she met it, challenging him with the tilt of her chin.

"What're you going to have?" Taylor asked Army.

"I'd like something raw and tender," Army said, staring at Mia.

And he didn't stop. He just kept it up—blatantly eye-fucking her in front of Taylor and Peyton. From her peripheral vision, she saw Peyton's smile frozen on her taut face.

Leaning forward, Mia cocked her head to the side. "Then order the steak tartare. It should satisfy your carnal, caveman-like appetite."

"Shit," Peyton whispered at the same time Taylor said, "Where the hell is the waiter?"

Army jerked his head back and flashed Mia a wicked grin. "You *do* know me, *Stiletto.* I'm fuckin' touched."

A collective sigh of relief escaped Taylor's and Peyton's parted lips when the waiter came over to the table to take their order, and Army chuckled, his damn boot finding her calf again. Mia focused on her order and tried to ignore the sizzling undercurrent of desire connecting them, mad as hell that she was feeling *anything* more than annoyance for this man. Sneaking a quick peek, she was met by his now familiar smug look, and she couldn't think of anything more tempting and appealing at that moment than knocking it off his face for good.

*This is going to be a very long night.*

"ARMY'S NOT INTO me," Peyton said as she combed her hair in the ladies' room at Sound Nightclub.

"I don't think he's the type to gush over any woman," Mia replied.

Peyton caught her gaze in the mirror. "Are you kidding me? He's totally into you."

*Damn you, Army.* "I don't think I'd say that. He just feels more comfortable with me because I'm friends with Taylor." *That doesn't even make any fucking sense.*

Peyton stopped combing her hair and turned around. "It's okay. Really. I think my *idea* of going out with a bad boy is more fun than actually *being* with one. Taylor's nice and cute, though."

"He's a sweetheart. Totally not like his jerk brother."

"I think you keep badmouthing Army so you can convince yourself that you aren't interested."

"I'm not interested," Mia replied.

"I should've taken a video of the way you two were checking each other out during dinner. I don't know why you're fighting it. You haven't had a date since you broke up with Jorge, and that was over five months ago."

"When's the last time *you* had a date?"

Peyton smiled. "Last night with the guy who works at the smoothie place next door to the nail salon. We've been sort of flirting with each other on and off for the last six months. I never thought of going out with him, but I actually had a really good time. I guess that's why I kind of freaked out about meeting Army tonight. Will is just a plain ol' guy. Average looks, body, and height, but he has a real good sense of humor and we had a fun time. After last night, I didn't think I could hold my own with Army. He's intimidating and definitely not average."

"Are you going to see Will again?" Mia asked.

Peyton shrugged then turned back to the mirror. "I don't know. He's nice, but I think he's more in the 'friends' category. I'd give my number to Taylor if he asked me."

"I hope he does, but if he doesn't, it's because he's totally focused on going pro. I'm surprised he skipped training to make tonight happen."

"I'm glad he did. I'm having a good time, and I like getting to know

Taylor. He said we'd dance when I get back from the bathroom." She put away her comb and smiled. "Let's get back to our table."

Mia sat stiffly while she watched Taylor and Peyton on the dance floor. Army stood up and held out his hand. "Let's dance," he yelled.

Pretending she couldn't hear him, she shrugged her shoulders and pointed her finger to her ear then diverted her gaze back to the crowd. All of a sudden, she was yanked to her feet, the surprise of it taking her breath away. Army clutched her wrist and dragged her through the labyrinth of people.

"What the fuck are you doing?" she yelled, but the loud music swallowed her words. Beams of red, green, yellow, and blue lights flashed all around as she stumbled behind him. The doorman stamped the insides of their wrists then Army pulled her outside. The cool night air felt good after the stuffiness in the club. When they rounded the corner, Mia jerked her hand away from him.

"What the fuck's your problem?" she asked, rubbing her wrist.

In a sharp catch of her breath, he yanked her to him so hard, the purse in her hand dropped to the ground as she thudded against his chest. "Are you crazy? Let me—" Her outrage was lost in his mouth as he seized hers in a furious, possessive kiss. She brought up her knee and pushed him back, then hauled off and rammed her fist into his hard stomach.

Army flashed her a wicked smile. "Fuck, baby. You've got a good punch." He pulled her back into his arms and crushed his mouth down on hers again as his hand grabbed a fistful of her hair.

His lips were firm and demanding, sending needles of pleasure to every nerve in her body. Mia's protests died a quick death with a groan of surrender, and her fingers gripped his shoulders as she leaned into the kiss. He tasted like whiskey and dark temptation, and his scent of crisp night air and heated male skin swirled around her.

Lips open, breaths melding, they sank deeper into the kiss. His tongue darted inside, and hers met it halfway, tangling together in a frantic dance of lust. The sound of his groan in her mouth was like an electric jolt, turning her to mush.

It was unlike any kiss she'd ever experienced. Passionate. Urgent. Wild. Hot.

*What the hell am I doing?* Mia's mind screamed, but her body shut it up, and she pressed closer to him, rubbing against his erection as tingles skated up and down her spine.

"Fuck, baby. You taste and feel so damn good," he smothered her mouth.

Army's rough hand skimmed down her back then raked up under the hem of her dress and squeezed her ass.

*He takes what he wants without asking. Don't do this!* When his fingers inched toward her aching mound, she pushed them away, but he tried again. Another push. Another try. *He's a persistent bastard. I'll just be another woman who he's fucked.*

Mia used her strength and shoved him back. For a few seconds, Army looked startled then confused. She straightened out her dress and picked up her clutch, retrieving a wand of lip gloss that had rolled out of it.

Army reached out for her and she moved away from him. "Don't touch me." Her tone matched the chill in the air.

He glowered at her. "You didn't have a problem with it a minute ago. You were clawing and rubbing against me like a cat in heat."

His words lashed at her, but she feigned indifference. Mia shrugged then put the lip gloss back in her purse and snapped the clasp. "We obviously find each other attractive. It was inevitable. I got it out of my system." She ran her palms over goosebumped arms. "When you so rudely yanked me out here, I didn't have my jacket."

He took his off and started to walk over to her. Mia lifted up her hand. "I don't need anything from you. I'm going inside."

Army quirked his lips and slipped on his jacket. "I disagree. The way you were kissing me, *sweetheart,* showed me you need a lot more from me."

Tossing her head, she stared at him. "Don't flatter yourself. I've had a stressful week. Any good-looking guy would've fit the bill tonight."

"Bullshit. You don't fool me one bit. And the shit about Peyton wanting to meet me is so fuckin' high school. Just grow up and admit you want to hook up with me. You know I'm in."

"What is it with you? Are we all just living in *your* world? I've met men with egos, but you're in a league of your own. *Newsflash*—not all women want you. Sorry to break it to you." Mia stalked away, ignoring Army's deep chuckles behind her. *How could I have kissed him like that?*

Taylor and Peyton were at the table when she returned. Mia picked up her blazer and leaned over to her. "I'm taking off. I had a great time."

"It's only eleven o' clock," Peyton said, a slight frown lining her forehead.

"I have a client coming in early tomorrow morning. If you want to stay, that's cool."

"I'll stay for a while longer." Peyton glanced at Taylor. "We're having fun."

"That's great." Mia smiled then tapped Taylor lightly on the arm. "I've got to go. Early appointment in the morning. Thanks for arranging all this."

Taylor leapt to his feet. "Let me walk you to your car."

She shook her head. "I'm good. I can defend myself, remember?"

"Even so, I insist." He bent down and said something to Peyton then gestured for Mia to go ahead of him.

She waved at her friend and made her way to the front entrance. When they got outside, Mia opened her bag and took out her keys. "You didn't have to escort me, but I appreciate that you did."

"You're in heels and a pretty dress. No sense in risking your wardrobe." He laughed and Mia joined in. "Have you seen Army?" he asked when they stopped at her car.

She hit the fob and opened the door. "He was outside a little while ago. Thanks again."

"Are you going to be at the gym tomorrow night?"

"Maybe, but I may go out with my friends. We have plans, but Ronica and Danielle texted me during dinner and said they may have to reschedule. If we do, then I'll be at Champion. I'll definitely be there on Sunday. I have to get back on my schedule."

"Goliath and Rick understand. You have a lot on your back."

"Yeah." *You don't know the half of it.* She slid inside the car. "I better get going. Bye." Taylor shut the door and Mia drove away.

After she finished taking off her makeup and changing into her fuzzy green robe, she turned on the gas fireplace, poured herself a glass of white wine, and cuddled on the couch with Snickers and Pumpkin. The cats purred as she scratched under their chins and behind their ears. Looking at them, she shook her head. "I'd say tonight was a disaster. I did the one thing I told myself I wasn't going to do—let him get to me." Mia picked up the glass of wine and took a big gulp then set it back down. "And damn did I let him get to me." She dipped her head and kissed both of her pets on the head. "Do you know what I did that was totally insane and stupid?" They looked up at her. "I fucking kissed him. Yeah … that's right … I kissed the jerk." She took a bigger gulp of wine. "And the worst part is, it was the best kiss ever!" Pumpkin jumped down and Snickers' eyes widened at Mia's sudden loud voice. She giggled. "Sorry. No one's in trouble."

Mia finished her drink and threw her legs up on the couch then sank back into one of the decorative pillows. It was true: Army was an amazing kisser. As he held her in his strong arms, their mouths fused, static charges jumped through her. As hard as she tried, she couldn't control her body around him. It was like it was magnetically drawn to him.

*Tonight's over. He'll go back to Alina, and I can get back to my routine.*

Mia closed her eyes, and her mind conjured up images of Army with stubble on his strong jaw and his mesmerizing, ocean blue eyes that bore into her as he came closer, drowning her in a pool of scorching sensation.

Then she drifted off to sleep.

# Chapter Seven

THE PRESIDENT OF Satan's Pistons pushed the party girl off his lap, and her ass hit the floor with a thud. As she glared at him, she grabbed her top off the couch and pulled it on over her head.

"Why'd you do that?" she asked as she stood up, her hand rubbing her backside.

"I'm done with you." Shark zipped up his jeans and stretched out his legs.

"You could've just told me to get off." She tugged at the hem of her skirt.

"I wanted to hear your ass hit the floor." Shark narrowed his brown eyes at her. "I'm done talking."

The woman opened her mouth as if to say something then closed it and walked away.

"You didn't like Ginny?" Chip asked as he looked at her retreating figure.

"She's a whore like all the others. I was done with her. She's been to enough of our parties to know the fucking score. If she doesn't like it, her ass doesn't need to come around."

"But I heard she's real tight. She does those exercises bitches do to keep their pussies like that." Chip turned around and looked at him.

"I said she's okay. I didn't even remember her damn name until you just said it. If you want to know about her pussy so bad, then go get her. She won't say no ... she's easy." Shark took out a cigarette and lit it. He was bored out of his fucking mind. It seemed that each day blended into the next, and he was itching for something new to keep his adrenaline pumping.

"Blueman called when you were fucking Ginny," Demon said, sitting down next to Shark.

The president jerked his head back. "Why the hell didn't you get me? I can fuck her anytime. Shit!" He kicked the scratched-up wooden table in front of him with his boot.

The VP inhaled deeply then slowly exhaled as a cloud of smoke wrapped around his head. "He wanted to know when we're coming to Durango."

"When he has the fucking shipment. Haven't we told the dumbass that like a million fucking times?" He put the cigarette out on the floor. "I don't trust these fuckers one bit."

"None of us do, but we need the shipment to get back in business," Demon replied.

Shark ran his fingers through his long brown hair. "I'll call the fucking idiot. I'd like to close this deal in a month." He knocked over the table. "I'm so damn bored. We should go to a rally. New faces, fresh meat, and new scenery are what I need."

"The only rally in the area is the one the Night Fucks put on at the end of October. We should go and kick their fuckin' asses for what they did to us," Demon said.

"Just wait 'til we start selling smack. We'll get us some big-ass weapons and decimate the fuckers and their goddamn families."

"And have some fun with their women," Demon added.

"Yeah, before we slit their throats. I can't fucking wait to get revenge on those motherfuckers." Shark pushed up from the couch.

"It'll be damn sweet and long in coming." Demon offered a joint to Shark.

Shark's phone pinged and he smiled. "Noe's passing through," he said to Demon as he texted his friend to come to the clubhouse.

Noe and Shark had been best friends since they beat the crap out of each other in the alley behind their school. They were eight years old, and Noe had been the new kid in town. After the fight, they became fast friends. They'd formed Satan's Pistons, but his buddy and fellow club member stepped away when his dad fell ill and Noe moved them both to Phoenix for better medical care. Noe and his dad were close as hell, and

Shark often envied their relationship, wishing that he'd had that with his dad.

"I like it," Noe said as he walked into the large room. Shark met him halfway, and they hugged each other; it'd been at least a year since he'd seen Noe.

"It took us a fucking long time to get this place livable," Shark said, motioning the prospect to bring over two beers.

Since the Night Rebels had burned down their clubhouse two years before, Satan's Pistons made due with a few double-wide trailers, but a year before, one of the brothers—Bandido, had inherited some land and a ramshackle hacienda from his grandfather. After months of work, the clubhouse looked pretty damn good, and there were enough rooms to accommodate all of the members. Most of the brothers lived at the club, with only a few having places of their own in town. The club girls lived in three double-wide trailers behind the hacienda.

"How's your pop?" Shark asked, cracking open his beer.

"The doctors say the same, but I notice he gets a little worse each day. I'm staying with him in an assisted living place. It helps to take some of the pressure off me." Noe brought the beer can to his lips.

"He's been sick a long time, bro. You've given up your life for him."

"He used to take care of us when my ma died. He's the best dad."

"My dad was the fucking worst. So there you have it," Shark said. A comfortable silence fell between them, and Shark stared out the window at the cacti and red rocks.

"So, how are things going with you?" Noe asked.

"I'm bored out of my ass, but other than that things are okay." Shark motioned for two more beers.

"You're always bored." Noe chuckled and ran his finger up and down the can. "How's Mia?" he asked in a low voice.

Shark shook his head. "You still got the hots for her?"

"Just asking. Last time we spoke, you said she was in Tucson, but when I went through there, the salon said she'd moved."

"It's been that long since we talked?" Shark scrubbed his face. "That's too fucking long, bro. Mia moved to Durango. She just told me that she wanted a change. I helped her get her own booth at a salon. She's competing in MMA fights, and she kicks ass." Shark laughed.

"Really? I knew she was into MMA, but I didn't think she wanted to compete," Noe said.

"Me neither, but she's tough. Growing up the way we did, she had to be, you know? You should give her a call. I can give you her number."

"I'd like to give her a call. Now that I got help with my dad, I'd like to start dating Mia." He glanced at Shark. "You cool with that?"

He grinned. "Fuck yeah. I'd love Mia to be your woman. I've known you for years, and I know you'd treat her right." He clasped Noe's shoulder. "It's good to have you here. How long are you staying?"

"Just the night." He looked around the room. "Where are the club girls?"

Shark laughed. "You need some pussy?"

"Fuck yeah. I miss pussy without complications."

"Then you're in luck 'cause we got five sexy ass bitches who'll show you a damn good time. Tonight we'll have a fiesta."

After they talked, and Shark showed Noe to his room, he went into his office and called Blueman. He told him they needed the shipment in a month or less. The 39th Street asshole backpedaled a bit but then finally agreed when Shark told him he was taking his business to the Los Malos in Pueblo—the rival gang to the 39th Street Gang.

Shark put his phone down and leaned back in his chair. The notion of Noe making Mia his woman was perfect. It would mean he wouldn't have to worry about his sister anymore, and Noe would keep her safe. Ever since puberty had hit Mia, Noe had been in love with her. When she was a freshman in high school, Noe had asked her to his senior prom; Shark had brought his main squeeze at the time, and they'd all had a real good time.

Shark knew Noe had it bad for Mia, so he just had to convince Mia that Noe was the perfect man for her. The more he thought about it, the more hell bent he became about them hitching up. He'd make sure it happened because when he wanted something, he always made sure he got it.

# Chapter Eight

ARMY NOTICED THE same guy he'd seen for the past two days hanging around in front of the gym when he opened the door and waltzed in. He scanned the place and a twinge of disappointment mixed with anger clenched his muscles when he didn't see Stiletto. She hadn't been to Champion in the past three days, and he was pretty sure he was the reason she was avoiding it. The kiss they'd share was so fucking awesome that the memory of it was still burned in his cock. All the moaning and pressing her body against his showed that she was fucking blown away by it too.

The only thing that surprised the hell out of Army was that she hadn't had sex with him yet. Unable to seduce a woman into his bed was unheard of for him. The longest it'd ever taken him was twenty-four hours and then the chick had come to him, but that wasn't happening with the sexy vixen. He just couldn't figure it out, but it was driving him wild.

Most of the day and night was spent with Mia in his mind. It was making him damn insane, but the crazier part was that he only wanted *her*. Going out and finding pussy was an option, but it wouldn't be Stiletto, and that's who he wanted and couldn't have. Why the hell he didn't just move on, he couldn't say. Maybe it was that he was used to winning, or maybe it was because her eyes were the most unusual color he'd ever seen and her body was athletic but soft under his touch.

Army walked toward the ring where Taylor was sparring with another fighter. *It's more than the way she looks. I love the way she sasses me and how confident she is. And damn ... the way she fights just gets me going.* There was a lot he liked about her so far, and he wanted to get to know her better, but she wasn't letting him. *Fuck!*

By the time he reached the ring, he was all riled up and he picked up a pair of boxing gloves hanging on the hook. He slipped off his cut, and a guy built like a brick house came over to him.

"You're Mayhem's brother, right?" he said.

"Yeah."

"Go get a locker and put your cut in it. Goliath requires gym shorts, not jeans, in the ring."

"I got them."

"I'm El Toro." He held out a meaty hand.

Army took it. "Army. Thanks, man." He went to the lockers and carefully hung up his cut then kicked off his boots and socks before taking off his jeans. He pulled his T-shirt over his head then closed the metal door and walked over to the ring.

Taylor took out his mouthpiece and grinned. "You want to go a few rounds?" The dude sparring with him jumped down from the platform and went to the punching bags.

"I gotta warn you that I'm pissed as shit and got a lot of pent-up frustration," Army said as he went under the ropes.

Taylor jogged in place. "Bring it on."

El Toro whistled and threw a headgear and mouthpiece, and Army lifted his chin to him.

Twenty minutes into practicing their boxing moves, sweat poured down both of their backs as they jabbed, ducked, and punched each other over and over. The sparring helped to get rid of his anger, and he was giving Taylor a good workout.

"Mia!" a woman shouted.

Army glanced over and saw Stiletto walking toward a muscular blonde standing on one of the mats. His breathing quickened, and when she glanced over at the ring with those eyes that looked like gold in starlight, the world froze around him. *Bam!* Right to the side of the head. Army staggered backward, then lost his footing and fell to the floor.

"Shit, dude, I thought you'd fend off the punch. Are you okay?" Taylor said as he bent over, his pale blue eyes dark with concern.

For a few seconds everything blurred, then Army heard Goliath's gruff voice. "Get Randy."

Taylor unlaced Army's gloves and took them off to help him sit up. "Bring some water," he said.

Army spit out his mouthpiece. "Who the fuck's Randy?"

"He's a doctor who trains at the gym."

"I'm fine. I was just distracted." He pushed up and took the glass of water Raptor handed him and drank it down.

"Who'd you want me to check out?" a tall dude with short brown hair asked.

"You the doc?" Army removed the headgear. "I'm good."

"Let me make sure, okay?" Randy walked into the ring.

"What's going on, Taylor?" Worry laced Stiletto's voice.

"I said I'm good, doc. Back the fuck off," Army said.

Randy lifted his hands up and moved away as Army and Taylor stepped off the platform.

"Army? Are you hurt?" Stiletto said, walking toward him.

In multi-colored yoga pants hugging against her skin, Army bet she turned a few heads when she came in. She did his, and that was the reason he got clobbered.

Deciding to play on her sympathies, he smiled weakly. "I'm just a little dizzy. I need to sit down."

"You just told Randy you were fine," Taylor said. "I better get him. You may have a concussion."

"Leave it the fuck alone," he gritted, and then he saw understanding flicker in Stiletto's eyes.

She shook her head. "Seriously? That's just sleazy." She whirled around and marched away, her cute rounded ass bouncing in pants that left little to the imagination. "Greatest thing ever invented," Army said.

"What is?" Taylor asked.

Army cocked his head to one side, his eyes still fixed on Stiletto's delicious curviness. "Yoga pants. It's like we almost get to see it all, but then we don't. They're the ultimate temptation."

Taylor folded his arms over his chest. "You're right about that, and Mia fills them out real good … so does Kat."

Army didn't give a shit about the blonde, his gaze was on the vixen who was playing with his emotions. As if she sensed being watched, she turned around and met his gaze. "She's a real cutie," he muttered.

"Stay away from her," Taylor said.

"We're both adults. If Stiletto wants to play, it's not any of your fuckin' business."

"She's my friend. Anyway, she thinks you're a jerk. She told me."

"So, she's talking about me." Army winked at her, and she turned around, her high ponytail swinging across her shoulders.

"Didn't you hear what I said? Mia's not into you. She thinks you're an asshole. Leave her alone. She's still getting over a breakup."

"First—I am an asshole and women still clamor for me. Second—who was her ex? Was he a fighter?"

"No. He seemed like a really good guy, but he kept pushing her to get married. She wasn't ready."

*Runs from marriage. Just my type of woman.* "How long did they go out?"

"About five or six months, I think. She met him pretty soon after she moved here. He'd always send her huge bouquets of flowers at the gym. I think it was his way of telling us guys she was taken."

"I don't see her as a flowers kind of woman."

Taylor shrugged. "She likes them, and some guys love giving them, but her ex overdid it." He chuckled. "I bet you never gave a woman flowers in your life besides the corsages Dad bought for your dates when you went to the school formals."

"Yeah, it's not my style."

"You have a style? I thought it was—meet a pretty woman, charm her, bed her—rinse and repeat." Taylor laughed.

"You know me too well." He clasped his brother's shoulder. "I'm gonna walk around and see what everyone's doing."

"You mean *Mia*."

"You said it."

"Mayhem! Are you here to train or to chat?" Raptor yelled. "Get your ass over here."

"Don't piss anyone off," Taylor said.

"Pissing people off is what I do, bro." Army laughed when Taylor threw him a dirty look over his shoulder as he jogged over to Raptor.

Army scanned the room: vinyl-padded walls in burnt orange, royal-blue, seamless foam floors, designated training areas, and a fully equipped gym made up the large room. Toward the back of it, there was a dedicated warm-up area replete with jump ropes, resistant bands, and colorful mats.

Then he saw a ponytail swishing back and forth, toned legs, a delectable ass, and the image of a dragon tatted on a sculpted back, and he quirked his lips as he headed to the yellow mat. Seeing a folding chair off to the side, Army went over and grabbed it, then sat down and focused his attention on Stiletto as she stretched her limber body. She wore a purple sports bra that showed off her flat stomach while the head of the dragon curving along her left side stared menacingly at him.

Ignoring him, she tossed her hair and spun around. On the mat next to her, a well-built man stretched his limbs while a group of men and a few women warmed up in a series of exercises led by a short woman with arms that would put most men to shame.

Stiletto lifted her arms above her head and reached up high. The move made her tits stand out, and Army leaned back in the chair to enjoy the view. After several basic stretches, she threw him an annoyed look.

"Don't you have something better to do than watch me warm up?"

"Nope. This is the best thing going. I like watching chicks."

An exasperated groan flew from her lips as she dropped her hands to her hips. "Stop assuming everything women do in life stems from an effort to make you find them sexually attractive."

"Well … you told me." The corner of his mouth curled up in a smirk.

She scrunched her face then spun around and resumed stretching. With each squat, his pants grew tighter as he pictured her on all fours, her round ass wiggling and two of his fingers pushing into her slick pussy. He shifted in the seat and glanced down at his ringing phone. When he looked back up, he caught her eyeing his hard-on and he winked. A pinkish-red flush colored her cheeks and she turned away, and he chuckled as he answered the burner phone.

"Whatcha got?" He watched Mia bend her left knee then grab the right foot and slowly straighten out her leg until it was perpendicular to her upper body, and held the position. "Hang on," he mumbled to Lil' Donnie as he watched transfixed. *She's so fuckin' flexible. We could have a lot of fun.* Army's bulge grew uncomfortable, so he readjusted his shorts and then walked quickly out the back door.

The cool night had replaced the warm day, and the distinctive smell of wood burning, damp leaves, and sweet, newly mown hay wafted around Army.

"I'm back," he said into the phone.

"The deal's going down, the middle of next month," the snitch said.

Army detected a tiny shake to his voice. "You good?" He knew Lil' Donnie didn't use what he sold, so he wondered if the drug dealer was double-dipping between the Night Rebels and the 39th Street Gang.

"Sure. Yeah, I'm good. I just don't want 'em knowing where the info came from, you know?" He sneezed then coughed. "I got this fuckin' cold. Youse guys gonna protect me if shit hits the fan?"

"We got your back if you don't fuck up."

"I've been working for youse for a long time. I'm no double-crosser." Two more sneezes.

"No one ever is until they are. So, you got the date and place yet?"

"Not the exact date, but the place will probably be the warehouse over on Trailside Road. Blueman does the bigger deals over there. I gotta go. You wanna meet at the same place for my payment?"

"No, I'll find you," Army said.

"What the fuck does that mean? You owe me!"

"Why're you so on edge? Night Rebels don't go back on their word. I'll find you … that's all you need to know." Army hung up then tapped in Steel's number.

"You got something?" Steel asked.

"Lil' Donnie said the buy's going down the middle of next month at a warehouse. He doesn't know the exact date or time yet. He seemed nervous."

"He's never backstabbed us before," Steel replied.

Army rubbed his hand over the side of his face. "I know. Maybe he's just scared. I'm giving him some money tomorrow."

"Watch your back. Are you flying your colors?"

"Sometimes, but not when I meet up with him."

"It's not a good idea. You want to keep a low profile. Never know if the fucking Pistons are around, and you don't have any backup," Steel said.

"Yeah." Army squeezed his eyebrows together.

For outlaws, the three-piece patches they wore on the back of their cuts were their identity. They marked the bikers' membership to their club and the territory they claimed. Flying their colors was mandatory on bike runs, rallies, and at the clubhouse, but most of the time, all of the Night Rebels wore their cuts outside the club. Army was no exception, and not wearing his cut seemed off kilter to him. He'd been donning it for the past seven years, but the last thing he wanted was to jeopardize the club's plan to shut down the damn Pistons and the 39th Street jerks.

"See you," Steel said. "Tell your brother to kick ass at his next fight."

"I will. He's got a couple in the next few weeks, and if he wins them, he'll go pro. I'm fuckin' proud of him," Army said.

"Yeah. He's come a long way from when you used to protect him from bullies."

Army slid the phone in his pocket and went back inside. Stiletto had finished her stretching and was beating the shit out of a speed bag when he entered the main room. Taylor called out his name, gesturing him to come over.

"What's up?" Army asked as his gaze drifted over to Stiletto.

"I usually go to Berriegood on Mondays. Do you want to come along?"

"Is Stiletto going?" Army blurted, cursing himself for it.

"I don't know. I told you to leave Mia alone, dude. If you don't want to go, I can grab a Lyft or someone can drop me off."

*If Stiletto doesn't go, then I'm stuck drinking protein out of a fuckin' glass. But if she does, it could be fun.* "I'll go along. What time are we heading out?"

"In a half hour."

"Sounds good. I think I'll kill the time punching the bag." Army strode over to one of the large speed bags, slipped on a pair of yellow gloves hanging on a hook against the wall, and sank his fists into it.

An hour later, Army followed Taylor into Berriegood and chuckled when Stiletto rushed ahead and took the seat between Raptor and El Toro. He pulled out the chair and sat next to Kat, who turned and threw him a small, seductive smile. Glancing sideways at Stiletto, he saw her sour face as Kat placed her hand lightly on his and asked why he never considered being an MMA fighter.

About twenty minutes into their protein bowl fest, El Toro stood up and told them his wife wanted him home to help out with their three rowdy boys. The minute he walked away, Army went over and slid into the seat next to Stiletto. Taylor's facial muscles were taut as he handed Army's smoothie to him. Instead of going for the protein bowl that all the fighters raved about, he went for the basic mango and coconut smoothie, deciding to do a drive-through at one of the fast food burger places on the way back to the apartment.

As he waited for Stiletto to turn toward him, he swirled the straw around in his glass, then pretended that he didn't see Kat trying to get his attention. Bolting from the chair to get a chance to sit next to Stiletto was out of character for him. Chicks came to him, but she was proving to be inordinately stubborn.

After ten minutes of stirring the damn smoothie, he nudged her slightly with his elbow and smiled when she faced him.

"Hey." He gave her his crooked smile, the one that landed him into countless beds.

"Hey," she replied, turning back toward Raptor and Madman. Most of the male fighters preferred to use their nicknames with the other gym members.

"I'm trying to talk to you," Army said, an edge creeping into his voice.

"And I'm involved in another conversation. I'm not going to just stop midway through like you did with Kat. I'm not rude."

His eyes narrowed and he leaned back in the chair. *Why the fuck am I putting up with this shit? Because I'm drawn to her for some damn reason.* For a long while Army sat there and sipped his overly sweet mango drink while ignoring her sensual scent as it curled around him. It reminded him of screwing around on an exotic beach under a large umbrella as the waves from the pristine blue ocean crashed on the shore.

"Are you having a good time?" she asked, turning toward him.

"I've had better."

"I guess drinking smoothies or eating healthy bowls isn't your thing." Her sweet giggles went right to his dick and he shifted in the seat.

"I'm more of a steak-and-rib-kind-of-guy, and I like my vegetables whole, not pureed."

"It's not too bad. I come mostly for the camaraderie. I'll admit I had to acquire a taste for the protein bowl, but I love the mango smoothie you're drinking."

"It's not bad. So, how about getting a drink after we finish playing healthy?"

"I'm too tired. I'm going straight home."

"We're taking off," Kat and Raptor said. Several other people from the group also rose to their feet.

"See you," Stiletto said and waved to them.

Kat came over and squeezed Army's shoulder. "It was nice talking to you."

"I didn't mean to be rude."

"No worries." She glanced at Stiletto, then back at Army. "I understand. If you ever need someone to hang out with, Taylor has my number." She turned around and followed Raptor out the door.

"I bet women are always giving you their phone numbers. Kat is really nice." Stiletto picked up her spoon and kept scraping her empty bowl.

"I'm not interested in her. I'm interested in you, and I'm pretty sure you feel the same about me. Why are you fighting me on this?"

She tilted her head back. "On what?"

"On just going out for a fuckin' drink or something without a gang of people tagging along."

"That's it?"

"Yeah. If something goes from there, then it does. What about tomorrow night? We can go for dinner or a drink. Somewhere we can talk." Army watched as hesitation played on her face. "You're prejudging me."

"I'm not. It's just that you're used to women who fall right into bed with you, but I'm not like that, and I'm not up for a night of wrestling. I can do it at Champion."

"How do you know what I'm used to?"

"I know your type."

Army snorted out a loud laugh. "And that's not prejudging me? I'm not a fuckin' *type*. I'm one of a kind, and women find that damn refreshing." He pushed back in the chair. "I never push a chick to do something she doesn't want to."

Stiletto picked up the napkin and crumpled it over and over in her hands. "I also don't want the whole focus to be on me being a woman."

Army jerked his head back. "But you are one."

"I know *that*. I mean it doesn't have to be the focal point in all of our interactions."

"Don't try and con me. I noticed you checking me out at the gym."

She lifted her chin and met his gaze. "That's different. I appreciate a man who takes care of himself."

"And I appreciate a toned, hot woman. There's no fuckin' difference."

"There is because I wasn't leering."

"BS, sweetheart. You were leering plenty." Army watched her as she smoothed out the napkin. "If you don't trust yourself alone with me, I get it."

Her head snapped up and her eyes flashed. "You're so damn vain."

"Just calling it the way I see it." He rose to his feet and looked over at Taylor, who was deep in conversation with Goliath.

Stiletto leapt up then slung her tote bag over her shoulder. "I'm out of here." She said her goodbyes to the others and headed for the door.

Army rushed after her. "I'll walk you to your car."

She stopped so abruptly that he almost ran into her. "I don't need you to do that."

"I'm walking you to your car, and it's not open for debate. You're the most stubborn woman I know." Army trudged behind her.

"You don't know me," she said as her heels clacked on the sidewalk.

"I'm trying to, but you're making it damn hard."

When they arrived at her car, he took the keys from her and opened the door. Her sweet scent played havoc with his desire, and he tried to stop thinking of how wonderful she smelled and how great she looked walking to the car in her yoga pants. He pretty much figured that having an erection while trying to get her to go out on a date with him wouldn't really work. He glanced up at the stars and silently began counting them.

"Thanks," she said taking the keys from him, her soft touch distracting him. "I guess I'll see you at the gym?"

"So, it's a no for tomorrow night?" *The brothers would be having a field day if they could see me practically begging for a date.*

"Will you promise to behave and treat me like a buddy?"

"If I don't behave, you can smack me, but there's no way I can treat you like a buddy."

"I'm sure you'd love it if I decked you. I just want you to promise you won't undress me all night and talk about how flexible I am or how pretty, and all that other shit that makes me feel like I'm just an object for your visual pleasure."

Army dragged his foot back and forth over the asphalt, gravel crunching under his boot. "I'm a man. We're visual. I'm not gonna promise I won't enjoy your beauty, but we're going out to get to know each other."

Stiletto slid onto the seat, threw her purse on the passenger floor, and gripped the steering wheel. After a couple of minutes of silence, she looked up at him and audibly sighed. "Okay. We can meet up tomorrow night for dinner."

Army wanted to high five her, but he simply jutted his chin out and nodded. "You like Mexican food?"

"Yes. There are some good ones downtown. Did you want me to choose?"

"I can handle it. I'll pick you up at seven."

"I'll meet you." She turned on the ignition.

"I don't meet dates—I pick them up. Seven o'clock." As she opened her mouth, he shut the door then stepped back and motioned for her to back out. Shoving his hands in his pockets, he watched as the red tail lights disappeared into the night, then went back into the restaurant.

# Chapter Nine

M IA CRADLED THE phone between her head and shoulder as she flipped through her client profile book searching for her noon appointment.

"Vic, I'm just not interested. I don't need you to fix me up with anyone."

"Noe's the best guy you'll ever meet. He's been crazy about you since you were fourteen."

"And I have never been crazy about him. I like him like a cousin. Leave it alone, Vic."

"It's Shark. You fuckin' know that," he grumbled.

Mia scanned the notes she made on her client's hair color, then put the binder down. She sat down and lightly massaged her shoulder. "How's Finn doing? Did he bail out?"

"Stop changing the fuckin' subject."

"Why're you so pissed about me not wanting to date Noe? You're acting childish."

"I didn't say to date him. Just go out with him for dinner when he comes to Durango."

"If he calls me, I will, but just as friends. You need to make it clear to him, or I will."

"I'm not gonna say a fuckin' thing. Anyway, just give him a chance. You haven't seen him in a couple years."

"You didn't answer me about Finn," Mia looked out the window and saw a man leaning against a red sports car across the street staring at the salon. *I've seen that car parked across from Champion a couple of times this past week.* Unease niggled at the back of her neck.

"I couldn't bail the fucker out. The judge set a bond of a hundred thousand dollars. I don't have that kinda dough." Shark's gruff voice broke in on her thoughts.

"Did he tell you why he did something so stupid?"

"Money."

"Did it ever occur to him to get a job?"

"Or a bitch like Tucker did. She keeps bailing his ass out all the time."

Mia sighed and glanced across the street again and noticed the man was still there. "I can't believe what a mess everyone is," she said in a low voice. "Tucker's either in jail or drugged out, Dean just got out of juvy detention, and now this shit with Finn. I'm scared for him because he's looking at some serious time." The right side of her face twitched, and she rubbed her fingers over it to calm it down. Ever since she was a kid, her facial muscles would spasm if she was scared or really stressed.

"He's taking a trip to the pen for a while. No fucking doubt about that."

"Mia, your noon appointment is here," a woman's voice over the speakers announced.

"I have to go. My client is here." Tears welled in her eyes, and she blinked them away. "I'll talk to you later."

"Be nice to Noe. Don't disrespect me, okay?" A threatening thread wove through Shark's voice.

"Bye." Mia hung up and clenched her jaw to keep her bottom lip from trembling as sadness crushed down on her. Unshed tears stung her eyes, and she clutched at her aching chest.

"Your client's here," Ronica said, breaking through Mia's hazy sadness.

She swallowed the lump in her throat. "Thanks."

"Are you okay?" Ronica came over and stood in front of her, peering into her face.

"I'm worried about my brother, that's all." But it wasn't, it was everything and nothing. It was a hollowness that held thousands of tears and jagged pieces of glass wedged between her body and soul.

"I'm sorry. I wish I could help."

"So do I." Mia stood up and glanced out the window—the man was gone. She smiled weakly at Ronica, then went to meet her client.

After several hours of dying, perming, highlighting, and cutting hair, Mia welcomed the thirty-minute lull in her day. Staying busy made the day fly, and by the time she sank into the chair and lifted a much-needed café latte to her lips, she was feeling considerably better than she had earlier. Talking with Vic—to her, he'd never be Shark—usually made her nostalgic and sad. Most of the time, she focused on the moment and let go of the past, but there were times when the darkness would seep in and distort her present-day reality.

Mia couldn't believe she'd accepted a date with Army. *What was I thinking?* Her mind tried to think up excuses to get out of the evening, but a part of her—the one she was ignoring—couldn't wait to see him again. She couldn't deny that the night before she'd sneaked way too many glances at him in his gym shorts that were slung low on his narrow hips. How could she not notice the hard muscles that rippled across his chest or the dusting of dark hair that trailed down past a taut, corrugated stomach? Mia closed her eyes and the vision of Army's incredible tattoos danced in her mind. *They're amazing.* The curling, flowing designs covering his arms and a good part of his chest had tempted her to touch.

Her eyes flew open. *I didn't give him my address.* Dread spun around her. *Maybe he was just talking out of his ass last night. What should I do?* As if on cue, her phone vibrated against the black lucite countertop. She didn't recognize the number and crossed her fingers it wouldn't be Noe. She glanced at the text and smiled.

**Army:** *What's ur address?*

**Mia:** *How'd u get my number?*

**Army:** *Taylor.*

**Mia:** *1479 S. Larkspur Lane.*

**Army:** *Be there at 7.*

**Mia:** *K.*

That was it. No smartass remarks, no macho shit, just clean and direct. Maybe dinner wouldn't be that bad after all. Picking up a hairstyling magazine, she browsed through it as she waited for her next appointment.

MIA STOOD IN front of her closet debating on what to wear for her date with Army. She held up a plum skirt with lace. *Too sexy.* After spending twenty minutes vetoing different outfits, she finally settled on blue jeans and a burgundy hollowed-out cold shoulder blouse with a block neckline. She slipped on a pair of black stiletto short boots, then grabbed her leather jacket and went downstairs.

At exactly seven o'clock the doorbell rang. Mia set down the cats' food bowls and went to the door and looked out the peephole. As Army stood there, looking down at his phone, she opened the door.

"You're prompt. Come in for a sec. I have to finish up something in the kitchen." Pumpkin rushed up to Army and rubbed against him, meowing. "I'm warning you—she's an incorrigible flirt."

"Is her owner?" His gaze traveled over her body, then he smiled at her.

"Not so much. Have a seat." She walked into the kitchen, rinsed the cans of food, threw them into the recycle bin, and then wiped down the counter.

"You've got a nice place. Do you live here alone?"

After drying her hands, she slipped on her jacket. "Yes. I debated about getting a roommate, but after working out the finances, I decided that I'd rather be more frugal and live alone than have one. I've lived with roommates or family my whole life. I love being alone."

"Do you have an alarm?"

She laughed. "I've never had anyone ask me *that* question before." Mia picked up her purse from the stool at the breakfast bar. "I do have an alarm, and I try to remember to put it on."

"You need to do it all the time even though you live in a nice area."

"Noted. Are you ready to go?"

"Yeah." He lifted Pumpkin off his lap, where she'd sprawled shamelessly, and stood up. "I thought I saw another cat roaming around here."

"That'd be Snickers. She's the shy one, so she's probably hiding behind something. Do you like cats?" Mia punched the code into the alarm panel.

"They're cute. I had one when I was a kid. My mom loved them." He stood aside on the porch and let her go first.

"What was her name?"

"Harley, and it was a tomcat." Army opened the car door and she slid inside.

They pulled in front of El Señor Sol. The large smiling sun was the trademark of the restaurant, and it was one of Mia's favorites.

"Good choice. I love this place," she said, patting her hand on top of his. When his gaze blazed with heat, she realized her faux pas and quickly pulled her hand back to unfasten the seat belt.

Seascape paintings decorated brightly-painted walls in turquoise, orange, yellow, and lime green, and multicolored wood chairs surrounded tabletops imprinted with a smiling sun. The place wasn't very big, but it was a mélange of color, scents, and salsa beats.

The hostess sat them at a table for two and took their drink order. Soon, Mia had a margarita in front of her, and Army had a bottle of Corona; a big basket of chips and salsa separated them.

"Do you come here a lot?" Army asked, picking up his beer.

"Too much. My friends and I love it, and it's a favorite for our weekly dinner out. Goliath and Rick would kill me if they knew how often carbs slip into my diet." She gave a half shrug and picked up a chip. "I don't have a fight, so I can fudge a bit."

"Breaking away is always a good time." He winked at her.

"I saw you sparring with Taylor last night. You're good. How long have you been boxing?"

"Since high school. I actually got Taylor into MMA after I left high school. He needed to take care of himself since I moved away to Alina. Once he started, he really got into it. He was able to hold his own in high school."

"How many years apart are you?" Mia scooped up some of the tomatillo salsa with the chip.

"Five. So, what made you go into MMA and compete? It's not real common for a woman. I know there are a lot more now, but dudes still outnumber chicks."

All of a sudden Mia's mouth went dry as she pondered whether she should tell Army the truth. *Will he look at me differently?* Except for her therapist, she'd never told anyone what had happened that night so long ago, but somehow sitting across from him, drinking a margarita and surrounded by all the gaiety and bright colors, she yearned to tell him— to unload something she'd been carrying around with her for too long.

After a large gulp of the margarita, she folded her hands on the table and looked at him. "I wanted to feel empowered."

"Were you bullied in school?"

"No." Another big drink, then she looked down at the tropical orange placemat. "I was attacked and felt powerless." She pulled on a loose thread in the orange cloth. "It was an awful feeling," she said softly, slowly lifting her eyes up.

Consternation filled the fine lines around Army's eyes that had glints of anger in them. "Is that why you moved to Durango?"

"Yeah." Mia picked up her drink and drained it.

"What happened?" Army asked in a low voice.

"I need another drink for that." She laughed, but her insides were twisted and her heart raced.

Army gestured to the waiter, then he placed his hand over hers. "If it bothers you too much, you don't have to talk about it."

Pressing her lips together, she shook her head. "It's hard, but I do want to talk about it." The waiter set down another margarita, and she grabbed the stem of the glass like it was a life raft. "I knew the guy. He was a friend of a friend who I'd met at a Christmas party two years after

I moved to Tucson. I wanted to study cosmetology and break away from the craziness of my family, so I went to the big city. I earned my associates degree and was feeling pretty damn proud of myself when I went to the party. Gavin and I had some chemistry going the minute we met, and he said all the right things to me. We danced, laughed, and I felt like I'd met a really great guy." Mia stared at the smiling sun imprinted on the table then traced her fingernail over the triangles around its face. "He called me and asked me out. We had a nice dinner, good conversation, and I felt okay. I didn't get the vibes that he was a creep or something wasn't right with him. After dinner he asked if I'd ever been to "A" mountain and I said no, so he suggested a drive to it. I'd heard it was a the perfect place to see the whole city, and even though a small warning light went off inside me, I ignored it and agreed to go."

Army grasped her hand and held it, and the warmth from his skin on hers calmed her. She looked up at him. "Long story short, he wouldn't take no for an answer. I kicked, screamed, and scratched, but I still couldn't protect myself. He just got madder, hit me harder, then … well …"

"What a fuckin' bastard," Army gritted, his gaze narrowed.

"Yeah … I'd say that. And the fucking sick part was that he didn't think he did anything wrong. He thought it was his right to do whatever the hell he wanted. The asshole dropped me off at my apartment and said he had a nice time and would call me." She blinked rapidly.

Army reached out and stroked her face with his other hand. "He should've been taught a lesson. Did you turn him in?"

She shook her head. "I was so embarrassed and humiliated that all I wanted to do was forget the whole thing. I kept thinking that I shouldn't have worn the skirt or the blouse that I did. I doubted everything I'd done that night, convinced that I'd somehow caused him to do what he did."

"The fucker was one hundred percent at fault. You said no, babe."

"I know that now, but it's taken me a long time and years of therapy to realize it. After it happened, I stopped hanging out with my friend because she was always asking why I didn't want to go out with Gavin anymore. I stayed in the victim mindset until a good friend of mine told me about a class they were teaching at a local gym on self-defense. I went with her, and the rush I got after that first training was something I'd never experienced. I felt liberated, so I signed up and then went on to learn jiu-jitsu, and I've never looked back. I didn't even think about competing until Sergio—my trainer in Tucson—suggested it. I thought if I could win, I could show that I really can kick ass." She laughed as the memory of the pride she felt after her first win flitted through her mind.

"And you *can* kick ass." Army leaned across the table and before she could react, he'd brushed his lips against hers, in a soft, quick kiss. "You're a survivor, babe." He leaned back in the chair and held her gaze.

Mia cleared her throat and shifted in the chair. "It's your turn." The noise in the restaurant filled in the silence as Army drank his beer. "Besides my therapist, you're the only one who knows the truth about what happened. It's only fair you share something about you that you keep deep inside." Dunking the chip in the salsa, she brought it to her mouth.

Softness erased the tightness he'd had on his face as she told him her story. "I'm glad you trusted me enough to tell me."

"I do." And she wasn't exactly sure why. Normally, she guarded her privacy like a trained pit bull, but for some reason it felt okay—no ... better than okay, it felt *right*, and that blew her away.

"I didn't know that not being able to talk about how sexy you look in your jeans, and how pretty your eyes shine, was gonna make me spill my guts."

Playfully hitting his arm, she chuckled. "I didn't tell you what you could and couldn't say."

"You told me I couldn't say anything about you being a woman. You wanted me to treat you like a buddy."

"I think you're trying to get out of telling me what I asked."

The waiter put a steaming and sizzling plate of steak fajitas in front of her and a dish of Mexican steak and shrimp in front of Army. His twinkling eyes resembled chips of blue topaz glittering under the sun. Picking up his fork, he winked at her then dove into his food.

"You're not getting off that easily," she said, pouring salsa over the steak and green peppers.

Army raised his finger while chewing as if to say, "Give me a minute," then he picked up the beer bottle and took a swig.

"Okay. Let's see. My dad collects wives." He put another forkful of food in his mouth.

"How many does he have?"

He raised four fingers.

"Which number was your mom?"

"The first. He's divorced again and working on number five. He met her not too long ago, and he already moved her into the house."

"How old were you when your parents divorced?" Mia picked up a corn tortilla and filled it with steak and guacamole.

Army kept eating and chewing … and looking everywhere but at her. *I think I found his dark spot.* "Divorce is really hard on kids," she said.

"My mom didn't wait around for the divorce, she fuckin' blew." Another large bite.

Waiting until he'd swallowed, Mia asked, "Did you get to see your dad a lot when you were growing up?"

"My brothers and I lived with our dad. My mom left all of us for a sonofabitch." Army nodded as he looked at Mia. "You're surprised and you fuckin' should be because moms aren't supposed to do that shit."

"How old were you?" she asked softly.

"Nine."

Her heart ached for the nine-year-old boy who was still trapped inside the man. "That's real tough."

Army shrugged. "It's whatever."

"Is your dad a bigamist?"

His face crinkled in laughter. "I gotta tell my brothers that one. I wish he was—that'd be fuckin' awesome. You know, raising your middle finger at the establishment. Unfortunately, my dad plays by the rules, so he divorced my mom. He found out she was living in Madison, Wisconsin, with the asshole, so he served the papers there."

"Have you ever tried to get in contact with her?"

His expression tightened. "No fuckin' way. My dad's lived in the same house we grew up in. She knows it."

Sensing that he was more than bitter and angry, she decided to back off. "Have you ever been married?"

He jerked his head back and laughed. "Fuck no. Never plan to either. It's a crock of shit invented by the establishment to get more taxes and stick their fuckin' noses into people's personal lives."

"Ooo ... kay." Her eyes widened and she looked sideways.

"What about you?"

"Not yet. I bet you have a lot of girlfriends." *Why do I care about the women in his life?*

"I don't have girlfriends, but ... yeah ... I have a lot of chicks wanting to hook up with me."

"Anyone currently?" *I wish I could keep my damn mouth shut!*

A big grin lit up his face. "I'm not fuckin' anyone right now if that's what you wanna know. I also use a condom when I fuck, and I get tested regularly. I'm clean." He winked and she froze, wanting nothing more than to disappear into the floor's terra cotta tiles. "Is the food too spicy? You're all flushed."

"Yeah, the jalapeños are a bit much." *Talk about too much information. Damn.* She picked up her water glass.

"You got anyone around?" There was a slight edge in his voice.

"No. I broke up with a guy about five months ago, and I've been focusing on my business and training."

"Everyone needs to play a little." His gaze bored into her.

"Do they call you Army because you were in the military?"

His gaze never wavering, he nodded. "Served four years. I did three tours of duty in Afghanistan. Fucked-up mess over there."

"I bet that was tough."

"Life's always tough. So, you do hair?"

"I do. I have my own booth at Salon on the Boulevard. I love being my own boss even if my pay fluctuates from month to month. You don't like talking about things that bother you, do you? I mean, I notice when we start talking about something deep, you change the subject. Sometimes it's good to let things out."

Army sat back and folded his arms against his chest. "You think talking about how I killed people who were in the wrong village at the wrong time is gonna make it seem right? You're wrong. And if you think talking about my mom, who abandoned her kids because she was a selfish bitch is gonna make me feel better, you're wrong about that too. Life is the way it is. Sometimes it's great and sometimes it's shit, but the way you react to the shit determines if you're a survivor or a victim. That's the way I look at it."

Mia wanted to tell him that not dealing with the deep hurt or the horror of things can affect the present and the future. She could tell just from their short conversation that Army was still hurt over his mother's abandonment, and that was probably why he only had hookups. *He probably doesn't trust women.*

"Do you want another drink?" Army asked.

Again, he was changing the subject, but she didn't want to push him. After all, this was their first date, and probably their last because she had no intention of sleeping with him that night even though her body had been humming since he'd briefly kissed her.

"No thanks. How do you like your food?"

"It's damn good." He pushed his plate away. "I'm having a good time."

"Don't sound so surprised." She propped her elbows on the table. "I'm having a good time too." Then she leaned forward and he met her halfway and their lips pressed together in a warm and tingly kiss. He threaded his fingers in her hair, pulling her closer as she gave herself into the pleasure of the kiss.

A few minutes later, she pulled back, and the thrill of his heated gaze tingled over her skin. For an endless moment they stared at each other, then Army took her hand and brought it to his lips. "You do something to me I can't fuckin' explain," he said hoarsely.

"Do you want any dessert? Sopapillas?" the waiter asked as he cleared away their dishes.

Breathing deeply, Mia struggled to regain her senses.

"Fried ice cream? Flan?" The server darted his eyes between them.

"Nothing for me, thank you."

"Just another beer for me," Army said, his gaze still on hers.

When the waiter left, Mia stood up. "I have to go to the ladies' room. I'll be right back." She couldn't get to the bathroom fast enough. The intensity between them startled and thrilled her, but she didn't want to get mixed up with a guy who was only interested in casual hookups. Staring at her reflection, she groaned when she saw the sparkle in her eyes and the glow on her face. "You know he's danger. He just wants to fuck. A no-strings-attached deal. You're better than that."

The door swung open and two women walked in, both dressed like they were planning on going clubbing later on. The woman with deep plum hair took out a wand and swiped it over her lips. "If they're duds at the club, we'll ditch them. Agreed?"

Her companion, a short brunette nodded. "Or if we meet someone like that hunk sitting across from us. Did you see his arms? They're delicious and I'd love to get up and personal with all his tattoos."

"He looks like a model for a cover of a romance novel. You know the ones about alpha males."

"Why aren't there any guys like that on Tinder?" the brunette said.

Mia went into the stall and leaned against the cool metal door. *I can't get involved with him.* Over and over she repeated the sentence, but each time, the feel of Army's lips on hers overpowered her mantra. *I can't. He doesn't even live here. I'd just be another name on his long list of conquests.* But he was being so nice and respectful, and he acted like he really cared when she'd told him what had happened to her. *Mia, don't. You can't get involved with Army.*

A few more women entered the small bathroom, and she picked up her purse and came out of the stall. After washing her hands and reapplying her lipstick, she walked out. When she approached the table, she noticed the two women in the bathroom who'd been drooling over some guy look at her, then at Army. *The hot dude they were talking about was Army.* Smiling, she pulled out her chair and sat down, an unexplained thread of pride wove itself around her as the women wistfully looked away.

After Army paid the bill, they walked out into the night. The moon cast a silvery glow, and the dark silhouette of oak trees stood out boldly against the starry sky. Mia tugged her hand away when Army clutched it, and she tucked it into the pocket of her leather jacket and kept walking to the car, the scrape of her heels on the concrete the only sound between them.

On the ride home, the melodic beats of "Something to Believe In" and Army's deep voice singing along with Bret Michaels's soulful one filled the car. Mia looked out the passenger window as her body shivered with every note Army sang. How could her body keep betraying her? *This can't work. It just can't.* When the familiar lampposts came into view, Mia sucked in a long, slow breath. After pulling in the driveway, she practically jumped out of the car in an anxious attempt to hide away behind the safety of her home.

"What the fuck?" Army asked as she leapt from the parked car and dashed across the lawn.

Leaves rustled and crushed behind her, and she knew he was following her. As Mia made her way to the porch, she fished through her purse for the keys, cursing all the crap she had inside it that made it near impossible to find them.

"You gotta pee or something?" Army said.

Sweaty from her mad dash, Mia stopped in front of the door and erupted in laughter.

"Well, do you?" Army took a few steps then hovered over her, his hands flat against the door. She tried to suppress her laughs but she ended up sputtering like an old faucet. Hiding her face in her hands, she leaned against the front door and heard the meows of Pumpkin and Snickers.

"What's so funny?" He chuckled.

Her hands slipped away from her face. "Hell, if I know," she managed to get out between gulps.

"I like hearing you laugh." His voice was husky and deep and so damn sexy.

Mia tilted her chin up and met eyes that held such desire in their dark blue depths, she trembled. Common sense reared its head and screamed, *Go inside!* She knew she should listen to it, but her body wouldn't let her.

"I better go," she said feebly, ignoring the shivers rippling over her skin.

"I'm not stopping you," Army whispered, kissing her ear and then her throat, feathery kisses that made her want to surrender and have a night of hot, passionate sex.

*Open the door, thank him for the night, and go inside.*

When he ran his tongue up her neck, then past her chin, a moan climbed up her throat. "Mia," he said in a low voice, then his lips brushed hers and it was like spark to tinder. Ears pulsing, she wrapped her arms around his neck and buried her fingers in his hair.

His strong arms jerked her flush against him, and his mouth crushed over hers, his tongue delving deep.

Sensations crawled wild through her veins as she kissed him back passionately ... wildly. Digging her nails in the nape of his neck, she pulled herself deeper into the embrace, thrusting her hips against him and feeling the hardness of his erection. His hand skimmed down her back and rested on one of her ass cheeks as his fingers kneaded through the fabric, squeezing while he groaned into her mouth.

Army's kisses and touch sent a carnal tremor down her spine, and when he began to slip his hand inside her waistband, she gripped it and pushed it away.

"You're not gonna let me touch you?" he whispered against the shell of her ear.

"I just don't want things to get out of control," she said softly, pulling back a bit.

"They're already outta control. You're not feeling it?"

"That's not the point."

"I guess you answered my question," he said huskily against her neck.

"Army—"

"Don't fight it—feel it," he whispered in her ear and ran his lips the length of it.

Mia held her breath then yanked her purse in front of her to separate them. She exhaled slowly and avoided his captivating gaze. "I really have to go. I hope you understand." After pulling out her keys, Mia turned around and opened the door a crack. Her two cats meowed loudly. She looked over her shoulder at him. "Thanks for dinner."

"That's it?" He shoved his hands in his pockets.

Opening the door a bit more, she slipped inside and turned off the alarm. A long yawn of foyer light winked onto the porch's concrete floor. Pumpkin and Snickers rubbed against her legs as she bent down to pet them, then went back to the front and looked at Army. "I had a good time, but I'm sorry if you're upset with me."

"I'm not pissed at you. If you want to stop ... okay." He smiled at her and her heart pounded. "You free tomorrow night?"

"I'm training, but maybe after?" She bit the inside of her cheek.

"That's cool. I can come by the gym. I'm thinking eight or nine. We can get a drink."

"Nine's better. There's a nice neighborhood bar about a half-mile from here."

"Sounds good. I'll meet up with you at Champion."

"Okay. See you."

Army just stood there staring at her, and she didn't move either.

"Go on inside. Make sure you put the alarm back on. I'll wait until you lock up."

Warmth spread through her at that small gesture, and she stepped back and closed the door.

After locking up and punching in the code, she turned off the lights in the living room and peeked out the window, watching Army walk over to the car, his stride slow and confident. He stood beside the vehicle, tall and straight, the moonlight shining down on his chiseled features, and as if he sensed her presence, he looked over at the window and lifted his chin, then went inside and backed out of the driveway. As he drove away, a sinking emptiness descended on her, and she stayed peering out at the empty road long after the taillights melted into the darkness.

"What am I doing?" Mia muttered, kicking off her boots. The phone buzzed against her thigh and she dug it out, scanning the screen. Ronica's picture flashed intermittently, and she debated whether to answer or not. The buzzing stopped then started up again, like a persistent fly. A sigh escaped her lips, and she put the phone to her ear.

"What's up, Ronica?"

"Are you still on your date? I hope I'm not interrupting you in the middle of something." She giggled.

"I'm alone. Army just left."

"So early? Was it *that* bad?" The sound of Ronica clucking her tongue annoyed the hell out of Mia.

"No. Not at all. We had a great dinner and talked a lot. He behaved." She threaded her fingers through her hair. "I have to be at the salon early in the morning."

"Hot, mind-blowing sex is a great reason to forgo sleep. Was it his or your idea to end the date before midnight?"

"Mine. I guess I didn't trust myself if I invited him in."

"He's a hunk. It's required that you have the best damn sex of your life with him. What's wrong with you, girl?"

Mia sank down on the couch. "I don't just want to be another woman he banged. I don't know. Maybe if we just met at a bar, were both drunk, and would never see each other again, then yeah. I know Taylor, and Army's real supportive of him." She reached for the water bottle she'd left on the coffee table earlier that day. "And I know him now. He's not a stranger anymore."

"Nice speech, but you wouldn't have done the hookup if you'd met him at a bar," Ronica said.

"I guess I'm just not that way. Maybe I'm rebelling against my mom, who was exactly that way. Every damn weekend there was a different guy at our house when I was growing up." She took a drink of water. "I have to know a guy, but with Army, he's not a good bet. He doesn't live here, and he's got some real trust issues with women. He's never been in a relationship for Christ's sake. I want something more than a guy who only has hookups."

"I can see your point. You're not a risk taker when it comes to men. Actually, you seem so wary of them all the time. I mean Jorge had to practically beat down your door before you'd started going out with him. Army's faring much better. I think you could be the one to tame this wild beast, but I get why you may be afraid to take the chance."

Mia moved her neck from side to side, cracking it. She was tired and didn't want to hear Ronica psychoanalyze her. Once a week with her therapist was enough, and besides, *she* knew the reason for her wariness, but then no one knew what'd happened to her except for Army. *Ronica would be so pissed at me for telling him and not sharing it with her.* A groan slipped from her lips.

"What'd you say?" Ronica asked.

"Nothing. I'm real tired. We can talk tomorrow, okay?"

"Oh ... sure. Did he ask you out again?"

"We're going for a drink tomorrow night." She rolled her eyes when Ronica's excited squeals filled Mia's ears. "No more questions. I have to go to bed."

Mia scooped up Snickers and headed upstairs with Pumpkin padding behind her. After a while, she slid between the sheets and placed her arm over her eyes. A carousel of images spun inside her head—all of them featuring Army. She flung her arm off and squeezed her eyes tight as if to push away the pictures. Excitement mixed with fear as she lay there realizing that she'd enjoyed their date a bit too much.

*Ugh! I like him too much.*

And she had no clue what to do about it.

# Chapter Ten

GROUPS OF YOUNG teens congregated on the street corner, several of them staring at Army as he waited for the red light to change. Scattered around the area were rundown houses with weeds and dirt in front as landscaping, plenty of liquor stores with iron grates over their windows, colorful tagging on storefront walls, and garbage strewn all over the street filling the gutters and sidewalks.

Still stuck at the light, Army glanced to the left then right, checking for any badges hiding in the shadows, waiting to pounce. Some of the teen boys pointed at him and a couple yelled out, but with the windows up, he couldn't hear what they were saying.

He looked in the rear view mirror and saw a car approaching from behind. Suddenly it accelerated, changed lanes, and blasted through the red light. Army watched the car race down the street, and from the corner of his eye he saw two teenagers coming up to the car. *Fuck this.* He put his foot on the accelerator and zipped through the light, as the two boys yelled and waved their fists at him until the darkness swallowed them up. Army didn't have time to deal with the fucking punks. He was looking for Lil' Donnie and had a strong hunch he'd be right in the thick of things on Buena Vista Avenue, where the hookers and junkies hung out.

Passing a slew of liquor, convenience, and gun stores, he knew he was in the hub of illegal activity for the neighborhood. Women in cheap, tight-fitting clothes that revealed too much, hung around in the shadows of graffitied buildings, venturing out only when a car slowed down. In the darkened corners, Army saw quick drug deals, and he turned around and circled back looking for the black fedora Lil' Donnie usually wore.

Army had planned to find the dealer the following day because he was certain he'd be spending the night with Mia, but she'd told him no. That alone was a surprise, but the thing that fucking floored him was he wanted to see her again. Normally, he'd have moved on at this point, deeming the chick too much trouble for a fuck and gone on to the next one. He rarely had to do that because more times than not, the women wanted to have some fun with him.

He slowed down and stared at an alley where two guys stood outside by the streetlamp. A woman with Daisy Dukes, thigh-high fishnets, and a red sequined bikini top teetered over to him in high-heeled boots. Army smiled, thinking of how sexy Mia had looked that night in her stilettos and snug jeans.

A knock on the window refocused him, and he rolled it down.

"You looking for something?" the blonde asked, batting her fake eyelashes.

"I'm looking for someone."

"You found her. You're a good-looking man."

"Have you seen Lil' Donnie around here tonight?"

The woman averted her gaze. "You a cop?"

Army laughed. "Fuck no. Just need to do some business with him."

The blonde stared at him and smiled, then rubbed her tongue across two chipped front teeth. She leaned over the window to display her more than ample cleavage. "What's in it for me?"

"I got you covered." He opened the armrest console and pulled out a fifty. "That's when you tell me, and you get another if you're not bullshitting me."

Her eyes widened. "He's in the alley off Vance Street. Just do a U-ie and go two streets down. That's Vance. Turn left and you'll find him in the first alley to your right."

"If you're fuckin' with me, your ass better not be here when I come back." Army put the car in gear, and the working girl backed away as he took off, hanging a U-turn as she'd instructed.

Vance Street was dark as hell because all the streetlight bulbs were broken. Army turned off the lights in the car and slowed way down as he looked out for the alley. He pulled over, then reached out and grabbed his Glock from the glove compartment along with a thin-bladed knife, slipping it into his pocket. He killed the ignition and went to look for the snitch.

As he approached the alley he heard low voices and hung back, then keeping himself plastered against the wall, he slowly inched toward the entrance.

"I'll cover you this time, man, but you already owe me ten bucks. If you don't got all the dough next time, there'll be fuckin' trouble. Got it?"

"Yeah, yeah, I will. I just need something to take away the tension, you know?" The desperation in the voice was that of a person who'd gone over the edge and the drug owned every bit of him.

"Next time I won't be so nice. And if youse take your business somewheres else, I'll find you and beat yo ass."

"I got it. I'll make good, dude. Thanks."

Army saw a skinny man stumble over the broken sidewalk as he walked away. Army slipped into the alley and watched Lil' Donnie using the phone's flashlight to count a wad of dough.

"Business good?" Army asked.

The drug dealer jumped and dropped his phone. "Fuck! Shit! Why the goddamn hell are youse sneaking up on me?" He bent over and picked up his phone.

"Here's the money the club owes you. You'll get the rest when this all goes down." Army took out a thick roll of bills and handed it to the informant.

"I'll let youse know," he panted, his fist clenching over the money. "Next time, don't give me no fucking heart attack. Fuck, man."

Army walked away sideways, his eyes darting between Lil' Donnie and the alley entrance. He unlocked the car and slid inside then headed back to Buena Vista Avenue to give blondie the other fifty.

Before returning to Taylor's apartment, Army had stopped at the neighborhood liquor store and bought a bottle of Jack Daniels and a twenty-four pack of Coors. He hauled the case on his shoulder and walked up the three flights of stairs and tapped the door with the toe of his boot. Footsteps grew louder on the other side until Taylor opened the door and moved aside.

"I have beer in the fridge," he said as Army marched into the kitchen.

"I like Coors. I got us a bottle of Jack. You got any ice?" He slid the case on the bottom shelf of the fridge then grabbed two glasses from the cupboard and opened the bottle of whiskey.

"Just one shot for me," Taylor said, leaning over the breakfast bar.

"What'd you do tonight?" Army handed the glass of whiskey to his brother then poured three shots into his.

"Nothing much. I didn't get back from Champion until ten." He took a sip. "How'd it go with Mia? I hope you remembered to call her that tonight."

"It went great. Tonight she was more Mia than Stiletto." With the glass in hand, he walked over to the couch and plopped down, then kicked off his boots and took a big gulp, relishing the sting as it burned down his throat and into his belly.

"Where'd you go?"

"El Señor something. The food was fuckin' good."

"Sol. It's El Señor Sol, and the food is great."

"I should've figured out the name with all the crazy ass grinning suns. How come you didn't tell me about the place?"

"You don't come down that much, and when you do, I rarely see you. It seems like you either have a woman around or are hanging with your club members." Taylor put the empty glass on the table and gave a half-shrug. "Anyway, I never thought to."

"How the fuck could you forget that Mexican food is my favorite? Remember the killer enchiladas Mom used to make?" As soon as he asked the question he knew the answer was no. *How could Taylor remember? He'd just turned four when she left.* He massaged his forehead as he idly stared at nothing.

Taylor shifted on the other end of the couch. "Did you respect Mia tonight?"

For a few seconds Army was eight years old, sitting at the kitchen table and wolfing down the plate of enchiladas as his father told him to slow down and his mother laughed. He could still hear her laugh ... like wind chimes on a clear spring day.

"You didn't," Taylor groaned. "Fuck, dude. She's not one of the floozies you hookup with."

At first his brother's voice was distant, then it came in clearer and stronger. "What?" Army looked up. "Sorry, dude. I zoned out. What were you asking?"

"Did you respect Mia?"

Army frowned. "Of course. I'm not some goddamn barbarian. We had a nice time." He got up and refreshed his drink. "What time do you have to work tomorrow?" Taylor had a job at a sporting goods store.

"Around nine. Aren't you leaving tomorrow?"

"I thought I'd stay around until the end of the week." Ignoring the scowl on Taylor's face, Army rested his feet on the coffee table and swirled the amber-colored liquor around in the glass. "I want to spend some time with Dad," he said, hoping that would allay Taylor's fears and stop any more questions.

"Are you sure you're not staying to spend more time with Mia?"

"I just told you I wanted to visit Dad."

"So you're not going out with her again?"

Army gripped the glass. "Now you're starting to piss me the fuck off. You told me you weren't interested in her."

"I'm not, but she's my friend and I don't want to see her get hurt."

"That's fuckin' noble, but last time I looked she was all grown up. You're not her damn dad or brother. She can make her own choices." He threw back his drink.

"But it's not a fair playing field. She doesn't know you like I do." Taylor put his empty glass on the table. "I know how you treat women."

"Every chick who goes out with me knows the fuckin' score. I don't lead them on. I can't help it if some of them think they can change me."

"Did you tell Mia the score?"

Army rose to his feet. "We went out for dinner, for fuck's sake. There's nothing to tell." He rinsed out the glass and put it in the dishwasher.

"Why're you getting so mad?"

"Because this is pussy bullshit we're talking about. I'm done." Army picked up his boots and went to the bedroom, closing and locking the door behind him. Gripping the hem of his T-shirt, he tugged it over his head then shrugged off his jeans and tossed them on the floor next to his shirt. He slipped on a pair of sweat pants and went over to the square four-paned window. Looking out, Army could see the building across from Taylor's and what the residents had on their balconies: grills, pumpkins, hanging plants, and patio furniture. A small courtyard filled with flower boxes, winding walkways and clusters of ash trees, whose leaves had now taken on various hues of red, yellow, and orange, separated the buildings. For the most part it was quiet, except for the few muffled voices from unknown apartments that bounced off the stuccoed walls and the rustling of branches in the wind, which sounded like trees whispering. Gradually, the lit apartments went dark and soon the only lights were the dim lampposts lining the sidewalks, the soft spotlights under the trees, and the glow from the tip of Army's joint.

That night had puzzled him because it was unlike anything he'd ever experienced with a woman. It was the first time he'd been with a chick where the night didn't end in sex. That alone surprised him, but what blew him the hell away was he'd had a great time even though they hadn't fucked. For Army, women were for pleasure, and it never occurred to him that he could have a good time with a pretty chick without screwing. He actually enjoyed talking to Mia and getting to know her. Army knew more about her in the short time they'd spent earlier that night than he did about any of the club girls or Willow, who he'd been fucking for several months. The crazy part of it all was that he wanted to know everything about Mia and spend more time with her.

She'd gotten into his head and under his skin, and that was a first for him. Mia was like a shot of whiskey, only smoother and more potent.

*I don't have time to get involved with her. We got a possible war with the fuckin' Pistons looming. I have to focus on that.* But thinking for even a moment that he'd never see her again brought up emotions inside him he wasn't ready to deal with. This had never happened to him with a woman and he couldn't believe it. *I'm just all riled up because we haven't fucked. She's teasing me, and I'm a natural hunter. Of course I love the challenge.* It had to be that because he didn't get *involved* with any woman. He thought Steel, Paco, Goldie, Diablo, Sangre, and Muerto were damn fools for tying themselves down to one chick. He didn't want or need that shit … but at that moment, the only woman he wanted was Mia. *No … Stiletto 'cause right now she's busting my fucking balls. I should hook up with Willow. She'd take the edge off for me.*

Army stared at a raccoon scampering across the sidewalk. He wouldn't hook up with Willow or any other woman because, for now, he just wanted Mia, and he was positive she'd be worth the wait. He didn't plan on keeping her; he just wanted some time to fuck her out of his system. As much as he enjoyed their time together, at the end of the day, women couldn't be trusted. All the years his mother told him she loved him were nothing but damn lies. She walked out of their lives without a backward glance. *And that's love?* The women he fucked all had other men they banged on the side. *No one gives a damn, that's the way it works. Just have a good time.*

Army pushed away from the window, a hard expression tightening his facial muscles. *That's all it's gonna be,* sweetheart—*a good time. I'll give you my cock, but there's no fuckin' way you'll ever have my heart.*

He lay down on the bed and rested his forearm over his eyes. Mia was front and center in his mind, and for a long while, he kept replaying their night together and every other instance they'd shared thus far. Turning on his side, he punched the pillow and tried to get comfortable, but the images kept running through his mind like a movie reel. After a couple of hours, he finally drifted off into a fitful sleep.

# Chapter Eleven

THE LOW BUZZING filled Mia's ears and she swatted at the air, but it wouldn't stop. Cracking one of her eyes open, she groaned when a sliver of sunlight pierced it, and quickly closed her lid. The buzzing had stopped for a few seconds then started up again.

"What the fuck!" She pulled her head up from the pillow and glanced at the nightstand where the phone shook, then looked at the time on the alarm clock: 7:15 a.m. The plan to sleep in until eight o'clock had just disintegrated. Reaching over, she snagged the phone and brought it to her ear.

"Hello?" She coughed, trying to clear her dry throat.

"Hi, Mia. How are you? I hope I didn't wake you," an annoyingly cheerful voice answered.

"Who the hell is this?" she asked, sitting up and reclining against the headboard.

"Noe. You sound like I woke you up."

*Fuck!* "Uh … yeah … you woke me up." *Please don't be in Durango.*

"Sorry about that. I got into Durango late last night."

*Fuck!* "Oh."

A deep chuckle. "I guess I took you by surprise."

"Yeah, you did. I'm just not a functioning person until I get some coffee in me."

A roaring laugh that definitely grated her nerves. "I hear you. Did Shark tell you I was coming?"

"He mentioned it, but he didn't say when. I didn't get the impression it was going to be this soon." *I really don't need this shit right now.* Mia grabbed the water bottle on the nightstand and took several sips—it cooled her parched throat.

"I work fast." Another chuckle. "Just joking. I'm here on some club business."

"I didn't think you were still in the MC."

"I'm not officially, but I'm still a member. Brothers never retire from the club. You should know that."

Rolling her eyes, she quirked her lips. "I'm not up on MC rules. Vic moved out of the house when he hit eighteen, so I wasn't involved with what he did. All I know is he's in a club and they ride motorcycles and probably do a lot of illegal shit to live because he hasn't had a job that I know of since high school."

"Watch what you say about the president. You need to show some fucking respect." Noe's cheerful tone turned steely. Mia liked steely better—it didn't piss her off as much. "And you know more than you're pretending."

"Like what you're all into?"

"Not that. That's always club business and not for bitches."

"Did you just call me a *bitch*? You phone me at a ridiculously early hour then tell me I'm a bitch?"

"Whoa … I didn't call you a bitch. I meant it's not for women."

"Then say that. You're telling me about respect and then you're saying *bitches* instead of *women*? I don't think so."

"You still got a mouth on you." Noe laughed dryly, and Mia was sure he wasn't as challenged by it as Army.

*Army. Why can't I get that guy out of my head? If only I had a shitty time last night.*

"Let's start over. How've you been?"

Noe's voice pushed through her thoughts. "Uh … good."

"Shark told me you're competing and that you're damn awesome. I'd like to see you fight sometime."

"I'm taking a hiatus right now. I have a lot going on with Finn. I'm sure Vic told you about him getting arrested. I'm trying to take on more clients so maybe I can help bail him out."

"Shark told me. You're gonna have to cut a shitload of hair for a hundred-thousand-dollar bond."

"I know I can't do it alone. I was hoping Shark and my mom would help. I can't stand knowing he's in jail." Mia had always been much closer to Finn than to Vic. Maybe it was because she and Finn were only three years apart versus the five-year difference with Vic, or it could have been Finn's willingness to understand and support her when their mother treated her so badly. Vic always seemed to take their mother's side, and when he was in charge, which was often, he was a cruel and unyielding dictator to all of them. At eighteen she'd moved to Tucson, and that was when Finn started spiraling downward. Even though her therapist kept telling her it wasn't her fault, Mia still blamed herself for leaving him behind. Now Finn was in a shitload of trouble, and she didn't know how to help him.

"He put his own ass in jail. You shouldn't have to be responsible for him. He's fucking twenty-three years old."

Anger pricked at her nerves. "I don't want to talk about this anymore. I have to get ready for work. It was nice talking to you." *You're a jerk just like Vic and all his other stupid friends.*

"I didn't mean to make you mad. I'm sorry you're going through all this with Finn."

"Thanks," she mumbled, not believing him one bit.

"Let me take you out to dinner. You'll have a bunch of coffee in you by then." He laughed.

*So he thinks it's just because I haven't drunk any coffee. What is it with men?* She rubbed the side of her neck. "I'm at Champion tonight."

"What's Champion?"

A sigh escaped from her lips. "A training gym. I really have to go."

"What about tomorrow?"

"That's not good either. How long are you staying?"

"Until the end of the week."

"Let's plan on lunch. Maybe … Sunday, or will you be gone by then?" Mia smiled at Snickers licking her black paws.

"Sunday's good. I can leave early Monday, but I'd like to see you more than once while I'm here."

"It's already Wednesday, and my days are really booked; plus, I've already made plans for the weekend. Sunday lunch is all I can do." Lunch was safe—a few hours max.

"Okay. I'll call you later."

"Bye, Noe." Mia put the phone down on the mattress and covered her eyes with her palm. *What a shitty way to start the day.* Shuffling to the bathroom, Mia wished she wouldn't have answered the phone. She turned on the shower and let it run for a few seconds before stepping in, then she placed one hand on the wall underneath the shower head and let the warm water cascade over her shoulders and down her back.

AS THE DAY went by, Mia was so busy that she didn't have a chance to chat with Ronica when she'd come over to Mia's station earlier in the afternoon. That morning, Mia had put the phone on the counter to make sure she didn't miss any calls, and as the day wore on, she became more and more perturbed by the lack of communication from Army. What had she expected? A gush of emotion telling her it was one of the best dates he'd had—probably the *only* date—and that he was looking forward to seeing her again? *He's probably pissed as hell because I didn't put out last night. I bet he'll stand me up. He's a player—I called it the first time I saw him.*

As the time neared seven o'clock, a throbbing headache surfaced as she dropped the styling brush on the floor.

"Sorry. I'm so clumsy," she said to Keri—her last appointment of the day. This was the third thing she'd dropped in the last fifteen minutes. *What the hell's the matter with me?* She glanced at her silent phone for the umpteenth time of the day.

"That's okay. As I was saying, I brought what I thought was a nice dip for my daughter's ballet recital, and some of the women thought I was committing a *too much high fat* crime." Keri laughed while shaking her head.

"Please don't move," Mia said.

"Sorry. So I told them ..."

*He didn't say he was going to call. We made a date at a specific time and said we'd meet at Champion. Why would he call? There's no reason to, but I thought he'd call to confirm or say he had a good time last night ... or any damn thing. I bet he'll be a no show. Shit ... I hate this. I don't care ... yeah I do. Shit.*

"Don't you think that was right?" Keri asked, looking at Mia in the mirror.

"Absolutely." *What the hell is she talking about? Something about a creamy dip with too much fat.* Her stomach rumbled. *I'm starving. I haven't eaten anything since I left this morning. I need protein.*

"I'm glad you can see my point." Keri looked at the back of her head with the mirror Mia handed her. "I love it, but I always do. You're the best. Did Rebecca Michaels ever call you? I told her how fabulous you are."

"She did. I thought I mentioned it to you. Thanks for the referral."

"You're welcome." Keri handed her a credit card and a fifty-dollar bill.

Mia shook her head. "Keri, this is too much, really." She tried to give the money back.

Keri gently pushed her hand away. "Nonsense. You deserve it. I know you do late nights for me, and I appreciate how accommodating you are." She glanced at the clock on the back wall. "Oh ... I didn't realize it was so late. I have to pick something up for dinner. I'm sure my family is starving and wondering where I am." Keri slid out of the chair and walked to the front of the salon.

Mia locked the door after Keri left and cleaned up her station. With everything in order, she walked out to her car and made her way to the gym.

The first thing she did when she entered Champion was scan the room for Army. She spotted Taylor sinking his fists into a speed bag, but there was no sign of his brother. At that moment, Mia's stomach suddenly gurgled reminding her how hungry she was.

"How did your day go?" Kat asked. She wore tight neon-green fighter's shorts and a sports top. Her makeup was impeccable, and her long hair was twisted up in a tight bun.

"How do you look so good all the time?" Mia asked, taking a protein bar out of her gym bag.

"Waterproof makeup and self-tanners are the secret." She tucked a few strands of stray hairs into her bun. "Not having to work or worry about money also helps." Kat had inherited a ton of money after her grandfather—a surgeon who'd invented a screening machine used in hospitals—had died three years before.

"I'm sure it does." Mia glanced around again as she walked toward the locker room.

"Army's not here," Kat said.

"And ...?"

"I know you're looking for him, and I don't blame you. I wish he was into me. I'd go for him in a minute," Kat replied, following Mia.

The truth was, Kat would have any well-built man, and she was continuously on the lookout even when she was with a guy because her relationships never lasted more than three months. She'd once told Mia that with so many men around she never could pick just one forever. She called herself "greedy," and the way she blitzed through men, Mia agreed with her self-assessment.

"I'm not looking to get involved with anyone right now." Mia put the gym bag and purse in the locker and went back into the gym. "Do you want to practice after I warm up?" she asked Kat.

"Sure. I'll just go over and watch Taylor. I love the way his biceps flex when he hits the bag."

A half hour later, Kat and Mia were rolling on the ground with Kat trying to get out of Mia's submission. When a low whistle broke Mia's concentration, Kat instantly escaped and pushed Mia down on the mat and straddled her.

Another whistle, this time louder, and Kat looked over and smiled. Mia took advantage of the distraction and pushed Kat off with her feet, securing the blonde fighter in another submission until she tapped on the mat several times. Mia stood up and wiped her sweaty brow with the back of her hand, then glanced over and saw Army standing with his arms folded across his sculpted chest, smiling. She smiled back as she bent down and picked up the water bottle.

"Good practice," Kat said, patting Mia on the shoulder. "I should be mad at you for distracting me," she said to Army, sticking out her lower lip in an exaggerated pout.

"I couldn't help it. You two looked hot as fuck."

Mia's smile fell and a pulse of anger went through her. "What did you say?"

He walked toward her. "I paid you"—his gaze flicked over to Kat—"and *you* a compliment."

"Thank you," Kat said arching her back and thrusting her more than ample breasts forward. She used that tactic successfully many times when she wanted the male fighters to do things for her, and by the way Army's gaze lingered on her cleavage, she'd been successful again.

"It's an insult to me," Mia said as Kat threw her a small smile then walked away.

"Really? I've never met a woman who didn't like a man to think she looks hot." Army's gaze fixed on hers.

"Congratulations, you met one now. Kat and I were practicing our skills and you disrupted us. Thinking we're hot while we're perfecting our moves is juvenile as fuck." Heat rushed up her neck and to her face, and she was pretty sure she resembled a tomato.

Army laughed. "If you think men are admiring female fighters' style and their skill, you're naïve as hell. The truth is, *sweetheart,* when we watch them fight, we all have wood and just want to drill them."

Her fingers flew to her parted lips as fire raced through her veins.

Army took a step closer to her. "Are you seriously clueless? Do you have any idea how many male fantasy buttons you push?"

"Since you've got a one-track mind, you think all men just see women as sex objects. At Champion, we're all fighters—male or female—it doesn't matter."

"Bullshit. I've seen the dudes in here throwing looks at you while you stretch or move around in the ring." He rocked back on his boot heels. "And when you and Kat or some of the other chicks are wrestling, or in the ring wearing your sexy clothes, these dudes are sporting hard-ons for sure. I mean … that shit's like every man's wet dream, only it's in 3D."

Mia shuffled back a few steps. "Of course, you see it that way because sex is all you think about. News flash: I came into the sport to prove to myself that I could handle anyone who tries to mess with me. I didn't come to look good in a pair of tight shorts"—she brushed the stray strands of hair away from her heated face—"or to get laid."

"I'm not doubting that. I'm just saying that men are visual, and all of you wrapped up in your sexy fighter clothes hits a man right in the dick. That's just the way we're wired. I'm not saying you aren't a hell of a good fighter or don't have great skills because you do. I told you that the first night I saw you fight. Having you sexy in the ring is just a bonus."

"Unbelievable." Mia brushed past him then yanked out of his grasp. "Don't fucking touch me. I thought last night was the real you, but I can see that it was an act to probably get into my pants." She waved her arm at him. "*This* is the real you. The one I saw the first night when I thought you were an asshole. Well … I was right." A lump began to form in her throat and she whirled around and dashed away, not wanting Army to see how upset she was.

"Mia," Army's voice called behind her, but she ignored it and went into the locker room and slammed the door. Throwing the water bottle in the trash, she went over to her locker and punched it. Pain shot up her arm and then everything inside of her snapped; she erupted, punching and kicking the metal door, the sound loud and hollow as it ricocheted off the walls. Waves of disappointment crashed over her as the locker assault intensified.

"Mia! Stop!" The deafening noise drowned out the voice.

Panting heavily, with sweat pouring down the back of her neck, she shrieked when someone caught both wrists and pulled her away while she fought like a wildcat.

"Calm the fuck down!" Army said, holding her against his solid chest.

Mia squirmed, her breath coming in ragged pants as tears welled up. "Leave me the hell alone." Army just held her until she was too exhausted to fight anymore.

"Oh, Mia," he said in a low voice, his hand running up and down her back.

She buried her face in his shirt in an attempt to stifle the sob that rose in her throat as hot streaks ran down her face. Her chest heaved as she desperately tried to hold back the floodgate of tears that threatened to open. She heard her own sounds—raw from the inside.

Army held her close, swaying back and forth while murmuring indecipherable words. A tiny lapse let her pull away, and she stared at the damp circle on his black T-shirt, her thick lashes sticking together in clumps as if she'd been swimming. Mia wiped the wetness from her red mottled face and nose.

"Fuck," she whispered.

Army kissed the top of her head. "You okay?"

Blowing out a shaky breath, she looked down at his boots. "I don't know."

Army placed his hands on her shoulders. "You're right."

Mia glanced up. "About what?"

"I'm an asshole." He pulled her into him. "I didn't mean to come off like a fuckin' jerk." Tilting her head back, he brushed his lips across her forehead. "Especially not to you."

"I didn't deserve what you said to me. No woman deserves that." She held his gaze.

"I know. I was just ... hell ... I don't know." Army's gaze flicked to something behind her.

"Don't mind me," El Toro said, striding past them.

"Let's go somewhere else to talk," Army said, his warm breath fanning over her face.

"I think I should go home," she said even though she didn't mean it.

"I want to go out with you." Army blinked. "I didn't mean the shit I said."

Mia tugged at his shirt. "It sounded like you did."

"I was pissed."

Her eyes widened. "At me?"

"Not exactly." He rubbed his chin. "It was more like at myself."

"Why?"

"Not here, Mia."

Her stomach rumbled, and she pressed her hands against it as if that would quiet the hunger pangs.

"Sounds like we should get a bite to eat. I could go for a burger."

A juicy hamburger with a thick tomato and crispy lettuce sounded like the best idea in the world, and her mouth salivated at the thought. "I know a great burger restaurant."

"Is it Big Bobby's?" His eyes twinkled.

"Yes! At least we have the same taste in food."

"We have a lot more than that, baby." He swept his mouth across hers.

She pulled away. "I'm still sore at you. Let me freshen up. Give me about fifteen minutes or so."

"Okay." His gaze lingered on her face, and there was such tenderness in those blue eyes that she almost wrapped her arms around his neck and kissed him.

"All right then." She turned around and rifled through her locker until she couldn't hear his footsteps anymore. With the gym bag clenched in her hand, she went over to the shower area. Mia went to the sink and cupped her hands under the faucet then splashed cool water over her face. Taking her towel from the bag, she patted her skin. *I really lost it. What the fuck was that all about? Finn.* I'm so worried about him. *I have to help him. Get him a good attorney.* As much as she didn't want to admit it to herself, Army's words had hurt and disappointed her because she really liked him ... too much, although she had no intention of telling him that. She was too terrified of falling for him. *I'm supposed to be strong and independent, not fearful and teary-eyed. What is it with this guy?*

After Mia had taken a quick shower, swiped a coat of sparkling plum gloss on her lips, and slipped into her black denim skirt and multi-colored knit top, she pulled on her ankle boots, grabbed her purse and gym bag, and left the locker room. Scanning the main area, she saw Army by the weights. The muscles of his butt flexed under the fabric of his tight jeans as he bent over and picked up one of the dumbbells. The sight made her breath catch in her throat as she imagined what he'd look like naked, hovering over her as he roughly pinned her arms above her. When Army's gaze locked on Mia's, her heart gave a sharp thump, and as he threw her a devastating smile, she felt her insides melting. She licked her lips then started walking toward him when a voice called out her name. Casting a sidelong glance to the left, she froze as panic threw a few punches to her gut. *What the hell is Noe doing here?* She darted her gaze back to Army and saw him glaring at Noe as he approached her.

"You look great, Mia," Noe said as his gaze swept over her then lingered on her breasts.

She folded her arms across her chest. "Thanks. So, what are you doing here?"

"I was in the area so I stopped by to say hi. Let me give you a hug." He put his arms around her and gave her a light squeeze. "You smell fucking good too," he said in a low voice.

She stepped back, her arms still folded. "I ... uh ... have—"

"Plans," Army said behind her, his voice hard. He came over and looped his arm around her shoulder and pressed her close. Mia leaned into him and saw the angry sparks in Noe's eyes. The two men stood staring at each other, nostrils flaring like two bulls ready to charge.

Glancing at Army, she gestured to Noe. "Noe is a friend of my brother's. He's in town on business." Army grunted. She turned to Noe. "And this is Army." Noe hissed. "And this"—she swept her arm around—"is where I train. Army's brother is a fighter. He's being looked at very seriously by the recruits to go pro. I know he'll make it. You should see him fight—he's awesome," she prattled as the two men kept their staring match going.

"You heading out?" Goliath asked as he came over, his eyes darting between her, Army, and Noe.

"I am." She pointed at Noe. "This is a friend of my brother's. He just stopped by to say hi." Goliath extended his hand, and Noe hesitated before taking it. "Goliath owns Champion, and he's a three-title heavyweight winner." That seemed to pique both Noe and Army's attention, and they turned away from each other.

"I didn't know that, dude. Impressive as fuck," Army said.

"That's quite a legacy. Do you still fight?" Noe asked.

"Nope. Retired and opened this training center. The wife's glad."

Happy that the crackling tension between the two men had been temporarily broken, she tugged Army's hand. "We better get going," she said softly.

Noe glanced at her, but he seemed intrigued by Goliath, and the fact that the owner was even talking to her brother's friend was huge and showed her how much Goliath cared about her. Goliath was a man of *very* few words, and when it came to his past fighting days, he rarely spoke about it.

"I'll call you," Noe said, looking down at her hand in Army's. "And I'll see you on Sunday."

Army's fingers tightened around hers in a vise-like grip, and she bumped against his arm. "You're crushing my hand," she whispered.

"Sorry," he mumbled, easing up.

When they got to the parking lot, Army walked with her to the car.

"I thought we'd take our own cars."

"I came with Taylor," he said, putting his hand on the door handle.

"That works then. I can't wait to get to the restaurant—I'm beyond starved." She slid inside and turned on the ignition.

"Who's the asshole?" Army pulled the seatbelt and fastened it behind him.

"Noe? He's one of my brother's best friends. He's been part of our family for years. Noe's like a cousin."

"He doesn't think that."

"He's fine. I haven't seen him in quite a while. Like I said, he's Vic's friend. They go back since grade school." Her fingers curled around the steering wheel, and she turned on the radio.

Army reached over and turned the volume down. "Are you seeing him?"

"Ugh ... I just told you he's passing through. Anyway, you and I are only on our second date."

"I just wanna know if I got competition." He settled back. "Not that it matters."

"You don't, but the way you acted earlier, I'm not sure if I want to hang out with you anymore."

Army leaned over and kissed her gently on the cheek. "You want to. You're pissed at me, and I get it. I was a fuckin' prick."

"No argument from me." She turned left into the parking lot of Big Bobby's Burgers. As they walked hand in hand toward the entrance, Army stopped and yanked her to him and gave her a hard kiss.

"Don't stay mad at me for too long, babe." He pulled away then grasped her hand again, and they walked inside the eatery.

The hostess sat them at a booth and handed them two menus, then walked away. Army put his down and sank into the black leather cushion behind him, his gaze fixed on her.

"Do you already know what you want?" Mia asked.

"A double bacon cheeseburger with barbecue sauce and jalapeños."

"Is that what you always order?"

"Since I was a kid—only back then it was a single not a double. You look beautiful."

She glanced up and met his intense gaze, then looked back down at the selections. "Flattery will get you some points, but I'm still not feeling all warm and fuzzy yet."

"Did you last night?"

"Yeah. I guess that's why the way you acted surprised ... no ... disappointed me. I just don't know why—"

"Do you want something to drink?" The waitress gave Army a toothy grin.

He gestured to Mia. "Take her order first."

The woman looked startled as if just realizing that someone other than Army was at the table. She turned to Mia, the smile replaced by a dour expression. "What do you want?"

"A Diet Coke."

The waitress looked over at Army and smiled. "Let me guess—a shot of whiskey or a good stout."

Army laughed. "A double Jack."

Smiling like she was on a damn toothpaste commercial, her dark curls swayed as she shook her head. "I knew it. You definitely look like a Jack man—rugged and tough."

"Why don't you take our dinner order too?" Mia asked.

Without looking at her, the waitress patted Army's hand. "Is that what you want me to do?"

"That's what *I* want you to do," she replied. Army's lips twitched as if he were trying to suppress a smile, and if Mia wasn't so hungry, she'd have taken off right then and there. *He thinks I'm jealous because the waitress is flirting with him. I'm so not.* What irked her was the way the twenty-*something*-year-old woman ignored her. *Why do so many women diss each other when a man is around?*

"Take my date's order," Army said.

Mia snapped her gaze to him. *Didn't expect* that. She thought for sure he'd play along with the server because that's what ego driven men did, right?

"So, what'll you have?" The woman acted like it was an enormous amount of work to take her order.

"The mushroom-Swiss burger—medium—and a salad instead of fries. Please bring me oil and vinegar for the dressing."

"What would you like?" she asked Army as another toothy smile spread over her lips.

The woman walked away after taking his order, and Army earned bonus points for not looking at her butt in her short uniform dress. He smiled at Mia and took her hand in his and kissed the tips of each one of her fingers as his gaze bored into hers.

Shivers sparked along her spine, and she willed herself to focus on finding out why he'd been such an ass to her at the gym. She gently pulled her hand away and returned his intense stare.

"Are you going to tell me now why you acted like a jerk at the gym?"

"Let me get some Jack in me." The familiar roguish smile flashed across his face as he winked at her, sending a tingle of arousal along her spine, prickling in her breasts.

The waitress put a glass in front of Mia while her eyes fixed on Army. "Here you go. I put an extra shot in it for you." She placed her purple-tipped finger to her lips. "It's our secret."

"Thanks," Army said, lifting the tumbler to his lips.

The woman lingered for a couple of seconds, but when Army's attention never wavered from Mia, she turned and walked away.

Mia watched as his full lips hugged the rim of the glass and his throat vibrated as the whiskey slid down it. *He's too damn sexy. He's messing me up. I'm still pissed at him.* "Well? You got some whiskey in you."

"Patience isn't one of your strong points outside of the ring." Another few swigs then he put his hands over hers. "I took shit out on you tonight. I already told you I was an asshole."

"But you told me you were mad at yourself. What are you mad about? Me?"

"Yes ... and no. Shit. I don't talk about my feelings, so this is hard."

"I understand, but it's important for me to know why you're mad at me."

"Not *at* you. I'm pissed about liking you. So I guess I said all that to punish you for getting to me. Aw shit … I don't know." He picked up his glass with one hand while the other remained on top of hers, then he threw back the rest of the drink.

"I get what you're saying. I kinda feel the same way—mad because I like you. I'm just not passive-aggressive like you are. Is this fucked up, or what?"

"I guess so. I've never liked a chick in the way I like you."

"You mean as a friend."

"I don't see you as a fuckin' friend. I like you. A lot." He ran his fingers through his hair. "I wanna keep seeing you."

Excitement simmered under her skin as she trembled. "I want to keep seeing you too."

He gave her a chin lift.

"But no more antics like you pulled tonight. We can talk about things if something's bothering you, but don't take it out on me."

"I get it—give respect in order to get it. I'm down with that. Respect is everything. It's the code. The way to live."

"And trust is important too."

Army's jaw hardened. "Trust is earned, and it comes from actions—not words."

"I agree. I think we both have some issues with it based on our pasts."

His eyes narrowed. "I don't have any issues with it other than it doesn't mean shit to most people."

*His mother.* "Yeah. Most people are not dependable." *My mother. Christ we both have mommy issues.*

"That's why earning trust is important and actions are key."

"I've learned to depend on one person only—me."

"That's good, but you need someone to have your back. You know to fight and stand by you no matter what. I've got my brothers and can depend on them to fight or give up their life for me as I would for them without a second thought. Citizens just don't fuckin' get it."

"A mushroom-Swiss burger, a salad—dressing on the side," a waiter said, putting the plate in front of Mia. He put the other burger in front of Army, asked if they wanted anything else, then promised to return to fill the water glasses.

"This looks so good," Mia gushed as she cut her burger in half.

"They have the best damn fries. Try one."

Army held one up and she smiled and leaned forward. His lips pressed against hers, leaving the salty taste of the fry in her mouth. He winked at her, kissed her again and then fed it to her. "Good?" His intense gaze deepened, and she could feel the level of sexual tension between them begin to rise.

Mia's tongue skimmed around her lips while she watched him. "Very good," she said softly while sitting back.

"I'm so fuckin' hungry," his voice sounded thick as he held her gaze, and she knew he didn't mean for the fries and burger.

Mia's breath caught as Army stood up slightly and placed his hand behind her head, pulling him toward his waiting lips. The kiss was tender and languid; he tasted of salt and whiskey and smelled spicy and earthy.

The clink of ice cubes drew their attention to their meals, and Army sat back down. The waiter filled their glasses, then dashed away.

Mia's body hummed, missing Army's lips, his taste … his heat. She looked down at her burger and wondered if she could eat it with all the somersaults going on in her stomach.

"Aren't you gonna eat?" he asked, picking up his mammoth burger and positioning it near his mouth.

"Yeah." She picked up her fork and speared a tomato then popped it into her mouth.

"I wish we had burgers like this in Alina. I try to come here when I'm in town. I usually bring my dad."

"It sounds like you're close to him."

"Sorta. I respect him for raising us after my mom skipped out. We don't see eye to eye on a lot of things. Taylor and Asher lived up to his expectations. When Taylor goes pro, my dad's gonna throw the biggest damn party."

"Does your other brother live in Durango still?"

"Yeah. He's hitched and has a son—Joshua." Army laughed and a wistful look glazed his eyes. "He's about nine months old, and he cracks me up."

"I bet you spoil the hell out of your nephew."

"I do." He took another big bite.

Mia watched the muscles in his jaws and wondered whether they'd moved the same way if he was eating her out. "Oh," she moaned, immediately embarrassed.

"Thinking about something dirty? I hope it involved me."

*Dammit!* "Not at all. I was rubbing my calf with my boot. It feels good."

The corner of his lip twitched as he looked at her, desire burning in his gaze. "That's the story you're going with?"

All of a sudden, her mouth went dry and she lowered her lids and grabbed the water glass. After several gulps, she cleared her throat. "Is your married brother older than you?"

He guffawed and shook his head. "I'm the oldest. Asher's two years younger, and Taylor's five."

*He's twenty-nine ... Three years older than me.*

"What about you? What's your family's deal?"

"Totally fucked up. Unlike yours, everyone but me has been to jail."

Army picked up the napkin and wiped his mouth. "Shit happens. I've been arrested a few times."

"For what?" With her throat parched and mind spinning, her voice was barely audible.

"Fighting. Mostly bar stuff."

"Have you ever been to prison?" Her body stiffened.

"Nah. Just misdemeanor bullshit, so it was all county time."

"My younger brother's been arrested for armed robbery—five of them."

Army gave a low whistle. "That's fuckin' tough. Is he in Colorado?"

"Arizona. I'm trying to get family members to help out with either his bond or retaining a decent attorney."

"Put your money with the lawyer. He needs to get a good deal and not end up rotting away in the pen. How're your parents taking it?"

"My dad left after Finn was born—he's the one in trouble, and my mom's biggest worry is which guy she'll bring home after a night of clubbing." Army's eyes widened. "Yeah ... I have a totally dysfunctional family. My mom had my oldest brother, Vic, when she was only fourteen, then Tucker came along two years later, and me when she was eighteen. By that point my dad blew, but he came back and gave my mother Finn as a going away present. I also have a half-brother, Dean, who's fourteen and following in my other brothers' footsteps. He just got out of juvie."

"Is his dad in the picture?"

"Nope. I mean, I get that my mom had us all too young and never had a chance to be a teenager, but she should've waited to sow her fucking wild oats until we all grew up. I was the cook, the laundress, the babysitter, the tutor—the fucking everything, and my mom still yelled and blamed me and my brothers for ruining her life."

Army slid out from the booth and came over to Mia's side and sat next to her, then he wrapped his arm around her. "You had it bad, babe." He kissed the top of her head and sighed loudly. "Why the fuck do people have kids if they don't want to be parents? Those are the ones who should be in prison for fuckin' up their kids' lives."

Mia settled back into him, loving the way the heat of his body warmed her. "I don't want you to feel sorry for me. It made me stronger, and it taught me to depend on *me*. I decided I had to get out, or I'd be trapped forever."

"You did real good for yourself."

"Thanks. I did."

He put two fingers under her chin, lifting her head up to meet his lips. Mia moaned as Army's tongue slipped inside her mouth and tangled with her own. She curled her arm around his neck, then raked her fingers through his hair as she pulled him down closer. A low, sexy grunt filled her ears, and it drove her wild.

"Mia," he rasped as his mouth glided down to her neck. "You're fuckin' killing me." He nipped the tender flesh above the sterling silver hoop earring she wore, then laved the shell of her ear. Clutching his firm biceps, she whimpered. He dropped tiny kisses over her neck, then trailed his lips up her throat to her jaw before nipping her chin. Taking her hand, he placed it on his dick. "See what you do to me, baby? I want you so fuckin' bad." His hand grazed the front of her skirt and pressed against the juncture between her legs.

Her body jerked at his touch as a blazing ball of lust rushed down her spine to her pulsing sex. "Army," she choked. It felt like the air in her lungs was on fire. He pushed down harder, and she closed her eyes as arousal swept through her.

He nuzzled her neck. "Are you wet for me, baby?" his soft, husky voice whispered. He pulled her earlobe between his teeth and sucked gently.

Mia wanted his hand to slip under the skirt, his fingers to push inside her as she rubbed against him ... unzipping his pants, touching him ...

*I must be out of my damn mind.* Mia pulled away then pressed her face in his shoulder.

"What's going on?" he asked.

She managed to sit up straight and scoot over a bit. "We're in a public place."

Army grinned. "That can be fun, but not for our first time. Do you want anything else?"

"No, thanks." As hard as Mia tried, she couldn't keep from stealing peeks at his impressive hard-on. She licked her lips. "We should go."

"I'm down with that."

On the drive home, Mia's mind swirled and twirled like leaves in a windstorm. Out of the corner of her eye, she saw Army watching her, probably noticing how white her knuckles were as she gripped the steering wheel, or how rigid her body was. He reached over and slid his hand under her hair at the nape and gently drew circles on her tingling skin.

*I can't have sex with him. Can I? No. I don't want a casual hookup. Why not? No-strings-attached can be a great set-up because I'll have intimacy without commitment. But I don't want that. What do I want? I don't fucking know!* Over and over her mind battled until she almost screamed at the top of her lungs.

When Mia turned down her street, she realized that Army didn't have a car. How could she have been so stupid? She pulled over to the curb and put the gear in Park.

"What's up?" Army said, his fingers still caressing the back of her neck.

"I forgot that you don't have your car. I don't know where Taylor lives."

Confusion marred his rugged face. "I can deal with getting back in the morning."

Swallowing, she pivoted in the seat at the same time he moved his hand away. "I'm sorry, but it's late and I have another full day at the salon tomorrow." *Chicken.*

Army slammed his fist on the dashboard, and she jumped, her heart thumping. "Fuck this shit," she heard him mutter under his breath. He opened the car door but seemed to change his mind when he slammed it shut again and glared at her. "Do you want me to leave you alone?"

Mia's heart lurched, and she shook her head.

"What the fuck do you want then, because I'm getting mixed signals."

She waited a few seconds before answering because she honestly didn't know what the hell she wanted from him. "I know that I don't want to be a casual hookup."

He tilted his head back and growled. "I've told you I don't really date, but I'm doing it with you. I don't know what more you want me to say."

"I just think things are moving way too fast." She held up her hands when he scowled at her. "I admit I'm to blame for that too."

"Are you afraid of me?"

"No. Definitely not. Don't think that." Her hand flew to the base of her neck as her eyes widened. "But we only met a couple of weeks ago, and we still have things to learn about each other. I don't want what we have to only be about sex, and it would never be anything more than that if I slept with you now."

"I don't get what you're talking about. Do you wanna fuck me or not? The way your body reacts when I'm kissing and holding you tells me you do."

"I do, but I just think we should date for a bit. If you're not into that, I understand. I know you don't do the whole dating thing."

An awkward silence fell between them, and in the glow of the dashboard lights, she could see Army frowning as if wrestling with what she'd said. The possibility of him telling her goodbye was more than strong—it was probable. Even though they hadn't gone out that long, Mia knew that she'd miss him. She'd never felt such a pull to a man before, and it scared the hell out of her.

"Okay," Army said, breaking the silence. "I'll try it your way, but I'm gotta tell you … I've never taken anything slow in my life. I don't really know what the fuck that means, but I know I like being with you, and I want to keep seeing you."

Happiness filled her, and she reached over and grabbed the front of his shirt, tugging him to her. "I want to keep seeing you too," she breathed before she kissed him. The porch light switched on at the house they were parked in front of, and a man stepped outside. "We better get going. He probably thinks we're casing the place." Army chuckled, then told her Taylor's address.

When she pulled in front of the gate leading to the courtyard of the apartment complex, she pointed at a black and silver Harley-Davidson.

"What a beautiful bike."

"You ride?" he asked.

"No, but I've been on the back of a lot of bikes. I love it."

"That's good to know."

"That reminds me. At the restaurant when we were talking, you used the word 'citizens' for people, and I meant to ask you then if you're a biker, but we ended up getting sidetracked."

"Yeah, I am, and that bike right there is mine."

"It's beautiful. Do you take women for rides? I know a lot of bikers are funny about that unless it's their old lady."

He looked at her. "You know something about the brotherhood, and I don't take chicks on my bike, but I'll make an exception and take you for a ride. Are you doing anything on Sunday?"

"I'm supposed to have lunch with Noe."

"That's too bad." He clucked his tongue. "We'll have to make it another time. I'm heading back to Alina that night."

She ignored the voice in her head and said, "I can reschedule with Noe. It's no big deal."

"Then, it's a date."

"Are you with an MC or anything?"

"Yeah—the Night Rebels."

Everything blurred around her, and the only thing she could hear was her mumbling voice echoing in her head. "The Night Rebels?"

"Yeah. Are you okay? ... Mia?"

Army's voice cut through the thickness and slowly brought her back to the moment. "Huh...? Oh ... I guess I'm more tired than I thought."

"You seem a little weird. Can you drive home all right?"

*Home. I have to get there. Now.* "I'm good. I'll see you around."

"Wait. What about dinner tomorrow night, and not with the gang at that place you get dinner in a bowl or a glass."

"I'm guessing Berriegood isn't one of your favorite restaurants." She smiled weakly as her heart raced. "I think tomorrow's good. I don't know."

He chuckled. "You are tired, babe. We can talk about it in the morning." He pulled her toward him and gave her a deep kiss, then got out of the car. "Drive carefully, and text me when you're inside the house with the alarm on," he said before closing the door.

"Will do." Then she drove away. Her temples pounded. Her body trembled.

*Army's Vic's enemy. Satan's Pistons hate the Night Rebels. I've heard this for years. What the hell am I going to do?*

Tears welled up in her eyes as she headed home.

# Chapter Twelve

AFTER STEEL ADJOURNED church, Army pushed away from the table, walked out of the room, and grabbed his phone. Early that morning, Steel had texted him that he had to get back to Alina. He'd thrown his clothes in his satchel and hit the highway without a second thought. According to what Chains and Hawk had picked up on the grapevine, Satan's Pistons were low on funds and looking for quick ways to get it. Without cash, there was no drug deal with the 39th Street Gang, and the Pistons needed that deal real bad to keep the club going. There was also talk that the Pistons were planning to put a glitch in the Rebels' revenue sources—their businesses.

Steel had called church to discuss the new developments and to go over the action plan for the large party at Lust that night. All members had to be available in case some trouble started at the gentlemen's club. Lou Blakely—the richest man in the county—was giving a huge bachelor party for one of his best buddies, who was getting married to wife number three. He rented out the club, and the net worth of all the guests would be in excess of a billion dollars. That was a hell of a lot of money to have together, and Steel and Paco wanted to make sure that no one—namely the damn Pistons—got any ideas. Security would be top notch, but they didn't want to leave their club, dispensary, or other businesses unmanned, so all members had to be present at all Night Rebels' interests.

"Are you sticking around for a beer, or going to Lust right away?" Eagle asked.

Leaning against the hallway wall, Army looked up from his phone. "I'll be there in a few." He walked farther down the hall so as not to be disturbed by the members shuffling out of the meeting room.

"Hello?" Mia said.

"Hey, how are you?" Army answered.

"Good, but busy as hell. How're you?"

"Okay. I had to go back to Alina." Army saw Chains approaching so he ducked into one of the storage rooms and locked the door behind him.

"Are you coming back?"

"Eventually. Sorry about tonight and the bike ride on Sunday. Another time."

"Whatever," she mumbled. "I'm super busy so I better go. See you around sometime."

"Wait. What the hell? I'd much rather be riding my bike with you pressed close behind me, but shit happens."

"It does."

"My prez called me back for club business. Don't give me a damn attitude."

"It just seems pretty convenient, especially after I told you I wasn't going to have sex with you last night. That's all I'm saying."

"You're wrong. I told you I have club business. It has nothing to do with us fucking or not. I wouldn't have called you if I didn't give a shit."

Army waited for Mia's response as the whirring noise of a hair dryer filled in the silent gap between them.

"Does your club business involve a rival club?" Her voice was so low he could barely hear her.

"I can't talk about it. Just know I'm not bullshitting you."

Another pause, then he heard her exhale slowly. "Let me know when you get back in town."

"I'm in a MC and shit comes up sometimes. You have to understand that, if you want us to keep going out."

"I get it. I'm in the middle of a highlighting job, so I have to go."

"I'll call you."

"Okay. Bye."

Then she was gone and something deep inside of him pulled hard as he stared at the dark screen. He shoved the phone in the pocket of his jeans and went back into the hallway. Whatever he was feeling, he didn't want to think about it.

"How was your time off?" Eagle asked, handing a shot of Jack to Army.

"Good. Do you think they'll be problems at Lust tonight?" Army picked up the tumbler.

"Not sure. The fucking Pistons have been looking for a way to get back at us, and Lust brings in a ton of dough; with all those expensive cars in the lot, I wouldn't put it past them to try something."

"They'd be fuckin' stupid to do shit in Alina," Muerto said.

"That's one of the problems with the assholes, they're dumber than dirt," Crow added.

"The only way we need to handle them is to annihilate 'em." He crossed his arms over his chest.

The members looked at Crow with grim expressions on their faces. They knew their brother had a personal vendetta with Satan's Pistons ever since three of the bastards attacked him and his girlfriend. They raped her and sliced him from his rib cage down past his navel and left him for dead. That was before Crow had moved to Colorado and joined up with the Night Rebels.

"They play fuckin' dirty, that's for sure." Army patted Crow's shoulder while the others nodded in agreement.

"Even so, to come into our town? No one's that much of a moron." Muerto picked up the beer bottle the prospect handed him.

"They won't come, themselves, they'll pay someone to do their dirty work," Army replied.

"I can't wait until we surprise them in Durango and get rid of them once and for all," Crow said.

"Yeah. Lil' Donnie's gonna tell me the exact date and time when he knows it, but with the rumor that the assholes are low on cash, it may be longer than a month. I'll probably head back to Durango in a few days."

"Really?" Eagle said. "That seems to be your favorite place all of a sudden."

Frowning, Army shook his head. "My fuckin' family lives there, dude."

"They didn't just move there. They've been living there since you've been in the club."

"What the fuck are you trying to say?" Army's body went rigid.

Eagle jerked his head back. "Why're you getting pissed off? I was just making an observation."

"I don't need you butting into what the hell I do. I don't give a shit where you go or what the hell you do." Army pushed away from the bar, his nostrils flaring.

"Chill, bro," Muerto said.

"Chill, my ass. I'm outta here." He turned around and stalked out of the clubhouse. Taking out his keys, he headed over to his bike. The crisp air cooled his ire down a bit, and he cursed himself for overreacting to Eagle's comment. Why did it bother him so much? Maybe it was because he didn't want to admit that the only reason he'd decided to spend time in Durango was because of Mia. *BS. Dad's there, and Taylor's close to going pro.* He slipped on his sunglasses and gripped the handlebars. *And I hadn't seen Joshua in almost three months. I don't want the little guy to forget his uncle. Mia was a bonus, that's all.* The cams screamed as he sped out of the lot and headed for downtown.

Army pulled up in front of the flower shop and killed the engine and then stared at the passing cars. *What the hell am I doing?* He'd never thought about giving flowers to a woman in his life, and here he was in front of Hailey's floral shop planning to go in and have a bouquet of flowers sent to Mia. Disappointment, along with distrust, was in her voice when he'd spoken to her and it ate at him. The last thing he wanted was for Mia not to trust him.

He turned his head and looked at the front window with its display of fall arrangements amid wooden buckets, straw, fake red apples, and a smaller replica of a tree with silk leaves in gold and orange. *I'll tell Hailey not to tell Goldie. I don't need the brothers hazing me about this.* He swung his leg over and walked up to the front door.

A small chime rang when he opened the door and a few customers glanced at him as he walked in. Army looked around the store not sure of what to do since he'd never been inside a flower shop. Behind several glass doors, arrangements in vases, brightly colored pails, and straw baskets lined the shelves, so he went over to them and wondered which one Mia would like best.

Army thought he was going to lose it the night before with Mia's soft body pressed against him, her intoxicating scent swirling around him, and her luscious lips on his, and then she'd pushed him away. She'd said she wanted to slow things down, but how the hell could he do that? Mia scorched his mind far more than he cared to admit, and the way she kissed. *Damn.* He'd kissed a lot of women, but he'd never experienced the raw intensity that he did with her. It burned his insides and stayed with him, invading his thoughts. He couldn't remember wanting a woman as badly as he wanted Mia. Just thinking about her, remembering her tongue tangled around his, the sound of her laugh, and the way her lips twitched when she tried not to smile made fire rush right to his dick.

He moved away from the arrangements and went over to the corner, pretending to be engrossed in a little pink boot filled with pastel colors and balloons that said *It's A Girl!* so no one would see him pitching a tent and think he had some damn flower fetish. He concentrated on counting the number of petals in each flower, banishing any thoughts of the sexy, sassy wildcat who had somehow managed to take up a permanent residence in his head.

"Army?" Goldie said.

*Fuck!* He turned around and saw his buddy coming out from behind the counter. Army quickly stood in front of a table that came up to his waist. "Hey, dude. What're you doing here?"

*Where the hell's Hailey?*

"I'm just helping my woman out until she gets back from setting up for a wedding." Goldie cocked his head to the side. "What's up?"

"Not much. Doesn't Hailey have employees?"

Goldie raised his eyebrows. "Yeah. One called in sick, one is helping her at the hall, and one's in the back. Why?"

Army darted his eyes around the shop. *I can just say I was passing by, or just order the fuckin' flowers.* "Just wondering. So you're the one taking orders?"

A slow smile began to spread over his face as he nodded.

Army sucked in a deep breath, then exhaled. "I need to place one."

"Are you fuckin' around?"

"No, and I don't have time for your smartass comments. I gotta get over to Lust, so let's do this so I can get going."

Goldie stared at him for a few seconds then erupted in laughter, and a woman came out from the back carrying wire cutters in one hand and ribbons in the other. "Is everything okay?" she asked, her gaze moving back and forth between Army and Goldie.

Still laughing, Goldie nodded over and over.

"It's fine," Army said, his insides tightening.

"Okay," the employee said. Doubt laced her voice as she slowly walked to the back room.

"Are you fuckin' finished?" Army asked as he walked to the counter.

Wiping his eyes with his palms, Goldie went over to the computer. "Sorry, dude. I haven't had a good laugh in a while."

"If you spread this shit around the club, I'm gonna beat your ass," Army growled.

"Then let's go out back and face off, because there's no fuckin' way I'm keeping this one under wraps. You gave me so much shit when I was dating Hailey, and you ragged on and on about Paco and Chelsea. No way I'm not spilling my guts." He started laughing again.

Army clenched his fists. "You gonna do this, or do I go to Rambling Rose and give *them* my business?"

Goldie cleared his throat. "Okay. Let's be professional." He snorted as he slid the book over to Army. "Pick something out of here because I don't know shit about doing a custom order."

Army flipped through the pages, but each snicker from Goldie pissed him off more and more. He pushed the book back at him. "I'm not ordering from you. Tell the chick in the back to help me, or I'm outta here, dude … I'm not fuckin' around."

Goldie held up his hands and pivoted. "That'll work for both of us 'cause there's no way I can keep a straight face." He popped his head in the doorway. "Petra, can you come out here and take an order?"

"Sure," a high-pitched voice answered.

Army pointed his finger at him. "And you keep your fuckin' mouth shut, or go outside and smoke a damn joint if you can't."

Goldie just laughed and settled on the stool behind the counter. Petra ambled over, her dark brown apron speckled in glitter and globs of glue. "Did you pick something out?" she asked, looking at Army over big red-framed glasses.

"He's new to this," Goldie said, then smiled when Army threw him a dirty look.

"Did you want something already made or a custom?"

"Not sure." Army refused to even glance at Goldie, who was enjoying this way too much for Army's liking.

"Do you know what kind of flowers she likes? That'll help."

"I'd say sunflowers and some purple flowers and green stuff." Army's jaw tightened at Goldie's snicker.

"Let me see," she said, flipping through the plastic pages in a big binder. "Here we go." She turned the book upside down so Army could see the picture. "Something like this? It has sunflowers mixed with miniature scarlet carnations, bronze daisies, orange chrysanthemums, and large lavender asters. Bold red roses would be a pretty addition. Just a suggestion. Of course there'll be autumn greens like in the photo. It comes either in an angular vase or a large, rectangular basket."

Army felt Goldie's gaze on him. "I like that. The colors complement her eyes."

"What color are they?"

Army wished like hell Goldie wasn't there. "Amber."

Petra looked up at him. "True amber? I mean a lot of people think hazel eyes and amber ones are the same, but they're not."

"True amber."

"Wow ... that's rare. This arrangement will be beautiful. Do you want it in a vase or basket?"

"Vase."

"Clear?"

"I guess."

"Okay. What about the roses?"

He hesitated. "Pass."

"Okey dokey." Petra's fingers flew over the keyboard.

Army looked over at Goldie. "Go smoke a fuckin' joint."

"Don't you want me to know your chick's name and address?"

Army scowled and Goldie chuckled while he stood up. "I'll stack those boxes on the shelves," he said to Petra as he disappeared into the back room.

"It's hard for guys to order in front of their friends. I think it's a macho thing," she said as she pushed up her glasses.

Army didn't answer but a multitude of emotions coursed through him. He almost changed his mind when Petra asked for Mia's name and address, but he didn't, and by the time Goldie came back out, the order was paid for: the flowers would arrive at Mia's house the following day—he'd paid extra for overnight delivery.

"I'm taking off," he said to Goldie. "See you later at Lust."

"I'm gonna be at the dispensary tonight."

Suddenly, the teasing from earlier disappeared, and the seriousness of what may happen later that night fell over the two men.

"I got the vibe some shit's gonna go down," Army said after Petra went in the back.

"Me too." Goldie ran his fingers through his hair. "I'm worried about Hailey."

"I know." Army clasped Goldie's arm. "Are some of the brothers watching the old ladies?"

"Yeah. They're all going to Steel's house. The kids too. Breanna's been preparing for it all day. They'll have dinner and do whatever shit women do."

"Are the prospects gonna watch them?"

"Yeah. I told Hailey to call me if anything goes down."

"They should be all right." But Army knew they were empty words because the damn Pistons wouldn't hesitate to hurt women or children. Both men stood quietly, each lost in thought.

The front door opened and the chime broke through their musings. Army lifted his chin at Goldie then turned around. An older woman and man walked past him as he went out of the store. He jumped on his Harley and made his way to Lust.

STARS SPLASHED ACROSS the sky like diamond-splattered blood but cast nothing to lift the impenetrable inky blackness blanketing the town. The occasional beam from a passing guard illuminated the luxury cars parked in Lust's parking lot. The muffled beats of music and voices filtered from the club.

"Everything good?" Army asked, coming around the back of the building.

Dennis—one of four extra security guards they'd hired from Sangre's company—stepped back a little as if startled. "Yeah. Seems pretty quiet back here. It'd be better if it wasn't so dark." He looked up at the moonless sky.

"The security spotlights should help, but not having a new moon would've been better. A lot of dark corners and shit to check out. I'm headed around the front. If you need any of us, you know what to do." Army made his way to the front of Lust when he saw Eagle and Crow coming out the side door.

"All's good?" Crow asked as he fell in step with Army.

"Seems to be. I'm checking on Paul in the front. How's it going inside?"

"Those guys can fuckin' party." Crow laughed.

"And they got a shitload of money to burn. The girls will make a killing tonight," Eagle added as he trailed behind.

When they came around the front, they saw the other guard holding a large pizza box as he walked toward the front door.

"Paul!" Army called out.

He stopped and looked at them. "The strippers ordered pizza." He laughed.

"What the fuck?" Crow said.

Army shone his flashlight on the security guard who looked like he was going to open the box. "Don't move! Don't open the—"

A loud explosion, shattering glass, a streak of fire reaching up into the blackness, and the fearful screams coming from Paul as he propelled backward and landed on the ground filled the night. Army, Eagle, and Crow dashed over to the fallen man and quickly dragged him away from the burning cardboard box on the tarmac. Dennis came running over at the same time Diablo, Brutus, and Chains burst through the club's front door.

"What the fuck happened?" Diablo cried as he ran over.

Dennis—wide-eyed and pasty—knelt by his co-worker.

"A fuckin' bomb in the pizza box. Paul opened it," Eagle said before he and Crow ran out to the street.

"Can you hear me, dude?" Army said to Paul.

"Yeah. What the fuck happened?"

"The goddamn box was booby-trapped." Army looked behind him at Chains. "Call Medico."

"We need to call the police and an ambulance," Dennis said.

"We'll take care of it. Go back to your post. Chains will go with you."

Dennis reluctantly stood up. "Do you want me to call someone for you?" he asked Paul.

Shaking his head, Paul took the damp cloth Brutus gave him. "No. I feel like I'm on fire."

"The dumbasses who made the pipe bomb fucked up, otherwise we'd be picking up parts of you all over the damn lot," Diablo said.

Army took out the phone and called Goldie. "We got a bomb blast over here. Paul got hurt, but Medico's on his way. It was a pizza box."

"I have the fucker who delivered one here. He was trying to tell me that one of the employees ordered it. I knew it was bullshit," Goldie said.

"What'd you do with it?"

"It's far enough away, so it won't do much damage if it goes off."

"The bomb here was defective. Burned Paul pretty good, blew out some car windows, and some of the debris dented a few BMWs. I don't know if Medico can help out. We may have to call Wexler on this." Not wanting to deal with law enforcement, the Night Rebels handled things on their own as did all outlaw MCs, but sometimes they needed the assistance of Sheriff Wexler. They had a tacit agreement with Wexler—they'd keep hard drugs and gangs out of Alina, and he'd look the other way on some of their not-so-legal dealings. For the most part, it worked well.

"I'll take the little shit to the clubhouse. Jigger will stay here and deal with the badges. They gotta disarm the bomb. Is everything okay at Skid Marks, Get Inked, and Balls and Holes? Seems like they're targeting our businesses."

"Diablo's taking care of it. Here comes Steel and Paco. I'll see who they want to go to the clubhouse to help you interrogate the fucker."

"I'm going now. Wexler's gonna have his hands full," Goldie said.

"How the fuck did this happen? Where the hell were you?" Paco asked, a scowl embedded on his face.

"I was on the other side checking on Dennis and making sure no one was lurking in the shadows. I can't believe Paul thought the strippers would order a fuckin' pizza in the middle of a party," Army replied.

"He knew to call one of us." Paco looked at Steel. "I was against bringing in citizens to help out. What a fuckin' mess." He bent down and put his hand on Paul's shoulder. "How're you doing, man? We got help coming."

"My face feels like's it's on fire," he whimpered.

Paco nodded then stood up. "He's burned pretty bad," he said in a low voice.

"The other places are good. Muerto said someone tried to deliver a pizza, but Brandy knew something was off. The guy left it at the front and took off but Muerto got him. He said the place was packed tonight." Diablo clenched his fists. "The fuckin' Pistons are gonna pay for this."

"What'd he do with the box?" Army asked. A sideways glance confirmed Medico had just arrived. The forty-four-year-old man had his medical bag in one hand, and he lifted his chin at Army and the others then knelt down beside Paul.

"He said he took it over a few blocks and left it behind a trash bin in an alley. The dude he caught is at the clubhouse. He's going back to the pool hall when Goldie gets there, then he'll call the badges."

"How he is?" Steel asked Medico.

"He's got some pretty bad burns. He needs to get to the hospital stat." Medico had been on the Night Rebels payroll since the club had started. Many times he was called in to patch up the brothers after a rumble, and he never opened his mouth about what he'd seen or did—a trait that was priceless to the outlaw club. Steel took off his jacket and gave it to the physician, who placed it around a trembling Paul.

"I'll call it in," Steel said somberly.

By now, many partygoers had filtered out of the club, and Steel went over to them in an attempt to put them at ease. Eagle and Crow returned without any luck in finding the person who'd delivered the bomb. They joined Army and Paco, who talked in hushed whispers, calm and low, but their words were of hate and retribution.

The flashing red and blue lights signaled that the badges had arrived. Army looked over his shoulder and saw three police cars and an ambulance. Paco walked over to the sheriff, and Army saw that the VP's jaw was working overtime.

Soon the paramedics had Paul on a stretcher, wheeling him to the ambulance. Sangre stood next to Army and watched the vehicle drive away.

"Fuck," Sangre said.

Army gripped his shoulder. Paul was one of Sangre's employees, and he felt for him. "Yeah ... fuck."

"The women are good. Ink told me no one's come near the house," Diablo said as he came up to them.

"That's something," Army answered. "Anything happen at Get Inked?"

"Nope." Diablo folded his arms over his chest.

"That doesn't make sense. I wonder how long the damn badges are gonna keep us," Sangre said.

"I heard Wexler say they've got some badges coming down from Durango to disarm the bombs," Diablo said.

At the mention of Durango, an overwhelming desire to hear Mia's voice seized him. "I'll check on the dancers," Army said. He walked past the deputies and went back into the club. The women sat with patrons, and when he entered, the barrage of questions made him sorry he hadn't just gone around back. After fielding their inquiries, he made his way to the back area and slipped into the office, shutting the door behind him.

For some reason he had it in his head that Mia could be in danger, and that Satan's Pistons could go after her to get back at him. He had no indication that the damn Pistons even knew he dated Mia, and his rational mind told him that his reasoning was askew, but he needed to make sure she'd turned her alarm on and was safe. Army tapped in her number and glanced at the clock: 1:00 a.m.

"Hi Army," she said groggily.

Her voice was thick and sweet like slow pouring honey. "It sounds like I woke you up."

"You did, but I don't mind."

"Did you remember to put your alarm on?"

"You're obsessed with that." She chuckled. "Is that the reason you called me?"

Her voice was clearer now that she was awake. He pictured her pushing up and maybe leaning back against the headboard. "I wanted to hear your voice."

"That's nice to know," she said softly.

"What did you do tonight?" He wondered what she was wearing. *Is it something sheer and nasty or cozy and flannel?* His dick twitched.

"I went out with some of my friends for a drink after the gym." She yawned. "What about you?"

"I worked, remember?"

A small pause. "That's right. Was everything okay with your club business?"

"Can't say. What're you wearing?"

"A nightshirt."

"Anything under it?"

"Panties."

"Fuck." He huffed out a breath. "I wish I was with you."

"Me too."

*Damn, she gets me going.*

"Taylor talked me into competing in an upcoming fight. I'm still thinking about it. I'll have to train my ass off and lay off the carbs and booze."

"Doesn't sound like too much fun. When's the fight?"

"In four weeks."

He heard her gulp something and smiled as he imagined the sheet falling down past her toned legs as she reached for a glass of water.

"I hope … you can come and see me … if I decide to compete," she said tentatively.

"I wouldn't miss it." Flashes of her in the cage straddling him and wiggling her firm ass over his cock made the bulge in his pants grow bigger. That had been a favorite fantasy of his since he'd first seen her at the MMA fights.

"Maybe you could come before then. I know Taylor likes sparring with you. He told me you guys used to do it a lot when he was younger."

"Maybe." Army perched on the edge of the desk enjoying the battle going on inside Mia at that moment. He knew she wanted to ask when he was coming back, but her independent side wouldn't let her. It seemed like her mind and body were constantly at war with each other. The way he saw it, there was no doubt her body craved him, but overthinking it too much made her push him away.

"Oh."

Army looked out the window and saw the sheriff and his men walking around the building. *I gotta get back out there.* "Do you miss me?"

"I had fun with you." Defiance crept into her voice.

*You miss the fuck outta me.* "That's good." A rap on the door. "Hang on." Army went over and opened it then put the phone tight against his denim-clad thigh.

"What the fuck are you doing in here?" Steel asked as his gaze flicked to the phone.

"I had a call to make. You want me to head over to the clubhouse and see what's up?"

"Goldie, Rooster, Razor, and Cueball are finding out answers. Wexler has some questions he wants to ask you. I don't want him nosing around anywhere else except here and the two other businesses."

"Okay." Army stood rooted to the spot.

"End your fucking call and get outside." Steel turned and walked out the back door.

Army shut the door. "Mia, I gotta go."

"Is everything okay? I heard someone talking."

"It's fine. One more thing—did you cancel your date with that fuck-face?"

"Date?"

"Lunch on Sunday."

"His name is Noe."

"Did you?" He looked out the window and saw Steel pacing.

"I did because I thought we were going for a ride. I was going to call him in the morning and tell him I can make it now."

"Don't."

"You're telling me what to do now?"

"Yeah, I am. Just don't go. I have to hang up. Later." He slipped the phone in his pocket, switched off the lights, then headed outside.

BY THE TIME Army got back to the clubhouse, the two delivery boys, both who turned out to be no older than fifteen, had been questioned and released. They didn't even know they were carrying bombs in their hands when they carried the boxes. Each teen said that they were given a hundred bucks to deliver the pizzas. They were given the addresses and told to hand over the pizza to a person who wasn't wearing a black jacket or leather vest and then to leave immediately. They named the third teen and said he was their friend. After hours of questioning and implicit threats, Goldie, Cueball, Rooster, and Razor determined the frightened teens were just unsuspecting pawns in a dangerous game. From the description of the drivers, the Night Rebels were pretty sure they knew who they were. The teens were scared to death the men would try and hurt them if they knew they talked, but Razor told them not to worry because the club would take care of it.

Cueball and Rooster escorted them home, then had the two pro-spects, Ink and Vegas, stand watch at each of their houses. Before long, three local drug dealers—Ramsey, Mats, and Billy—were locked in the club's interrogation room, shackled to the wall.

"The explosives were PVC and black powder, but the good thing was the moron who made it didn't secure the caps tight enough so they were half on. That bit of stupidity saved Paul's life and a lot of others," Army said as he picked up his much-needed glass of whiskey.

"It was the fuckin' Pistons. The three sniveling pussies we got chained up verified what we already knew." Razor rubbed his eyes.

"Why don't you call it a night, dude. The fuckers aren't going anywhere," Army said.

"I think I will," he answered. "Goldie and Rooster already took off. I'm not sure where Cueball is."

"He's with Alma." Ruby sashayed over and ran her blue-tipped nails down his back. "Need some company?"

Razor snagged her around the waist and pulled her toward him. "It'll be quick."

"No worries. You need to unwind. I'll do all the work."

Army laughed. "That's an offer a dude can't turn down." He watched Ruby snuggle into Razor as they walked away, and for a moment he wished Mia were tucked under his arm as he escorted her to *his* room. He picked up the glass and tossed it back—the whiskey a little nugget of warmth sliding down inside him. He cupped his hands around the tumbler and let his gaze drift, seeing nothing.

"Steel chewed your ass out good," Eagle said, sliding onto the stool next to his. "Who the fuck were you talkin' to?"

"A friend, but he was right to be pissed off at me." Army pushed away from the bar. "I'm beat, dude."

"I'm just having a nightcap then I'm gonna crash too," Eagle replied.

Army tilted his head then headed to his room. After kicking off his boots, he sank down on the mattress. He couldn't believe that in the middle of a clusterfuck he'd slipped away to call Mia. *What the hell's going on with me?* Since he'd met her, he kept telling himself that all he wanted was to have her writhing underneath him, but a feeling niggling at the back of his mind made him second-guess himself. What he felt was more than simple lust; it was a connection like nothing he'd ever experienced with a woman. It made him want to step away from her and run to her at the same time; his feelings were a confused mess of contradictions.

*Shit.* Heaving out a sigh, he sat up and leaned back as sleep evaded him. He opened the top drawer on the nightstand and took out a joint, hoping that it would help his brain switch gears and ease his thoughts away from Mia. Images of her in tight shorts and tops played in his mind. *Fuck!* He slammed his fist on the top of the nightstand; just thinking about her got him hard. The pain of a rigid, unsatisfied cock didn't help dispel thoughts of Mia from his mind. Calling in one of the club girls to relieve the discomfort crossed his mind, but they were poor substitutes for the pussy he wanted to pump into—Mia's.

"This is a crock of shit!" he cried out, stubbing out the joint. Growling in frustration, he pushed down on the desire for her still burning in his veins. Shoving the ashtray away, it fell to the floor with a dull thud. He stood up, picked it up then hurled it across the room. It struck the wall and shattered there, shards of glass falling on the wooden floor. He walked in a circle, pacing as his mind raced. *I'm in deeper than I should be with her.* Anger rolled through him—that, and desire. *I need to just fuck her and stop this bullshit.* He ran both hands across his face, through his dark hair. *I can't let her screw with my head. I need to concentrate on the club and the mess we've got going with the fuckin' Pistons. I don't have time for these feelings for her. I didn't ask for any of this!*

The sound of Mia's sweet laugh, the scent of her perfume, images of her in high heels, and the feel of her soft body pressed against his ran through his mind. Army shook his head back and forth, trying to chase the thoughts from his brain.

The first slither of sun peeked over the desert in a radiant, white form as ribbons of sandy yellow and rosy pink filled the sky, welcoming a new day. Army grabbed the trashcan and picked up the shards of broken glass, then went over to the window and closed the curtains. He needed to get some sleep because the day would be long: three lives would end; evidence would be destroyed, and plans for retaliation would be put in place.

The trashcan scraped against the floor as he pushed it back in the corner. He lay down on the mattress and closed his eyes, hoping sleep would come quickly.

# Chapter Thirteen

MIA SNEAKED A peek at her phone and groaned inwardly. *Only thirty minutes has gone by?*

"Do you gotta go somewhere?" Noe asked, staring at her.

"I'm trying to get a long workout in today. I'm thinking of competing and the fight's a month away. I have a lot of work to do."

"Is that guy gonna be there?"

"Army?" Just saying his name sent an excited flip through her stomach, making her fork clank against her plate.

"Yeah ... that asshole."

"Pretty strong word for someone you don't know." She picked up the knife and cut a piece of steak then looked up at him. "He's not a member, so he won't be there." *But I wish he was.*

"You dating him?"

Mia popped the morsel of food in her mouth and chewed slowly as she thought about the answer. On one hand she wanted to tell him they were dating, but on the other, she didn't want Vic to get too nosy about Army. It would spell disaster for both of them if Vic ever found out he was a Night Rebel. She swallowed. "No."

"He acted like it."

Mia shrugged slightly and looked back down at her plate. "You grabbed my hand when we walked in here. That's the way men are."

"But you pulled away from me. I didn't see you do that with him."

Shaking her head lightly, she gave a tight laugh. "With all the questions, you're acting more like you're my brother instead of his friend." She picked up the glass and drank; the bubbles from the carbonation tickled her nose.

"I hope you see me as more than just Shark's friend."

"Did you finish with your business in town?" She avoided his stare and concentrated on scooping up a hazelnut on the fork.

"Yeah. I'm thinking of heading back tomorrow unless there's a reason for me to stay." His gaze pierced through her.

"I won't be able to hang out. I'm just too busy at work and with training." She gave a small laugh. "That's really my life in a nutshell."

He pressed his lips together to form a straight line and stared at her for several seconds. "Yeah … right." He ran his finger over the beer bottle, his gaze still fixed on her. "I can stop by the gym and watch you train later tonight."

*I shouldn't have called Noe back after Army canceled on me.* She'd procrastinated in doing it but finally made the call figuring it was easier to just go out with him than to go through Vic's interrogation as to why she'd canceled. Also, Army telling her *not* to go was presumptuous, and it pissed her off. However, at that moment, she was afraid Noe was reading too much into their lunch. Earlier that day, two of her clients had rescheduled so she'd called him and suggested meeting up for a late lunch that afternoon rather than on Sunday, and Noe readily agreed.

"I'll be in a private room with my personal trainer," she lied, hoping he didn't know squat about Champion.

"Then what about dinner after?"

"Another time. After a long workout, I'm not good for anyone." She laughed, trying to make light of the situation even though Noe's eyes pierced through her and his brows knitted together. "Speaking of training, I have to go. My trainer gets mad if I'm even five minutes late." Mia opened her wallet and pulled out a twenty. "That should cover my share."

"I invited you," Noe growled. "Put your fuckin' money away."

Taken aback, Mia shoved the bill back in her wallet. "I didn't mean to offend you. I just thought we'd go Dutch since we're just friends, you know?"

Ignoring her, Noe threw down the money on the bill tray and

pushed back on the chair; it made angry scraping sounds on the tiled floor. "You coming?" he gritted as he walked away from the table.

Mia quickly slipped out of the chair and followed him to the car. From the corner of her eye, she saw a red sports car across the street and sitting in it was the same man she'd seen in front of the salon the week before. After opening the car door, she turned and looked straight on at the guy. There was no expression on his face, but his hands gripped the steering wheel, and he had a menacing presence. An electric chill ran down her spine as she slid into the seat and closed the door. As Noe drove away, she stared out the passenger mirror, seeing the sports car pulling out and falling behind them. Panic pricked at her skin as her gaze fixed on the vehicle.

"What're you looking at?" Noe asked.

"I think that red car is following us. No ... actually, I *know* it is."

Noe glanced in the rearview mirror. "Why do you think that?"

"I've seen it many times in the last couple of weeks. I don't know who he is or why he'd be following me."

"It's a flashy car, so I'm not surprised you've seen it around. The city's not that big."

"Even so, I don't want whomever it is to know where I live."

He glanced again in the mirror. "He just turned left."

Mia looked over her shoulder. The car was gone. "I just think it's odd that he was in front of the salon last week."

"Are you sure it was the same person? I couldn't even tell what he really looked like."

"Maybe you're right." She stared straight ahead, a niggling doubt still in the back of her mind.

Noe put his hand on her thigh and squeezed a bit too much. "Next time you see it, get the plate number and give it to me. I'll check it out, okay?"

"All right," she said, shifting her body.

Noe pulled his hand away and pounded it on the steering wheel, cussing under his breath. Mia counted the minutes until they'd arrive at her house.

"We can do breakfast tomorrow morning before I leave." Noe put the car in Park.

"Sorry, but I have a private customer tomorrow morning. Have a great trip back, and I really hope that your dad feels better."

"He won't. He's got a fuckin' progressive disease." His voice was hard like steel.

Mia opened the door. "Then, I hope he's at least comfortable. I know how hard it must be for you."

"You really don't. You don't know jack shit about loving a parent. Shark tells me you rarely call your mom. That's not being a good daughter, is it? Raye always complains to Shark about not hearing from you."

Her body tensed and she turned to look at him, her chin held up high. "First off, my mom has a phone, too, and the *only* time she'd ever called me since I moved away was a couple of weeks ago to tell me about Finn. Any other rare time I hear from her is when I go home or *I* call her. That's the way it's been for the past six years, so where the fuck do you get off telling me about my mom?"

"Of course, you're mad and defensive. Telling someone the truth always brings about that kind of reaction."

With her temper flaring, she rushed out of the car then slammed the door.

"Mia, get the fuck back over here."

Anger and contempt burned behind her eyelids, red and hot. She stalked up the walkway, not turning around when she heard Noe yell, "You can be a real bitch!" followed by tires screeching as he sped away. *How* dare *he tell me about Mom! And Shark's an asshole for saying that shit about me. He knows how Mom is with me.* Grinding her teeth, she bent her head down and kicked the dried leaves littering the path. "Why the hell don't they sweep the sidewalks? I pay a hefty HOA," she fumed under her breath.

She took out her keys then looked up and saw a beautiful bouquet of flowers in a glass vase with a deep purple ribbon and bow around it. Staring at it, her anger intensified. *Fuck! Why can't Jorge catch on that it's over? This is my day for assholes!* She bent down and picked up the vase and tucked her arm around it while she opened the front door. Pumpkin and Snickers came running over, and she went into the living room and placed the flowers on the coffee table then bent down and petted the cats. "I had a shitty time," she said to them as they nuzzled their faces against her cheeks. "Are you hungry?" She stood up and went into the kitchen.

After she fed them, she changed into one of her favorite fleece night-shirts she wore for lounging around, and sat on the couch staring at the vibrantly colored flowers. Spotting a small white envelope, she debated about reading the crap Jorge had written, but curiosity got the better of her, and she leaned over and snagged the note: *Hey, babe. Army.* Straightening up, she reread the note again as her anger melted away and the glow of happiness radiated through her. "I can't fucking believe it!" she cried out loud, startling both her cats.

Her mood, which had been foul just moments before, was bright and jovial, and she thought she would burst from shock and joy and sheer giddiness. Mia stood up and bent over to smell them. "How did you know I love sunflowers?" she murmured under her breath.

The last person she would've thought of as romantic was Army, yet the unexpected bouquet proved her wrong. Mia was no stranger to receiving flowers from men, and when she'd dated Jorge, it seemed like he sent them every week, but none of the bouquets or arrangements she'd received meant as much to her as the one right in front of her. Threads of desire wove through her as she stared at the most beautiful flowers she'd ever seen while vivid pornographic images of Army played in her head.

The phone humming on the table invaded her erotic reverie and she reached over and picked it up, hoping it wasn't Noe going in for round number two. Ronica's name flashed across the screen, and she pushed the button and held the phone to her ear.

"Hi, Ronica."

"Mia. You sound ... bubbly, and that's not a word I thought I'd ever use to describe you. Did you finally screw your hottie?"

She giggled. "No, and he's not *my* anything, but he did do something totally unexpected and terribly romantic." She paused for dramatic effect, laughing when Ronica kept asking what it was that he did.

"I swear I'm going to hang up if you don't tell me right now, Mia."

"He sent me a huge bouquet of flowers." Mia stared at them as she spoke, the thrill of his gesture still sparking inside her.

"Red roses?"

"No. He sent a gorgeous assortment of sunflowers, copper daisies, carnations, and some others I don't know the names of. Simply beautiful. I've never been so shocked and happy at the same time."

"I have to admit I'd never have guessed a guy like him would even think to send flowers. Wow. He really likes you or really wants to screw you."

"I think it's both, and I feel the same way."

"Is there a card?"

"Yes." Mia grinned again as she reread it.

"What does it say?" Ronica asked.

"*Hey, babe* ... then his name."

"What the hell? That doesn't say anything."

Mia pressed the card against her chest. "You're wrong—it says *everything*."

"Did you call and thank him yet?"

"I was just getting ready to when you phoned."

"When are you going to see him again? Didn't you tell me you don't know when he'll be back in town?"

"Yeah. I'm not sure when he's coming back here. I didn't tell you this, but he's a Night Rebel."

Ronica laughed. "He's a rebel all right. He swaggers, has a cocky demeanor, and has a bunch of tattoos on his arms. I don't think anyone would think he's a conformist, but then you aren't either. That's why I told you he'd be perfect for you."

"No, I don't mean that. He's a biker in an outlaw motorcycle club—the Night Rebels."

"I'm not surprised he's a biker. I bet he has a big Harley to go along with other things that are big on him." Ronica chuckled.

For a second, Mia pictured Army hovering over her with his big dick pushing in and out of her; she shook her head to scatter the image. "Is your mind one track? And he does have a Harley." Mia sniggered.

"I knew it. I bet it'll be exciting to ride on the back of that thing holding onto him. It sounds like something out of a movie. I must admit, bad boys are so fucking sexy."

"I've been on bikes a lot of times. My brother Vic has had Harleys since he was sixteen. Hang on a sec … I'm going to get a Coke." Mia went into the kitchen and grabbed a can from the six-pack on the granite counter. She'd never told any of her friends that Vic was in an outlaw club, but she needed Ronica's advice on what to do about the situation with Army. She sank back down on the couch. "I'm back."

"So your brother likes motorcycles."

She took a large gulp then suppressed a burp. "He's in an outlaw club too. He's the president."

"Really? That's a small world. Do you think Army and Vic know each other?"

Her insides tightened. "I'm positive they do, but not in a good way. Their clubs are rivals. My brother would kill me if he knew I even talked to him."

"Are you serious? That's dumb."

"It is to us but not to these guys. I'm not sure what to do here."

"Are you involved with your brother's club?"

"Not at all. He started it with Noe when they were around twenty years old, so he's been in it for eleven years now. He's the president. I only know that his club hates the Night Rebels and a few other MCs because he's ranted about them for a lot of those years. A couple of years ago, the Night Rebels destroyed their clubhouse, and Vic was beyond livid. Normally, he wouldn't tell me something like that, but he was so enraged, he couldn't help venting to me when I called him to ask about one of my brothers."

"This is like a TV show. It's like that one that was popular on TV a while back. I can't remember the name. Damn ... I never thought this stuff happened anymore." Ronica's voice had a thread of incredulity running through it.

"It does. I think it's ridiculous, and I'm not involved in any of it. I don't really speak to my brother all that often, and I haven't seen him for a couple of years now."

"Then what's the problem with you going out with Army? I mean, that's your brother's issue, and frankly, it's none of his damn business what you do."

"I feel that way too. I have nothing to do with the Satan's Pistons. How can—"

"*That's* the name of your brother's club? It's too wild." Ronica laughed.

"It is. It's so not my world." Mia brought the can of soda to her lips.

"What's your gut telling you?"

Mia fixed her gaze on the flowers. "To go out with Army. I really like him, and it's blowing me away because it takes me a long time to fall for a guy."

"I know. You dated Jorge for five months, and you never fell for him."

"He was nice, but I like more of a challenge, and I like things darker and rougher when it comes to sex, but I've told you all this before."

"Yeah, but the point I'm making is ... if you have feelings this quickly for Army, it must be the right thing, you know ... the real deal?" Ronica said.

"Maybe. I'll admit there's a real strong connection I've never felt with any other man, and I know Army feels it too. The thing I'm wrestling with is whether I should tell him about Vic being in the rival club."

"Why? Like you said—you aren't involved with any of that, and you haven't seen your brother in a long time. It's not like you're super close to him or you're all gung-ho about his club thing. What difference does it make? I mean we're civilized people, right? We don't believe in feuds. You're not the Hatfields and the McCoys. It's silly, really."

"I like him a lot," Mia whispered. "Why would he judge me because of who my brother is, right? I'm my own person. I want to keep seeing him."

"Then go for it. The only world that should matter is yours—not your brother's and Army's club. This is about the two of you—not anyone or anything else. You deserve to have a really great guy. Oh, hang on a minute." Ronica put her on hold.

Mia read the card again and leaned over and smelled the sweet fragrance of the flowers. *I can't give him up. He's only been gone two days and he's been in my head nonstop.*

"Mia, I have to go. Stuart's on the phone, and he's in a mood. Go with your instincts. We'll talk later. Bye."

Mia crushed the can in her hand and went into the kitchen and threw it in the recycle bin. After replenishing Pumpkin and Snickers' dry food, she went back into the living room and dialed Army's number. He answered on the first ring.

"Hey, babe. Nice surprise." His low voice caressed like warm fingers.

"You're the one full of surprises."

"What do you mean?" A hint of mischief wove through his question.

"The flowers. They're beautiful! I'm still reeling and in shock that the big, bad biker sent them." She laughed.

Army joined her. His rich, low rumble stroked her senses like velvet. Mia loved to hear his voice … laughing … talking … singing … anything. She could lose herself in his voice.

"So a biker can't send a chick flowers?"

"Is that your MO with women? Dine them, kiss them passionately, then send flowers?"

"Not with women, babe. Only with you."

A warm feeling spread through her. "That's good to know. How did you know sunflowers were my favorites?"

"I didn't, but you seem to bring light wherever you go, and I know you're crazy about fall from the way your porch and house are decorated."

Mia blinked rapidly to hold back unexpected tears then inhaled a deep breath; his words had touched her in ways that surprised her. She had never been a sentimental fool when it came to men, but since she'd met this captivating man, her emotions had been bouncing all over the place.

"You're sweet," she said softly.

"Get your ass movin', dude. Church is starting now," a booming voice said in the background.

"I gotta go."

"When will I see you?"

"Not sure. We got some club business going. I'll call you, baby."

"Okay then—" The phone went dead, and she wondered if the club business was about the Satan's Pistons.

She put her phone down and scooped her cats up in each arm, nuzzling their faces. "I'm screwed big time here," she told them. "I like Army too much to walk away." Remembering how Pumpkin played up to him when he'd been to her house, she kissed her on the side of the face. "You liked him too, didn't you? He's irresistible. Look what he gave me." She gazed at the flowers making a mental note to put the vase on a plate surrounded by orange and lemon peels to keep the cats from nibbling on the petals—both her cats loathed the citrus scent.

After playing with them, Mia changed into her training clothes and headed out of the house, looking one last time at the bouquet before she closed the door.

# Chapter Fourteen

ARMY WATCHED THE woman strut on stage shaking her tits and ass as she auditioned for one of two dancer jobs.

After the explosion at the strip club a couple of weeks before, Army and the other brothers thought business would be bad for a while, but the crowds just kept getting bigger, thus the reason Army was watching a clodhopper attempt to dance on stage.

"You've got the best damn job," Jigger said, sitting in the chair next to Army's. "She's a looker."

"Yeah, but she has no rhythm or sex appeal."

"I'd watch her." Jigger lifted his chin to Charlie, who placed a bottle of beer in front of him.

"Do you want anything?" the bartender asked Army.

"Just a 7-Up. Thanks," he answered slicing the air horizontally with his finger.

Kyra, the stage manager, turned off the music. "Thank you. We'll be in touch," she said to the redhead, who picked up her robe off the floor then walked off stage. "Patricia Fuentes," she called out, and in seconds, a stunning brunette came out and shrugged off her robe.

"She's fuckin' hot," Jigger said.

"Yeah. Let's see if she can dance." Army took a sip of soda.

"She can just stand there, and that'd do it for me."

"A paying customer wants more than that. Besides, you're always looking to get laid." Army motioned to Kyra to start the music.

"And you're not?" Jigger looked back at the stage.

The music filled the venue as the applicant swung her leg around the pole. Instead of seeing her, Army saw Mia arching her back, her long caramel hair skimming her ass while her tits pointed up toward the ceiling. Then she was underneath him, her strong and shapely legs wrapped around his back as he pumped into her, those magnificent amber eyes locked onto his as small moans escaped through her parted lips.

"You gotta hire her, dude. She's fuckin' awesome. I wish Ruby or Kelly was here to get rid of this boner I have from watching this chick. *Damn.*"

Jigger's voice pulled Army away from his fantasy, and he shifted his jeans as he tried to focus on the woman gyrating on stage. At that moment, his cock throbbed painfully which helped with his attention span. It seemed that in the past few weeks, whenever he had a free moment, all he could think about was Mia and fucking her hard and rough. Every time he had some dead space, there she was in his mind—naked and underneath him.

*Fuck. I need her so bad.*

During the past two weeks, he'd managed to go to Durango twice. Both times, they had a great time and talked about practically everything well into the night. He couldn't believe how much he enjoyed talking with her. It was a first for him with a chick, and sharing his thoughts and anger about his mom was cathartic. He was still trying to figure out how Mia keeps getting him to reveal so much shit about himself. They'd made out pretty hot and heavy, and she finally let him play with her luscious tits, but each time he'd delve a little farther down her body, she'd shoot him down.

He was going crazy just thinking about her and imagining how awesome it would be to fuck her so hard that she wouldn't be able to walk for the rest of the day. Army pulled at the whiskers on his face while deep in his thoughts. He had a connection with her he couldn't explain. It was the first time he'd ever felt bonded with a woman. All of his encounters with women over the years had just been sexual and only about pleasure, but with Mia, it was different. He didn't want a no-strings-attached arrangement with her. Just the thought of another man holding her or kissing her made his anger index rise to boiling, and he was pretty sure she wouldn't be too happy if he had a one-night stand.

Nudging him with his elbow, Jigger waved his bottle toward the stage manager and said, "Kyra keeps looking at you to give the word on the dancer."

Army straightened up from his slouched position. "Is she done dancing?" *Dammit*. He'd gotten caught up in his head and missed the audition. *Mia ... you're fuckin' killing me.*

"Yeah, dude. She's just standing there on the stage."

"Did you like her?" Army asked.

A wide grin broke out across Jigger's face. "She's a keeper. She can dance and turn a guy on. She'll bring in some good money on the private dances."

"Okay then." Army gave Kyra the thumbs up and he heard her tell the woman—he'd forgotten her name—that she'd gotten the job. The woman squealed and clapped her hands then turned to Army.

"Thank you so much," she said, her gaze scanning both Army and Jigger's faces.

"You gotta get drug tested before the job's official. Kyra will go over everything with you, including the rules," Army replied.

The woman walked off the stage and Kyra went over to Army. "Do you want to see more? We have the first slot filled now with Patricia. There are two more applicants waiting to audition."

Army motioned Brutus over. "I'll let Brutus and Jigger check out the last two. If they're no good, then we can do some more auditions tomorrow."

"Sounds good." Kyra ambled away and soon a short woman with pink and purple hair came on stage.

"Make sure you think with your heads and not your cocks. The chick has to have rhythm and sex appeal. I'll be back—I have something to do," Army said to the two guys.

He went to the bar and had Charlie pour him a double Jack then he tipped his head and threw it back, loving the slow burn as it slipped down his throat. Maybe that was enough to take the edge off so he'd stop acting like he was a lovesick idiot who couldn't control his fucking hormones. He slid the glass to the end of the bar then walked through the backstage area and went outside.

It was a nice Indian summer day: warm with a clear blue sky. Army watched the leaves flutter down and crackle on the pavement. Leaning his head back against the wall, he wondered how Mia had slid in and taken a place in his life. A place he didn't even know was vacant until she came along.

The phone rang and he smiled when he saw it was her. They talked on the phone a lot, sometimes for an hour, which was a record for him, considering that he rarely talked for more than fifteen minutes with *anyone* on the phone, but with Mia the time just flew by.

"Hey, babe," he said.

"Hiya, sexy. Are you doing something?"

"Yeah—thinking about you."

Her sweet laughter hit him right in his dick, waking it up *again*. "I was jogging and thought about you, so I wanted to give you a call."

"How's the training going?"

"Rick's mad at me. He says I'm too distracted, and I'm blaming you for it all the way."

"Is that right?" All he wanted to do was pull her through the phone and kiss her deeply.

"Yep. I wasn't this way before I met you, but … you're a very good distraction. Rick tells me I'm not ready for the fight. I'm bummed about it, but I have to agree with him. There's another one in a couple of months I'm training for."

"Since you're not gonna compete, why don't you come down to Alina for a bit?"

"I'd love to. I've never been there, and I miss you too much."

"Me too, babe." Army rocked back and forth on the balls of his feet.

"I'd have to reschedule a few things."

"I want you to come to the club party we're having on Saturday."

A pause. He chuckled. She breathed out loudly.

"It's not so bad. I'll be with you. I want you to see a part of my world. I've seen a lot of yours," Army said.

"Okay," she said with a tinge of hesitation. "Saturdays are tough to reschedule. Maybe Ronica and Danielle can help me out."

"Or you could come after your appointments. The party doesn't really get started until around nine or ten. The food will be available all night."

"That could work." Hesitation was still in her voice.

"Don't you wanna come?" Army cradled the phone on his shoulder as he lit a joint.

"I do. I want to see you in your environment. Is your club going to be the only ones at the party?"

"Some brothers from the Fallen Slayers will be there and some from the Twisted Warriors. The Warriors are from Ohio. They're passing through on a bike run."

"When did you say your club's rally is?"

"In a couple of weeks. I'd love it if you could come down for that. You can meet the old ladies, and there's a ton of shit to do. There'll also be a lot of booths and all that. It's our fundraiser."

"I'd like to go. Taylor said he was planning on coming down, so I may ride with him."

"That'd be cool. I haven't talked to him, but I'll give him a call. So, Saturday works for you?"

"What the hell? Sure. I'll go to the party."

"Then we can go to Chaco Canyon for a ride the next day. It fuckin' rocks. How many days can you take off?"

"Probably until Tuesday night. I'll have to be back at work on Wednesday. That's now the beginning of my week."

"A four-day week isn't too shabby." He hated that he was so damn excited. *I can just imagine what Eagle or Goldie or any of the brothers would be saying about now. I'm acting like a damn pansy-ass.* But he didn't really care because he was excited that Mia was coming, and he'd get to spend four days with her. The woman just did shit to him that made him crave her with an insatiable hunger.

"I'll book a room at a hotel," she said, enthusiasm replacing the hesitation from moments before.

"You can stay at the club if you want." Army smiled, knowing full well she wouldn't go for it. He was teasing because there was no way he'd want her around the brothers and club girls on her first trip down. The party would be enough of a window into his world.

"Thanks, but I'd feel uncomfortable."

"Okay. I'll set everything up for you at one of the hotels."

"Decelles, get your ass moving!" A man's voice bellowed.

"Uh-oh. I'm in trouble," she said. "Whenever Rick calls me by my last name that means pushups. We'll talk later." Mia kissed into the phone.

"Bye, babe."

Army stubbed out the joint on the patio floor then went back inside. Several of the regular dancers were now in the dressing area getting ready for their shifts. He lifted his chin at them then went back into the bar and headed over to Kyra.

"Are the auditions over?" he asked.

"For today. The last two didn't work out. I'll set up five more for tomorrow. The same time?"

"Yeah. I'm gonna be in the back room sorting through some boxes if you need me." Army went over to Jigger. "You still here?"

"I don't have anything else to do. I was gonna go to Durango to see Abe, but Morgan said he has to do some shit at his school tonight. I'll have to wait for the weekend to see him."

"You're not going to be here for the party?" Army scooped up a handful of pretzels from the bowl on the table.

"Nah. I promised Abe we'd do the zip-line adventure. He's been talking about it for the past three weeks."

"Morgan's letting you take him on that?" Army asked.

"Yep. I'm surprised too." Jigger chuckled. "Have you ever tried it?"

He shook his head. "Not into soaring on a cable. I just like to fly on my bike."

"I agree with that. I've never done it, but Abe's been asking about it since one of his friends did it with his folks over the summer."

"It should be fun."

"Any time I spend with my kid is fun. I just love hanging with him. He's gonna be eight soon and before you know it, he'll just wanna hang with his friends," Jigger said.

"Yeah—they grow fast. Since you don't have anything to do, you can help me go through a bunch of boxes we have in the back room."

"Let's do it," Jigger said, rising to his feet.

As they unloaded the crates, Army kept thinking about Mia and how soft she felt in his arms. As far as he was concerned, Saturday couldn't come fast enough.

*Yeah ... nothing but a fuckin' pansy-ass.*

# Chapter Fifteen

**M**IA SWUNG HER legs sideways then stepped out of the car, stumbling on the uneven asphalt of the club's parking lot. She'd opted to take her car because she couldn't imagine how she'd ride on the back of Army's bike in a miniskirt without showing her ass to the world. Army had reluctantly agreed and left his bike at the hotel where Mia was staying at for the next four days.

Circling his arm around Mia's waist, he drew her to him. "Stay close to me inside, otherwise you're gonna be bothered." He softly traced her jawline with his finger. "You look so damn sexy, and those fuckin' high heels are killing me." Sweeping her hair over her shoulder, he pressed his warm lips to her neck. She cocked her head to the side, shivering as he grazed his tongue across a reddish love bite he'd left there a few nights before when he'd come to Durango.

She moaned and gripped his bicep, her fingertips pressing into the taut skin.

"I love the sounds you make, babe." He kissed the spot behind her ear that turned her to mush then gently licked her skin, his tongue tracing invisible patterns down to the hollow of her throat and back up to nibble on her ear.

Tilting her head back, she closed her eyes. "Oh ... Army," she gasped softly.

His lips covered hers, eliciting a small groan from the back of her throat. "You do something to me, babe," he muttered against her lips before pressing the warm tip of his tongue along the seam of her own.

She opened her mouth to him, and he delved in deep and urgent while his hand glided down the side of her until he cupped her ass and jerked her even closer to him. Mia's body melted into his as sparks of desire stoked her need.

A loud shriek splintered the air, and Mia jumped back from Army, who burst out laughing. She punched his arm. "It's not funny." She glanced over at a burly man with long hair switching off the engine of a huge motorcycle. "Damn, that bike is loud. The noise scared the shit out of me."

Army hugged her close, her face pushed against his solid chest. "You're too damn cute."

"Yo, Army," the long-haired man yelled out.

Army looked over her and a grin split his face as he raised his fist in the air. "How's it going, bro?" His broad chest vibrated against her cheek as he spoke.

"Good. Ironclad and me just got here. You going in?"

Through dark lashes, she glimpsed at the biker whose gaze swept over her before returning to Army's.

"In a minute. Did you get a new bike?"

"Last month."

Army backed away from Mia then draped his arm around her shoulder and walked toward the brawny man. Army whistled low. "She's a fuckin' beauty, Tats. It looks like you added some aftermarket pipes." Pointing at them, he looked at Mia. "See those? That's what gives the bike that *fuck-you* noise."

Tats chuckled, his gaze quickly sweeping over her as Army bent down to examine them. She suddenly wished she hadn't worn her black miniskirt, lace scalloped-edged crop top, and her peep-toe lace boots. The boots were a reward for having a full week of awesome training a couple of weeks before. When Mia saw them, she fell in love with their delicate black lace and satin piping, and the four-and-a-half-inch heels sealed the deal. It set her back a couple hundred bucks, but they were so worth it.

But now with the biker's eyes roving over her body, she felt exposed. She reached down and threaded her fingers through Army's hair as if to tell this guy to back the fuck off. Army captured her hand and brought it to his mouth, kissing it as he stood up.

"A real beauty, dude," Army said.

"She sure is," Tats replied, his half-lidded eyes darting to her then back to Army who was still looking at the Harley.

Mia stood behind Army and wrapped her arms around his waist. He put his hands on top of hers. From the way Vic and his biker buddies talked about women, she was pretty sure this jerk thought she was a hookup at best and a slut at worst. *Tell him we're dating.* But she knew Army never would. She was in biker territory, where the women were for fucking and nothing else. In the outlaw world, women were best seen and not heard. At the parties they'd be ignored for the most part until someone wanted a little fun. It was just the way it went, and Mia had heard Vic talk about the wild parties the Satan's Pistons threw, and she didn't expect anything less from the Night Rebels.

"Ready to go in?" Army asked her in a low voice. She nodded and tucked her hand in his as they walked toward groups of men milling in front of the two-story stucco building.

Out of the corner of her eye, she saw the men stealing furtive glances at her while they yelled out their greetings to Army as the two of them went to the front door.

Once inside, the rush of warm air and the smell of pot, sweat, and cheap perfume put her on edge, and she gripped his hand tighter as he pushed through the throng of people, stopping every once in a while to talk to fellow bikers before making their way to the bar.

Mostly men surrounded the large bar, which had a walnut slab top scattered with memorabilia from various metal and hard-rock bands all under a clear gloss resin. Riveted metal panels comprised the base of the bar, and thin beams of color from overhead lights bounced off the shiny metal bar foot rails. A few of the women, who wore clothes that made Mia's look like her Sunday best, sat on some of the men's laps or were dancing on top of the counter.

"Let me get you a seat," Army said in her ear.

The people crammed the room and the scene was a riot of black leather and denim. Blue, green, and red party lights flashed around the room from spheres suspended from the ceiling that had an American flag painted on it. Hard hitting music filled the air, the deafening bass beats made her skin tingle and her bones vibrate. She looked behind her when she felt a hand on her arm, tugging her.

"I got you a seat," Army mouthed, pointing toward the middle of the bar.

Holding onto him tightly, she looked down as they forged through a thick group of men who stood around drinking and somehow managed to carry on conversations despite the loud music.

Army picked Mia up from her waist and settled her down on a comfortable black cushion. "What do you want to drink?" he yelled.

His loud voice tickled her ear and she rubbed it vigorously with the edge of her palm. "A margarita would be good," she yelled back and he nodded then leaned over and gave their order to a well-built man covered in tattoos. Smoke billowed and swirled around her, enveloping the room in a perpetual haze.

Army handed Mia her drink, and she took a large gulp and placed it down on the counter. He waved a joint at her, a quizzical expression on his face. She bobbed her head, and he lit one and handed it to her. Men kept coming over to either pull Army in a hug, hit him on the back, or lightly punch his arm as they stopped and talked with him. They'd steal glances at Mia, and she could tell they were wondering who the hell she was.

By now, her eyes had adjusted to the lighting in the room, and she noticed a lot of women wandering around as some of the bikers smacked their asses or copped a feel of their breasts when they walked past them. The women would laugh, and some even threw their arms around the offending men and kissed them. Mia had never seen anything like it before, and it made her feel uncomfortable and vulnerable. Images of her fighting off Gavin flashed through her mind, and she squeezed her eyes shut, trying to banish them.

"Are you okay?" Army asked, his breath warm on her damp skin.

"It's so stuffy in here," she said, fanning her face with her hand.

"Finish your drink then we'll go out back," he said.

She gulped it down then slid off the barstool.

"If someone touches you, tell me." He gripped her hand.

"Wait." She pulled back. "What the hell does that mean?"

"You're not wearing my patch so some guys may disrespect you. Usually, you'd be good 'cause you're with me, but sometimes a dude gets drunk and acts like a fuckin' asshole. Night Rebels are cool, but we got some new faces here tonight. Just tell me and I'll take care of it."

"How?"

"Beat the shit out of him." He said it so matter-of-fact that it took Mia by surprise and before she could respond, he was dragging her behind him.

She spotted three large couches and two of them looked to be upholstered in a Southwest design, while the third one seemed to be either dark brown or black leather. A woman was reclining on the couch, her legs spread, with a man's face buried between her legs. Her head lolled to the side as she played with her nipples. The man's cut identified him as a member of the Fallen Slayers MC. Mia's stomach twisted, and she decided that she'd only look at the floor as they cut across the room.

The flaming torches around the perimeter of the large yard took the chill out of the autumn night. Strings of white lights that were twisted around a cluster of trees and draped around the tall chain-link fence gave an almost magical look to the area, and a large fire pit off to the side offered a cozy ambiance.

"Better?" Army smiled.

"Much. If you take away the people screwing in public, I'd think I was at an outdoor wedding reception."

Army laughed and drew her into a tight embrace. "You're too funny, babe. Do you want to fool around?" He ran his hand down and cupped her butt.

Mia brushed her lips across his. "As much as I'd like to, I'd rather do it without an audience."

"I can arrange that." His fingers dug into her firm behind.

"Can you?" Mia kissed him gently then drew his bottom lip between her teeth, slipping her tongue into his mouth. His growl reverberated through her, sending static flutters over her skin. Army's other hand curled into her hair, yanking her closer, and then his lips covered hers while his tongue tangled with Mia's in an erotic dance.

Mia bucked into his groin and felt the rigid outline of his dick, moaning into his mouth. "Army ..." she whispered.

He broke the kiss and buried his face in her neck, breathing deeply. Needles of pleasure pricked every nerve in her body, and she realized that she'd never have enough of his kisses—his taste. Each time his lips pressed against hers, it stole her breath then gave it back, showing her that every other kiss she'd had before Army's had been wrong.

"Baby." Army's lips vibrated against her skin. "I think about you all the time. You're killing me with all this fuckin' waiting." He groaned softly, adding conviction to his words.

A surge of desire to have Army swept over Mia and she clasped her arms tighter around him. "I'm waiting too," she reminded him.

"Yeah, but I'm a man, and when it comes to you, babe, I have a one-track fuckin' mind."

Before she could reply, her stomach rumbled and she froze in embarrassment.

Cupping her chin in his hand, he titled her head back and captured her gaze. "When's the last time you ate? And a protein bar doesn't count."

She smiled. "This morning. I was so excited to see you that after my last client, I just headed down."

"Let's go get some food. If it's cold, we can warm it up in the kitchen."

Army guided her over to a long table that had platters of food strewn over it. She picked up a plate and piled it with pulled pork and a few hot links.

"Is that all you want?" he asked, placing a large scoop of potato salad on his plate.

"Just the protein," she answered.

Soon they were at a small picnic table with four other people. Army had brought over another margarita for her and a couple bottles of beer for him. The four other guys at the table spoke with Army and ignored Mia, but he made it a point to turn away from them and converse with her. The bikers seemed surprised that the two of them kept talking and laughing, and they frowned when Army didn't immediately interrupt what she was saying to answer one of their questions.

"Hey, dude," a tall, good-looking man said, bumping fists with Army. "It's been too fucking long."

Army laughed and gestured for him to take the seat across from them, which had just recently been vacated. The dark-haired biker sat down and his gaze fell on Mia's. Shock swept across his face, then disappeared as quickly as it'd come.

As the two of them talked, Mia's stomach churned. *This guy was surprised to see me. Why? I don't know him, do I?* She racked her brain trying to remember if she'd ever bumped into him. Maybe he's seen me fight. That's not a big deal, right? All of a sudden, the lukewarm pork on her plate made her nauseous. *What if he knows Vic? Wait ... all the guys here are against Vic's club. I shouldn't have come.* As Army laughed and held her hand under the table, panic and fear spread through her.

After what seemed like an eternity, the well-built biker stood up. "You gotta come to Silverado soon," he said.

"I'll try. I've been so busy with running the strip club and other things." He squeezed her hand and she smiled.

The man glanced at her then back at Army. "I heard your brother's one step from going pro."

"He is. His next fight is coming up soon, and if he wins it, he'll be good as gold."

Again he darted his eyes to Mia, then quickly back to Army. "Let me know when he's fighting. Me and some of the other Slayers will come up to watch it."

"Sounds good, Buzz. Taylor would appreciate the support. Are you coming to the rally next week?"

"Yep. We're all gonna be there. Steel said we can crash here. You may have a roommate for a few days." The two men chuckled. "You got some hot women at the party." Again a quick look her way.

Mia leaned against Army, and he turned and planted a kiss on her temple.

"Go pick one out."

"I got two picked out. I'll see you around." Buzz and Army bumped fists again, then the tall man disappeared into the crowd.

"Who was he?" Mia asked, pushing the plate away from her.

"Buzz is with the Fallen Slayers. He's a good guy. We've had some great fun over the years."

"With women?" Mia picked up her drink.

"That and riding. We've done a lot of poker runs together. You hardly ate shit, babe. What's up?"

"I'm not that hungry. I guess it's all the excitement of the party."

"If you get hungry later, I'll get one of the club girls to make you something."

"Do they do all the cooking?"

Army took a swig of beer. "No. Lena's our cook. She's fuckin' awesome. She's been with us for four years now. Her old man used to be a Night Rebel, but he left her for another brother's—Chains'—old lady."

"That's awful. What happens in a situation like that?"

"The fucker gets thrown out after a beatdown. So Cross Bones got his patch taken away and his ass beat. Chains' old lady went with him after he threw her ass out. Lena was lost—she'd been part of the club for years, so she asked if she could come on as the cook. It worked out for her and for us. She's a damn good cook. The club girls help out."

"How many of these club girls do you have?"

"Six. You want another drink?"

Mia wanted to ask him about the girls and if he bangs them regularly, but she held her tongue. "Some water would be good for now."

Army motioned over a woman with long dark hair, Daisy Dukes and a barely there gold sequined bikini top. "Clear the table, Alma," he said as he slipped off the bench. "I'll be right back with your water." With two fingers, he pushed her head back and kissed her softly then ambled away.

Alma stared at her as she gathered the Styrofoam plates and plastic utensils and cups. Mia smiled at her and helped her gather some of the debris. The pretty woman shook her head. "Army asked me to do it, not you."

Taken aback, Mia's hand stalled above the dirty plates next to her. "I'm sure Army wouldn't mind if I helped out," she replied.

"It's not that. It's just that he asked me, not you."

Mia drew her hand away. "It's all yours." Alma continued clearing the table, her gaze still fixed on Mia.

"Here you go, baby," Army said behind her, leaning over to put a bottle of water in front of her. He nuzzled her neck. "You smell so fuckin' good. Do you know what your perfume does to my cock?" He peppered her skin with feathery kisses.

With Alma's gaze burning a hole through her, Mia felt self-conscious, and she moved slightly away from him.

"What's up?" he whispered in her ear before licking it.

His tongue tickled and scorched her at the same time. "She's watching us."

"Who?"

"Alma."

"So?" He sucked at the sensitive skin on her neck and knew she'd be upping her concealer coverage when she went out in public.

"Do you want me to do anything else?" Alma asked in a soft, sensuous voice.

"That's it," Army answered, his lips still doing delicious things to Mia.

"I'll see you around, lover boy," Alma said, tossing her hair over her shoulders.

Mia read the signal very clear: stay away. Alma was making sure she understood that even though Mia had him at that moment, she had him every day and night.

"She seems upset that I'm with you," Mia said.

"Alma? Nah. She's a club girl, she knows the score."

"And what's the score?"

He pulled away then came over and sat by her again. "Pleasing the men without any attachments."

"Is it that simple?"

He shrugged and brought the beer bottle to his lips. "Seems to be."

"I think it would be hard to have sex with the same guys over and over and not form some attachment. I don't believe there aren't any emotions."

Army wrinkled his forehead. "I guess there are emotions and attachments but not in the traditional sense. I mean, the women are there for us, and we're there for them. We give them lodging, a monthly stipend, and help out if there's a problem. The club girls respect us and do things for us. Some of the brothers like some of the girls more than others and vice versa, but it doesn't mean there's any 'falling in love' going on."

"That's sounds so lonely … and sad."

"Not at all. You're seeing it as a citizen—love and marriage, but it's not like that. We're a family for sure. If anyone messes with one of our girls, we're gonna beat their ass. Most of the women here come from real shitty backgrounds and never felt accepted or cared for until they came to us."

Mia nodded as she drew invisible patterns on the plastic tablecloth. "Now that you put it that way, I can understand it better. Not having anyone to care for you is beyond tough. It's nice that they have a sense of family at your club."

"We've got tons of chicks clamoring to be a club girl. Look at all the women here tonight—they want a walk on the wild side, and they're gonna get it." Army laughed.

Mia looked around. "Every woman here will have sex willingly?"

"Yeah. If someone doesn't, then that's cool for the most part." Army wrapped his arm around her shoulder. "I'm cool with us not having it even though it leaves my cock hard for days."

She ran her finger down the side of his face. "Frankly, I'm surprised you keep going out with me."

"I like you," he said before he kissed her softly on the lips.

"I like you too." *Are you fucking Alma or any of the other women who come around? I hope not, but I'm not that delusional to think you're not.* He had a bevy of women whose sole purpose was to please him and the others in his club, but she refused to ask. Maybe she didn't want to know, or maybe she didn't want him to think she was jealous; Mia wasn't sure, but the one thing she *was* sure about: she was beyond crazy about Army. She couldn't imagine not having him in her life. Mia's body yearned for him, to feel his lips on every part of her.

"You wanna dance?" he asked, breaking through her thoughts.

"Sure." She clasped his fingers and he escorted her back inside onto the crowded dance floor. He took her into his arms and drew her close, resting her head against his chest.

Mia lifted her head and looked into his smoldering blues. "You do know that we're slow dancing to Metallica's 'The Four Horsemen,' right?"

"I want to feel all of you when we dance," he answered.

A shiver ran through her body and she rested her cheek on his chest, feeling hard muscles and heat. The pounding of his heart matched hers, and desire burned in her like a slow fire. She closed her eyes and let him move her body back and forth, his hands skimming over her hips and landing on her backside. Her feelings for him were over the top. He still held her after the song ended, his hands squeezing her butt. While he ground his hard dick against her, he claimed her lips in a kiss that sent need spiraling through her.

"You wanna go to my room?" His words were smothered on her lips as he devoured her mouth.

Ozzy Osborne's high voice sang out in "Crazy Train" as people bumped into them while they danced frenetically.

Mia pulled back and tugged Army toward the wall. "There's a good chance we're going to be trampled." She nipped his bottom lip. "Let's go back to my hotel." A heated shiver of anticipation ran up her spine, and she trembled slightly.

"Are you cold, baby?" he asked.

She shook her head, her caramel-brown hair skimming the bare skin under her crop top. She looked up at him. "No."

Army must have seen the gleam of desire in her eyes, for his own eyes darkened as well. As he caressed a finger down the side of her face, the heat from his touch added to the fire already burning inside her. "Let's go," he rasped, breaking away and taking hold of her elbow.

As Army led her out of the club, Mia noticed that the party was getting wilder and raunchier, and a lot of men and women staggered around the room, trying to keep their balance. She leaned into Army, and he draped his arm over her shoulder as they made their way to the car.

# Chapter Sixteen

"I SHOULD'VE BROUGHT a bottle of Jack when we left the club," Army said, looking around the room.

"There's a mini bar. Let me see if it has any whiskey." Mia headed over to the small fridge, taking off her leather jacket as she went, then folded it over the back of a cushy chair. She bent down and opened the door, scanning the miniature bottles that lined the shelves. "You're in luck," she said, glancing at Army over her shoulder.

"Grab all of them," he said, his eyes fixed on her ass.

A small shudder ran through her, and she pulled out three small bottles of Jack and two of gin. Mia stood upright and snagged two wide glasses then slowly walked over to the loveseat facing the picture window. Points of light coming from residences dotted the silhouette of the mountains in the distance. "Do you want any ice?" she asked while placing the bottles down on the end table next to a tall lamp with a large ivory shade.

He shook his head as his gaze captured hers.

She poured the amber liquid in a glass and handed it to Army. He took the proffered tumbler, swirled the whiskey and sniffed the aroma, then he winked at her before taking a drink. After pouring her own, Mia clinked her glass against his and raised it to her lips while keeping her gaze locked on his. The cool burst of slightly sweet freshness slid down her throat. "Wonderful," she said then licked her lips. Mia's pulse soared when his gunmetal blue eyes grew dark as he followed the movement of her tongue.

Army took her hand and guided her down on the couch, his intense body heat radiating into her. "It's nice without all the noise," she murmured.

"Was it awful for you?" he asked over the rim of the glass.

"The open sex thing was a bit much, but otherwise I found it interesting. I loved seeing the camaraderie you all share. It's awesome to be so close to so many people."

"They're my family. You know ... family isn't always blood. We earned each other's respect and love, and I know no matter what the fuck happens in life, they'll be there for me the same as I will for them. There's not one damn bit of doubt about that."

Army's passion and love for his club turned Mia on even though she thought that was a crazy reaction to his words. She was keenly aware of his knee touching her skin, the warmth that emanated from him, and the spicy scent of his cologne ... even the way his throat moved as he spoke.

Army finished his drink and leaned forward, inches away from her face, "You keep looking at me like that and it's going to be fuckin' hard to behave," he whispered before brushing his lips across hers.

"Maybe I don't want you to behave," she said softly.

Army's eyes met hers in a fiery bond, and his lips curled up in a sexy smile. "Maybe?" His finger trailed down her throat, slowly bringing a starburst of pleasure to spread through her.

Before she could say anything else, Army claimed her lips in a hard and demanding kiss. His lips and tongue plundered her mouth, devouring her, and Mia kissed him back with just as much fervor and intensity. She wound her tongue around his and pushed in deeper, trying to feel as much of him as she could.

Low guttural groans rumbled from his chest and he grabbed a handful of her hair and yanked it hard as his other hand cupped her breast and roughly squeezed the soft flesh. Mia moaned into his mouth and he pulled back a little. "You like that, babe?" he said against her lips.

"Yeah," she breathed, her fingers digging into his scalp, "but I'd love it harder."

"You like it rough, don't you?"

Nodding, she pulled his hair hard, jerking his head back. "And dark." Her tongue licked across his lips before she nipped at them.

"Fuck," he grunted, tearing his mouth away from hers.

Pleasure spread through her as he trailed hot kisses down her neck, sinking his tongue into the pulsing hollow of her collarbone before he moved to the swell of her breasts rising above the low scooped neckline of her snug top. Tugging at the hem, Army pulled the top down to reveal more before licking circles down her cleavage. His stubble lightly scratched and tickled Mia's sensitive skin, and she looked down at his strong hands massaging her tits while he nipped then laved her flesh.

Army glanced up and she knew he noticed that she was watching by the way his grip tightened. She cried out as pain shot through her, then moaned as warm pleasure replaced it.

"You like that, baby?" he said hoarsely, his fingers pinching her hard.

Mia sucked in a ragged breath and let the pain wash over her, then relished the soft touch of his tongue soothing the ache. "Yes," she rasped.

Suddenly, he clutched the hem of her top, and in one fluid movement pulled it up and over her head, throwing it to the floor. In the cool air of the room, her skin pebbled and her nipples hardened, making the hiss of Army's indrawn breath hit right between her legs.

"Fuck, baby," he gritted as he yanked her bra straps down to expose her breasts. He stood upright and gathered her in his arms then threw her on the bed. Mia gasped for breath and wiggled up toward the headboard, grasping at the bedspread.

His eyes pierced into her as her breasts bounced, and she started to get up, but he pushed her down. "No," he growled.

His deep voice held a hint of danger, and all kinds of tingles danced over her skin. Kneeling on either side of her, he bent over and gently sucked on her earlobe. "What's your safeword?" he whispered.

"Independence," she breathed.

A deep chuckle rumbled from his chest. "It fits you." His breath was hot against her skin as he scorched a path with his lips and tongue and teeth to her breasts. "So fuckin' beautiful," he muttered, lowering his head before swiping his tongue over her nipples then blowing on them, sending chills rushing down her spine. Army licked and blew several times as she arched her back, silently begging him to suck her aching buds.

He smiled. "I love how your body is asking me to touch you. Is that what you want, babe?" His deep voice sent heat right to her throbbing sex.

"You know I do," she said, grabbing for his hand.

He pushed hers away. "I'm in control here ... not you," he said as his finger circled around the areola.

Her body hummed with nerves when he pinched her nipple again, and she cried out as waves of white-hot lust encompassed her.

"I like hearing you scream," he said, pinching the other nipple.

"It feels so good," she panted. She reached and grabbed his hard dick, but he pushed her hand away and leaned back on his heels.

"Please let me touch you," she said.

His eyes fixed on her painfully erect nipples as they swept over her body. "Beautiful."

"Army ..." She reached out once more for him, but he shook his head.

"Hold onto the headboard and don't let go until I fuckin' say so." His gaze locked with hers.

Tremors vibrated over her as she raised her arms and grasped the wooden slats. *This is what I've always craved. How does he know what I want? Army ... oh fuck.*

Mia watched as Army pulled her skirt over her hips then skimmed it down her legs to her ankles and tossed it on the floor. She lay on the mattress in only her sheer bikini panties with her heart racing, her mouth dry, and pulse pounding.

She felt a finger touch the tattoo around her ankle as Army traced around it then lightly inched up her leg, and she sucked in a sharp breath the closer he moved to her mound—until he stopped. She groaned in frustration.

"Such a nasty girl. You need to learn patience."

"I need you to touch me."

"I know." Army brushed a finger over her panties and she jumped at the contact, fire burning in her. "Fuck, you're dripping wet."

She'd never been this wet before. "I want you so bad," she said softly.

Mia saw his smoldering gaze flick over her from her wrists down to her feet then back to her eyes. "You look amazing."

Something twisted deep inside her as tension coiled in a tangled mess of want and need. "Please?" she whimpered.

Army leaned forward and dipped his head, capturing her lips in a passionate kiss as he pushed her panties aside and slipped two fingers inside her. His thumb pressed firmly against her clit, and her heated walls tightened against his digits as Mia moaned softly. When he pushed his thumb harder, she squirmed and groaned louder. She felt her juices trickling down as he pulled out then thrust back in, finger fucking her hard as he kept the pressure on her engorged nub. Mia was perched on the edge, ready to dive over at any moment, but she didn't. It seemed that Army knew just where to touch to give her enough pressure to lift her higher without spilling her over. Her whole body throbbed against his as he slowed his pace. He was playing her and drawing it out.

"You like that?"

She groaned.

"Your pussy's real tight. I can't wait to fuck you with my cock." He groaned soft and slow. The sound rode along her spine, hot and heavy, and she curled her hand around his dick but he moved back.

"Please!"

"Let me finger fuck you a little longer. Get your damn hands back on the headboard."

A tendril of frustration wove through her desire. *He knows how to push my buttons.* Suddenly, he crushed his mouth against her and everything blurred. He nipped at her bottom lip then plunged his tongue between her lips. She sucked on his tongue and he grabbed a fistful of her hair and pulled it hard. The pain was mixed with the pleasure of the kiss, and when he ground his hips against her, sparks lit up her nerves.

Not able to keep from touching him, Mia slipped her hands under his T-shirt and ran them down his back, then cupping them around his ass, she pressed down in an attempt to hold his body close to hers. All at once, he pulled up and sat back on his heels again.

Shaking his head, he stared at her. "You don't like taking orders, do you?"

Immediately, she raised her arms over her head. Army chuckled, and without breaking eye contact, he pulled his shirt off and tossed it by her skirt on the floor.

Fucking hell. Mia's insides lurched, stealing her breath, her blood boiling hot. It wasn't that she was surprised—she'd seen him at Champion sparring with Taylor, but under the warm golden light from the lamp on the nightstand, he looked magnificent: cords of muscles with a dusting of dark hair that disappeared into the waistband of his jeans. Evil-looking tattoos moved, as if on screen, over his powerful arms. *Holy hell,* she thought as sweat beaded along her hairline.

"Like what you see?" he asked as he shrugged off his jeans.

Nodding, her eyes fixed on his thick, hard dick. "Fuck," she whispered.

Army straddled her again. "Do you like my cock?" He grabbed his length in his hand and slowly worked the skin up and down along his shaft. "Do you want to touch it?"

Mia nodded again, a moan slipped from her lips as her heart fluttered with erratic beats.

"Go ahead—touch it," he rasped.

She brought her arms down then wrapped her hand around his cock. She pushed up on one elbow and lowered her head, swiping her tongue over the glistening crown. He tasted warm and salty, and she slipped her mouth over the smooth skin.

Army grunted then gently shoved her away. "I'm gonna blow if you keep it up." He eased her back down and placed both of his hands on her bent knees and spread her legs wide open, then he leaned back and stared at her pussy. "So perfect. I can see your juices shining. I can't wait to taste you, babe." He glanced up at her, and her breath caught at the feral look in his eyes. "Keep those beautiful eyes on me, baby. Don't look away," he said as he bent down and slipped his finger between the heated folds of her pussy.

The tip of his tongue touched her clit, electrifying her body. "Army," she moaned as she shifted under his mouth.

"You taste so good." He sucked hard on her firm nub, scraping it with his teeth.

"Oh … shit!" She bucked, arching her back and pushing against his mouth as sweet pain shot straight to her core.

"I need you, baby," he said huskily.

"Then have me," she moaned.

Army pulled back a little and she felt his dick pushing against her entrance. A sliver of clarity sliced through her sexual haze.

"Condom," she croaked.

"Are you on the pill?" he asked. She nodded. "Then we're good. I'm clean. I haven't been with anyone since we started dating."

Surprise flitted through her mind at his revelation, but she shelved it for another time. She looked down and saw him holding the base of his dick as he slowly guided it inside her until he filled her up. He held her gaze.

"I can still taste your pussy. I like having you on my tongue while I fuck you." He pulled out and slowly went back in.

Mia loved his filthy talking—his words scorched her and had her craving for more. She wrapped her legs high around his waist, opening herself wider for him. Army captured her mouth then, and without warning, he plunged deep. She cried out. In and out. Fast. Hard. Deep. Over and over. Never had she experienced anything like what he was doing to her.

"You like that?" he panted as he kept up the pace.

"Damn. Yeah." Raw desire and lust overwhelmed her as he pounded into her relentlessly.

Then his teeth sank into her shoulder, delivering the pain she craved, and she exploded. Crying out to him, shaking and gasping—her entire body spasmed as wave after wave of sensation hit her, each cresting higher than the last. She pressed her face into the pillow to smother the sobs escaping from her throat at the intensity of her climax.

Army stiffened then filled her with the heat from his release as he erupted inside her. "Mia," he grunted.

He collapsed on her, panting and shuddering, and she wrapped her arms tightly around him. Army lifted up and kissed her then rolled over and lay on his back, drawing her close. Mia inhaled deeply, loving the scent of them.

"That was incredible," she murmured, her finger tracing the tattoos on his chest.

"You"—he tilted Mia's head back and swept his lips across hers—"were definitely worth the wait. Fuck, baby." He tucked her closer to him.

Mia pillowed her head against him and listened to the rhythmic thudding of his heart. Soon his body relaxed, and his breathing deepened. Fully spent and exhausted, Mia sighed contentedly as her lids grew heavy and she quickly drifted off to sleep.

MIA WOKE UP with a start and looked around the room, not recognizing anything. *Where am I?* Then, a flood of happiness spread through her at the sound of light snoring as someone moved beside her. *I'm at the hotel and Army's sleeping next to me. And the sex? It was mind blowing. The best I've ever had.* The lamps in the room were still on, so she quietly slipped out of bed and turned the one by the couch off, then went into the bathroom to clean up.

Looking at her reflection, she smiled at the red marks covering her breasts, the memory of dark pain morphed into pleasure tingling through her. "He likes it dark too," she said in a low voice as she ran her fingers lightly over the love bites. Her nipples were still sore to the touch, and she wondered if Army was into clamps and flogging. A bolt of desire ran through her as she pictured him standing behind her with her ass up high as the flogger *whished* in the air before striking her tender flesh.

Bending over the sink, she cupped cool water in her hands and splashed it over her face several times then blotted it dry with a towel. After cleaning up, she padded back to the bed and switched off the small lamp.

Army stirred in his sleep as he rolled over on his side, grabbed a fistful of her hair, and dragged her to him.

"Not so hard," Mia said softly, but the only reply from him was steady breathing. She snuggled closer and placed her hand on his warm thigh. "I love you, baby," she whispered.

She paused and the quietness in the room enveloped her.

"Are you asleep?" she asked. Nothing. Again she posed the question. Just intermittent snoring. Mia pulled the blanket under her chin, and with warmth spreading through her, she closed her eyes and fell fast asleep.

# Chapter Seventeen

I N THE LATE morning sunlight that streamed through the gap in the curtains, Army watched Mia as she slept, her naked body bathed in a soft golden glow. The scent of lemongrass on her skin, the peaceful look on her sweet face, and the rise and fall of her tits as she breathed, combined to play havoc with his emotions. He reached out and gently ran his fingers down the length of Mia's body. He loved the feel of her hard muscles ... the softness of her tits ... the curve of her hips and the dip of her stomach. He skimmed over her smooth mound and ignored the pain in his hard dick.

Mia shifted slightly and a small moan escaped from her slightly parted lips. Fuck ... he loved the sounds she made: quiet whimpers, throaty giggles, sweet laughter. He slipped his finger between her folds, a smile ghosting his lips when her wetness coated it. She moaned again and the sound broke something inside him, and a sudden wash of emotion stung his entire body. But he couldn't say what he was feeling for her. He wouldn't.

Army pulled away, and a small frown creased over her brow, then sleep quickly absorbed it, and calmness returned to her face. He sucked in a deep breath and shook his head. He was in deep. How the fuck had that happened? Mia had come into his life like a gust of fresh air, making all the liaisons he'd had with other women seem stale and nondescript.

She cracked her eyes open, then smiled. *Damn*. Her smile lit up the dark places inside him, warming his heart like no one else ever had.

"What're you doing?" Her voice sounded groggy as she stretched.

The way her back arched brought her tits up into the air, and for just a moment, all Army could think about was burying his face against them and playing with her nipples until she writhed in pain and ecstasy.

"Seeing how beautiful you look in the morning," he answered, trailing his fingers down her arm.

"I don't," she said, suppressing a yawn.

Looking at her messy hair, drowsy eyes, and no makeup, he dipped his mouth to hers. "You *so* fuckin' do," he said against her lips before claiming them. Her whimper drove him beyond insane, and he kissed her deeper and more passionately. She looped her arms around his neck and pulled him in even closer as he pushed farther into the sweet recesses of her mouth.

His phone rang. "Fuck," he said, breaking their kiss.

"Let it go to voicemail," she whispered.

"I can't," he replied. One of the rules of the brotherhood was to always answer the phone. In the unpredictable world in which outlaws lived, a brother may be called upon at any time. Leaning over, he grabbed the phone from the top of the nightstand and pushed the button.

"Yo." He kept his gaze on Mia's, her eyes shone in the beam of sunlight, her lips slightly swollen from the power of his kiss. *Fuckin' beautiful.*

"You wanna go riding with us? Buzz and Ironclad are coming," Jigger asked.

"Nah, I'm kinda busy right now."

"With your fighter? You taking advantage of her flexibility?" He chuckled.

Army's jaw tightened. "Have a good ride." He put the phone back on the nightstand and caught her gaze—desire-filled and tender. He wanted to tell her how much she twisted him all up, but he couldn't. He didn't understand what was happening because he'd never felt such a connection with a woman before: it was as special as it was consuming. In his mind, women were for fun, and if men got too close and trusted them, they'd destroy them like a black widow. His mom had certainly done that to his dad and to him and his brothers.

"You look so intense. What're you thinking about?"

He scooted closer and loomed over her, pressing her shoulders against the soft mattress. "Fucking you last night was off the charts, babe. I just … hell … I don't know." He slammed his mouth on hers in a crushing kiss as he slipped his hand under her and cupped her ass, jerking her naked flesh closer to his. He wanted to possess her, make her his exclusively and irrevocably. He wanted to cherish her, protect her, and be everything to her.

"Army," she murmured.

He pushed her legs open with his knees. He needed her with an urgency he'd never felt before. Later that day, he'd fuck her good and slow, tease her until she begged for his cock, but at that moment, all he wanted was to fuck her hard, rough, and fast.

His lips raced down to her breasts, nipping and licking them as they made their way to her nipples. She groaned when he sucked one hardened bud into his mouth, biting it hard then licking away the pain.

"I need you real bad, baby," he gritted.

Mia laughed, the sound catching in her throat as his fingers pinched the slick folds of her pussy.

"I like how wet you are for me," he said as he pushed down then planted his mouth on her clit. She bucked under him, and he kept teasing her clit with the tip of his tongue while he twisted and pulled her nipples.

"Harder," she groaned. He yanked her red buds. "Yeah … just like that."

Watching her writhe under his touch, her face contorting in pain and pleasure, Army couldn't hold back any longer. He ran his tongue from her rigid clit to her slick entrance then pulled back before he rammed his cock inside. The way she arched her back and the deep cries that tore from her throat only fueled his desire, and he drilled in and out of her hard and fast. Her breathing quickened, and as she rocked her hips to meet his thrusts, he felt her warm walls clenching around him.

"You're loving this, aren't you, babe?" he grunted, pummeling her tight heat as sweat crawled down his back.

"Army ... fuck, it's good," she rasped.

Fierce. Primal. Raw ... And relentless.

Moaning and whimpering, Mia's head thrashed about on the pillow while she balled the sheet in her fist. He watched her hand slide down her taut belly and land on her smooth mound. Without saying a word, he slapped her hand away, and her eyes snapped to his—desire brimming and defiance warring inside them.

"That's only for me." Army held her gaze, the sound of her wetness intermingled with the slapping of his balls with every deep thrust. "It feels so fuckin' good, babe. I love watching you as I fuck you," he growled.

Mia splayed her hands on his chest and dug her nails in, scratching and clawing him hard, and he found it wildly hot and sexy.

"That's right, baby, leave your mark on me." He put his finger on her sweet spot and pushed hard.

Mia cried out and her heated walls clamped tightly around him, and he felt his balls tighten, pulling up inside him. Suddenly, he was right there with Mia, grunting, moaning, and panting as they clung to each other and cried out their mutual release.

Army lay on top of her, his dick still twitching inside her, his chest heaving. He nuzzled her neck then swept his lips overs hers before rolling on his back and tucking her under his arm. He'd never expected a woman's skin pressed next to his could be so fucking addictive. And he'd never imagined a woman would affect him this way. Mia had slipped into a place in his life he had no idea was vacant, and now that she was here, he would never let her go. He wrapped his fingers around her hair and tugged it back, then brushed his lips against hers in a long, lingering kiss.

"I feel so good being with you," she said in a soft voice.

"Me too, babe. He wanted to hold her like that all day, but the pull of having her tits pressed against him on the back of his bike was strong. He smacked her ass lightly. "I gotta go to the club and wash up. I'll pick you up in an hour and we can go for that ride I've been promising you."

"I can't wait." She kissed his chin then untangled herself from his arms. "How're you going to get back? We took my car last night, remember?"

"I'll call one of the brothers." He kissed her quickly—it was ridiculous how he couldn't get enough of her lips—and scooped his clothes off the floor before heading out of the hotel.

WHEN ARMY WALKED in he saw Eagle sitting down, his elbow on the table with his chin cupped in his hand, and staring across the room at the dark television screen.

The sound of the chair's legs scraping across the floor as Army pulled it out with his foot drew Eagle's attention, and he glanced at him. Army clasped his shoulder before sitting down. "Your famous hangover cure not working so well today?" He chuckled.

"Fuck you," Eagle muttered, slowly picking up a steaming mug of coffee.

"Where is everyone?"

"Riding." He took a sip then put the cup down and glanced sideways at Army. "Jigger said you were busy with your sweet piece."

Army smiled at Kelly, who put a bottle of beer and a turkey and Swiss cheese sandwich in front of him. She blew him a kiss and sashayed away. Army took a long drink then pushed the plate away from him. "Mia and I are going riding. I just came back here to clean up before heading back to the hotel. You want the sandwich?"

Eagle grimaced as he shook his head. "Buzz kept asking questions about her this morning. He keeps thinking that he knows her."

"I doubt it. Mia didn't say she knew him."

"It's not like that. He's probably seen her in a fight. He used to go to Arizona a lot to visit his buddy until Patrick moved to Nevada. That dude was really into MMA fights."

"Could be."

"Hey," Goldie said as he pulled out a chair. "It's pretty quiet around here."

"They're all out riding," Eagle said.

"No one called me." Goldie looked at the sandwich then at Army and Eagle. "Is this someone's?"

Eagle grimaced again and Army chuckled, sliding the plate over to Goldie. "Kelly made it for me, but I don't want it."

Goldie took a large bite and waved at Lucy to bring him a beer. "I would've gone riding. Hailey's busy with an anniversary party today."

"I guess they think you're outta commission since you've got an old lady," Army said.

"That's a load of shit." Goldie washed down his second bite with a gulp of beer.

"It wasn't anything planned," Eagle added.

"After I'm done here, I'm gonna head out for a ride. Either of you wanna come along?"

Army pointed at Eagle and laughed. "He's still got a party jumping in his head."

Eagle glared at him. "And he's getting pussy all day."

Army bristled. "Watch it, dude. Mia's not just pussy." Anger licked at him and he pushed it down, not wanting his two buddies to see how tied in he was with Mia, but he wouldn't let anyone disrespect her.

Goldie pushed the empty plate away and cocked his head to the side, a smile twitching on his lips. "So she's gotten to you."

"No one's gotten to me. She's cool and we have fun."

"I bet you do." The smile now split his face, and it pissed Army off that Goldie was enjoying his discomfort way too damn much.

"When's she going back to Durango?" Goldie asked.

"In a couple of days. I'm going to go there to see what's going on with Lil' Donnie." Army ignored the smirks on both of their faces.

"I thought you heard from him recently," Eagle said.

"Yeah, he called to ask for more bucks. He said the damn Pistons are scrambling to raise the money for the buy, and I told him that was fuckin' old news."

Goldie leaned back and stretched out his legs, crossing them at the ankles. "Then why are you going to Durango?" Eagle snorted and Army glared.

"I know the date's gonna be postponed. Anyway, I wanna spend some time with my dad."

"*Your dad?* What a load of shit." Goldie laughed.

"I want to install alarms at his place and at Asher's. I already put one in for Taylor when I was staying with him a few weeks ago."

All of a sudden the mood turned somber as the danger of what the outlaw world could do to the members' families came crashing through.

"The 39th Street assholes don't know you've been around, right?" Eagle asked.

"Yeah. I don't wear my cut when I'm in Durango." Army took another swig of beer. "I hate not wearing it."

"I hear ya, but there's no way in fuck the Piston bastards don't know you're from Durango. I bet the wannabe badasses know too," Goldie said.

Army absently ran his fingers down the condensation on the brown bottle. "I'm sure they do, and I wouldn't put it past either of those motherfuckers to try some shit with my family. And then there's Mia." He wiped his hand on his jeans. "I have to make sure my woman's safe."

The corner of Goldie's mouth turned up as he gestured with his beer bottle. "You just called her 'your woman.'"

"What? I did not ... *Fuck.*"

Goldie took a long swig then clinked the bottle against his. "That's how it happens—you don't even know it then pow ... she's your woman."

Eagle guffawed then groaned and brought the coffee to his mouth.

Army pushed away and stood up. "Yeah ... well, I have to take a shower. Later." They exchanged chin lifts and he walked to his room. He heard Goldie and Eagle talking in low tones behind him, and he caught the words "fighter" and "Stiletto" as he left the room.

It didn't matter if Goldie was feeling a spattering of satisfaction about the hard time Army gave him when he was going out with Hailey, or that Eagle thought he was a pussy for spending the day with Mia instead of riding with the other brothers. What mattered was the way Mia made him feel when he was with her. He'd never been so drawn to a woman on so many levels—physically, intellectually, emotionally, and sexually. She'd made her mark on him and it was wickedly delicious.

Yeah ... *Pow!*

Army opened the door and went into his room.

# Chapter Eighteen

THE CLASH OF aluminum cans and bottles hitting the floor reverberated around the room as Shark kicked over a table.

"Where the fuck's my phone?" he boomed then smacked Tikka's ass hard.

"Ow!" she cried out and pushed herself up from the couch. "What are you yelling about?"

"My goddamn phone. Go find it," he growled as he staggered over to the small bar against the back wall. A curtain of flies hung in the air in the corner of the room. Shark went over then yelled out, "You and Pinkie clean this fuckin' barf off the floor."

"Red Dog kept upchucking," Tikka grumbled.

Shark turned around, anger shooting through him. "What the fuck did you say? You disrespecting a brother?"

Tikka's eyes widened and she jammed her hands under her armpits. "No, I wasn't. If it sounded that way, I'm sorry."

"You better be, otherwise you'll be cleaning it with your fuckin' tongue." Shark headed back toward the bar. "And where the hell's Pinkie?"

"Right here," she said, rising from the floor. "I must've passed out at the party."

Shark ran his gaze over her tangled hair and naked body. "Help Tikka clean that shit up, then I want you on your knees in front of me."

When he got to the bar a shot of Jack waited for him, but he shoved it away. "Gimme a shot of tequila," he said to the prospect. "Is my phone around here?"

Rash shook his head as he poured the liquor.

"I found it!" Tikka shouted.

"Then bring it the fuck over here, stupid."

Tikka's face fell, and she bent over to pick up her clothes.

"I told you to bring it to me, now! I want you naked when you're cleaning up Red Dog's puke." He laughed then threw back his drink.

Tikka dropped the clothes and rushed over and gave him the cell then just stood there looking at him.

"What the fuck?" Shark said, looking down at the screen.

"Don't I get a kiss or something?" Tikka blinked rapidly.

Shark's gaze snapped to her face and he pulled her toward him and slammed his mouth on hers. She moaned then jerked back and cried out when he bit her bottom lip hard. He guffawed as he spun her around and smacked her ass again, then pushed her forward. "Get cleaning, slut."

"I'm still so damn wasted," Noe said as he walked into the small room and plopped down on a chair. "I forgot how crazy the parties get around here."

"Did Cheetah and Vi treat you right?" Shark moved away from the bar and sat down on a chair across from Noe. He handed his friend a cup of coffee.

"Oh yeah. They're hot as hell. I may have to stay one more night before I head back to Phoenix." Noe brought the mug to his mouth.

"I got four damn calls from Blueman. Who the fuck calls at two in the damn morning? Doesn't he know we're all too damn drunk and high to hear anything?"

Noe laughed. "He needs to come to a biker party." He put the coffee down. "Have you talked to Mia?"

"No. Forget about her, bro. She's a cunt. She always thought she was better than us. That's why Ma was always beating her snobby ass."

"She can be a bitch, but she's still your sister. Talk to her."

"All she wants to talk about is Finn. I'm bored with it. I hope the asshole rots in prison. She wants me to give money to help him get an attorney. Fuck that! I'm not giving shit."

"Yeah, she was talking about the fucker to me too. She's kinda obsessed with it."

"She's a snotty bitch. You can do better."

"I thought you were all for it," Noe said.

"I was, but then when you told me the way she dissed you when you were in Durango a few weeks ago, it pissed me off. You don't need some cunt treating you like that."

"If we're together, I'll teach her who's boss."

"She needs a good thrashing," he said, placing the phone against his ear. Gesturing Noe to be quiet, Shark lightly tapped the table with his finger as he waited for Blueman to pick up.

"Why the fuck didn't you pick up the phone?" the gang leader asked.

"Why the fuck did you call me at two in the goddamn morning? I don't hear shit when I'm partying hard, and that's what me and the brothers did last night. Whaddya want?"

"Confirm our meet up next week."

"Yeah … about that—I need to postpone it." Silence crackled between them. "Did ya hear me?"

"I heard. Do you have the money?" Blueman's voice was cold with a sharp edge to it.

"That's why I need the continuance. We've almost got it all but just need a bit more time to get the rest."

"I heard you fucked up the attack on the Night Rebels' businesses. What the hell were you thinking in sending two-bit dealers and pimpled-faced teens to do your job? I don't have too much confidence you're gonna pull this buy off."

Anger rushed through Shark. "We'll pull it off just fine, and what we did in Alina doesn't concern you. We got our own score to settle with those fuckers. It had nothing to do with getting money."

"Even so … you fucked it up."

Shark gripped the side of the table with his hand so hard his knuckles turned white. He wanted to tell this smug punk what he really thought of him, but Shark needed to keep cool because the Satan's Pistons needed the drugs to double or maybe even triple their investment. They needed to get back on their feet, then they wouldn't have to send out amateurs to destroy the damn Rebels—they'd do it themselves.

"We'll have the money in a month."

"Three weeks or the deal's off," Blueman answered.

"Okay, but cut the attitude. You're not working with a bunch of losers here. I know the score—you need our money. I checked you out. Your club is near broke after that sting operation took down some of the heavy players and the feds took away your assets, so don't act like gangster-of-the-year with me."

Noe guffawed, and Shark and he bumped fists. Another long pause. For a few seconds, Shark cursed himself for losing his temper and blowing the deal.

"Maybe your check should extend to your family as well."

"Are you telling me I've got a fuckin' traitor in the brotherhood?"

"Your blood family. I've had one of my men watching your sister, Mia Decelles—a.k.a. Stiletto."

Confusion spread through him. "What the fuck does she have to do with any of this?"

"It's what I do. It's good to know about the people I'm dealing with, even their family members. It gives me some insurance, you know?"

"Leave her the fuck alone. She's not a part of this."

"You don't fuck me over, and I won't need to do anything."

"I'm telling you again—leave her the fuck outta this."

The clucking of Blueman's tongue irked the shit out of Shark. Then in a very steady, cold, and low voice, he asked, "Do you know your baby sister is sleeping with the enemy?"

"What the fuck are you talking about?" he growled.

"A Night Rebel is filling her holes."

Now it was Shark's turn to grow silent. As Blueman's words began to sink in, adrenaline pushed through him as white-hot rage filled his veins. "You're fuckin' wrong. If you want this sale to go through, you'll shut your lying motherfuckin' mouth!" Shark's voice grew louder and louder with each word until he was shouting.

"I'm just telling it like it is. Why the fuck would I lie about it?" Blueman asked, his voice cool as ice.

"Just shut the fuck up about it. We're doing a business transaction and that's all. It doesn't involve my family. You still in, or do I take my business to Los Malos?" Shark's nostrils flared.

"You got exactly three weeks. Eleven p. m. at the warehouse. I sent you the address," Blueman replied.

"We'll be there, and you and me don't need to talk no more." Shark cut the call then tapped in Mia's number. On the second ring, he hung up then paced around in circles trying to understand what Blueman's game was.

"Man, you're pissed off. What the fuck did Blueman say to you?" Noe asked.

Shark stopped in his tracks and looked at Noe. "When you saw that dude with Mia at the gym, was he wearing a cut?"

Noe jerked his head back. "No. Why?"

"Did you see a Harley in front, or in the parking lot of the gym that night?"

Noe shook his head. "What's this all about?"

"Blue-*asshole*-man told me Mia's fucking a Night Rebel. Did you see any MC tats on the guy?"

Noe's eyes widened. "No damn way. Mia wouldn't do that. The dude with her looked like a fighter. He definitely wasn't wearing a Night Rebels patch tatted on his back. He looked like he could be a biker or a rocker."

"What was his name?"

"Uh ... something military-sounding."

"Who'd she say he was again?"

"A brother of one of her friends who was an MMA fighter. I still can't believe that about Mia. This asshole's trying to get you riled up."

Shark scrubbed his three-day-old unshaven face. "But why? What's the point in pissing me off? And why the fuck would he make up that BS about Mia? Something isn't making sense here. He knows she's my sister, so he's not bullshitting about someone keeping tabs on her. Fuck!" He picked up his empty shot glass and hurled it across the room where it hit the front of a steel cabinet and crashed to the floor.

"Just ask Mia."

"Yeah. I'll give her a call later on, and if I find out it's true, the fucking Rebel is dead. I'll show Mia what happens to bitches who disrespect me and the brotherhood." Shark kicked the chair over.

"If she's guilty, I'm with you all the way, brother. I just remembered the fucker's name: Army."

Shark made a mental note of it, then yelled over for Tikka and Pinkie to come and relieve the tension from his body.

# Chapter Nineteen

"**Y**OU FINALLY SCREWED him," Ronica said a bit too loudly, and Mia hushed her as she glanced around the salon.

Grabbing her wrists, Mia dragged her friend to the break room and shut the door. "I don't want my private life to be the topic of discussion for the next week. Anyway, I didn't tell you anything."

"You don't have to—you're glowing like a damn thousand-watt bulb." Ronica leaned over near Mia's ear, her eyes focused on the closed door. "Was it incredible or a huge disappointment?" she asked softly.

"It was phenomenal," Mia said, her emotions bubbling like a glass of champagne.

"I knew it would be, or at least I hoped it would. It was a gamble. Sometimes the real good-looking ones with an attitude make the most mediocre lovers, but Army had the whole badass vibe going so I suspected he was the real deal." Ronica sat down and crossed her legs. "Did you fuck him out of your system?"

Mia giggled. "That's all we did while I was there. We did it in the shower, on the loveseat, on the floor, and on his bike when he took me for a ride to the most beautiful place I've ever seen. The view alone—"

Ronica held up her hand in front of Mia's face. "Wait ... go back. You guys screwed on his motorcycle? That sounds uncomfortable and dangerous."

"We weren't moving." Mia laughed. "We were on top of a peak, and it felt like we were the only people in the world. I'd never had sex on a bike, but it was so good. Army left the engine running while in park, and the vibration was like a huge vibrator. Anyway, it was awesome."

"Is that a biker thing?" Ronica pursed her lips.

"I don't know. He told me it was the first for him, so that made it even more special for me." She laughed again.

"What're you thinking about? Your cheeks just turned red."

"He kept revving the engine up and it made everything so much more intense." The memory of one of the most powerful orgasms she'd ever had made her clench her legs as she leaned against the counter.

"So he sends you flowers, wines and dines you, agrees to wait until you screwed, and he knows how to screw. Sounds like a keeper."

Mia's eyes sparkled. "He is. I've done something totally scary—I've fallen for him."

"Big time?" Ronica's gaze widened.

"Yep." She covered her face with her hands. "I know it's crazy. I've only known him for a month. I never fall this fast."

"You never fall *period*. When's the last time you've been in love after high school?"

Mia shook her head. "Never—not even in high school. I was too busy playing mom to have friends let alone a boyfriend." Her hands slipped down by her side. "Is this too insane?"

Ronica smiled. "No, I thinks it's great. I told you the first day I met Army that he'd be a good match for you. Do you know how he feels?"

"He tells me he's happy I'm in his life, and that he's never been with a woman as wonderful as me. I know he feels the connection."

"When are you going to see him again?"

"I'm not sure. It's been only two days since I got back, and I'm missing him so much. I was supposed to go to the bike rally on Saturday, but I can't swing it. I have a full day." Mia opened the fridge and took out a bottle of water. "Do you want one?" She waved the bottle at Ronica who shook her head no. Mia twisted open the cap and took a drink. "I've been going on about me too much. How was your trip with Stuart?"

"It was fun. Aspen was so beautiful with all the trees changing colors. We had a very romantic time. Not as sex-filled and wild as your vacation with Army, but then, I like romance with my man."

"Army does subtle stuff, and since he's such a rough and tough guy, those are the things that touch me and are romantic. Like, after we banged our brains out on his Harley, he spread out a blanket and held me close while we watched an incredible sunset and the mist rise in the valley. Neither of us spoke—we didn't have to. Sharing that moment together spoke volumes."

"Well put. It is the simple things that show a man cares for you." Ronica glanced at the clock on the back wall. "I better get going. My client will be here in a few, and I want to prep my station. When's your next appointment?"

"In a half hour." Her ringtone bounced off the walls and she pulled out her phone, hoping it was Army. She frowned when she saw Shark's name.

"From your face, I know it's not your honey." Ronica chortled.

"It's my brother Vic. I'll see you later." Mia put the phone to her ear as she walked over to the small locker area for the employees. "Hi, Vic."

"Who the hell are you fucking?" There was a harsh edge to his voice.

Her insides turned to ice, and her stomach churned. The room spun around as she gripped the opened door of one of the lockers to steady herself. He knows! How the hell did he find out?

"Hello ... Vic?" She stalled for time, pretending she couldn't hear him.

"Mia? Can you hear me?"

Will he believe I can't, or will it prove to him I *am* with Army. Second guessing her brother and mother when she'd been young had been a full-time job. Most of the times when she'd gone with her instinct, she'd gotten it right. Her gut was telling her to answer him.

"Vic?"

"I'm here. Fuck!"

"I can hear you. I was in the back room and my reception is usually shitty there. How are you?"

"I asked who you're fucking." He was hard and angry, and she cringed.

"I've never discussed my sex life with you—it's just weird." She laughed lightly as if this was a joke between brother and sister.

"Are you fucking a Night Rebel?"

Oh God! He knows. How? Noe? "A biker? No," she lied. She ran the cool bottle over her forehead then down the side of her face and neck. "Why would you ask me that?"

"I heard you were fucking one of those assholes."

"That's absurd. Where did you hear that from?" Mia tried to control her breathing—the last thing she wanted was for Vic to pick up on her anxiety.

"Never mind where I heard it from. Who's this Army dude Noe told me about? You dating him?"

"Not really. I told you I wasn't attracted to Noe in that way."

"Why didn't you tell me you were with someone before Noe came to Durango?" Suspicion still laced Vic's voice, but he didn't seem as angry as he was when he first called.

"You wouldn't listen to me that morning. You seemed hell bent to make us a couple."

He grunted.

"I have to go. I have a client coming in. Business is real good." Mia willed her pounding heart to slow the hell down.

"I'm gonna look into this a little more. I better not find out you're bullshitting me." A thread of warning wound around his words.

"I guess you don't have anything better to do."

"Go take care of your customer."

The phone went dead and she covered her mouth and rushed to the bathroom. His words, his anger, and his hatred sickened her.

Several minutes later, she wiped her ashen face then brushed her teeth. As she left the break room, Chloe—another stylist—waved to her then stopped. "Are you all right? You look sick."

"I'm fine," Mia croaked. "Wrong time of the month." She placed her hands over her belly, the corner of her mouth lifting into a weak smile.

"Bummer. I hate cramps. I've always got some Advil on me. Let me know if you need it."

"Thanks," Mia mumbled as she walked over to her station. She hoped she didn't screw up Elizabeth Danby's hair. She refused to acknowledge all the fear and panic and dread playing havoc inside her. *I have to get through the day. I'll think about all this later.* Mia went to the lobby and gave Ms. Danby a huge smile then escorted her to the booth.

MIA SAT IN front of the gas fireplace watching the blue flame shoot up from under the fake logs, drinking a glass of white wine she'd bought on sale at the liquor store on her way home from work. The autumn air had a chill in it that matched the one that had been running through her ever since Vic had called. It was just a matter of time before he'd find out that she lied to him, then he'd bluster around, ranting and raving and planning vengeance on her ... and Army. She took a big gulp of wine then promptly began to choke—sputtering and coughing as she pressed her hand at the base of her throat. Startled by the sudden burst of noise, Snickers ran into the other room. "Shit," she croaked as she rose to her feet and went to get some water. After a bit, all was back on track and she went back to the couch, sank down into the cushions, and stared at the fireplace again. The blue flame reminded her of Army's eyes: flashing, burning, dangerous.

"Fuck you, Vic," she muttered. The more Mia thought about the ridiculousness of the situation, the more she wanted to bash her brother's head in. He'd always thought he was the boss of her, and he could be cruel just as he could be kind with her. She'd left their small town so she could escape from him and their mother. This shouldn't concern him at all. But in his crazy mind, he thought everything about her was his business.

A small voice pricked the back of her mind, a voice she'd been ignoring since she'd found out Army was a Night Rebel. At that moment, she let it talk, and it asked if Army would be just like Vic. Would he leave her just because she was tainted by blood to Vic—Shark?

Mia leaned forward and retrieved her wine, taking a small sip. She didn't want to think—especially after they'd gotten to know each other and shared so much as they came together in their want and desire for each other—that he would, or could, just walk away.

*And what would I do if he did? Dammit … I don't want to think about this. I'm putting the damn horse before the cart.* Army had infiltrated her life, filling her mind even when he wasn't around, and each time she thought about him, excitement surged through her blood like an elixir. *What the hell did you do to me?* The past few days they'd just spent together were a mixture of tender moments and fucking each other's brains out. And … can *he* kiss. Damn. Each kiss had a raw intensity— fast breaths, hearts racing. When she'd arrived back home, hours after he touched her body, his smell still lingered on her skin.

She drained the last of the wine. *He turns me into a trembling jumble of need, and I fucking love it. I'm not going to let Vic ruin this. Army is the only man I've been in love with, and there's no damn way I'm letting Vic's ignorant hatred take that away from me.*

Mia picked up the remote but stopped when the doorbell rang. Her heart pounded in her chest, her hand curled tighter around the device, and her mind swirled. Would Vic really be that nuts to drive all the way to Durango to confront her? Yes.

The bell rang again. She prepped herself for the fight of her life and slowly walked to the front door, her senses on high alert. She looked through the peephole. "Army!" She flung the door open and fell into his arms.

"You didn't put your alarm on," he said.

She laughed and playfully punched his chest. "You could've just called and reminded me," she teased him as she pulled him inside.

"Yeah, but I wouldn't be able to hold you and feel your soft tits pressed against me." He grabbed the sides of her face, his eyes boring into hers. "Give me your lips."

The command shimmied down her spine and landed right between her legs. She tilted her head back and waited for him to claim her mouth. At first, his kiss was slow and gentle and the more she leaned into him, the faster and rougher it became. It was like dancing the tango with their lips and mouths—closely connected and intimately romantic. She moaned when he bit her lower lip then softly sucked on her tongue. Mia matched his moves as arousal swept through her in a wild rush. Then, he roughly pulled her head back by the hair and whispered, "Did you miss me?"

His lips were so close they tickled her ear and sent chills skittering across her skin. "Yes," she breathed.

The tip of his nose caressed her earlobe. "Have you been a good girl?"

Oh fuck. Her sex clenched at his words. "Very good," she rasped.

He gave a low, deep growl in her ear that reduced her to a horny puddle craving to be devoured.

Army smacked her butt hard then pulled away and shrugged off his jacket, throwing it casually over the wingback chair. Mia stood there watching him, her insides a trembling mess of want.

"Do you have any beer?" He winked and threw her a quick smile before ambling into the kitchen.

Not answering, she took several deep breaths, focusing on a piece of lint on the floor as she regained her composure.

"No beer, babe. What about whiskey?"

"In the cupboard next to the dishes," she managed to say as her breathing normalized.

"Want one?"

"No, thanks. I'm drinking wine." Mia walked over to the coffee table and picked up her glass then padded over to the counter and refilled the goblet. "Why didn't you tell me you were coming up?"

"I wanted to surprise you." He patted her ass then took her hand and led them to the couch.

"You definitely did that. It's a happy surprise. Is everything all right with your family?" She sipped the chardonnay.

"Yeah. I came to see you. I missed you, babe." Warmth spread through her. "How's your training going?"

"You've made me lazy." She laughed. "I need to step up my game if I'm going to compete in a couple of months. Rick's given me a week to rest, but after that, it's no more coddling."

"I know you get a rush from being in the ring, and I get a hard-on watching you, so you gotta get back in there for both our sakes." He brought the tumbler to his lips.

She squeezed his bicep then dug her nails hard into his taut skin. "I'm so happy you're here."

His gaze scanned her face then slipped down to her breasts and lingered before coming back up to her eyes. "I'm glad I'm here too. Where do you want to go for dinner?"

"How about Twin Dragons. They have the best Kung Pao ..." Her voice trailed off as the thought that Vic heard she was dating Army stabbed at her brain. *Someone must be watching us.* Then the image of the red sports car with the creepy guy flashed through her mind. *Of course!*

"What's up? You shut down."

Army's voice drew her away from her musings. "I was just thinking that you always take me out, and I'd love to cook for you."

A slight smile played over his lips. "Aren't you tired from working all day?"

"Not really. I have some steaks in the fridge."

"Are you sure?"

"Absolutely. We can go for Chinese another time." She snuggled next to him.

He kissed the top of her head and ran his fingers over her forearm. "I want you to meet my dad and brother Asher."

"Meeting your friends last Saturday, now the rest of your family ... it sounds serious," she said with an impish grin on her face.

He lifted her chin on his index finger and held her gaze. "I'm fuckin' crazy about you, babe." Mia smiled and he caressed her jaw with his thumb. "That's what gets to me—your smile, your eyes … every fucking thing. Mia, you light up the dark places inside me and make them all right. No one else has ever done that."

Mia was overcome with emotion at his words. She blinked rapidly then hooked her arm around his neck and brought his face down to hers. "I've never cared about anyone as much as I do about you." Then, their mouths fused in a long, lingering kiss.

When their lips broke apart, Mia ran her hand through his hair then stood up. "I'm going to start dinner." She handed him the remote then practically skipped into the kitchen.

In the middle of the black glass-topped table, two rust-colored candles in bronze candleholders flickered as Mia breezed by carrying a small platter of asparagus and cherry tomatoes in one hand and a cucumber and avocado salad in the other. After placing the last dish—black bean and corn quinoa—on the glass top, she slid into the chair across from Army.

"This is the first time I've used the dining set," she said, scooping a generous portion of salad on his plate. "I bought these autumn-colored placemats, and they've just been sitting in the drawer. It's nice to be able to use them."

The dining room only fit a small table for four and a tall, skinny curio cabinet in the corner. An abstract oil painting of the sun setting over the city hung on a wall painted in a ginger shade.

Army popped a piece of steak in his mouth then took a sip of red wine. "The food's awesome. I'm impressed that you whipped all this up in under an hour."

"Thanks. It's fun being able to make a big dinner. I rarely do it for myself."

As they ate, Army stared intensely into her eyes like a hungry wolf surveying his prey. She found it incredibly sexy and it made her body heat up, her nipples erect, and her skin tingle. Squirming in the chair, she smiled weakly at him then took a long drink of wine in an effort to calm down.

"Do you want some more quinoa?" Mia pushed the bowl toward him.

Shaking his head, he put down his fork and knife. "I'm good." His gaze still bored into her.

"I'm full myself," she replied, putting her cinnamon-colored napkin on the table.

Army leaned forward to pour more wine into her glass, but she covered it with her hand, shaking her head slightly. He proceeded to fill his up then reclined against the black leather chair.

"Do you trust me?" Army asked before taking a sip of merlot.

"I'm not sure I understand what you're asking me. Are you talking about you not sleeping around?"

He chuckled. "Not exactly, but now that you brought it up—I'm not. I haven't been with anyone since I met you."

"Me neither, but I have to admit I'm surprised you haven't. I mean, you have easy sex available to you twenty-four seven."

"That's not what I want. You are a challenge, baby." He reached for her hand, tucking it into his. "I meant sexually. Do you trust that I wouldn't do anything to hurt you during sex? That all I want is for you to have pleasure?"

Mia licked her lips and nodded.

"Are you open to me grasping your throat while I fuck you?"

"You mean choking?" she asked softly.

"Not exactly. For me, placing my hand on your throat isn't about choking or breath play, it's about deep intimacy and a lot of trust. I've never done it with anyone in the past, but I'd like to with you, but if you don't then it's okay too." His gaze still held hers.

"No one's ever done that to me before, and I know I wouldn't have done it because I've never trusted anyone before when it came to sex, or just … in general." Shivers lightly skated up her back. "But I do trust you. I know you would never hurt me or do anything to me I don't want."

Army brought her hand up to his mouth and kissed it. "With trust, you can surrender, and I can let all those demons inside you come out to play."

*How does he know this is exactly what I want ... what I need?* "I surrender to you," she whispered.

"Come over here." He gestured to his lap and she went over and curled up in it, cocooned in his powerful arms. "You are my dark fire," he said against her hair.

They sat like that until his phone started to ring and broke through their comfortable silence. "Sorry, baby. I gotta take this."

Mia climbed off his lap and he went into the garage and closed the door. Her body was still tingling from anticipation and fear. Never in her life had she trusted anyone as implicitly as she had Army. Growing up, she'd learned to trust her intuition to try and stay one step ahead of her mother's wrath, thus gaining loads of mistrust for her mother, and later on men.

She stood by the kitchen sink rinsing a pot, and Army sneaked up from behind and hugged her close to him. He bit and kissed her neck, then whispered in her ear, "Mine." Sparks of desire traveled from her nipples down to her pulsing sex, and she moaned and pressed her head against his shoulder.

"I gotta go out for a little bit. Some club business came up, but I should be back in less than an hour," he said as he squeezed her tight.

Mia wanted to ask him if it involved the Satan's Pistons, but she was afraid. At some point she had to tell him about Vic, but she kept pushing it away, pretending that it wasn't between them. "Did you see anyone in a red sports car when you came over here?"

He turned her at the waist so she faced him. "What're you talking about?"

"Did anyone follow you to my place?"

"No. Why? Is someone messin' with you?"

She told him about the guy in the red car and how she was positive he had been following her. A knot of muscles at the side of his jaw pulsed.

"Why didn't you tell me this sooner?"

"I didn't think about it. Anyway, I haven't seen him in about a week. It's probably just a groupie." She laughed half-heartedly, her gut telling her that wasn't true.

"Next time you see him, get his plates. I'll find out who the fucker is and straighten him out."

As she nestled her head against his chest, she felt safe and protected. He kissed her forehead then pulled back. "I have to get going." He grasped her hand and they walked to the front door.

"When you get back call me so I can open the garage door. You can park your bike in there." She didn't want to take any chances with his motorcycle parked in front of her house.

"Sure, babe. Put the alarm on. I'll be back." He stepped onto the porch. "When I get back I better find you naked and in a pair of heels." He turned around and walked to his bike.

Dampness laced Mia's panties and she felt a full body flush as she latched the screen door. Every nerve throbbed in anticipation of what was to come as she stood watching him until he turned the corner, then she locked the door and set the alarm.

A WARM AND fuzzy golden glow from two dozen red candles illuminated the bedroom, sending out showers of highlights while casting everything beyond its ambit in darkness. Hypnotic swirls of smoke escaped into the air from a stick of vanilla incense, wrapping the room in the sensual and luxurious scent. Metal power ballads from Manowar, Skid Row, Winger, Tesla and other artists played softly from a small speaker illuminated by a table lamp in the corner of the room.

The flickering candlelight reflected in Army's blue eyes making them sparkle and blaze at the same time. He raked his gaze slowly down her naked body and up again as she stood in front of him near the bed. Mia trembled and her skin felt hot—flushed, as arousal coursed just below its surface.

"So sexy," he said hoarsely as his eyes met hers.

Mia's body had been a medley of emotions since Army had left, only growing bigger as the minutes ticked away the time. She'd showered, dabbed some cinnamon oil on her pulse points, and made the room ready for their night of love. Sitting still while waiting for Army to return practically drove Mia to the brink of hysteria. When he'd finally called and asked her to open the garage door, she almost broke down and cried from relief. Her body was zinging and zapping all over the damn place, and the way Army was taking his time frustrated and enthralled her.

"Come closer," he ordered. Army reached out and touched her and she sighed deeply. His hand skimmed over her in a feather-like touch. She sucked in her breath and looked deeply into his gaze. All of a sudden, he grasped her nipples and rolled them between his thumbs and forefingers. They strained in tight peaks and an electric current singed through her. A deep moan broke free from her lips, and she tilted her head back and closed her eyes, reveling in the delicious ache throbbing in those hardened points.

"Look at me. I want you to watch me play with your tits," he said in a calm but stern voice.

Her eyes snapped open and met the intensity of his stare as he twisted and tugged on her nipples.

"Harder," she breathed.

Raging desire fluttered through her veins.

"Harder."

A shot of pain made her gasp.

"Harder."

The burn of lust between her legs.

"Harder!"

"If I pull any harder, I'm gonna rip the fuckin' nipples right off your tits."

"I didn't say my safeword. Harder ... *please.*"

A streak of mind-numbing pain morphed into a euphoric haze that seeped through her veins, evicting her anger, fear, and uncertainty about Vic's phone call.

Army licked her bright red tips, soothing them gently. After several minutes, he trailed his lips to hers and kissed her deeply and passionately while his hand slid over her throat. The mere hint of what was to come ignited every nerve in her body and she moaned into his mouth as he applied firm but gentle pressure. Mia closed her eyes.

He pulled back. "Open your eyes," he said in a low voice.

Mia's lids fluttered open and she stared into his gaze. As he held her look, he kissed his way up her neck until he reached her ear. Army's musky, hungry scent wrapped around her, inviting her to journey into the darkness with him. Her skin tingled and her mound pulsed as she kept her stare fixed on his.

Lightly biting her earlobe, he applied a bit more pressure to her neck. "You turn me on so much, babe," he said in a soft, low tone. "I bet you're dripping. I want to taste you and feel your wetness on the tip of my fingers."

Mia clenched her legs. *This is erotic as hell. I don't think I can hold out.*

"Do you like being spanked?"

Army's calm, deep voice made her body a bundle of sizzling nerves.

His hand pushed down a bit harder. "Answer me." His voice turned steely, and she loved it.

"Yes," she choked.

"Good girl," he said, his timbre soft and low again. "I'm going to smack your sweet ass until I see my handprints marked red on your cheeks."

"Oh God," she moaned.

"Then I'm gonna fuck you real hard. Just like you want it—rough as shit."

Her mouth was dry.

"Now open your legs."

A shiver traveled across her back as she obeyed.

"Wider."

She did as he ordered.

Army slid his hand down to her quivering mound while his other one still pressed down on her throat.

"Just what I thought—you're dripping wet." Without warning, he drilled several fingers into her and she cried out. "You love it," he said close to her ear before moving his mouth away.

The small hairs tickled the back of her neck as he trailed soft kisses over her shoulders while ramming his fingers roughly in and out of her dripping heat. His hand was still on her throat, and his gaze bored into her.

For the next hour, Army teased her, bringing her to the verge of climax only to pull away. Mia was nearly in tears from frustration, but he kept playing with her as her body greedily accepted anything he did to it.

Right as she was ready to go over, he withdrew his tongue from her sweet spot. "What the fuck, Army? I need to come."

"I'll tell you when to come. I'm in control, not you." He grasped her hand and led her over to the bed. "Get down on all fours. Leave your heels on."

Mia obeyed, positioning herself as he requested, then glanced behind her shoulder at him. Army had stripped and the golden light in the room danced over his amazing pecs. "Can I lick you?" she asked.

"After you've rested." Her eyes widened, and he chuckled. "That's right. I'm gonna fuck you all night."

Her body hummed and she pursed her lips in a kiss. He leaned forward and crushed his mouth over hers and gave her a wet, messy kiss that left her lips tingling.

"Put your ass higher in the air."

The slap stung and she jumped. He immediately rubbed the spot. She lowered her upper body down on the mattress which helped to elevate her butt.

"I fuckin' love your hot little ass," he growled. He smacked it again then rubbed his palm over her cheek. Another slap then he gripped her butt. Another smack.

Mia wiggled and moaned—her need was so great, and the way Army was treating her was liberating and sexy as hell. She felt him rub his hardness against her ass crack.

"Fuck, you make me so hard. I can't wait to shove my cock into that sweet pussy."

"Do it ... *please.*"

He ran his hands over her back then grabbed a fistful of hair and yanked her head back to kiss her deeply. "You have no fuckin' idea what you do to me," he said in a low voice. Then he pulled back and jackhammered into her.

Two hours later, Mia lay tucked in next to Army, her body sated and glowing from several orgasms. She'd blown out the candles and the only illumination in the room was a sliver of moonlight spilling in.

"It wasn't too much for you?" Army asked as he stroked her head.

Glancing up, she smiled. "It was perfect."

"You and me are real good together," he said in a low voice.

"Yeah." She held her breath. *Do you love me? I love you so much.*

"We got this connection that goes beyond fucking. It's damn cool." He kissed the top of her head.

"I love being with you."

"Me too, babe."

*I have to tell him about Vic. First thing in the morning. For sure.*

"You want to play some more?"

Mia chuckled. "I'm good. You've worn me out. I'm happy just holding you like this."

"Yeah it kicks ass ... *you* kick ass."

She pressed her lips to his chest. "So do you."

They lay together in a warm, comfortable silence, their legs tangled together and arms curled around each other.

*I have to talk to Vic. He has to see reason—I need to make him listen.* She craned her neck and saw that Army's eyes were closed. She snuggled closer to him.

*How could I ever leave him?* Army allowed her to become the darkness she had always wished to explore.

He touched her deeply, and what she felt for him was a helluva lot more than fluttering hearts and smoldering eyes—it was more like two souls catching fire.

# Chapter Twenty

ARMY WOKE UP with Mia's ass against his hard dick, her face covered by messy caramel-brown hair with several tendrils stuck to his chest. He ran his hand down her arm, smiling when her skin pebbled under his fingertips. She was beyond wonderful, and as hard as he tried to push down his feelings, they kept rising back up. Mia trusted him implicitly when they were together, and he trusted her, which was a new feeling for him when it came to a woman.

*Mia's so special. I don't want any other chick but her. Damn ... I never thought I'd feel like this.* She'd done something that he never thought would be possible with a woman—she'd made her mark on him. He sucked in a deep breath and exhaled it slowly as he watched her sleep. *I can't stop looking at her, and I'm always thinking about her. I've been to Durango more in the last couple of months than I have in the last five years.* He bent over and kissed her hair. *And I love the way her face twitches when she's nervous or too excited.* He chuckled softly under his breath.

The phone pinged and he groaned inwardly hoping he didn't have to go back to Alina until tomorrow. While looking at the text, he dragged a hand through his hair and blew out a breath. "Fuck," he mumbled as he texted back, telling Steel he'd be there in an hour.

Army put the phone down, and his chest tightened when he looked over at Mia again before rising to his feet.

When he came out of the bathroom, Mia was sitting up in bed, looking down at her phone. She averted her gaze to him, and a smile lit up her face, which made his dick twitch. *Damn.*

"My ten o'clock rescheduled, so I'm yours for the next three hours. Oh ... and tonight, I thought I'd make fajitas, and we can watch a movie."

For the first time since he became a Night Rebel, he wanted tell Steel he couldn't come back until the next day. He walked over to the bed and bent down to capture her lips in a long kiss. "I gotta go back to Alina, babe. I got the text fifteen minutes ago from the prez. Chad, who's a citizen, is sick, and I've got to be at Lust. It sucks." He pulled away and shuffled over to the chair where he grabbed his jeans after tossing the towel around his waist to the foot of the bed.

"When will you be back?" Disappointment wound around her voice.

"After the rally. You're coming with Taylor, right?" He slipped his T-shirt over his head.

"I can't get away. Saturday is way too busy, and I have a few private clients on Sunday. I'm trying to raise money to get an attorney for Finn."

"I can help you out with that." He pulled on his boots.

Mia shook her head. "Thanks, but I couldn't take money from you."

Army stopped in mid-zip and looked over at her. "Why the fuck not? We're together, and I wanna help out your brother."

"I've never taken money from a man before. I've always been sorta nutty about it."

He finished putting on his boots then walked over to her. "Fuck, woman, I'm not just a man ... or am I?"

"Of course not," she said quickly.

"Then I'm gonna help you out. That's what people who are together do—they help each other out." He swept his lips across hers. "The discussion is over."

She looped her arms around his neck and pulled him down so hard that he toppled on the bed. She laughed then gave him a wet and passionate kiss. "You're the best."

His cock strained painfully against his jeans, but he knew if he gave it what it wanted, he'd be disrespecting Steel, so he pulled away and lightly patted her ass. "I'll call you later today. You can meet my dad and Asher on my day off."

All of a sudden, Mia's face grew tight and her right eye started twitching. "I wanted to talk to you about something. Can you tell your president that you'll be a little late?" She put her thumb to her mouth and chewed the cuticle.

"I can't, but we can talk later. Uh ... are you pregnant or something?"

Mia dropped her hand and shook her head. "No."

"Can it wait until I come back next week?"

"I suppose." She gave him a small smile.

"Maybe I can come on Monday. I'll probably have to go back that night to work at Lust, but we can talk then."

"I'm not sure how I feel about you working full-time at a strip bar." Her forehead creased.

*She's fuckin' cute when she's jealous.* He dipped his head and brought his face inches from hers. "I don't think of anyone but you. The dancers are just bodies on a stage."

"Thanks for saying that, but I can't believe that you don't watch them or get turned on."

"Of course, I do, I'm a man. But ... there's no one I want to be inside of but you." He brushed his lips gently over hers. "I better get my ass going."

After making sure she'd reset the alarm, he straddled his bike, and took one last look at her standing by the window before he rode away.

HARD ROCK BEATS from local bands floated on the crisp breeze like the autumn leaves falling down from the oak trees. The aroma of smoked meats from the food stalls wafted around the rally, drawing people to them. Slick custom Harley-Davidson motorcycles gleamed under the fading western sun as hordes of leather-clad men and women milled down the aisles appreciating the iron machines. The bike rally had pulled in a record number of bikers and citizens that year, making the Night Rebels pleased that they could cut a hefty check to Bikers Against

Child Abuse.

Army waved at Kelly as she walked past in a wet T-shirt plastered against her braless chest. All of the club girls volunteered at the rally either by engaging in the T-shirt competitions or washing bikes in skimpy outfits. Some even squared off with citizen women in the mud pit.

"This event keeps getting bigger every year," Bones said to Army. Some of the members from the Insurgents MC came down from Pinewood Springs. Bones' new Forty-Eight Special Sportster was one of the bikes entered into the competition. Hawk had customized it by adding chrome pipes for more sound, and ghoulish demons and a scantily-clad woman holding a big glass of beer decorated the coverings that surrounded the bike.

"Yeah. It's turning out to be one of the biggest rallies in the Southwest. That bike of yours is a real beaut. How's the ride?"

"Fucking awesome!" Bones replied.

"I bet. Where'd you get that wicked hood ornament?" Army took the beer the prospect handed him.

"Jerry designs them. Talk to him. He's got a ton of kickass ornaments. Hawk's got them at his shop, but Jerry'll custom one just for you." Bones lifted the plastic cup of beer to his mouth.

"I'll hit him up for sure. How's life treating you in Pinewood?"

Bones tossed the cup into one of the large trashcans. "Not bad. I hear you got a woman. When Eagle told me that, I almost shit a brick."

"*I* almost shit a brick. Mia sucker-punched me." Army chuckled.

Dressed in a long-sleeved crop top and short shorts, Kelly came back over and stood next to him. "Buzz is looking for you," she said, her eyes on Bones.

"Thanks. I'll catch up with him." Army laughed to himself because he could practically see Kelly salivating. Whenever he and Bones hung out, he noticed women checking out both of them. Several of the club girls loved it when Bones came into town, and they tried to outdo each other in an attempt to have him hook up with one of them during his stay. Sometimes he'd hook up with just one club woman the whole time, sometimes he'd try out a few of them. Kelly had a real soft spot for him. Army wondered if Bones would pick her or one of the others.

"How've you been?" Kelly asked softly.

Bones glanced at her, his dark chocolate eyes roaming over her body. "Good. You?"

"Real good." She placed her hands on her lower back which pushed out her chest more. Army sniggered then scanned the area for Buzz. Spotting the tall guy, he chugged down the rest of his beer then said, "I'm gonna see what Buzz wants. You coming?"

Bones' long dark hair fell over his shoulder when he shook his head no. "I'll see you around," he said, his gaze fixed on Kelly's tits.

Army lifted his chin to Bones then walked over to Buzz, who was checking out a killer bike in metallic lime green.

"Hey," he said, coming around to Buzz's side. "I noticed that bike earlier this morning. It's fuckin' wicked."

"I spoke to the biker who owns this work of art. He customized it himself. I love the way he mixes the green with the chrome. Even the fuckin' hubcaps are decked out."

"I'd love to get an older Harley and take my time in fixing it up. I'm good with the mechanical stuff, but can't draw a damn straight line, so I'd have to hire out to do the art stuff. Did you see Bones' bike? Hawk customized it and another dude in the Insurgents, Jerry, made the ornament. I'm gonna hit him up to make one for me."

"I saw Bones' bike earlier. Selling all that weed is paying off big for the Insurgents. The bike is a showpiece, and it must've cost him a fortune," Buzz replied.

Army whistled over to the prospect. Razor rushed over. "Two beers," he said, and Razor tilted his head and hurried away.

"How was Durango?" Buzz asked.

Army's head flinched back slightly. "You asked me that last night. The answer is still that it was good."

Buzz chuckled. "Last night I was drunk as shit and only had pussy on the brain."

Army guffawed. "Sounds about right."

"That chick you brought to the party last Saturday, she's an MMA fighter, right?" Buzz took the plastic cup from the prospect.

"Yeah. Have you seen her fight?"

"I'm pretty sure I did in Tucson. My uncle's nuts over MMA, so he took me to a fight when I was visiting him. I remember her eyes— they're pretty hard to forget."

Mia's face skittered through his mind, and the memory of her lips and the scent of her perfume curled around him. He shifted in place as his dick woke up. "Yeah, they are." *They're mesmerizing. Damn. I wish Mia was by my side right now.*

"Have you known her long?" Buzz asked over the rim of the cup.

"Enough. Why all the questions?"

Buzz rubbed his hand over his jeans then scratched the side of his face. His eyes looked everywhere but at Army. "Just wondering. I gotta find Roughneck. I'll catch up with you later."

"You guys heading back to Silverado tonight?"

"Yeah. I think we're planning to leave soon. I'll see what Roughneck wants to do." He finished the beer then walked away.

Army watched his retreating back, surprised when he passed right by Roughneck, and then went over to Crow, Chains, and Eagle. In his gut, he knew something was off and it somehow involved him. The pinging of his phone pulled him away from the scene. He inhaled sharply when a picture of Mia from the waist down popped up on his screen. She had on a tiny G-string and sexy-as-hell purple lace stilettos. As he stared at the scrap of lilac material covering her smooth sex, another ping rang out.

**Mia:** *What're u doing?*

**Army:** *Staring at the most beautiful pair of legs in heels I've ever seen.*

**Mia:** *I'm glad u like the pic.*

**Army:** *I do. U look good, but just imagine how much better u'd look with my fingers inside ur pussy.*

**Mia:** *Mmm … but ur dick would look even nicer. ;)*

Army chuckled, and before he could respond, another picture hit his screen—her sexy-as-fuck tits covered in bite marks and hickeys. "Damn, woman," he muttered under his breath.

**Army:** *Love the artwork. It may be better than ur kickass dragon.*

**Mia:** *It's definitely better. I love looking at your marks.*

**Army:** *I see some skin on ur tits. I'll have to fix that.*

**Mia:** *Don't make me blush.*

**Army:** *I'll make u blush while riding my face.*

**Mia:** *U make me smile.*

**Army:** *That's why I'm here, baby. To make you smile and smack ur ass once in a while.*

**Mia:** *Hehe.*

**Army:** *Ur all mine.*

**Mia:** *Say it again.*

**Army:** *Ur all mine and ur fucking perfect, babe.*

Army looked at the screen and waited for her response. Nothing. Then just when he was ready to send her a text, she sent one.

**Mia:** *I'm yours but not perfect. Don't put me on a pedestal.*

**Army:** *How bout if I bend u over on one and fuck you hard?*

"Are you heading back to the clubhouse?" Bones asked as Kelly clung to his side.

Army looked up from the phone. "Uh … yeah, but I won't be there 'til real late. I'm leaving soon to go to Lust. I'll be there 'til closing."

He opened the text.

**Mia:** *R u gonna make me beg for it?*

**Army:** *U know it. I wanna make you drip, baby.*

"I'll see you in the morning," Bones said as he swatted Kelly's ass. "I'm planning to be real busy later on tonight." Kelly giggled and snuggled closer to him.

"Yeah, dude. See you." Army looked down at the phone again.

**Mia:** *I'm already dripping.*

His cock strained against his jeans, throbbing with each of her texts.

**Army:** *Fuck, baby. I wish I was there. I'd take care of u.*

**Mia:** *U always do. Miss u sooo bad.*

**Army:** *I'll be there in 2 days.*

**Mia:** *It seems like a lifetime. Client's here. Gotta go. xxooxx*

**Army:** *Talk to u soon.*

He pushed his phone into the inner pocket of his cut and adjusted himself; his dick rubbed painfully against the seam as he headed toward his bike.

★   ★   ★

"HERE YOU GO," Lena said as she put a breakfast burrito and a cup of black coffee in front of Army. "How've you been doing? I rarely see you anymore," the cook said.

"Good. Been busy at the club, and my brother's working on going pro in MMA, so I've been heading to Durango a lot. I know this is gonna taste as good as it looks." Army picked up the burrito and took a big bite.

Lena smiled then turned away and shuffled back to the kitchen. The first bite was fucking heaven, and he enjoyed the rare silence in the main room as he sipped his coffee and ate. Most of the guys were either at work or snoozing off a helluva hangover. When he'd come back to the clubhouse after the gentlemen's club closed, the party was at full throttle. He didn't even grab a beer; instead, he'd just gone straight to his room and crashed.

After he'd finished breakfast, he brought the dish and mug into the kitchen and opened the dishwasher. Before he could pull out the top rack, Lena rushed over.

"I'll do that. You shouldn't have to do it." She tried to grab the plate from him, but he gently pushed her hand away and put the items inside the appliance.

"Chill, Lena."

"You're always cleaning up after yourself. You shouldn't be—you're a man."

He guffawed. "Tell that to my old man. He had all of us doing chores since we started school. Cleaning the house and dishes were just two of the ones on a long fuckin' list."

"What about your mother? She let a boy do all that?"

The gaiety of the moment dissolved. "She did what my dad wanted." He walked toward the door.

"Thank you for helping, Army," Lena said, and he waved his hand in the air and left the room.

When he went back into the main room, some of the brothers began to come in. He saw Kelly walking in with Crow.

"Did Bones already leave for Pinewood Springs?" he asked the club girl. She bobbed her head then looked surprised when Crow suddenly shoved her away from him and stalked over to Army.

"Why the hell are you fucking a Piston's sister?" he gritted, his hazel eyes narrowed and flashing.

Army jerked his head back and took a few steps away from him. "What the fuck are you talking about?"

"The MMA bitch."

Anger immediately punched his gut, and he clenched his hands in fists. "Don't ever call Mia a bitch. I don't know what the hell's your problem, but don't get in my face about my woman or I'll beat the shit outta you."

"Your woman?" Crow laughed dryly. "Buzz saw your woman competing in Tucson about a year and a half ago. A group of Satan's Pistons were there cheering her on. After the fight, she went over and gave that sonofabitch Shark a big hug. Buzz later found out she's his goddamn sister. So … why the hell are you fucking the enemy?"

A sudden coldness hit at his core and he turned away and faced the bar. "Buzz is full of shit. He came over and talked to me yesterday and never said a damn word about it. We even talked about Mia. He's messing with you."

Chains sidled up next to Army. "Buzz is straight on," he said in a low voice. "I checked it out. Victor Decelles—a.k.a. Shark—is Mia Decelles' brother. Sorry, dude." Chains cupped his hand over Army's bicep, but he jerked away as if a hot poker had burned his skin.

"I don't believe this shit!" His mind spun around like an out-of-control carousel in a nightmare.

"Why the hell would I make this up?" Chains' calm voice asked.

Army stood there dumbfounded as a thousand emotions rushed through him. *It can't be true. Something's fucked up.* "There are probably two fighters that have the same name." But even as he said it, he knew the chances of that were infinitesimal.

"That go by the name Stiletto in the MMA circuit?" Chains asked.

The calm quiet in his voice was getting on Army's nerves big time, but before he could reply, Steel and Paco walked in and came over to the trio.

Steel cleared his throat. "I'm guessing by the tension I'm feeling right now, you"—he looked at Army—"must've found out that we know fucking Shark is that fighter's brother. Did you know?" He looked fixedly at Army. Several other members came into the room and walked over to where Army stood.

A frown wrinkled his forehead as he slowly shook his head and mumbled, "No." He hadn't quite absorbed the fact that Mia and Shark were siblings and that she never once mentioned it to him.

"She knows the layout of the club and most likely has already described it to Shark," Skull said.

"I don't think she did that. She told me that she rarely sees or speaks with any of her brothers," Army replied in a monotone voice.

"Of course, she'd tell you that. She wanted to gain your trust," Skull said.

Deeper wrinkling on his brow. "I don't believe that."

"Then why didn't she tell you about Shark? Why the fuck wouldn't she have mentioned that she had a dickhead brother who was president of a loser club?" Skull gritted.

"She came on to you to spy for Shark," Muerto said.

"She didn't come on to me at all. I pursued her. None of you knows what the fuck you're talking about." He scuffed the floor with his boot.

All eyes were on Army, and they flashed with contempt and anger, yet none of them knew Mia, but ... did he? He scrubbed his face with his fist. "I never got the impression that she was involved in the biker world." As soon as he said the words, a memory crawled forward from the corner of his mind: she knew the lingo and how the outlaw world worked. *Fuck.* His chest tightened even more, and it was like there was a vise around his heart, squeezing it harder and harder. *I can't believe she betrayed me. I have to talk to her.*

"None of us blames you. She lied to you," Eagle said.

The rumble of voices and Eagle's words sliced through his thoughts.

"I'll talk to her."

"What the fuck?" Crow slammed his fist on the bar. "About what? Lying to you? She's scum and should be thrown out like the trash she is." Several members hooted and voiced their agreement.

When Army heard Crow's words, his brain was on fire with the feeling to kill. "Don't ever call Mia scum." His voice was low and dark.

"Then bitch or cunt or—"

Army's fist landed right on Crow's mouth. The brother looked shocked for a split second then his nostrils flared and he swung a punch at Army, clipping him in the jaw. Army stumbled back but then regained his balance and went ballistic. Anger and heartbreak fueled him, and he went into boxer mode and used Crow's face as a punching bag.

"Dude, stop. Fuck!" Eagle said as he tried to pull Army away from a stunned Crow.

Army kicked backwards and sent Eagle staggering back then resumed his assault on Crow. It took five brothers to pull him away from Crow whose face looked like raw ground beef.

"What the fuck's wrong with you?" Steel yelled. "Crow deserved a punch or two, but you would've killed him. Over a chick who lied and deceived you?"

"Think with your fuckin' brains, not your cock," Paco added.

Army glanced over at Crow and his insides twisted when he saw what he'd done to him. A tornado of emotions swirled around inside him, and he jerked out of Diablo's and Muerto's hold, picked up a chair, and threw it toward the back wall. The club girls scattered out of the way before it hit the wall in a loud splintering crash. He grabbed his leather jacket off the back of the chair he'd sat on earlier that morning and stormed out. Fuming, he hopped on his bike and sped off in the direction of Durango.

# Chapter Twenty-One

NOT FINDING MIA at home, Army went over to Champion and spotted her car in the parking lot. Adrenaline pumped through him as he swung open the doors and stepped into the club. He immediately saw her sparring with Kat on one of the mats in the far corner of the room. As he stalked toward her, he tried to pull back his rage that bubbled close to the surface and focus on keeping his temper in check.

Mia turned to him and flashed him a big, warm smile, and her amber eyes shimmered with excitement. "Army!" She said something to Kat then began walking to him. Bitterness and tenderness battled inside him as he watched her.

She came up to him and grabbed his hand, then her smile waned and her face clouded a bit. "Were you in a fight?" Mia put her fingers on his jaw, but he jerked his head back. Her eyes snapped to his. "What's wrong?"

"We need to talk." He grabbed her arm and ignored her quips as he dragged her over to the locker room. Once there, he let go of her and stood facing her, his arms folded against his chest.

"What's going on with you?" she asked, rubbing her upper arm.

"Are you Shark's sister?"

Her sheepish look sunk his heart. He slammed his hand on a locker. "Why the fuck didn't you tell me?" He wiped away the spittle that had formed in the corners of his mouth.

Mia looked up at him. "Calm down."

"I have no intention of calming down. I trusted you!" He pounded and kicked the locker, the clash of metal resounding through the room. Mia flinched and he kicked the locker harder.

"I was afraid you'd stop us right when we were beginning," she answered softly.

"So, you knew? *Fuck!*"

"Not when I first met you. I only knew when you told me you were a member of the Night Rebels. I really liked you a lot and decided that I'd tell you later on."

"*You* decided. Did it ever occur to you that I would want to know something like that?"

"It did—that's why I didn't say anything. I was afraid you'd leave if you knew. I was planning on telling you when you came tomorrow. Remember, I told you I wanted to talk to you about something the other day when you had to go back to Alina? Well, I was ready to tell you then. I felt like we'd reached a place where we both trusted and cared for each other."

"Trust? Don't fuckin' use that word. You deceived me."

"Technically … yes, but it didn't make any difference what club you belonged to. I have nothing to do with your club or my brother's. I'm not involved with any of it. Please don't let this affect us."

"Did you give Shark info about the clubhouse?"

Her eyes glistened. "How could you think that?"

"Because I had to find out you were that fucker's sister in front of the club. Everyone knew but me. I don't know what to believe from you. You deceived me and lost my trust, *sweetheart.*"

"I didn't think it mattered. Just because my brother is president of some club doesn't mean I'm a part of it. It's like Taylor and Asher aren't a part of the Night Rebels. I didn't tell you because I didn't think it was important. Even if the Satan's Pistons didn't exist, I'd still be me. You're condemning me for who my brother is. That's so unfair. When I found out you were a Night Rebel, I didn't see your club—I saw *you*. You would still be you whether you were in the club or not."

"You don't know what the fuck you're talking about. The Night Rebels *is* who I am."

Mia took a few steps toward him. "Okay, I understand that, but I don't give one fuck about the Satan's Pistons. I don't even see or talk to my brother very often. His club doesn't involve me, and him being my brother shouldn't be a big deal with you, unless you're mad because you lost face in front of your club."

Army shook his head. "I'm pissed because you didn't trust me enough to tell me. I gave you what I'd never given to any other woman—my trust and my love. You threw both in the goddamn trash!"

"Stop, Army, please. You're not the only one who gave something—I love you too. I've never said those words to any man. Our love must supersede the hatred between your club and my brother's. Don't let it come between us." She wiped her cheeks. "I don't want to lose you."

He pressed his lips together in a slight grimace while he rubbed his hand against the front of his shirt, near his heart. He wanted to gather her into his arms and kiss her until she pulled away, breathless and satisfied, but he just stood there watching her silently cry. "It's not that easy. The brotherhood is who I am."

She sniffed and took out a tissue from the pocket of her top and blew her nose. "I understand that and love you for your sense of loyalty and family, but you're still your own person and would be with or without the club. I'm not expecting you to give up the club, but we can still be together. A lot of your members have women in their lives."

"The club won't accept you," he said in a low voice. Her bottom lip trembled and he wanted to slip it between his teeth and soothe it.

"I'm not dating the club—I'm dating you." She stared at him with those big, beautiful shimmering eyes.

"It's just not that easy. I *am* the brotherhood and it's me."

"Do you accept me?" she asked in a voice he could barely hear.

His gaze locked with hers as he stood mutely. A plethora of emotions were going through him: how she made him feel, his anger at her deception—yet he couldn't imagine a life without her, how he'd die for the brotherhood, and the fact her fuckin' brother was president of the damn Pistons. It was too much. *I need to get the fuck outta here and go for a ride. I have to clear my head of all this shit.*

"Are you going to answer me?" she asked.

He took perverse satisfaction in the hurt that flashed through her eyes an instant before tears spilled down her face. *Dammit. I hate to see her cry.* He longed to wipe them away and pull her into his arms and feel the heat of her body while he told her it'd all be okay. *But how can it? The club won't recognize her. This will alienate some of the brothers from me. There'll be tension, fights, and ... no trust. It can never work.*

"I guess you answered me." Her voice hitched.

"Is everything okay?" Taylor asked, his gaze darting between Mia and Army.

Mia mumbled something Army couldn't hear and then rushed out of the locker room. Taylor glared at him. "What the hell did you do to Mia?"

"Did she tell you her brother was the president of the Satan's Pistons?"

Taylor shook his head. "I'm assuming that's another motorcycle club, and she didn't tell me. Why would she, and why does it matter?"

"The fuckers are our rivals."

"And what does that have to do with Mia? Is she in the club too?"

Army chuckled in spite of himself. "No, dude, she's not a damn Piston."

"Then what's the problem? Why should what her brother does interfere with what you and Mia have going on? It seems dumb."

"You just don't fuckin' get it because you're a citizen. It matters."

"You can't be serious. You're finding Mia guilty by association just because her brother happens to be in a club the Night Rebels are feuding with?

"This doesn't concern you," Army grumbled.

"Mia's my friend and she's been hurt."

"Then she shouldn't have played a fuckin' game with me. I treated her right. I didn't keep shit from her. Go console your *friend* and listen to her bullshit. I'm outta here." Army slammed his fist into locker again then stalked out while ignoring Taylor's pleas; he disregarded the looks from the fighters, and paid absolutely no attention to Mia, whom he saw near the front door.

*Fuck all of them.*

He stormed into the parking lot and jumped on his bike and revved the engine, drowning all sound except the voice in his head. *How the fuck did this happen?* Ice ran through his veins. *I know how. I fucked up by giving her my trust and my heart.*

*Never again.*

# Chapter Twenty-Two

"**T**HIS IS SO screwed up," Ronica said as she buttered her croissant. "I never thought this motorcycle club thing would matter. It's so medieval. If he chooses some stupid-ass feud over you then he doesn't deserve you. You're an intelligent, strong, and vibrant woman who deserves so much better than all this bullshit. And what the fuck's up with your brother?" She took a bite and looked at Mia, waiting for her response.

Mia forced a smile and played with the sugar cube that came with her café au lait. *I can always count on Ronica to pull me up.* "You're right, it's just that it hurts so bad. It's been three days, and I thought for sure he'd call me by now. I get that he was pissed and shocked to find out that Vic's my brother, and I know it hurt worse that the knowledge came from his club and not from me, but get over it already. I can't believe that he'd walk away." She crushed the cube between her thumb and forefinger, and the white powder looked like snow as it fell on the tablecloth.

"I still can't believe it. He really seemed into you. I'm so sorry," Ronica said.

"He told me he loved me." Mia's voice hitched.

"I didn't know that."

"I would've been ecstatic about it if the circumstances were different." Mia pushed her uneaten croissant away from her. "I just don't know what else to do. I've texted and called him so many times that it's starting to feel like I'm a fucking stalker or something. He hasn't reached out at all. I guess it's over." She blinked rapidly.

"I don't know what to say. The guy's an asshole for what he's doing to you."

"He's just really hurt, but I didn't mean to hurt him. I'd hoped he'd look past all the bullshit with my brother and his dumb club. If I wasn't in such pain, I'd be rolling on the floor over the ridiculousness of the situation."

"Let me know how I can help. If you want to go out and get drunk on Saturday, I'm there. I can bring you a care package of chocolates or bubble bath—or how about some red wine, and cheese and crackers?"

Mia laughed. "That sounds great, but I don't think my trainer would agree. I guess I want to spend a few days feeling sorry for myself, but I may be sick of my self-pity by Saturday and give you a call. For the next few nights, I'm going to be sweating my grief out at Champion. I'll bounce back … I always do."

"Okay. I just hate that you have to go through this."

Mia glanced at her phone, her insides twisting when she saw there were no messages or calls from Army. "It sucks, but I did love being with him." Her bottom lip trembled and she bit it.

"I hate to leave, but I have an appointment in about fifteen minutes. Are you coming back to the salon?"

She shook her head. "I'm done for the day. I'm going to Champion. I need a good, mindless run. I'm just going to finish my coffee. See you tomorrow."

Ronica opened her purse and laid down a ten-dollar bill. "That should cover my share and tip. I'll call you later tonight." She scooted the chair back and stood up then walked out of the coffee shop.

Mia stared at her phone, willing Army to contact her. It'd only been three days since she'd seen him, but it felt like years. Her body ached for him and her mind craved his conversation. She missed everything about Army: his scent, his laugh, his touch, his kisses, the sound of his voice … *How could you leave me … us? You told me you loved me, yet you left me. I miss you too much.* She dabbed the corners of her eyes with the napkin and took several deep breaths. After all they had shared, the only thing she had left was the raw pain of an aching heart.

Mia quickly wiped the wetness from her cheeks and picked up the bill and went to the front counter. On the way to Champion, she tortured herself as she drove by the restaurants they'd gone to, the streets they'd walked down hand-in-hand, and the clubs they'd danced at. Staring at Sound Nightclub's unlit sign, she could feel his hands skim over her body as they danced close together with her head resting on his chest as she listened to his heartbeat. Mia pulled over and placed her head on top of her hands on the steering wheel. *I can't believe it's over. I love him and he loves me. How can it end?* Several minutes later, she swallowed hard and squared her shoulders then pulled away from the curb and headed over to Champion.

No one but Taylor knew what had happened between her and Army. The day he had pounded the crap out of the lockers, no one had noticed; the music had been blaring and they'd had several mini matches going on, so most of the fighters were at the other end of the gym. Mia was grateful for that because the last thing she wanted to do was answer a bunch of questions or see the pitiful look in anyone's eyes.

She'd just changed into her sports clothes to run a few laps around the gym before training. Mia noticed Taylor standing by the ring watching Raptor and Chainsaw spar. As soon as his gaze met hers, he gave her a wan smile. She waved at him, but before he could make his way over to her she walked up to the lap lane, put in her earbuds, and started jogging slowly. Images of Army stabbed her brain as she began to run, hoping to clear her mind. She turned up the music, desperate to not think or feel anything.

As she ran around the gym, tears poured down her face. *Why am I so upset? Once he found out who my brother was, I knew he'd never stay.* What had she expected? That he'd leave his club for her or risk the members' lives just because they had something before all the chaos erupted? She wiped her cheeks, but the tears kept coming. The pounding music didn't drown out her thoughts. She tore out her earbuds and they dangled past her waist and bumped against her thighs as she picked up the pace. Her feelings were all jumbled like hangers at the bottom of a closet. *Did he really love me?* Mia ran faster, ignoring the pain in her left calf. *How could I never see him again?* He'd crashed into her life with all the finesse of an angry bull, and now he'd walked away and shattered her life by his silence.

"Mia! Stop!" Taylor's voice boomed behind her, but she just picked up the speed even though her body screamed in discomfort.

Taylor was also gaining speed, so she pushed on until her chest suddenly became constricted, then she began to wheeze as she tried to gulp in air. Taylor grabbed her arm, and she collapsed on the ground into a weeping, gasping mess.

"Don't take it so hard, Mia." He drew her into his arms, and she rested her head against his chest. "I'm so sorry," he whispered as he held her.

As her breathing slowly returned to normal, she realized that she wasn't having a heart attack; it was just her heart breaking into a million pieces.

"What the fuck were you doing?" Rick's voice sounded jagged like broken glass.

"She's okay now," Taylor answered.

"Bullshit." Rick bent down and gently straightened her left leg.

"Ow!" The rush of pain felt like a hot poker stabbing her.

"You're injured. Why the hell did you keep running on an injured leg?" Rick's fingers lightly massaged her calf. "We need to ice this. I'll help you up, then lean on Taylor and me. Don't put any weight on your leg."

Numb from pain and sadness, Mia nodded.

Later that day, as she sat with her wrapped leg up on the ottoman, she absently stroked Pumpkin's soft fur. The soreness in her leg was nothing compared to the pain inside her: a plethora of broken memories and burning flesh. Her aching heart throbbed all the time during her waking hours, and she couldn't find any relief from it.

Mia leaned her head back and closed her eyes. The last conversation she had with Army haunted and taunted her, replaying through her mind like an echo. Her insides burned as if red hot coals had somehow replaced them, and other times she felt raw as if a winter wind was blowing right through her skin. His silence tormented her.

*One day we were together and happy, and now we're not. How am I ever going to get over losing the love of my life?*

*Fuck you, Vic.*

*Fuck you, Army.*

*Fuck everything.*

# Chapter Twenty-Three

A RMY CLEANED OUT the ashes in the fireplace before he'd locked up the cabin. For the past three days he'd gone to his dad's cabin nestled in the San Juan Mountains. His dad used to take him and his brothers fishing a lot when they were young, but he hadn't been back to the cabin in years.

Army needed to be close to nature to think. After leaving Champion that day, he'd bought a burner phone and called Steel to give him the number. He'd told Steel that he didn't want to be disturbed unless it was an emergency. He turned off his main phone because he didn't want to hear from anyone, especially Mia. He still couldn't wrap his head around the fact that she was Shark's sister. *Why couldn't she trust me enough to tell me?* He dragged his hand through his hair before emptying the cold ashes on the dirt in back of the cabin.

A soft breeze sang through the trees, and he looked up and saw gold and orange leaves spinning in the air, and a tinge of sadness pricked his heart. The colors reminded him of Mia's eyes: golden with streaks of copper running through them. He clenched his jaw and walked back into the cabin to gather his things before heading back to Alina. He'd take the back roads and try not to remember how Mia felt pressed against his back with her arms hugging his waist as they rode to Chaco Canyon.

Army shrugged on his jacket and the faint scent of her still lingered. *Dammit!* He missed her like hell. He couldn't just forget her and get on with his life like he had when his mom had walked out on them. This was different. Mia hadn't walked away ... *he* had. For what? *Because she's some fucker's sister? She told me she was afraid I'd leave her and that's exactly what I did. Mia ... I miss you, babe.* Maybe she was right about him losing face in front of his club. Crow had been a total asshole about it and he'd seen the smirks of some of the other brothers as if to say that she just used him. He knew in his heart that she didn't. *No one knows what we have. I know her love for me is real and mine sure as fuck is for her.*

He packed a few things in his saddle bags, then he straddled his bike, switched on the engine, and rode down the dirt road. Gold aspen trees mixed with dark-green pines lined the backroads while the magnificent peaks towered over the foliage of the San Cristobal Valley. As he passed through mountain meadows, canyons, and colorful foothills, all he could think about was how he wished Mia were with him so they could share the breathtaking vistas together.

As he neared Alina, the sun painted the sky a reddish pink and smoky purple streaks as it began its descent over the craggy mountain tops. The whole ride back, the colors of fall reminded him of Mia. The nutty scent of damp earth mingled with the aroma of burning logs made Army smile as he remembered the times they had rushed into Mia's house after a light rain and she'd turn on the fake fire. He'd kid her about it, then they'd both fall on the couch in a laughing heap. Then, he'd catch the scent of her shampoo as it wrapped around her and before they knew it, they'd be making out like a couple of teenagers.

Army kicked the loose stones on the concrete as he walked toward the front of the clubhouse. Eagle reclined against the stucco wall smoking a joint as he approached.

"Want one?" he asked Army, holding out his hand.

Army tilted his head and put the joint between his lips then lit it. He inhaled deeply, looking out at the saffron-colored glow behind the mountains. A few stars sparkled in the darkened sky to the east.

"How're things with the family?" Eagle asked.

"Good." Army blew out and a shroud of smoke hazed around them. He glanced sideways and saw Eagle's eyes on him.

"No matter what you decide, I'm with you, bro." Eagle dropped his roach and ground it with his boot. He pushed off the wall and went into the clubhouse.

The aroma of smoky fajitas that came from the open windows of the main room reminded Army of their first date at El Señor Sol. Since that night, they'd gone back many times, and she teased him about his obsession with Mexican food. He took out his regular phone and turned it on—several messages and missed calls from Mia flashed on the screen. He slid the phone into his pocket again.

Eagle came back out with a tumbler filled with whiskey. He handed it to him and leaned back against the wall.

Army took a long drink from the glass. One of the many things he loved about Mia was how easy she was to talk to. They could discuss anything—barbecue ribs and action films, past relationships and family stuff, or character flaws and personal failings. They shared their darkest thoughts and he fed her wicked desires while she fed his. That's why he was hooked and totally in love with her. *I can't let her go. I've been a fuckin' idiot.* She had gotten into his heart when he wasn't looking, and he knew she'd stay forever if he made things right.

"Is Steel or Paco around?" Army asked.

"Yeah. They're watching Raven kick Brutus' ass in pool. When the hell's he gonna learn that Raven just a better pool player than he is?" Eagle chuckled.

"Probably never. Is it family night?"

"Yeah. Lena just put out the food."

Once a month the clubhouse hosted family night for the old ladies, girlfriends, and children of the brothers. The club girls stayed out of sight, mostly hanging in their rooms or going into town for a movie or dinner. If they came back and the old ladies were still there, they'd use the back entrance and go directly to their rooms.

"I'm going in." Army lightly pounded Eagle's arm. "Thanks, bro."

Steel and Paco stood against the bar with their arms draped around their old ladies. Breanna glanced over at him and waved too enthusiastically, and he knew that Steel had told her about Mia. Army lifted his chin and walked over to the buffet table where he grabbed a plate and heaped some rice and fajitas onto it. He sat at a table away from everyone and didn't meet the glares of Crow, Skull, and Shotgun. Glancing sideways at Crow, he knew he'd broken his nose, but he'd do it again if he talked trash about Mia.

The chair across from him scraped on the floor, and Army looked up into Steel's gaze. He jerked his chin at the president then kept eating.

"Did you decide what the fuck you're going to do about Shark's sister?" Steel asked.

Army shoved a forkful of rice into his mouth. Nodding as he chewed, he picked up his drink and took a swig.

"What's your decision?"

"I'm getting an apartment. I get how you and the club feel about Mia, but I know she's sincere. We got something going and I don't give a fuck that she's asshole's sister, and she doesn't give a fuck that the Night Rebels hate her brother's club." He took another bite and chewed slowly, watching Steel who sat stone-faced across from him.

"What's going on?" Paco asked, sitting down.

"I was listening to Army's decision about Shark's sister," Steel replied.

Army reclined in the chair. "She's got a name—Mia. I'm staying with her. The club may not like it, but there's nothing in the bylaws against me having a rival fucker's sister as my woman."

"Did you think how this is going to play out?" Paco said.

"Yeah. If she can't come to the club, I get it and she'll get it too. She's not involved in the club wars. She just happens to be the sister of a sonofabitch." Army splayed his hands on the table. "She's important to me, and I can't let her go."

"You're a fuckin' pussy!" Crow's angry voice boomed through the room. Suddenly, all eyes were on Army.

He darted his gaze around the room, and from the look on some of the members' faces, he knew they agreed with Crow. "Maybe, but I think Steel, Paco, Diablo, Sangre and some of the others understand what I'm saying."

"None of the old ladies have deep ties to a rival MC," Steel said in a low voice.

Paco cleared his throat. "We see this relationship as a problem because we can't trust her. You're looking at it with your cock, and we're looking at it objectively."

"Bullshit. What I have with Mia is more than sexual." Loud rumbles echoed around the brothers. "It's true. I can't walk away from her, but I don't want to lose the brotherhood."

"How much shit did you tell her when you were inside her pussy?" Skull asked.

Army scowled at him. "I'm gonna let that pass this time, but you say one more thing even remotely disrespectful about Mia, we're gonna have a round in the yard."

"What did you tell her?" Steel asked.

Army's chest tightened as anger crawled up his spine. "The same thing you tell Breanna." He looked at Paco. "Or Chelsea." He slammed his fist on the table, knocking over the empty glass. "Give me a fuckin' break! I'm a Night Rebel through and through. I'd die for any of you. Any one of you pussies want to challenge me on *that*?"

"We're not disputing your loyalty," Paco said. "It's just that you really need to think about what you're doing. If she's bullshitting you, you're putting the whole club in jeopardy."

Army snapped his gaze to the vice president's. "Isn't that what Steel told you when you moved Chelsea into the clubhouse? You argued for her because you believed her—you trusted your gut. That's where I'm at, and my gut is telling me Mia's not involved. I respect the way you all feel, and that's why I'm moving out of the clubhouse."

Paco stood up. "I hope you're doing the right thing in trusting her."

Army held his chin up. "I am." He watched him and Steel walk back to where the old ladies sat. Chelsea caught his eyes and smiled at him, then turned away when Paco came over to her.

The other brothers dispersed and headed back to the bar and the pool table. Army took out his phone.

**Army:** *I've been a fuckin' fool, babe. Coming to Durango.*

In less than a second the phone pinged.

**Mia:** *U have. Bout time u realized it.*

He threw his head back and roared. Damn she got his blood going.

**Army:** *I'm leaving now. Be ready. Makeup sex is the best.*

**Mia:** *U put me through 3 days of hell. Ur crazy if u think ur getting it that easily.*

Army grinned knowing full well that she would make him grovel, and he was totally up to the challenge. She was his wildcat, and he would've been disappointed if she greeted him with open legs.

**Army:** *Leaving soon.*

**Mia:** *xoxo. Luv u.*

**Army:** *Me 2.*

He got up and went to his room to take a shower and pack a few things. When he came back to the main room, he walked over to Steel.

"I'm going to Durango for a few days. Lil' Donnie said that the buy is gonna happen in ten days. I'll be back before then. Chad and Brutus can cover Lust for me. Call me on my phone if you need me back sooner."

"We can manage without you for a couple of days," Steel said, grasping his shoulder. "I need you fuckin' focused when we take the Pistons and the 39th Street punks down."

"I'll be laser sharp. No worries about that." He bumped fists with Paco and Eagle then walked out of the club, acutely aware that his brothers' eyes were glued on him. He jumped on his bike and sped off.

BEFORE ARMY GOT off his bike, Mia ran over to him and threw her arms around his neck, covering his face in soft kisses. He chuckled as he pivoted toward her, wrapping his arms around her waist.

"Hey, baby," he growled, then he seized her lips in a furious, possessive kiss.

"I'm so pissed at you," she said as she pulled back a little.

"And …?" Army claimed her mouth again, smothering her answer as his hand roamed down her body and cupped her ass, squeezing it hard. As Mia sank into him, he pulled her up onto the leather seat, shifting her until she sat facing forward in front of him. He grabbed a fistful of her hair and yanked it hard, then slipped his tongue between her gasping lips and into the sweet recesses of her mouth. She tasted like wine and smelled of lemon and cinnamon. And he missed her every fucking minute they'd been apart. He plunged in deeper, loving the whimpers climbing up her throat and the way her nails dug into his back underneath his shirt.

"Let's go inside," she murmured against his lips.

"Anything you say, babe," he said before deepening the kiss for a while longer. He eased back, and the corner of his mouth turned up slightly. Mia kissed him quickly on the lips, then pulled her leg up and over and jumped off the bike.

"Park your bike in the garage," she said over her shoulder as she ambled across the lawn. "I'll open it for you." She disappeared into the house and soon the garage door slowly opened.

When Army came inside, he tossed his bag on the floor near the back door and gathered her into his arms again, but she twisted out of them and went to the refrigerator.

"Do you want a beer?" she asked.

"I want you," he said, coming over to her.

"I'm mad at you. Why didn't you return my texts or calls?" Her amber eyes sparked.

"I had my phone turned off." He took the beer from her and popped open the tab.

"That's it?" Mia slammed the fridge door.

"I went to think at my dad's cabin in the mountains. I had to clear my head."

"Why couldn't you have told me, *then* turned off your damn phone? I didn't know what happened to you." Her voice cracked.

Army put the beer down on the counter and tugged her close to him. "I'm sorry, darlin'. I wasn't thinking. I was so fuckin' pissed and confused that I needed to be alone for a while."

"I thought you dumped me," she said, the words muffling against his shirt.

He drew back and his gaze met hers. "I could never do that, babe. I was just pissed that you didn't tell me about the fuc ... about Shark. I had to digest it. I admit I was shocked off my ass when I found out you have the same blood as that ... him."

"I should've told you."

"Yeah ... you should have, but now I know and it's okay."

"Really?"

He picked up his beer and led her into the living room where they sat down on the couch. He just noticed the gauze around her calf. He ran his hand over it.

"What happened?"

"I sprained it or something when I was doing laps. Rick patched me up."

"That sucks. I'm sorry, babe."

"I'm supposed to keep off my leg as much as possible, but my job doesn't really allow for that. The worst thing is that I can't wear heels. I'm going crazy."

Army laughed then brushed his lips across hers. "You're kooky, but I love it."

Snickers jumped up and rubbed her face against his knee.

Mia laughed. "She's so shy around people. I can't believe she did that." Not to be outdone, Pumpkin leapt onto his lap and Army chuckled. "They missed you too," she said softly.

Army kissed her gently then pointed at the tabby. "Can you help me with this?"

Mia scooped Pumpkin up and plopped her down on the other side of Army. "She likes to snuggle."

He snagged Mia around her shoulder and drew her closer. "I know her owner loves it." He kissed her deep and hard then pulled away. "It's important for you to understand something."

Worry flashed in her eyes. "What?" she asked in a barely audible voice.

He locked his gaze with hers. "Make no mistake about who and what I am. I'm a Night Rebel and I protect the brotherhood to the death. Satan's Pistons—your brother's fuckin' club—is my enemy. It'll never be any other way."

She leaned closer to him. "What does that mean?"

"I'd kill him in a heartbeat."

She sat back, soaking in that knowledge.

"Still want to be with me?"

She lifted her chin. "Yes."

Surprise marred his chiseled face.

"Mia." His thumb moved, smoothing back and forth under her lip, and he dipped his head down. She tilted her head back and their lips met in a fiery kiss.

"Let's go to the bedroom," he rasped.

"I'm still pissed at you, remember?" she said between tiny nips to his lips.

"I thought you were screwing around."

"I wasn't. You're back to first base."

"Damn, you're hard, babe." He pushed her down on the couch and hovered over her. "First base isn't so bad," he said before crushing his mouth on hers. What mattered at that moment was—Mia was back in his life, and she understood who he was.

Everything else would fall into place.

# Chapter Twenty-Four

"YOU HEARD FROM him," Ronica said, her dark eyes dancing with excitement.

Mia grinned as she mixed two colors together in the salon's back room. "One better—he came by yesterday. When he texted me and told me he'd been an idiot, I almost died. Take it from me—it's huge that he admitted he was at fault."

"I bet the homecoming was wild." Ronica raised her eyebrows in an exaggerated way.

Mia chuckled. "Not as wild as he would've liked, I'm sure; since he put me through the ringer for the past few days, he needs to get back into my good graces."

"Has he started doing it?"

"He made me steak and eggs for breakfast this morning. Oh, and there was a vase filled with fresh flowers on the table."

"That's impressive. He must've gone to the store before you woke up," Ronica said.

"I had the food in the fridge already, and I know he picked the flowers from the pots around the community." Mia laughed. "I love him even more for doing it. He's my sweet badass rebel."

"Now for the important question—did he do the dishes afterwards?"

Mia bobbed her head several times. "Yes! He *so* wants a home run."

Ronica shook her head. "You're so bad, but you sure know how to handle him."

She rinsed off the stir spatula and picked up the bowl. "I'm so fucking crazy about him. I've never been this happy in all my life."

"I'm thrilled Army did the right thing. You deserve to be happy."

"I do. I better get back to my client. I'm not sure how long Army is staying, but if he's here for the weekend, let's double date and go out for dinner. I know Stuart is into motorcycles so he'd have that in common with Army."

"Sounds good. Stuart's been talking about getting one since we first met two years ago." Ronica giggled. "He'll love meeting an actual biker who owns a Harley-Davidson."

"Let's plan on it then. I better go." Mia left the room and went back to her station.

The rest of the day went by quickly, and she could hardly wait to get home and fix a gourmet dinner for Army. She still felt squeamish about going out, although she hadn't seen the guy with the red sports car since Vic had called her. Mia hoped Vic would just forget about the whole thing, but she knew that wouldn't happen. Army seemed to be able to take care of himself, but she still worried over what Vic would do.

When she drove down her street, she smiled and a warm tingle ran through her when she noticed a few less flowers in some of the pots. Mia threw her tote on the counter and leafed through her mail.

The door to the guest bathroom opened and excitement skated over her skin. *Army's home.* She put the mail down next to her bag and walked into the living room. She stopped dead in her tracks when she saw Vic glowering at her. *Shit! I forgot to put the alarm on.* Her stomach pitched. Swallowing, she gathered the tattered edges of her courage.

"Hi. How have you been?"

"This isn't a fuckin' social call, you fuckin' slut." He took a few steps toward her.

Anger began overtaking her fear. "You break into *my* house and then call me a *slut*? I don't think so. If you can't be civil, you'll have to go."

"Shut the fuck up! You don't tell me shit. I can't stand to look at you!" he yelled, spittle flying out of his mouth.

"Then don't look at me. Go." She stepped back, but he rushed up to her.

"You've been fucking a goddamn Night Rebel. You're a damn traitor!" Spit sprayed her face.

Her heart was like a train pounding down the tracks. She knew she should diffuse the situation or it would just escalate, but by now, her anger had totally overpowered her fear. "I'm not a traitor. I have nothing to do with your club and whomever I date is my business, not yours."

"We're blood, you stupid cunt. You owe an allegiance to me."

"It's funny how you didn't remember that when we were growing up and you were so mean to me and Finn." She tossed her head. "You have too much fucking time on your hands. Why don't you get a damn job so you wouldn't obsess over my personal life?"

He came closer and she could feel the burn of the angry heat emanating from him. "You've always thought you were so damn smart, but you're not. You're just a bitch who needs to be taught a lesson. I know who you've been fucking. And this Army fucker's got family in Durango. A real cute nephew."

Her blood ran cold as icy shivers raced and down her spine. "You couldn't be that evil to hurt innocent people, especially a baby. Leave his family alone. Leave all of it alone. This is crazy, Vic, don't you see that?"

"You don't think that your fucker or any of the other Rebels would do the same if one of their sisters were fucking one of my brothers? They'd do worse, bitch. Those assholes are ruthless and wouldn't hesitate to kill a woman or a child. They play dirty, and the man you think gives a shit about you wouldn't bat an eye if his club told him to slit your throat. So … I'm leaving shit alone."

*Vic knows nothing but anger and hate. He'll never let this go. I couldn't live with myself if he hurt Army's family. Maybe I should just walk away. I don't know what the right thing to do is.* The sweet scent from the flowers Army had picked for her that morning wafted around her, dispelling the confusion of her thoughts. She threw back her shoulders and lifted her chin. "Get out. Now."

Shark took a step closer to her then hauled off and slapped her hard across the face. "I told you not to tell me what to do, cunt!"

Mia cried out and her cats scurried away. Snickers disappeared into the other room, but Pumpkin went to a corner and hissed at Vic. He looked over at the cat, and Mia took the opportunity to immobilize him before he beat the hell out of her. Adrenaline pumped through her as she used all her strength and lunged forward. The pain in her calf screamed, but she ignored it and bent low beneath his arms. In one fluid Brazilian jiu jitsu move, she pushed hard then pulled Vic under her, taking him with her as they crashed down to the hardwood floor.

"Fuck!" he yelled out as they rolled around on the ground.

Mia jabbed his side hard with her knee, and he gasped and stalled just enough for the seconds she needed to gain the dominant position on top of him. She knew if she didn't keep Shark down that he'd beat her to death, so she gave it her all and managed to straddle him. He smelled of stale beer, cigarettes, and sweat.

"Get the fuck off me, cunt. I'm gonna give it to you—"

She smashed her fist and elbows into his face several times until she heard something splinter; blood gushed from his nose and he bucked forward.

"You're fuckin' dead!"

"I'm going to call the cops," she panted as she kept up the assault to his face even though blood was still pouring from it. Sharp jolts of excruciating pain burned the nerves in her leg, and she wouldn't be able to hold him down much longer. Taking several deep breaths, she jumped up and ran outside. She limped down to the curb and waved at her next door neighbor—a firefighter.

Vic came bursting out the door, screaming and cussing. The neighbor put down the hose and walked over.

"Everything okay?" Taber asked, his gaze fixed on Vic's face.

Vic had a wad of paper towels against his nose. He glared.

"Yeah," Mia said, glancing over at Vic. "My brother was just leaving." She took a few steps closer to Taber.

Vic stared angrily at her, hate flashing in his eyes. As he walked to his bike, he stopped next to her and hissed in her ear, "You're gonna pay for what you did, cunt. And if you ever try that MMA shit on me again,

I'll fuckin' kill you."

She shuddered as his words scraped along her spine. Long after he'd gone, she stared at the street as her body slowly came down from the adrenaline high she'd been on for the past hour.

As she limped up the sidewalk, she waved at Taber and made a mental note to send over a plate of cookies for him and his family. If he hadn't been outside, she wasn't sure what would have happened. She locked the door and turned on the alarm then hobbled into the kitchen to get two ice packs from the freezer: one for her face and one for her leg.

Grabbing a pillow, she slipped it under her head as she lay down on the couch. Snickers jumped up and snuggled next to her while Pumpkin stretched out on top of the sofa.

"I guess it's pizza tonight, girls."

She picked up the remote and turned on the television.

MIA WOKE UP to the touch of Army lips on her, kissing her gently. She curled her arms around his neck and tugged him closer, relishing the taste and scent of him.

"Perfect way to wake up from a nap," she murmured.

"What the fuck happened, baby?" he whispered before pressing his mouth softly on hers.

The memory of Vic's visit tore through her mind, and she gripped Army's shoulders and pushed him back. "I had a bad time at training."

He swept his tongue over her lips. "Want to try the truth this time?" he asked before straightening up.

*What will he do if I tell him Vic was here? I feel like I'm on a damn runaway train.*

His cool hand soothed the right side of her face. "We've gotta be honest with each other no matter what. I don't want you keeping shit from me, and I wouldn't keep it from you unless it's club business." He bent down and kissed her forehead. "Let's try this again. Who the fuck hit you?"

"Vic," she whispered. For a split second, his hand stopped moving then it started up again.

"Tell me about it."

"He knows it's you, and he's so mad at me. He knows your family lives here and he brought up Joshua in a way that made me think he was planning to hurt him and maybe your brother and sister-in-law. I couldn't stand it if anything happened to them because of me.

"Nothing will," he replied calmly as he kept caressing her face.

"How do you know?" She pushed upon her elbows, then sat upright with her back supported by the arm of the couch.

"I just do. Did he hit you anywhere else?" He picked up the ice pack that had fallen on the floor while she'd been asleep, and stood up. "Did you want me to get you some ice from the freezer while this gets cold again?"

Mia tugged at his hand. "It's okay—just leave it alone."

He eased back down and shifted back against the seat cushions, crossing one leg over the other before putting her feet up on his thigh. He turned to her, a light smile playing on his lips.

"When Vic hit me, I knew I had to defend myself." She scratched Pumpkin under her chin. "This one helped me out by distracting him, then I moved in. I think I might have broken his nose. I never thought I'd be using my fighting skills to defend myself from my own brother."

Army's eyes shone with pride. "You are so fuckin' awesome—my incredible, sexy wildcat. Don't feel guilty about what you did. No dude should ever hit a chick."

"I don't feel guilty, but I do feel sad about it." She shook her head slightly. "I guess I just feel bad that my whole family is so screwed up."

"*You* didn't make it that way. Look at what you've accomplished for yourself. Don't blame yourself for what your brothers do."

"Now you sound like my therapist." Mia shifted on the couch. "When Vic threatened your family, I thought that maybe it'd be simpler if we backed off a bit. It's no longer just about us—it's your club and family. I don't know." Mia looked down at the cushion, picking off imaginary lint.

Army brought his hand to her face and slowly traced from her forehead to her jawline with his fingers, then gently ran his thumb over her bottom lip. "I want to always be with you," he said in a low voice.

Mia tilted her head back, and he leaned forward and peppered her skin with kisses. She moaned softly. "It just seems like everything is against us."

"Only if we let it be," he said, his husky tones sending tingles down her spine.

Her heart twisted. *Things are already so complicated. I fear for Army and his family.* She reached out and stroked his cheek, the stubble rough like sandpaper against her fingertips. Tenderness shone in his eyes, and she knew that no matter what happened she could never be without him in her life. He was the ache between her legs, the shivers on her skin, and the love in her heart.

"I love you, babe. No matter what goes down, you need to remember that and never fuckin' doubt it." He nipped the sensitive part of her skin, right below her earlobe.

"And I love you so much. I can't find the words to tell you how much," she whispered.

His gaze smoldered with fire as he stared fixedly at her. And then they were kissing, tongues touching. He looped his arm around her waist and pulled her up a bit as he bent down, deepening a kiss that made her toes curl. Mia clung to him as though he was the only thing grounding her in their topsy-turvy world.

"Mia," he whispered as he nipped her bottom lip before plunging back into the recesses of her mouth.

Army's hands were all over her body, and she reached down and grabbed one of them, slipping it under her skirt. Surprise flickered in his blues, then they darkened as he pulled her panties aside and slid his finger over her hardening nub. His touch lit her up like a blazing torch under him, and she moaned. She pulled at his belt, fumbling with the buckle until he gently pushed her hands away and undid it himself, then he unzipped his jeans and tugged them past his hips, his shaft poking against her flesh. Her fingers curved around his hardness, and she squeezed tight as her thumb glided over the smooth top of his dick.

"Fuck, baby," he groaned, as he lowered his head and pressed his lips to the base of her throat before they coasted over her collarbone. "I've missed your touch," he rasped, his words smothered against her skin. He gripped the hem of her shirt and shoved it up under her chin. Mia held her breath as she watched him pull down the cups of her ivory bra, the golden light from the setting sun spilling over her breasts.

"Baby," he said, his voice thick. Army covered one of her nipples with his mouth and sucked hard while his finger flicked the other one.

A deep groan crawled up her throat and escaped from her parted lips as she arched her back. As he played with her breasts, she slid her hand slowly up and down his dick, loving the way his breathing quickened. Wild tremors sparked through her when he pulled away from her, then looked down and watched as she stroked him. She reached under and tickled his balls and he stilled her hand. Her gaze snapped up to his.

"You're too good at this, babe," he said.

Suddenly, they tugged and pulled at each other's clothes, constantly kissing and caressing. He hovered over her, his gaze locked on hers. "I need to be inside you," he growled.

Army didn't wait, and she didn't want him to.

Mia spread her legs open: she was wet and wild and ready to have him. Placing his hands on top of the couch's arm, he plunged into her and everything locked into place as they clung to each other, fused together by their raw passion and love, never wanting to let go. Over and over he thrust into her, grinding his pelvic bone against her pulsing nub. Their sweat-slickened bodies moved together in a faster and more-crazed rhythm with skin slapping against skin. Mia clutched his shoulders as she arched her back, rocking her hips tight to him. His thick cock filled every inch of her, and her tight walls clenched around him.

"Fuck, baby," he panted.

With a scream, she came, wrapping her legs tighter around his waist as she bucked and writhed from waves of ecstasy that crashed over her body.

A rumbling groan burst from deep within Army and he collapsed, his head resting on her chest, as both of them gasped for breath and their heartbeats thrummed wildly. Mia tangled her fingers in his hair, squeezing her legs tighter around him.

"Damn, babe," he grunted.

"Army," she whispered.

He pushed up and brought his face close to hers. "I love you so fuckin' much," he said, then covered her face with soft, gentle kisses before claiming her mouth.

Mia put her hands on each side of his face and pulled him up at bit. "I love you too," she said softly then kissed him deeply.

They lay on the couch, entwined together until moonlight seeped in from the living room's window, illuminating their bodies in a soft, shimmering glow. Mia looked toward the window and watched the streetlight in front of her house twinkle on, and she heard Mr. Stevens' sputtering car drive by.

Army ran his fingertips across her bare skin and she shivered. He nestled her closer to him. "Are you cold, baby?" he asked in a low voice.

"Not really." Mia didn't want him to pull away from him. She wanted nothing more than to block out the world and stay in his strong arms—just as they were—forever.

"I can put on the fake fire."

She looked up and scrunched up her face in feigned disapproval. "The gas flame is real."

"Admit you hate your lame fireplace that gives shit for heat."

"Okay ... *maybe* I wish I had the real thing, but I love the easy cleanup with this one."

Army chuckled. "So are you agreeing with me or not?"

"Kind of, but not a hundred percent."

He laughed and held her tighter. "Damn I love you, woman." Army swatted her ass, and Mia giggled.

Pumpkin and Snickers padded over and sat down right in front of the couch and stared at her. She reached out and petted them, then untangled herself away from Army. "The girls want to eat," she said, pointing at the cats. Mia sat up then groaned as the right side of her face throbbed.

"The fuckin' bastard," Army muttered under his breath. "Do you have any pain pills?"

"Yeah, but it's not that bad. I think I just got up too fast. I'll take some ibuprofen. I wanted to make you a killer dinner but got sidetracked when Vic paid me that unexpected visit."

"Don't worry about it," he said, a hard edge to his voice.

"I was thinking salad and pizza? Or we could order Mexican, Chinese, or Lebanese food from Chowtime. There're some restaurants that use their service," she said pulling her top on over her head.

"Pizza works for me, but if you want something different, then I'm cool with that too."

"Let me give my sweeties their dinner, then we can decide what we want on our pizza." She scooped up her skirt and underwear then went into the kitchen.

An hour later, they sat next to each other on the couch and ate a sausage, pepperoni, mushroom, and jalapeño pizza while watching a thriller. Pumpkin snuggled next to Army and Snicker burrowed by Mia. The wavering blue flame in the fireplace made Mia smile, and she craned her neck and kissed Army on the cheek. He looked at her sideways.

"What was that for?" he asked, his eyes twinkling.

"For being such a hunk who knows how to push my buttons."

"Oh yeah?" He turned toward her and put his hand on the back of her neck, drawing her face close to his.

"Yeah," she whispered.

The caress of his lips on her mouth sang through her veins, and she threaded her fingers through his hair. Army pulled away and winked at her, then he leaned over and grabbed another slice of pizza.

As Mia nibbled on her slice, she couldn't remember when she'd ever been happier than she was at that moment. She loved him with a fire that could never be extinguished. *He is my heart and my life.*

She put her empty plate on the coffee table then rested her head against his shoulder as they watched the movie.

# Chapter Twenty-Five

ARMY STRETCHED OUT his legs and folded his arms across his chest as he watched Taylor and Madman practice their moves. Kat walked by and threw him a toothy grin before heading into the locker room area. Even though she knew he and Mia were together, she kept trying to start something with him. The last time she'd come on too strong, Army had set her straight about his relationship with Mia. The amazing thing about his woman was it didn't seem to bother her too much when Kat flirted with him. Of course, he never reciprocated, but he'd never been with a chick who wasn't constantly jealous. Mia really trusted him, and he was blown away by her faith in him. Even though he trusted her as well, he still got pissed off when a guy checked her out.

Behind him, he heard Chainsaw's voice rising in irritation. He was talking loud enough for Army to hear him.

"I'm just gonna tell you this one more time. You gotta be a member of Champion. You're not, so you can't come in. It's pretty fucking simple," Chainsaw said.

Army pivoted in the chair and saw a guy dressed in jeans, T-shirt, and a leather cut standing by the door. The man's eyes kept looking over Chainsaw's shoulders, scanning the inside of the gym. Army had a feeling this dude wanted him, so he pushed up from the chair and sauntered over.

When he reached the door, he knew the guy was a biker from the tats on his arms and a small patch on his cut—a devil face with guns surrounding it.

"I got this," Army said to Chainsaw.

The fighter looked from Army to the guy then back to Army. "He can't come in."

"I know." Army steeled his eyes on the guy.

Chainsaw grunted then walked away.

"What the fuck do you want?" Army asked.

The medium-sized man ran his beady eyes over Army then shook his head. "I'm looking to talk to Army."

"That's me. Now what the fuck do you want?"

"You're not wearing your cut," the man said.

"I bet you're the brightest member of the fuckin' Pistons. You've got ten seconds to tell me what the fuck you want and then I start punching." Army stepped outside.

"Shark wants to meet with you," the guy said, shuffling back a bit.

"You a damn prospect?"

"Yep." The older man's eyes shone with pride.

"Where?"

"He said for you to call him. He said it's personal so it'll just be you and him."

Army glanced around the street, but didn't see anyone. "Gimme the fuckin' number."

The prospect gave him a piece of paper then walked away. Army stepped back inside and headed for the break room. He opened the fridge and took out a small bottle of orange juice and twisted off the cap then took a deep drink. Taking out the burner phone, he plopped down on one of the chairs and tapped in the asshole's number.

"I've got a score to settle with you," Shark growled into the phone.

"That makes two of us. I don't like fuckers who beat up on chicks." Army took another drink.

"You're fucking my sister, asshole."

"So you hit her?"

"She knows her fuckin' duty to the family, especially me. She deserved the beating."

"I heard she beat the shit out of your wimpy ass," Army said.

"Let's settle this fucker—just you and me. No backup, no weapons, just fists. And one more thing—I want you to stay the hell away from Mia," Shark gritted.

"You don't tell me shit, motherfucker. Tomorrow night at ten. There's a baseball field—Sloane's—just on the outskirts of the city going east. I'll meet you there and I can finally get this shit over with." Army finished the juice. "I don't want you near Mia again."

"I'll bust your goddamn balls, asshole!"

"I'm ready for you, dumbass." Army clicked off the phone then threw the empty bottle in the trash. Adrenaline pumped through him and he jumped up and paced the room while he pounded his fist into the palm of his hand. "You sonofabitch. I'm ready for you," he said aloud.

"Don't meet him." Taylor's voice startled Army and he stopped in his tracks. "I overheard you talking to Mia's brother. You know this isn't the answer.

Army shook his head. "You don't get my world so stay out of this."

"*Your* world? What the hell does that mean? How is beating the shit out of each other going to solve anything? You need a mediator. You're both hot heads and have a lot of emotions involved in this. Let *me* talk to Vic. I'm sure if he understands how happy Mia is he'll let her live her life."

"Are you stoned? Just leave it the hell alone. I'll deal with it in the way it needs to be, okay?"

Taylor walked over to Army and put his hands on his shoulders. "Please don't do this. If you don't care about yourself, think about Mia and Dad. Don't you want to see Joshua grow up? I don't want you to get hurt."

Army pushed his brother's hands away. "I don't plan on getting hurt."

"How can you know that? I don't plan on it when I'm in the ring but sometimes it happens. Let me just try to talk with Vic."

Army guffawed. "Like that's gonna do shit." He patted his brother on the back. "Stick to MMA competitions. You don't know a fuckin' thing about the outlaw world."

"But what's going to be resolved?"

"Taylor, stay the fuck outta this. This discussion is over." He glanced at his brother and shook his head. "You need to worry about winning your next fight not about what's going on with me. I'm gonna hit the speed bags and pretend it's that asshole Shark." He laughed, ignoring his brother's serious face as he walked out of the room.

Stripped to his gym shorts and wearing boxing gloves, Army pummeled the bag with kicks and punches from all directions—each strike tightly executed and perfect in form. Sweat rolled down his shoulders and back, his forearms glistening under the florescent lights as he threw jarring jabs and large, hooking body shots into the heavy bag, grunting loudly. He kept up the grueling pace until his muscles screamed and he was soaked.

As he passed by Taylor on his way to the showers, he noticed his brother didn't meet his gaze. He grabbed a towel from the rack, stripped off his drenched shorts then turned on the water in one of the shower stalls and stepped in.

After Army dressed, he looked at his phone and saw that he'd missed Steel's two calls. He packed all his stuff into the duffel bag and tapped in the president's number as he walked into the break room.

"Sorry I missed your calls—I was working out. What's up?" Army asked.

"I heard you're meeting Shark tomorrow night," Steel replied.

Army narrowed his eyes. *Fuck you, Taylor.* "Yeah, but it's personal. It doesn't involve the brotherhood."

"When one brother has a problem, we all do. There's no fucking way you're going out there tomorrow night without backup."

Army didn't say anything, but he understood what Steel was saying because he'd be telling one of the members the same thing if they were planning to do what he was.

"I'll put it out to the brothers and let them know what's up. I'll make it strictly voluntary. I don't trust the fucking Pistons," Steel said.

"I don't either."

"This is going to turn into a rumble for sure. I'll let you know who's going to be with you, bro."

"Thanks, Prez." Army slid the phone into his pocket and walked back into the gym. He strode over to Taylor and clutched his shoulder. "I talked to Steel," he said.

"I don't give a shit if you're pissed at me," Taylor replied.

"I'm not. I'll talk to you later."

After putting the gym bag in one of the saddle bags, his phone rang and he saw it was Steel.

"Hey," Army said.

"All the brothers volunteered to watch your back, but we can't leave the clubhouse unmanned and we got businesses to run. So the ones coming up tonight are Eagle, Brutus, Muerto, Sangre, Diablo, Jigger, Goldie, Crow, Cueball, and Ruger."

"Okay," Army said. He pulled in a deep breath and the feeling of being able to conquer the world filled him. The ties and friendship they all shared were forged in trust, honesty, and reciprocity, and, in that moment, he was proud as hell to be a Night Rebel.

He swung his leg over the bike, revved the engine, and sped away. When he turned down Mia's street, he saw her standing on the porch, arms folded over her chest, and a scowl creasing her forehead. *Fuck, Taylor.* Grinding his teeth, Army got off his bike, took out the gym bag and ambled up the sidewalk.

"Hey, babe," he said, leaning down to kiss her pursed lips. "Taylor shouldn't have involved you." He slinked an arm around her waist and nuzzled her neck.

Mia moved back. "Of course he should have. What the hell are you thinking?"

"Your brother challenged me."

"Dueling went out in the nineteenth century."

"Not for outlaws." His grin faded when he met glaring amber eyes. "Let's not fight about this, babe. I just want a nice dinner with my woman."

Mia's features softened. "Okay. I'm just worried you'll get hurt. Vic's always played dirty and I wouldn't put it past him to have his friends ambush you when you get there."

"Me neither—that's why I got my posse coming too." Army leaned forward and gave her a quick kiss. "So we'll both be playing dirty." He drew her to him and she relaxed in his arms. "Now how about a real kiss, baby?"

Mia tilted her head and his mouth covered hers while his hand ran down her back, cupping her ass. "Do you promise you won't get hurt?" she murmured.

"I'll do my fuckin' best," he whispered before claiming her mouth again.

Army knew anything could happen at the rumble, and he was positive Shark wasn't going to show up without packing a gun or two. Army didn't plan on meeting the asshole without any weapons either. Since Shark was Mia's brother, Army would try to teach him a lesson without killing him. After all, this was a personal fight and had nothing to do with the club.

"It's kind of chilly out here. Let's go inside," Mia said as she pulled away.

When he came into the house, the aroma of garlic and onions wafted in the air, and his stomach growled. "It smells damn good in here."

"I made lasagna," she said, walking into the kitchen. "It'll be ready pretty soon. I'll make us a salad. Do you want a beer?"

"You read my mind, babe." Army took the can from her. "I'm gonna step out back and smoke a joint." He squeezed her ass then sauntered out of the room.

The patio took up most of the postage stamp-sized yard leaving only a little bit of room for a bush against the dark wooden fence. The tall shrub looked like a small tree, and its foliage was a colorful burst of reds, oranges, and yellows. Army stood under the covered patio and phoned some of his buddies. Even though he'd installed alarm systems in both his dad's and Asher's residences, he wanted someone to keep an eye on them until after the fight. His friends told him it was no problem and then they all agreed to get together real soon to play some pool and get drunk. He slipped the phone in his jeans pocket and sucked in a deep breath, exhaling it slowly.

Leaves blew across the grass as a cold gust of wind whispered through the nearly bare branches of neighboring trees. Smoky purple smudges painted the sky as the last remnants of the setting sun disappeared over the mountains. Army tilted his head back and saw a small spatter of sparkling stars in the darkened eastern sky. A memory from his past filled his mind: his mother pointing out constellations to him when he was a young boy. She'd loved star gazing and had bought a telescope from a thrift shop. On clear nights, they'd stand on the balcony and peer into the eyepiece, and all the stars crashed down on their heads—it'd been magical. He'd loved the way his mother's eyes glittered like the stars above them whenever she found the Milky Way. A vibration in Army's pocket snapped him from his reverie as he fished out the cell phone. Eagle's name came up on the screen, and Army pushed the button.

"Hey."

"Yo, bro. We just got here," Eagle said. "We're staying at Green Pines Motel. Do you know it?"

"It's off the interstate, right?"

"You got it. We saw a diner not too far away. You wanna join us for some chow?"

"I can't. Mia made dinner for us. I'll come by in a few hours and we can go over the plans for tomorrow night. What room are you in?"

"I'm staying in Cabin 8. Just give me the heads up when you're headed our way," Eagle said.

"Will do."

"See you then."

"Uh … Eagle? Thanks for everything, bro."

"Yeah."

Army slipped the phone in his jeans pocket and took out a joint and before he could light it, the sliding glass door opened and he glanced over.

"Dinner's ready," Mia said through the screen.

Army put the joint back into his pocket and came inside.

"I hope you're hungry," Mia said as she locked the door.

Tugging her to him, he dipped his head down and kissed her deeply. "I'm starving, but I'll eat first." He smacked her ass.

Mia giggled. "We're having dinner in the dining room." She moved out of his arms and walked over to the stove.

"Do you need any help?"

"You can bring the salad bowl to the table, please."

"Okay." Army picked up the ceramic bowl. "I'm meeting up with some of the brothers tonight. I won't be long." He placed the salad on the table and sat down on one of the dining room chairs. The flames from the candles flickered, and he unfolded the rust-colored napkin and put it on his lap.

Mia placed a pan of piping hot lasagna on two hot plates. "Hand me your dish," she said, cutting a large square.

Army gave it to her then stood up. "I'll get the wine."

As they ate, he kept staring at her thinking that she looked so beautiful in candlelight. Normally Mia would be chatting away, but she was quiet that night, and Army suspected she was thinking about the fight the following night.

"This is really good, babe," he said before taking a big bite.

She looked up and smiled. "I'm glad you like it." Then she went back to pushing her food around on the plate.

Army set his fork down. "It's going to be all right, Mia."

"Please don't go," she said softly. "It'd kill me if anything happened to you. Maybe the universe is telling us that we *aren't* meant to be."

"No fuckin' way. The problem is your brother can't let you live your life. I know what needs to be done. I'll make sure Shark doesn't bother you—us—anymore."

Her eyes widened. "What does that mean? I don't want you to kill my brother."

"I'm not. Once he's defeated, he'll concede, and we won't have to worry about him anymore."

For a second Mia stared at him as if she didn't quite believe what he'd said, and then she looked away. "I just wish you'd call him back and tell him that you're not going to meet him."

"You know I can't do that, babe." His gaze caught hers and held it for a few seconds. "Now eat your dinner. After I get back from hooking up with the brothers at their motel, we'll have some fun." He placed his hand on top of hers and squeezed it gently."

The smile she aimed at him was weak as she picked up her fork and began to eat.

Hours later Army and Mia lay wrapped in each other's arms, sated and warm, their naked bodies cocooned in a mass of tangled sheets. Army stared at the wall, striped with moonlight filtering through the blinds on the window as he twirled a strand of brown silken hair in his fingers.

"By this time tomorrow night, you'll be home safe," Mia whispered, tilting her head back and gazing at him.

"Go to sleep, baby." Army kissed her softly on the lips. "I love you."

"Me too." Her voice quivered slightly. She rested her head on his chest and tightened her grip around his waist.

Silence filled the room, and Army fell asleep, Mia's body pressed to his, her finger tracing the line of Adam's apple and collarbone and pecs.

THE FOLLOWING NIGHT, Army tucked his gun into his waistband as he waited for Eagle and Sangre at the motel. The two had gone to a convenience store to stock up on energy drinks.

"I scoped out the area today and saw more of the fuckers," Crow said as he stared at the television screen.

"How many?" Goldie asked.

"Five." Crow lit up a joint.

"We'll go in slowly to make sure no one's at the field yet. There are bleachers and bushes plus a ton of trees around there we need to secure." Army pushed the curtains aside and looked out the window. "Did the fuckers see you?"

"I don't think so, but I wasn't wearing my cut."

There'd been a strained tension between Army and Crow since the member had arrived in Durango, but the fact that Crow was willing to fight by Army's side meant a lot to him.

Army saw Eagle's SUV pull into the parking lot and he let go of the curtains and turned around. "They're back," he said.

The two entered the room and dispersed cans of energy drinks around the room. "The chick at the counter was ready to jump Eagle's bones," Sangre said as he popped the top on the can.

"You can hook up with her after we beat the Pistons' asses," Jigger said.

"She's cute but too skinny. I like a woman I can grab onto." Eagle opened a drawer and took out a 9mm and stuck it into his jeans pocket.

"Are we ready to rock and roll?" Goldie asked as he rose to his feet.

"Yeah," Army replied.

"Let's go kick some Piston ass," Muerto said, opening the door.

The men laughed as they walked out of the room and into the parking lot. They'd driven to Durango in two SUVs for obvious reasons, and Army slid into the front seat of the one Sangre drove.

"There's no way the lazy asses are gonna get there two hours before the fight." Cueball offered a joint to Army who took it with a jerked of his chin.

"I could wait all night if it meant beating the shit outta Shark or one of the other assholes," Diablo said as he cracked his knuckles.

"Is the deal with the fuckers and the 39th Street shits still going down next week?" Ruger asked.

Army blew out and smoke billowed around him. "According to Lil' Donnie it's a go."

"The fucking Pistons have been a real pain in the ass. It's time we get rid of them for good," Diablo growled.

"Like we did with the asshole Skull Crushers," Cueball added. The men grumbled their agreement as the car drove further away from the lights of the city.

Army pointed his finger to the left. "Turn here."

The night before, the men had agreed to park the two cars in a neighborhood six blocks away from the old ballpark and walk to it. Sangre pulled over then turned off the ignition. The men filed out of the car, and Army shoved his hands into his pockets in an attempt to warm them up a little as the group of men made their way to the field.

It was a starless, moonless night. Streams of gray clouds stretched over the sky giving it a hazy, ominous feel; in the distance, the city lights ebbed to a mere inkling. A trembling gush of wind rattled the trees' branches as the Night Rebels approached the field.

After securing the area, Goldie, Jigger, and Eagle disappeared behind the tall evergreens; Crow, Brutus, and Muerto found bushes in which to crouch down low; and Sangre, Diablo, Cueball, and Ruger found refuge under the bleachers. Army stood by a rusting chain-linked fence and waited. Memories of playing baseball at the park swirled in his head. In his mind, the rotting bleachers were new and clean, and his mother sat in the middle of them in her bright yellow sundress cheering him on. He'd been nine years old the summer he'd joined the baseball team— The Tigers. His father had made it to a couple of his games that summer, but his mother hadn't missed one. Afterwards, she'd have the team over to their house and serve lemonade and freshly baked cookies. Once the summer had ended and the trees had begun shedding their leaves, his mother ran away from the family … from *him*. Army shook his head and banished the images to the back of his mind. *I need to stop thinking about shit and focus.* An eerie stillness settled over the field as he waited for Shark to show up.

A half hour later, Army heard movement in the dry leaves. His body tensed and he placed his hand on the gun in his waistband. His eyes scanned the area looking for raccoons, skunks, or possum, but he didn't see anything and he knew that the Pistons were getting into position. He strained his ears to figure out where they were hiding, but it had grown quiet again except for the occasional hoot of a hidden owl. Army crouched down, his senses on high alert, his gaze darting all around.

At exactly eleven o' clock, slapping footsteps echoed angrily into the emptiness of the night, and Army stood up and walked slowly toward Shark.

"You alone?" Shark asked.

"Same as you," Army answered.

The two men glared at each other for several minutes, then Shark shuffled his feet on the dirt and looked down as if he'd dropped something. Army didn't follow his gaze; instead he kept it focused on the asshole. Shark bent down then lunged forward toward Army, but he'd anticipated the move and jumped back, and then followed up with a fist to Shark's jaw. Adrenaline surged through Army, his pulse a steady drumbeat.

Shark raised his clenched hands, but Army ducked forward and down, Shark's fist just missing the side of his face. Army moved to the right and his left foot stepped into a hole and he stumbled. Shark lifted his muscled arms straight in the air, brought them down on Army's shoulders, dumping Army on his ass.

"You're fuckin' dead," he hissed as he glared at Army with cold brown eyes.

Shark kicked Army, digging the toe of his boot into Army's side. "You think you can fuck my sister?" he gritted, bringing his heel down on Army's stomach.

*Fuck!* Army winced in pain and he sucked in a deep breath then exhaled. He looked up in time to see Shark's boot ready to come down on him again, and with the speed of light, Army grabbed Shark's foot and twisted it hard then pushed back. Shark groaned in pain as he stumbled backwards, and Army jumped up quickly and lunged at Shark with both fists swinging. Army landed a hard blow to Shark's jaw and he staggered back, and then Army drove his fists over Shark's face before quickly bringing his knee up and thrusting it hard into Shark's groin.

"Fuck you!" Shark gasped as he bowled over, his hands flying to his crotch.

Army's knee hit Shark's chin toppling the Piston to the ground. He kicked the downed man hard in the leg and was ready to strike him again when he saw five men emerge from behind a cluster of pine trees. As they rushed toward Army, he stepped back and saw the Night Rebels come out from their hiding places.

Then all hell broke loose.

Fists against skin.

Shattering kicks from steel-toed boots.

Splintering bones.

Grunts. Threats.

As Army wrapped his hands around Shark's neck, two headlights lit up the field, and the fighters scattered out of the way as a bronze SUV came closer.

"What the fuck?" Army said out loud as he saw Taylor behind the wheel. His brother parked the car then jumped out and rushed over to him.

"You're okay." Relief filled Taylor's voice.

"Get the fuck outta here!" Army yelled.

Shark pushed Army away then jumped up, laughing dryly. "Did your little brother come to help you out, asshole?" He wiped the blood from the corner of his mouth with the back of his hand then spat on the ground.

Taylor looked over at Shark and smiled. "I'm really good friends with Mia."

"Well isn't that fuckin' nice?" Shark glowered.

"Go home, Taylor. This isn't your fight," Army said as he grabbed his brother's arm.

Taylor jerked away. "I'm here as a mediator. Nothing will be accomplished by beating the shit out of each other."

"Move outta the way, Taylor," Diablo said.

"Is this asshole for real?" Army heard one of the Pistons ask.

"I'm here to make peace between you." Taylor looked at Shark. "And you." He looked at Army. "Mia's upset over the two of you not getting along. She's a wonderful—"

"You don't know what the fuck you're talking about. If you don't get your ass in the car right now, me and some of the brothers are gonna make you." Army took a few steps toward his brother.

"I'm just trying to help," Taylor said.

"You're doing the opposite." Army had his back to Shark, and the Night Rebels and Pistons started throwing insults at each other which quickly turned into blows. Army glanced behind him and saw the men fighting, and then he turned back to Taylor. "Just get the fuck outta here. I don't want something to happen—"

*Bam!* Taylor fell to the ground with a thud as blood poured down the side of his head. *Bam!* An industrial flashlight slammed across his left leg and Taylor howled.

"Fuck! Taylor!" Army ran over to his side and dropped to his knees. "Can you hear me?" White-hot bolts of rage ripped through him.

"Yeah …"

Out of the corner of Army's eye, he saw Shark ready to slam the fucking flashlight over *his* head, and he reached down inside his boot and took out a knife. Army scooted away a bit then leapt up and plunged the knife into Shark's gut.

"Fuck!" the Piston cried out, covering his stomach with his hands as he fell to the ground; the weapon he was holding rolled away in the dirt. A dark crimson stain spread around him as his lids fluttered then closed.

Army leaned over and felt for Shark's pulse. Nothing. "Fuck … oh … Mia," he said as he walked away.

The fight continued to rage all around Army, but he no longer saw it. All he could see was his brother lying motionless on the brown grass.

Kneeling beside him, Army shrugged off his cut and whipped his T-shirt over his head. He put it against the wound on Taylor's head and applied pressure.

"Wake the fuck up!" Army yelled, shaking his brother. "Don't fuckin' die on me!"

Gunfire punctured the night air, and in the distance sirens wailed.

Eagle came over to Army. "We gotta take off, dude. The badges are coming."

"Taylor's hurt."

"We can take him with us."

Army shook his head. "He's hurt bad. He's gotta get to a hospital." He shook his brother again and Taylor's eyes opened and stared vacantly at him. "Can you hear me, buddy?" His brother licked his lips then nodded. "Okay ... that's good. Listen to me—I'm gonna get you to a hospital. Just hang in there and don't fuckin' fall asleep."

Army looked up at Eagle. "Did any of the brothers take a bullet?"

"No. A couple of Piston fuckers did. They drew their guns first."

"Get the hell outta here. No sense in dealing with the fuckin' badges." Army glanced back at Taylor. "I gotta make sure he gets to the hospital."

Eagle jerked his head at Shark. "Is he dead?"

Army looked over at his lifeless body. "Yeah. The fucker attacked Taylor and was aiming for me. Guess I cut a major artery." Army narrowed his eyes. "He got what he deserved."

The sirens seemed to be moving closer.

"We gotta get the fuck outta here," Diablo said as he came up to Eagle and Army.

"All of you go now. I'm staying with Taylor. There's no reason for you to have trouble with the badges." Army looked over his shoulder. "Are the fucking Pistons gone?"

"The pussies ran at the first sound of the sirens," Diablo answered.

"Any of the brothers hurt?" Army asked.

"Just banged up with some cuts. Nothing that can't heal." Diablo grinned.

"Then go," Army said.

"We picked up all the weapons and shit, even from the pussies. That reminds me—gimme your guns. You don't want the badges finding those on you." Diablo put his hand on Army's shoulder. "They're gonna take you in."

"I know. Call Hawk and see if his old lady can help out or recommend a lawyer. Now get the hell outta here." Army glanced at Taylor whose eyes were beginning to close. He lightly shook him. "Don't fall asleep. The fuckin' badges will be here soon to get you help."

"Are you sure you don't want me to stay?" Eagle asked.

"Yeah. Can you let Mia know I'm okay?" Eagle nodded and Army gave him her number.

Eagle clutched Army's arm and then disappeared into the darkness with the other brothers.

Taylor jerked and Army held him close. "Just don't fuckin' die, okay? Promise me that."

The police sirens splintered the night air and blue and red strobes flashed as the cars came to a screeching halt. For the first time in Army's life, he was happy to see the badges, and when they approached him with guns drawn, he held his hands up as he told them Taylor needed an ambulance.

One badge handcuffed Army while the other frisked him then they escorted him to the police car and put him in the back seat. Army stared at the ambulance that carried Taylor speed away then he settled back against the seat. Two badges slipped into the car, and the driver turned the ignition and drove away from the scene. He caught Army's eye in the rearview mirror.

"You want to tell me what happened tonight?" he asked.

Army looked away. "I'm not saying shit. I want an attorney."

"You may change your mind when you get to the station."

"I won't," he replied.

As the squad car drove down the city streets, Army stared into the dark night.

# Chapter Twenty-Six

MIA SAT ON the metal chair near Taylor's bed watching the machines beep and sigh as she held his hand in hers. Taylor had suffered a bad concussion and his left femur had been shattered. He'd had emergency surgery when he'd been admitted, and the doctor had placed a rod with twenty pins into his thigh. Mia knew there was a very strong probability that Taylor's injuries could end his fighting career.

"You're here," Taylor said in a groggy voice.

"Hey." She smiled even though her heart was breaking. It was bad enough that Taylor lay in the hospital, but Army was in jail and Vic was dead. It all seemed too surreal for her brain to really comprehend it. In just a short twenty-four hours everything had changed.

"Why isn't Army here?" Taylor asked.

Mia patted his hand. "He's been arrested."

He tried to sit up but yelled out in pain and then collapsed back down on the pillows. "Why?"

Mia inhaled deeply then slowly blew out the breath. "He killed Vic, or at least that's what the cops are saying." Saying the words out loud still didn't make the situation real for her.

"Vic attacked me. He was going to do the same to Army. I need to clear it up."

"You can when the cops come and talk to you, but right now you need to calm down." Mia leaned back in the chair. "How does your head feel?"

"Fucked up." He glanced over at her. "I guess I threw the chance at making it to the pros in the damn toilet."

"Not necessarily. Look at all the pros who had horrible injuries but made comebacks—Matt Hughes, Daniel Straus, Darrell Hocher, and many others. I'm not going to say it'll be easy, but you can do it if you want it badly enough. You're only twenty-four years old, so that's a huge plus in the MMA world."

"I'm not worried about the broken femur. I know I can rehab real well by working my ass off, but it's the fucking concussion that could be the deal breaker. Look at Chris Holdsworth—he never could fight again after his."

"But you don't know if your injury will be like his. Just take it one day at a time," Mia said even though she knew the odds were stacked against him.

A man with graying temples in a brown houndstooth jacket entered the room. "Hi. I'm Detective Cordova and I have some questions I'd like to ask you," he said to Taylor.

Mia stood up, but Taylor reached out for her. "Don't go. Please stay."

The detective looked at her. "Who are you?"

"Mia Decelles," she said softly.

Cordova raised his eyebrows. "So you're Victor Decelles' sister." She nodded. "I was going to come to your house after I left here. I can interview you after I talk with Taylor."

"Army was trying to defend me ... and himself," Taylor said and the detective's eyes darted to him. "Vic attacked me then I saw him ready to clobber Army over the head with the same thing he used on me."

Detective Cordova nodded as he walked closer to the bed. "I need to break it down a little more." He glanced at Mia. "Could you please wait outside?"

She smiled at Taylor then patted his hand. "I'll be back later." And then she walked out of the room.

★　★　★

LATER THAT NIGHT Mia sat on the couch drinking a glass of chardonnay as a tingle of excitement wove through her. Army's attorney had just called her to tell her he'd arranged for her to visit Army at the jail the following morning. The attorney had told the deputies Mia worked for the law firm, so she would be able to meet with Army in a private room.

Mia took a sip of wine, letting the warmth spread through her. She hadn't seen or talked to Army since he'd left that fateful night to meet up with her brother. When she'd first learned about Vic's death she was stunned and couldn't believe that her boyfriend had killed her brother. But as Mia learned about what had happened that night, she knew in her heart that Army had not gone to the fight with the intention of killing Vic. Instead, he had tried to defend Taylor and himself from Vic's vicious attack.

Mia sighed and wrapped her arms around herself. She missed Army so much that she ached all over. She wanted to grab him and kiss him and let him know how much she loved him. She was his and no matter what happened, she would always be there for him. Right or wrong, she loved Army more than life itself. *How could I ever hate him? He brought light into my life, and is my strength when I feel weak.*

The ringtones pushed through Mia's thoughts, and she wiped her cheeks.

"Hello?"

"Hi, Mia," Dean replied.

"Dean! It's been too long. How're things going for you?"

"Okay."

"Tell the cunt she's never welcomed in this house again!" her mother screamed in the background.

Mia's stomach churned. "I heard Mom," she said softly.

"Uh … Mom wanted me to call to say she … uh … she doesn't want you to come to Shark's funeral."

"You killed him!" her mother screamed.

"Do you believe that?" Mia asked Dean.

"I dunno. I know he was a pain in the ass to you, Finn, and Tucker. I didn't really know him. He left when I was young, but you've always been good to me."

"Gimme the fucking phone, you piece of shit."

"Bye," Dean said quickly.

Mia braced herself for the onslaught of verbal abuse that would soon spew from her mom's mouth.

"This is your fault, you ungrateful bitch. Shark set you up in business and this is how you repay him? You fuck his enemy? You bitch!"

"That isn't what happened, Mom," Mia replied.

"Shut that stupid mouth of yours! Noe told me everything. You're nothing but a traitor slut. You're evil. You fucked the enemy knowing it would hurt your brother."

"I didn't fall in love just to fuck Vic over. I don't even know why my love life was his business in the first place."

"Noe says you're still fucking the bastard. You're such a whore. I should've had an abortion. If I did, Shark would still be here."

"But you didn't abort me, Mom. And since you're telling me how you feel, let me share some of my thoughts, okay? If you would've acted like a mother, our whole family wouldn't be so fucked up."

"None of the shit that you fucking brats bring to me is my fault. I needed to have a life, but you always held that against me—Vic never did." Her mother's voice cracked.

*I'm done.* The thought echoed through her brain and slipped into her heart. "Mom, I feel awful about Vic, but you'll never believe that. Ever since I was young, you resented me and treated me worse than any of my brothers. I didn't choose to be your daughter—I was born into it. So I'm going to free both of us right now. Since I make your life so miserable, I won't contact you anymore, and you don't ever have to talk to me again."

"You ungrateful cunt. I gave up everything for you!"

Mia shook her head, knowing her mother would never take responsibility for any of her actions.

"Don't you dare come to Shark's funeral or I'll kill you. You took my favorite child away from me!"

"Are you really telling me that in front of Dean?"

"Stop mixing me up!" her mother yelled.

"Goodbye, Mom," Mia said softly.

She placed the phone down on the table and waited for the tears to come, but they didn't. For the very first time, Mia felt liberated from the chains her mother had put around her. After twenty-six years, it was finally over, and Mia could breathe again. Of course, she'd be there for her brothers if they needed her, but the tug of war Mia and her mom had been playing all these years had finally ended.

THE ROOM HAD blue-painted concrete walls, a table, and two wooden chairs. Mia sat waiting for the guard to bring Army to the attorney room, her heart beating wildly. The door clicked open and Army entered in an orange jumpsuit emblazoned with the name of the jail on it, and her heart melted. Even though his left eye was black and blue and practically swollen shut, and there were some red abrasions dotting his face and arms, Mia thought he was the most handsome man in the world, and she was dying to kiss him, but she didn't want to jeopardize the chance of seeing him again while he was incarcerated.

The guard closed the door and stood watch in the hallway. Army grabbed her hand and squeezed it, his blue eyes piercing into her.

"Are they treating you all right?" Mia asked.

"I'm good. Fuck, baby, things got outta control the other night. How's Taylor?"

"He's doing fine. I saw him yesterday. He had a shattered left femur and a concussion. The doctors fixed up his leg, but it'll take time with the head injury."

"Thank fuck he pulled through." Army's gaze swept over her face. "I didn't mean to kill Shark. He hurt Taylor and it set me off."

Mia nodded slightly. "Taylor said he saw Vic trying to kill you."

"Yeah, but I only meant to keep him away from me and Taylor, not fuckin' kill him. I didn't think he'd die. Fuck, baby. I told you everything would be all right and it's all fucked up. Taylor wanted to go pro."

He groaned.

Mia brushed her fingers across Army's hand. "It was self-defense. That's what Taylor told the detective. What the hell was your brother doing there anyway?"

Army shook his head. "I had no idea he'd do something so fuckin' stupid. He was trying to talk to Shark about making peace with me and you. It was damn insane. I kept telling him to get the fuck outta there, but he just didn't *get* it." He ran his hand through his hair.

"That's the way Taylor is—always trying to be the peacemaker. He's the same way at the club. It's amazing he can turn it off during a fight." Mia looked around. "Should we be talking about all this in here?"

"We're cool. You're in the lawyer room, so no wires or shit." Army squeezed her hand again. "I'm sorry I let you down, babe."

"Don't blame yourself. Life just crashed that night."

"I guess." Army's lips curled up. "Damn you look beautiful, woman. I miss you."

"I miss you too. I've been sleeping in one of your T-shirts pretending it's you pressed close to my body."

"That image will keep me going while I wait to get the fuck outta here."

"Has bail been set?"

"Not yet. I go in front of the judge tomorrow morning. Cara—Hawk's old lady—hooked me up with one of the best criminal defense attorneys in the county so I'm banking on him getting me out."

"What time is the bail review? I want to be there."

"In the morning at eight thirty. If I get bail, I'll come over and show you what you mean to me."

Mia licked her lips then smiled. "I can't wait to hold you again. Don't you think the charge against you will be dropped? You were just defending Taylor and yourself."

"Yeah, but prosecutors don't like dismissing cases, especially when an outlaw biker is involved. We'll see what legal maneuverings my attorney can come up with to spring me." Army leaned forward and entwined his fingers with hers, inhaling deeply. "I love the way you smell." His gaze met hers, and she saw desire in his eyes as she stared at him.

"You need to come home," Mia whispered.

"Yeah." Army cocked his head to the side. "I know you must be going through hell—Shark was your brother," he said in a low voice.

Mia nodded slightly as she took several deep breaths. "I'm sad that Vic's life turned out the way it did, but I don't blame you and I never will. Of course, I wish things wouldn't have turned out the way they did, but I understand what happened that night and why you did what you did." She brought a finger to her twitching eyelid and rubbed it gently. "Vic was always cruel and domineering, and he tried to make me want the things he wanted for me. I wish he would've understood how I felt about you." The truth was that she was sad Vic had died but she couldn't materialize the thoughts or feelings into words. When she was still living at home, her brother had run the house like a tyrant, and when he'd moved out at eighteen, they rarely heard from him. Then there were times when he had been incredibly supportive of Mia like when he'd given her the money to start her own business, but then he'd kept throwing it up in her face whenever they talked. Mia had made it her mission to pay him back, and had given him more than half of what he'd loaned her. *Why can't I cry? I feel terrible that Vic's gone.*

"You gotta let it out or it'll eat you alive." Army grasped the back of Mia's neck and pulled her close to him then kissed her. "I'm sorry things turned out the way they did, baby. You'll always have me to lean on. Don't ever forget it."

"Army," Mia muttered as she ran her fingers over his forearm.

A rap on the window reminded Mia where she was, and she moved her hand away quickly and leaned back in the chair as the deputy walked in. Army stood up and winked as the guard put the handcuffs on him, and then he led Army away.

A long while passed until Mia stood up and slowly exited the room. The sun's brightness hurt her eyes and she shielded them with her hand as she walked across the parking lot to her Chevy. She slid onto the seat and fumbled around in the car console, searching for her sunglasses. Mia put them on and leaned back, looking at the cars drive by on the busy street in front of the lot. Since everything had happened, she'd pushed down the emotions which threatened to take over, keeping herself tightly under control. But as the sun streamed into the car and the birds flew high in the sky, she broke down. Tears streamed down Mia's face as she gasped and hiccupped until her sobs died away to sniffles.

After blowing her nose several times, Mia straightened her shoulders and, and with a heavy heart, she pulled into the street, each mile tearing her farther away from the man she loved.

# Chapter Twenty-Seven

*Six weeks later*

ARMY HELD MIA'S hand and she glanced over and smiled weakly.

"Don't be so nervous. None of the guys will say shit to you with me around."

"That's not exactly the most comforting thought. I want them to accept me, not hate and mistrust me."

"Most of the brothers are cool, but the ones who aren't will come around in time."

"I hope so." Mia leaned over and kissed his cheek. "I never thought the DA would dismiss the charges against you."

"Yeah … I gotta call Hawk and tell him Cara did real good in referring Mitch. He's a helluva lawyer."

Mia squeezed his hand. "I know I've thanked you a million times for paying for Finn's attorney, but thank you again. I talked to the lawyer earlier this morning, and Finn's taking the plea bargain. Instead of twenty-five years in prison, he's going to get twelve."

Army nodded. "That's a damn good deal considering what he was facing. With good time credits, he'll probably be up for parole in about eight years."

"Yeah. I'd like to visit him, but he doesn't want me to. He didn't even want me at any of the hearings."

"I get that. You can write to him. He's gonna get real bored in the pen." He ran the back of his fingers down her face.

Since Army had made bail several weeks ago, he'd been living with Mia in Durango. One of the conditions of getting bail was not to leave the jurisdiction. Army was fine with the decision, and after the bond hearing, Mia had been outside the jail waiting for him. She'd driven straight to her house, and that was where he'd stayed until that morning when the judge dismissed all the charges against him. Army needed to get back to the Night Rebels, and he wanted to show the brothers that Mia was his woman, and she was here to stay.

"Taylor's doing real well with his rehab," Mia said as she ran her fingers through his hair.

"He's a fighter—that's for sure. I think he may even be able to get back in the ring in a year or so. I'm still pissed that I didn't drag his ass outta there." The guilt about that night still gave Army a sick feeling that would probably sit in the pit of his stomach for the rest of his life. He wanted nothing more than to have Taylor realize his dream and go pro. Army knew it was a long shot, but he'd told Taylor before leaving Durango that he'd be coming back regularly to make sure his brother did what the doctor ordered.

Mia ran her hand down the back of his neck and massaged it gently. "Taylor wants to get back in the ring in the worst way, so he'll definitely follow the doctor's orders. I'll check up on him and report back to you."

"My dad's a good watchdog." Army laughed. "Taylor's already griping about how disorganized Dad keeps the house." The physician had told Taylor that he couldn't put any weight on his healing leg for at least six months, so the doctor gave him two choices: stay at the rehab center or get a caregiver. Army had suggested his brother move in with their dad, and Army paid for the caretakers. "The only thing I'm worried about is my dad's crush on Maddie. I warned him to back off because she's great with Taylor, and he doesn't want to lose her. Good caregivers are hard to find."

"Since meeting your dad, I can see where you got some of your Don Juan ways."

Army glanced at her sparkling eyes and twitching lips, and laughed. "You probably have a point there."

The closer they got to Alina, the harder Mia kneaded the nape of his neck. She hadn't wanted to stay in his room due to the animosity some of the brothers had toward her, so Army had booked a room for them at the hotel Mia had stayed at when she'd come to Alina for the first time.

"I'm gonna get you settled in at the hotel then I'm going to the club. I made reservations at Flanigan's. It's one of the best steakhouses in town."

"That sounds nice." Mia fluffed his hair with her fingers.

Army caught her hand and brought it to his lips and kissed each finger. "Do you know how crazy you make me?" he asked.

"If it's anything like what you do to me then I know," she answered softly.

All of a sudden, Army pulled over on the shoulder of the highway and turned off the ignition.

"What's wrong?" Mia asked. Her eyes were luminous in the sunlight, which intensified the toffee highlights in her hair.

Army slid his arm behind her back and pressed her against his chest, and crushed his mouth on hers. Mia moaned softly and kissed him back, their tongues tangling. She was lean and soft and he loved the way she felt in his arms. He loved every part of her, and as long as he lived, he'd never get enough of her.

"You're mine," Army whispered over her lips.

"And you're mine," Mia mumbled back as they kissed deeply. The soft sounds she made had his cock growing harder, and all Army wanted to do was drag her over the seat to the back and pound into her.

Army eased away from Mia, his heart pounding, his temperature soaring. "We better get going," he rasped, turning the ignition.

"Maybe we can have some fun before you head over to the club." Her lips curled into a wicked smile.

Army stepped on the accelerator and sped down the highway while Mia giggled and snuggled next to him, her head resting on his shoulder. He couldn't get to Alina fast enough.

ARMY WALKED INTO the clubhouse amid cheers and whistles from the brothers. Before he could make it to the bar, the prospect gave him a beer in one hand and a tumbler of Jack straight up in the other.

"All fuckin' charges dismissed!" Army yelled, holding the drinks in the air.

"Fuck yeah!" several brothers shouted, raising their fists in solidarity.

Army downed his shot and threw the glass against the wall, and the room erupted in laughter as Eagle, Chains, Brutus, and Cueball followed suit, smashing their bottles and tumblers against the back wall.

"How the hell did you get them to drop the possession of a dangerous weapon charge?" Brick asked as he brought a beer bottle to his mouth.

"My lawyer's kickass," Army replied, glancing at Goldie and Paco.

The truth was that Steel had told Army's attorney about the drug buy between the Satan's Pistons and the 39th Street Gang, and the lawyer used it as a negotiation tool to get the illegal knife charge dismissed. Mitch had never revealed where the information had come from, and the narcotic detectives were still patting themselves on the back for busting one of the largest drug transactions of their careers.

Tipping off badges about criminal activity wasn't something the Night Rebels did, but it'd seemed like the only way to keep Army from doing a three-year stint in the pen and two years of mandatory parole. Added bonuses for leaking the information were that the bust had shut down the 39th Street punks for a while, and most of the Pistons at the warehouse had been arrested, crippling their club for a long time.

"I heard what happened to Shark," Buzz said as he pulled Army into a bear hug. "I also heard you're still going out with the sister."

"Yeah. My woman's here to stay." Army narrowed his eyes. "You got a problem with that?"

Buzz jerked his head back. "No fuckin' way, dude. I'm just trying to digest you saying *my woman*. Never thought I'd hear those words come outta your mouth."

*Neither did I, but Mia slipped into my life and hooked me before I even knew what had happened. Now I can't imagine a life without her.*

"Mia really came through for you and the brotherhood," Paco said, handing Army another drink.

"She had your back, bro, even after what happened to her fuckin' brother. She's okay, and she's a good asset to the club—man, can she fight. You better watch it if you piss her off," Chains said.

The men laughed and Army glanced over at Crow, who stood off to the side drinking a beer.

"When's Stiletto's next fight?" Buzz asked.

"Not sure, and you better not call her Stiletto outside of the ring or she'll have you in a submission before you'll know what hit you," Army said to the Fallen Slayer member.

Buzz guffawed and slapped Army on the back. "Good one, bro."

As more Fallen Slayers entered the clubhouse, Army grabbed another beer and made his way over to Crow. Before he reached him, Alma ran up to Army and gave him a big hug.

"I really missed you," she whispered in his ear.

He gently eased her away and smiled. "Did you think I moved to Durango for good?"

"No, but you were gone a long time." Alma twirled a strand of her dark hair around her finger. "Did you bring that lady back with you?"

Army tilted his head back. "Yeah … I brought my woman with me."

The club girl's face fell and she looked down at the floor. "Oh," she muttered then she looked up at him. "Are you gonna want to have some fun on the side like Rooster and Tattoo Mike?" She bit the corner of her bottom lip as she locked gazes with him.

"Mia's more than enough woman for me, but Buzz's got a thing for you."

Alma's dark eyes brightened. "He does?" She craned her neck. "Where is he?"

"By the bar. He likes pretty dark-haired women who walk like they're doing the rumba."

Alma put her hand behind his neck and tugged his face down and kissed him on the cheek. "Thanks," she whispered, and then walked away.

Army watched her sashay toward Buzz, and smiled when the big guy wrapped his powerful arms around Alma's tiny waist and lifted her up then planted a big kiss on her mouth. Army turned around and walked over to Crow.

"Hey."

"Hey." Crow stared straight ahead.

"We good?" Army took out two joints and handed one to Crow.

Crow took the weed and put it between his lips. "You still going out with *her*?"

Army leaned against the wall, the joint dangling from his mouth. "Yeah. She's staying around for a damn long time, bro."

Crow glanced sideways at him. "She's a damn good fighter." He lit the joint.

Army blew out. "Mia's the best." Pride swelled inside him, and he couldn't wait to get back to the hotel and be with her.

"I'd see her fight again," Crow said, still staring straight on.

"She'll probably come to the clubhouse once in a while and be at some of the family events. You gonna be cool with that?" Army chugged his beer.

Crow shrugged. "She came through for the Night Rebels. Yeah ... she sure can fight."

"Yeah," Army replied.

They finished their joints and their drinks without saying another word and, in that moment, Army knew the club would embrace his woman.

When Brutus and Skull walked in with several strippers from Lust, Army looked at his phone and decided to head back to the hotel. He wanted to have a special evening with his precious woman. As he walked through the crowd, he stopped and talked a bit before finally making it outside.

"Are you leaving so soon?" Eagle asked.

Army glanced over at him and saw that he had his arm wrapped around Kelly. She winked at Army then ran her blue-tipped nails up and down Eagle's arm.

"I'm taking Mia to Flanigan's," Army replied.

Eagle's eyes widened. "That's some serious shit, dude. You gonna do something pansy-assed like make her your old lady?"

"We just like steak. I gotta go. Later." They pumped fists in the air, and then Army jumped on his Harley and sped toward downtown.

When Army arrived at the hotel, he stopped by the front desk and thrummed his fingers on the counter while he waited for the clerk to finish his phone call. The tall man with wire-framed glasses hung up the receiver and walked over to Army.

"May I help you?" he asked.

"I want two bottles of champagne sent to my room—403. I'm taking my woman out for dinner, so I want them in the room when we get back."

The front desk clerk smiled. "Celebrating a special occasion?"

Stone-faced, Army stared at him. "We leave at six thirty, so make sure the champagne is brought in after that."

The man cleared his throat. "Would you like to add chocolate dipped strawberries to your order?"

Army splayed his hands out on the smooth granite counter. "Why the fuck not."

A small frown creased the desk clerk's forehead. "Is that a *yes*, sir?"

"Fuck yeah." Army hit the counter with his hand and the man jumped back. Army guffawed and turned around, and then swaggered to the elevators.

Army fished for the key card in his pocket but he couldn't find it. He knocked on the door and heard Mia's light footsteps approaching.

"It's me, babe," he said through the door.

The door swung open and Mia stood before him in a short as hell ivory robe, cinched tightly around her waist by a sash. The shiny robe draped sexily over her curves, and a hint of cleavage peeked out from the slightly opened neckline. Army ran his tongue over his lips as his gaze traveled up and down her body.

"Are you just going to stand there gawking at me, or are you coming in?" Mia asked.

Army glanced up at her and saw desire burning in her amber eyes. "Fuck you look sexy," he said in a low voice.

Mia ran her hands over her body, and then cupped her breasts. "Do we have time to play?" she asked softly, gripping his hand and jerking him inside.

Army kicked the door shut, yanked her to him, and took her mouth. Deep. Hungry. Mia slipped her hands under his shirt and drew her nails down his back, scratching him savagely.

"I like that," he gritted as he undid the robe's sash.

Army's hand covered one of her tits and he squeezed it hard, loving the way Mia groaned and dug her nails deeper into his skin. They clawed, bit and humped each other like two animals in heat, and then Army slammed Mia's back against the wall and leaned into her with the full weight of his body, pinning her. He pushed his hands inside her robe and ran them down her soft skin, and when he felt her panties, he looped his fingers around them and ripped them off. Mia cried out and tore his back even more with long scratches.

"I've been wanting to fuck you ever since we left Durango," he snarled.

"That makes two of us," she said before biting his bottom lip.

Army's fingers slid between her folds, and her juices covered them, exciting him more. "You're so fuckin' wet for me."

"That's what you do to me." Mia grabbed the hem of his T-shirt and tugged at it.

Army's teeth nipped and bit at her neck, her shoulders, and her tits, her moans fueling his burning lust. In frantic moves, they tore off each other's clothes, touching, grabbing, kissing, and biting as if it were the last time they'd ever taste and feel each other again.

Army lifted Mia's leg and she wrapped it around him, and then she put her other leg around, hugging him tightly as he held her up, his hands squeezing her ass checks.

"I need it so bad," he grunted as he thrust into her. He crushed his mouth on hers and then he banged her hard and fast. Mia cried out, her hands gripping his shoulders, her firm body matching his rhythm.

Her arousal mixed with his created a tangy, musky scent which drove him fucking wild, and he pounded in and out of her. Sweat beaded on his brow and trickled down his back.

"So fuckin' good," he panted as he pushed harder and deeper. "Touch your sweet spot for me, baby."

Army watched as Mia slipped her fingers between her engorged lips and flicked her clit while he fucked her. "I love watching you touch yourself," he growled.

"I'm so close, Army," she moaned.

He was too, and the combination of her whimpers, her face contorting in pleasure, and her finger furiously rubbing her hardened nub pushed his passion over the top. Mia banged her head against the wall with a thud as she cried out her release, bucking against him, mumbling incoherently. And then the knot at the root of his cock dissolved in fire, melting.

"Mia! Fuck!" he shouted.

Their orgasms downed them both, and they crumbled like sand to the floor, holding each other tightly, panting, their bodies sated.

After their breathing returned to normal, Army kissed her slowly and gently. With his fingertips, he traced the outline of her lips, loving the way they still glistened from his kiss. "I fuckin' love you," he said in a low voice.

The tip of Mia's tongue brushed over the pads of his fingers. "I love you too."

After a while, Army eased away from her and stood up, holding out his hand. "We've got dinner reservations, baby." He helped Mia up and handed her the robe and ripped panties.

"I better get ready. I'm always starving after a workout." She winked at him, and he swatted her ass as she went into the bathroom.

An hour later they sat by the restaurant window eating shrimp cocktail. Mia was beautiful in a form-fitting plum dress with her hair loose around her shoulders. Army smiled at her as he brought the whiskey to his mouth.

"It's so lovely and romantic in here," she said, picking up the glass of white wine.

"I'm glad you like it. It's one of my favorite steakhouses in Alina."

"I wish I could stay for the rest of the week and spend more time with you, but I have too many clients." Mia popped another shrimp in her mouth.

"How's it gonna play out when you go back to Durango?"

She glanced up at him. "I guess I can come down on my days off."

"And the times you don't come down or I can't come up?"

Mia put her fork down and looked at him. "What're you trying to tell me?"

"That commuting sucks." Army finished the drink.

"I know, and I'm worried about if we get a bad snowstorm. Remember a few years ago when that blizzard hit? If that happens again, it could be weeks until we see each other. I don't like thinking about it."

The waiter removed their dishes and placed their salads on the white tablecloth. "Ground black pepper?"

Mia nodded and the server doused the lettuce leaves in black sprinkles, then did the same to Army's salad. Mia picked up her fork and mixed the greens together.

"I'd get to you even in a blizzard," Army said.

"That's sweet, but it sounds dangerous." She smiled.

Army reached into the pocket of his leather jacket that hung behind his chair and pulled out a box wrapped with a white ribbon. Mia's eyes widened slightly as they focused on the blue box in his hand, and a pinkish flush tinted her skin. A smile played at her lips as she put her fork down then locked her gaze with his. "Is that a present for me?"

*She looks so damn gorgeous, sitting there, her mind working overtime.* "Yeah, but I'm gonna open it."

"If it's for me—shouldn't I open it?" Mia asked.

Army laughed then handed her the box. For a long pause, she stared at it then opened the lid slowly.

"It's beautiful," Mia gasped.

Army gently took the box from her and took out the cushion cut black diamond. The band had three rows of smaller white diamonds all around it. The ring sparkled in the light from the candle on the table in a way that was majestic. He took her hand and slipped it on her finger.

"You're the best damn thing that's ever happened to me," Army said.

Mia stared at the glittering ring on her finger then glanced at Army. "It's breathtaking," she said softly.

"I know we're meant to spend our lives together. We've been through a lot, and I can't imagine spending one fuckin' day without you. I want to spend my forever with you by my side. I want you to be my old lady. Marry me, babe."

Mia held up her hand and stared at the ring. "Aren't you supposed to ask me?"

Her sassiness drove Army insane with desire. "I'm not asking shit— I'm telling."

"If you're not asking a question, am I still supposed to answer?" A devilish smile whispered across her lips.

"Fuck yeah."

Mia locked her gaze with his. "I love you with all my heart." She smiled and reached for his hand. "You're my dark knight in leather on a big iron horse, and I want to live my life with you. I'd be honored to call you my old man."

Army laughed, leaning forward then curling a hand behind the nape of her neck, under all that soft brown hair he loved so fucking much. He fused his mouth to hers as he kissed her passionately. Mia was his nasty princess in his twisted fantasy, and his demons played very well with hers. She was the only woman he wanted on his body and in his life. Mia was his old lady, and nothing would ever pull them apart.

The busser came over and Army sat back, his gaze still fixed on Mia's as the man cleared the table. The waiter placed a plate of prime rib and sautéed mushrooms in front of Mia, then set Army's thick steak, baked potato, and asparagus dish before him.

As Mia cut into the prime rib, her sparkling eyes matched the brilliance of the ring. "Are you sure you're okay with getting married? I mean I know how you feel about the establishment."

Her words made his cock twitch, and he couldn't wait to take her home and spank some of the sass out of her. "I'm just thinking about you, baby. Unfortunately, we live under Big Brother's rules, so if something happens to me, I want to make sure you get my assets."

"Great answer," she said softly before putting the morsel of beef into her mouth.

"Now that we're gonna be hitched, I want you to move to Alina."

Mia started coughing and her hand flew to the base of her throat. "That sure came out of left field." She picked up the glass of wine and brought it to her mouth.

"Not really. I've been thinking about it for a while. There's no fuckin' way I'm not having you with me every day—"

"And there's no fucking way I'm moving to the clubhouse and living in your room."

Army finished chewing. "Right. Oh … by the way—the brothers are cool with you. You standing by me proved you're all right."

Mia's eyes widened. "Did they tell you that?"

"Yeah. Even Crow's cool. I meant to tell you that when I got back to the hotel, but you distracted me."

Mia laughed. "I'm happy to hear the club doesn't harbor any bad feelings toward me, but I still don't want to live in your room."

"If you wouldn't have interrupted me, you'd have found out that I want us to look for a house. I'm cool with whatever you pick."

Mia set her fork down and leaned back. "Wow … a lot of changes are happening right now. I have my business … Champion … and my friends, especially Ronica."

Army nodded "Okay, but hear me out. You can get into a salon in town, and I can help out while you grow your customer base. The second thing—Champion—is something I've been thinking about very seriously. Alina doesn't have a decent MMA training center. The two in the county are pathetic at best. I was thinking you could open one up here. You'd make a shitload of money, and you'd be able to train and compete as well."

"My own gym? I don't know anything about opening one up."

"I'm gonna help you figure it out. Taylor can give you some ideas, and I'm sure Goliath would be more than happy to give you the lowdown on how to start a gym."

She picked up her fork again and put another morsel of food in her mouth, chewing slowly. "The main thing would be to have great trainers. Dominant and Madman have told me that they want to move their families out of Durango and into a smaller town. They both mentioned Alina as a strong contender. I could talk to them and see if they'd be interested in working at my new gym."

Army smiled inwardly when she'd called the gym hers. The way her cheeks flushed and her eye twitched, he knew the idea of opening an MMA training gym would be right up her alley.

"And Ronica and my other friends can come down to Alina to visit, and I'll go up and see them. You and I will be going up to support Taylor, so I can arrange some lunches with them during that time. I think this is going to work out great." She grabbed his hand. "I can't wait to get our own home together."

"Me neither. I'd love to do it tomorrow, but I know you have to wind down your business and decide what you want to do with your townhouse."

"I'll sell it. I don't want to deal with renters." She pushed her hair behind her shoulders. "I hope people will join the gym. I'll definitely offer self-defense classes."

"I already know three customers for those classes—Breanna, Hailey, and Raven. Chelsea's sitting on the fence, but I'm sure Paco's gonna talk her into going. Those women are the old ladies. You'll meet them in a couple of weeks at one of the family nights. They're gonna love you. They get together for dinners and shit a couple of times a month."

Mia grinned. "That sounds awesome. I can't wait to meet them."

"Would you like any dessert?" the waiter asked as the busser cleared away their empty plates.

Army glanced at Mia who shook her head. "We're good, but we'll take two glasses of champagne."

The waiter tilted his head and walked away. Army tucked Mia's hands in his.

"When we get back to the hotel, I have two bottles of champagne waiting along with your cut bearing my property patch. I can't wait to see you in it."

"I'm so happy," she gushed leaning toward him.

Army met her halfway and they shared a passionate and loving kiss. The waiter put two flutes in front of them, and Army clinked his glass against Mia's; her lips turned up into a big, glowing smile.

*I get so fuckin' lost in her smile and her laugh. Hell ... I just get so damn lost in her.*

Mia was his forever, and nothing would ever change that.

Make sure you sign up for my newsletter so you can keep up with my new releases, special sales, free short stories, and other treats only available to newsletter readers. When you sign up, you will receive a FREE hot and steamy novella. Sign up at: http://eepurl.com/bACCL1.

# Notes from Chiah

As always, I have a team behind me making sure I shine and continue on my writing journey. It is their support, encouragement, and dedication that pushes me further in my writing journey. And then, it is my wonderful readers who have supported me, laughed, cried, and understood how these outlaw men live and love in their dark and gritty world. Without you—the readers—an author's words are just letters on a page. The emotions you take away from the words breathe life into the story.

**Thank you** to my amazing Personal Assistant Natalie Weston. I don't know what I'd do without you. I value your suggestions and opinions, and my world is so much saner with you in it. You make sure my world flows more smoothly, and you're always willing to jump in and help me. I appreciate the time you took in reading and offering suggestions with the book. You were a huge help in making this book ready for publication. Thanks for being there for me during the craziness of me juggling a million things at once. Your support meant so much. And a big thank you for watching out for me when I'm in writer mode and live life with blinders on. I'm thrilled you are on my team!

**Thank you** to my editor Lisa Cullinan, for all your insightful edits, excitement with this book. You made my book shine. A HUGE thank you for your patience and flexibility with accepting my book in pieces. I never could have hit the Publish button without you.

**Thank you** to my wonderful beta readers Natalie Weston and Jeni Yeager. You're both rock! Your enthusiasm and suggestions for ARMY: Night Rebels MC were spot on and helped me to put out a stronger, cleaner novel.

**Thank you** to the bloggers for your support in reading my book, sharing it, reviewing it, and getting my name out there. I so appreciate all your efforts. You all are so invaluable. I hope you know that. Without you, the indie author would be lost.

**Thank you** ARC readers you have helped make all my books so much stronger. I appreciate the effort and time you put in to reading, reviewing, and getting the word out about the books. I don't know what I'd do without you. I feel so lucky to have you behind me.

**Thank you** to my Street Team. Thanks for your input, your support, and your hard work. I appreciate you more than you know. A HUGE hug to all of you!

**Thank you** to Carrie from Cheeky Covers. You are amazing! I can always count on you. You are the calm to my storm. You totally rock, and I love your artistic vision.

**Thank you** to my proofreader, Daryl, whose last set of eyes before the last once over I do, is invaluable. I appreciate the time and attention to detail you gave to my book. Thanks for putting up for me with this book when things were crazy in my world. Without your support and flexibility, I don't know what I would have done.

**Thank you** to Ena and Amanda with Enticing Journeys Promotions who have helped garner attention for and visibility to the Night Rebels MC series. Couldn't do it without you!

**Thank you** to the readers who continue to support me and read my books. Without you, none of this would be possible. I appreciate your comments and reviews on my books, and I'm dedicated to giving you the best story that I can. I'm always thrilled when you enjoy a book as much as I have in writing it. You definitely make the hours of typing on the computer and the frustrations that come with the territory of writing books so worth it.

**Thank you** to Paul Salvette at BB Books. You are beyond incredible. The formatting you do is fantastic and you are ALWAYS there to help me meet a deadline. I don't know what I'd do without you! You're the best!

And a special thanks to every reader who has been with me since "Hawk's Property." Your support, loyalty, and dedication to my stories touch me in so many ways. You enable me to tell my stories, and I am forever grateful to you.

You all make it possible for writers to write because without you reading the books, we wouldn't exist. Thank you, thank you! ♥

## ARMY: Night Rebels Motorcycle Club (Book 7)

Dear Readers,

Thank you for reading my book. I hope you enjoyed the seventh book in my new Night Rebels MC series as much as I enjoyed writing Army and Mia's story. This gritty and rough motorcycle club has a lot more to say, so I hope you will look for the upcoming books in the series. Romance makes life so much more colorful, and a rough, sexy bad boy makes life a whole lot more interesting.

If you enjoyed the book, please consider leaving a review on Amazon. I read all of them and appreciate the time taken out of busy schedules to do that.

I love hearing from my fans, so if you have any comments or questions, please email me at chiahwilder@gmail.com or visit my facebook page.

To receive a **free copy of my novella**, *Summer Heat*, and to hear of **new releases**, **special sales**, **free short stories**, and **ARC opportunities**, please sign up for my **Newsletter** at http://eepurl.com/bACCL1.

Happy Reading,

*Chiah*

# A Christmas Wish (Biker Style)
## Coming November 2018

**Ryder Rossi dropped out of life.** He came back from the war a broken and angry man. They gave him a Purple Heart, but it sits in the bottom of an old chest his dad gave him years ago.

He doesn't feel like a hero. Hell, he doesn't even feel like a man. Honorable Discharge was what he got after losing a leg to a landmine.

Hawk from the Insurgents MC has been his best buddy since Ryder came back to Pinewood Springs. The ruggedly good-looking biker used to be an Insurgent but he gave that up a long time ago along with everything else.

All he wants is to be ride his Harley and be left alone.

When Savannah Carlton and her young son, Timmy, homestead on Ryder's property, he sees red. It doesn't matter that the pretty blonde pushes some buttons in him that haven't been in use for quite a while. He doesn't want her near him, and her son reminds him of him of the son he's been forced to forget.

Savannah is running away from her ex-husband's family who want Timmy. Her beat-up RV died on Ryder's property, and even though the surly biker tells her to leave, she sees kindness behind his anger. She finds herself making excuses to talk to him, but she doesn't want to fall for Ryder. Her life is screwed up enough, and the last thing she needs is a high maintenance biker.

Can two mismatched, lonely people find the Christmas light in their darkened lives?

**This book contains violence, abuse, strong language, and steamy/graphic sexual scenes. HEA. No cliffhangers. The book is intended for readers over the age of 18.**

# Other Books by Chiah Wilder

## Insurgent MC Series:

Hawk's Property

Jax's Dilemma

Chas's Fervor

Axe's Fall

Banger's Ride

Jerry's Passion

Throttle's Seduction

Rock's Redemption

An Insurgent's Wedding

Outlaw Xmas

Wheelie's Challenge

Insurgents MC Romance Series: Insurgents Motorcycle Club Box Set
(Books 1 – 4)

Insurgents MC Romance Series: Insurgents Motorcycle Club Box Set
(Books 5 – 8)

## Night Rebels MC Series:

STEEL

MUERTO

DIABLO

GOLDIE

PACO

SANGRE

## Steamy Contemporary Romance:

My Sexy Boss

Find all my books at: amazon.com/author/chiahwilder

I love hearing from my readers. You can email me at chiahwilder@gmail.com.

Sign up for my newsletter to receive a FREE Novella, updates on new books, special sales, free short stories, and ARC opportunities at http://eepurl.com/bACCL1.

Visit me on facebook at facebook.com/AuthorChiahWilder

CPSIA information can be obtained
at www.ICGtesting.com
Printed in the USA
LVHW012316040119
602857LV00008B/53/P

9 781723 765643